Irish Women Writers and the Modern Short Story

Elke D'hoker

Irish Women Writers and the Modern Short Story

Elke D'hoker
University of Leuven
Leuven, Belgium

ISBN 978-3-319-30287-4   ISBN 978-3-319-30288-1   (eBook)
DOI 10.1007/978-3-319-30288-1

Library of Congress Control Number: 2016945022

Printed on acid-free paper

This Palgrave Macmillan imprint is published by Springer Nature
The registered company is Springer International Publishing AG Switzerland

For my children: Jonathan, Lucas, Leander and Jessica

ACKNOWLEDGEMENTS

This book has been several years in the making, so I have reason to be grateful to many colleagues and friends whose conversations on Irish literature, the short story, or academic life in general sustained me in this period. In no particular order, I'd like to thank: Anne Fogarty, Tina O'Toole, Patricia Coughlan, Kathryn Laing, Heather Ingman, Margaret Kelleher, Claire Connolly, Theresa Wray, Grainne Hurley, Derek Hand, Lucy Collins, Maureen O'Connor, Philip Coleman, Rob Luscher, Katharina Rennhak, Fiona McCann, Michelle Ryan-Sautour, Emmanuel Vernandakis, Christine Reynier, Adrian Hunter, Paul Delaney, Jochen Achilles, Ailsa Cox, Sue Lanser, Elke Brems, Bart Van den Bossche, Ortwin de Graef, Hedwig Schwall, Pieter Vermeulen, Stephanie Eggermont, Raphaël Ingelbien, Anke Gilleir, Reine Meylaerts, Dagmar Vandebosch, and all my colleagues at the KU Leuven Arts Faculty, the Leuven Centre for Irish Studies and the MDRN research lab.

Many parts of this book first saw the light as conference papers, which I presented at several IASIL, EFACIS, SSSS, and ENSFR conferences over the years. Thank you to all the colleagues who provided feedback on those occasions. Some parts of this book have been previously published as articles. Chapter 3 draws on some material from "The Poetics of House and Home in the Short Fiction of Elizabeth Bowen", *Orbis Litterarum* 67, 4 (2012), pp. 267–89, and Chapter 6 revisits arguments that were previously published in "'And the transformation begins': Present-Tense Narration in Claire Keegan's Daughter Stories", *Contemporary Women's Writing* 7, 2 (2013), pp. 190–204 and "Rereading the mother in Edna O'Brien's *Saints and Sinners*", *Journal of the Short Story in English*

63 (2014), pp. 115–30. I am grateful to the editors of these journals for granting me permission to reprint my work.

Writing papers and articles is one thing, but finding the time to write a book is quite another—especially if that time is fragmented by so many other jobs: teaching, writing grant applications, supervising, administration and endless meetings. Since sabbaticals are hard to come by in my university, in the end I 'bought' a semester free of teaching by taking up parental leave so that I could finally write the book. My greatest thanks therefore go to my husband, who encouraged me to take this step and always believed I could do it. I am also indebted to my parents, who are always ready to help me out in the daily struggle of combining a family and a career. This book is dedicated to my children—Jonathan, Lucas, Leander and Jessica—who did not seem to mind that my parental leave was not entirely devoted to their care, or, if they did, were easily consoled by the promise of one day seeing their names appear in a 'real book'.

CONTENTS

CHAPTER 1

Introduction

Jane Barlow, George Egerton, Somerville and Ross, Elizabeth Bowen, Mary Lavin, Maeve Brennan, Edna O'Brien, and Mary Beckett: these are only some of many Irish women writers to have achieved widespread popularity and critical acclaim with their short fiction since the late nineteenth century. In the standard histories and theories of the Irish short story, however, their achievements have often been side-lined: limited to one or two small chapters, as in Patrick Rafroidi and Terence Brown's seminal *The Irish Short Story* (1979) and James Kilroy's *The Irish Short Story: A Critical History* (1984) or ignored altogether as in Deborah Averill's *The Irish Short Story from George Moore to Frank O'Connor* (1982). In these and other works, indeed, the history and conception of the Irish short story are constructed around such "masters of the genre" such as Carleton, Moore, Joyce, O'Connor, O'Flaherty and O'Faoláin, and women writers are at best but a footnote to this history (Kiely 2011, 8). This is also the picture we find in the standard, often reprinted, anthologies of the Irish short story: Frank O'Connor's *Classic Irish Short Stories* (1957), Vivian Mercier's *Great Irish Short Stories* (1964), Benedict Kiely's *The Penguin Book of Irish Short Stories* (1981) and William Trevor's *The Oxford Book of Irish Short Stories* (1991). In all of those, the number of short stories by women writers amounts to less than a fifth of the stories.

However, there are signs that this monochrome picture is changing. Thanks to the recovery work of feminist writers and critics, Irish women's short fiction has been promoted in such anthologies as Janet Madden-Simpson's *A Woman's Part: An Anthology of Short Fiction By and About*

© The Editor(s) (if applicable) and The Author (s) 2016
E. D'hoker, *Irish Women Writers and the Modern Short Story*,
DOI 10.1007/978-3-319-30288-1_1

1

Irish Women 1890–1960 (1984), Caroline Walsh's *Virgins and Hyacinths* (1993) and *Territories of Voice: Contemporary Short Stories by Irish Women Writers* (1991), edited by Louise DeSalvo, Kathleen Walsh D'Arcy and Katherine Hogan. More recently, two fascinating anthologies have represented short stories by Irish women writers from the nineteenth century to the present: *Cutting the Night in Two* (2001), edited by Evelyn Conlon and Hans-Christian Oeser, and *The Long Gaze Back* (2015), edited by Sinéad Gleeson. These anthologies have been of seminal importance both in creating an awareness of the long-standing involvement of Irish women writers with the genre of the short story, and in encouraging contemporary efforts in the form. Equally important have been the recovery attempts devoted to the work of individual writers. Over the past two decades, story collections by Mary Lavin and George Egerton have been brought back into print (Egerton 2006; Lavin 2011, 2012), while the short stories of Maeve Brennan and Elizabeth Bowen have been newly collected in several volumes (Brennan 1998, 2000; Bowen and Hepburn 2008). This in turn has produced new author studies about the short fiction of these writers and, hence, a better understanding of their work (Lassner 1991; Laing et al. 2006; D'hoker 2013b). Finally, two recent publications, Heather Ingman's *A History of the Irish Short Story* (2009) and Anne Enright's *The Granta Book of the Irish Short Story* (2010), consider and include Irish women writers on a par with their male colleagues.

Yet, however valuable these works are, they have not yet been able to dislodge the narrow and normative conception of the Irish short story which has held sway since the middle of the twentieth century. Based on the work of a handful of canonical male writers, this conception is often alien to the short fiction of Irish women writers and, as I will argue, it has exacerbated their marginalization in many ways. It is important, therefore, not just to open up literary histories and anthologies to the short stories of women writers, but also to consider how their work challenges the norms and orthodoxies of the Irish short story itself. As Patricia Coughlan notes about Irish literature in general, "There remains [...] a need for persistent intervention in the canon to redress the occlusion, omission and marginalization of women writers by those male-focused metanarratives which still dominate perceptions of Irish literary tradition" (2008, 1). Hence, the double aim of this book is to study the short fiction of Irish women writers and to see how their work challenges the established understanding of the Irish short story tradition.

For a general idea of this standard critical conception of the Irish short story, it suffices to peruse the Prefaces of the classic Irish short fiction anthologies just mentioned: by Mercier, Trevor, Kiely and O'Connor. In an attempt to explain the standing and success of the short story in Ireland, these editors often rehearse the same arguments: the Irish short story emerged out of a vibrant oral storytelling tradition and inherited its emphasis on plot and on voice (Mercier 1992, 8), the genre came natural to the Irish, given their "instinctive" "flair" for storytelling (Trevor 1991, ix, xv), and it could prosper because of the absence of a strong novel tradition (O'Connor 1957, ix). From these editorials and the stories they preface, the image emerges of the Irish short story as a traditional form, rooted in a common Gaelic heritage and general storytelling culture. It is a form that is shaped by Irish history and reality and comments on it, often from an off-centric, marginalized perspective. Indeed, protagonists of the Irish short story are often judged to be isolated or alienated from the community around them (Mercier 1992, 17). As a rule, Frank O'Connor is quoted in support of these statements. Indeed, the presiding image of the Irish short story is heavily indebted to O'Connor's landmark study, *The Lonely Voice: A Study of the Short Story*. Because of the profound and prolonged influence of this book on the conceptualization of the Irish short story tradition—and its attendant marginalization of the work of women writers—it is instructive to take a closer look at O'Connor's main theories.

FRANK O'CONNOR'S OUTSIDERS

In the Introduction to *The Lonely Voice*, O'Connor proposes three central concepts for the short story—"the lonely voice", "the submerged population group", and "the outsider"—which he then elaborates in close readings of individual authors in the chapters that follow. With the "lonely voice", O'Connor highlights the short story's embeddedness in, and difference from, an oral tradition: in the best stories we hear the voice of the individual writer who presses a story—and a message—on the individual reader. This idea favours well-crafted, realist stories over the work of "skilful stylists" who "so fashioned the short story that it no longer ran with the voice of man speaking" (O'Connor 2004, 29). Moreover, the interaction between solitary writer and solitary reader is embedded within their shared belonging to what O'Connor calls "a submerged population group" (2004, 17). This oft-quoted term is first introduced to explain the prevalence of the short story among ex-centric societies or ethnic groups, who lack "the classical concept of a stable society" required by the novel (2004, 20). Yet, O'Connor then shifts its meaning to define what he considers the essence of the short story, its focus on the experience of the outsider:

> Always in the short story there is this sense of outlawed figures wandering about the fringes of society superimposed sometimes on symbolic figures whom they caricature and echo—Christ, Socrates, Moses [...] As a result there is in the short story at its most characteristic something we do not often find in the novel—an intense awareness of human loneliness. (2004, 18–19)

This emphasis on "loneliness" as "the one subject a storyteller must write about" thus merges with that of the submerged population group and with the title metaphor of the lonely voice into a compelling image of the short story as a realist form predicated on a romantic anti-hero, "remote from the community" and "always dreaming of escape" (2004, 109, 20, 18).

The idea that the short story most typically expresses the fate of the lonely outsider has been echoed by many subsequent critics of the short story, both to distinguish the short story from the novel and to explain the genre's flourishing among marginalized groups, whether in terms of nationality, ethnicity or gender (Shaw 1983; May 1984; Harris 1994). As Clare Hanson puts it, quoting O'Connor:

> Is it not the case that the short story is or has been notably a form of the margins, a form which is in some sense ex-centric, not part of official or 'high' cultural hegemony? [...] The short story has offered itself to losers and loners, exiles, women, blacks—writers who for one reason or another have not been part of the ruling narrative or epistemological/experiential framework of their society. (1989, 2)

In Irish literary criticism, as we have seen, O'Connor's ideas have mostly been used to explain the success of the Irish short story in terms of the marginalized perspective of the Irish as a submerged population group and to normatively define this "national genre" as a realist form with oral roots, expressing an individual's loneliness and alienation from society. In her critical history of the Irish short story, for instance, Deborah Averill traces in the short fiction of writers from Moore to O'Connor what she considers "one of the broadest and most pervasive themes in the Irish short story [...] the conflict between the individual and the community', arguing, "Most Irish writers regarded their society as peculiar, self-defeating and out-of-step with other Western societies, and they could not achieve the stable, universalised view of human life that the novel demands" (1982, 24). David Norris similarly considers the individual's imaginative revolt against the authority structures of Church, State and Society as the theme "common to all significant writers" of the Irish short story (1979, 39–40) and James Kilroy argues, "Among the subjects treated in almost every short story is the individual's relationship to society"—a relationship which is mostly one of alienation, disillusionment and despair (1984, 6).

Although Hanson draws on O'Connor's terms to explain what she sees as a specific relation between women writers and the short story form, O'Connor's arguments themselves reveal a male bias. His images of the short story writer ("the lonely voice of a man speaking"), protagonist (a Christ-like outsider, at odds with his community) and topic (loneliness and alienation) immediately call up men rather than women. Small wonder then that the two women writers he discusses in *The Lonely Voice*, Mary Lavin and Katherine Mansfield, fall short of the ideal he describes. Mary Lavin's stories he considers un-Irish in their lack of political content and their focus on domestic issues. He discovers an "almost Victorian attitude to love and marriage" and a "different set of values" which, he argues, "make her more of a novelist in her stories than O'Flaherty, O'Faoláin, or Joyce" (2004, 209, 211). Katherine Mansfield too is considered "something unusual in the history of the short story" and not in a positive sense: unlike "the stories by real storytellers", her stories do not "leave a deep impression": "I read and forget, read and forget" (2004, 125). O'Connor's uneasy bafflement, in the case of Mary Lavin, and outright disapproval, in the case of Katherine Mansfield, reveal the male bias that underlies his ideal of the short story as a genre predicated on the experience of the lonely outsider, at odds with society and longing to escape. Inevitably, Lavin's explorations of family relations in small Irish towns or Mansfield's dissection of love, relationships and feminine subjectivity are at odds with this ideal. The same can be said of Somerville and Ross's humorous depiction of local traditions and events in an Anglo-Irish community, Val Mulkerns's tracing of a tragic family history in her story sequence, *Antiquities*, and Maeve Brennan's moving depictions of disintegrating marriages in *The Rose Garden*. While the neglect of these and many other women Irish writers in histories of the Irish short story is of course part of a larger marginalization of women's voices in literary history, it is certainly also due to the continued and unquestioned currency of O'Connor's narrow and essentialist definitions within Irish short story criticism.

Beyond the Lonely Voice

With the renewed academic interest in Irish short fiction in recent years, there are signs that this hegemonic and normative view of the Irish short story is slowly being eroded. In her highly informative *A History of the Irish Short Story*, Heather Ingman questions "the traditional affiliation of the Irish short story with the mimetic fiction of writers like Frank O'Connor and Séan O'Faoláin" and highlights a central strand in Irish short fiction concerned with "playfulness and subversion", with "experimentation and modernity". She continues: "A longer historical overview allows us to assess the extent to which the form's alliance with realism may be limited to a certain historical moment and reminds us that while realism in the short story might seem the norm, it is not the only mode in which the Irish short story operates" (2009, 12). Similarly, the Irish short story's association with questions of nationhood and national identity—as an expression of the different perspective of the Irish "submerged population group"—has been criticized by Patrick Lonergan, who argues instead for a recognition of three important strands in Irish short fiction: a regional, a national and a cosmopolitan strand:

> The development of Irish short fiction [in the period 1880–1921] could be considered from three interlinking perspectives. The works of Somerville and Ross and others can be seen as 'regional': insofar as they address a metropolitan audience and locate Ireland as a marginal but essential element of the United Kingdom. A second mode of writing evident at this time might be described as 'nativist' or nationalist—writings addressed directly towards Irish audiences, which attempt to promote the notion that the country is not only worthy of political independence but also deserving of its own distinctly 'national' literature. Finally, there is also a 'cosmopolitan' mode of short fiction; that is, works by Irish writers who see the subject of their literature as transcending national boundaries, while also crossing the boundaries of realism into the fantastic and the mythological. A similar three-part perspective could also be used to chart the development of Irish writing from Independence to the end of World War II. (2008, 63)

By countering, respectively, the realist and nationalist bias of the standard conception of the Irish short story, Ingman and Lonergan usefully open up the tradition of the Irish short story to a wider variety of authors, texts and perspectives. In this study, I intend to follow their lead by tackling the third—and last remaining—pillar of O'Connor's influential short story ideal: his equation of the short story with loneliness and the outsider. For, as I hope to show, the short fiction of Irish women writers is abundantly concerned with questions of relationality and connection. In the different chapters of this study, I will investigate the way their short stories imaginatively dissect their characters' relations to lovers and friends, fathers and mothers, siblings and children, community members and society at large. Although the relations depicted may be dysfunctional, destructive or simply less than ideal, the short stories' primary interest, I will argue, lies in dramatizing the difficulty of interpersonal relations or the need for human connection rather than in idealizing the romantic outsider or promoting a sense of universal loneliness. In her Introduction to *The Granta Book of the Irish Short Story*, Anne Enright also questions O'Connor's central tenet— "Are all short stories, Russian, French, American and Irish, in fact about loneliness?"—and suggests instead that "Connection, and the lack of it are one of the great themes of the short story" (2010, xv). This is the theme I propose to investigate in the short fiction of Irish women writers. My aim in this is twofold: I intend to reinstate their work within the tradition of the Irish short story, giving it the attention it deserves, and to further corrode the normative view of the Irish short story in terms of realism, nationhood and the outsider.

To a certain extent, these ambitions work in tandem: paying more attention to the work of women writers will help to unsettle and expand the tradition and ideal of the Irish short story which have largely been based on the work of male writers, while abandoning O'Connor's normative ideal of the Irish short story will inevitably make room for writers whose work was considered odd, un-Irish or "novelistic" because it dealt with questions of love and the domestic, the family and the community. However, as the history of feminist criticism has shown, the process is certainly not an automatic one. Rather, a sustained critical scrutiny of women's literature has to go hand in hand with an explicit challenge of reigning norms in order to successfully open up the existing canons and paradigms of Irish literary history. The need for an in-depth critical study of the work of women writers as a first step in the process of changing canons and histories also explains my exclusive focus on the work of Irish women writers in this study. I am well aware that this choice may invite charges of essentialism, whether of genre or gender, so I will take some time to further delineate the terms of my title—women writers, the short story, Irish literature—and to explain the relations between them.

Gender and Genre

In her contribution to *Re-reading the Short Story*, Mary Eagleton addresses the vexed question of the relation between gender and genre. Having surveyed different, unsatisfactory responses, she ends her essay with open questions:

> What is the relationship of gender to writing? [...] Does the relationship differ with different literary forms and is there, therefore, a particular scope in relating gender to the short story? Can we create a criticism which is non-essentialist, non-reductive but subtly alive to the links between gender and genre? (Eagleton 1989, 66)

Difficult questions indeed. Starting from the observation that a proportionally large number of women writers have turned to the short story—and even devoted their entire œuvre to the form—critics have attempted to explain this conjunction in different ways. Clare Hanson, as we have seen, draws on O'Connor to suggest that "the short story has been from its inception a particularly appropriate vehicle for the expression of the ex-centric alienated vision of women" (1989, 3) and Kate Krueger argues similarly, "Due to its qualities of symbolic suggestiveness, intensity, and rejection of novelistic premises and structures, the short story provides women a venue in which to represent their alienation from dominant ideologies of femininity" (2014, 3–4). While these arguments risk essentializing gender and genre, other critics have construed the connection in terms of a shared marginal position in reigning hierarchies: as the marginalized 'other' in the literary system and patriarchal society at large, women writers may well have been drawn to the equally marginal genre of the short story, often conceived of as the novel's "little brother" (Harrington 2008, 4). Female authors themselves have often raised even more pragmatic reasons for their preference for the short story: it demands a less sustained amount of time and can more easily be accommodated to pressing domestic and child-raising duties.

However, this certainly does not hold for all female authors, nor do any of these explanations give sufficient ground for assuming a necessary, or even privileged, relation between women and the genre of the short story. Hence, I hesitate to agree with Hanson's claim that women writers' use of the form is significantly different from that of male writers or that there is a commonality to all short stories by women writers in the sense of a "squint vision" or alienated perspective (Hanson 1989, 5). The most one can say is that the themes and perspectives offered in women's short fiction tend to reflect their specific position in society and the different experiences that come with that position. In her Introduction to *The Secret Self: A Century of Short Fiction by Women*, Hermione Lee writes, "There is no value in suggesting that women writers are better suited to the short story form than men. But there is value in identifying some of the particular qualities of women's stories" (1995, x). I agree, but with the caveat that identifying recurring concerns or particular perspectives in short stories does not equal absolutizing these concerns or making them normative for women's short fiction as a whole.

With regard to the specific concerns of this study, therefore, I do not want to argue that all women's short stories are about interpersonal relations, and even less that while men write about loneliness, women are interested in connection. Instead, I want to highlight and explain the different ways in which interpersonal relations have been staged, imagined, criticized and questioned in the short fiction of Irish women writers because this concern—like women's short fiction in general—has remained under the radar in Irish criticism. I suspect, in fact, that the stories by male writers too are preoccupied with human connection to a greater degree than the prioritizing of loneliness by O'Connor and many subsequent critics has given credit for. To some extent, the distinction is but a difference in emphasis, a different way of looking at the same fictional reality. O'Connor himself wrote in *The Lonely Voice*, in the context of his reading of Gogol's "Overcoat", "If one wanted an alternative title for this work, one might choose 'I Am Your Brother'" (2004, 16). Think of how differently the Irish short story might have been conceptualized had O'Connor chosen the latter over "The Lonely Voice"!

Apart from my intention to recover the short fiction of Irish women writers and to trace recurring concerns, this exclusive focus on women writers will also enable me to identify the relations of influence and inheritance among these writers. As their letters and reviews show, women writers did read, applaud or reject the short stories of their female predecessors and contemporaries. Yet, given the male-dominated hierarchies of literary criticism, their work has often been judged only in relation to the male masters of the form. Nevertheless, as I hope to show, it will be most instructive to trace the echoes of Elizabeth Bowen's "Breakfast" in Mary Lavin's "Miss Holland" or to chart the evolving conceptualization of mother-daughter relationships from Edna O'Brien to Claire Keegan. That said, I do not want to set up the short fiction of Irish women writers as a separate tradition next to the dominant, male one. Instead, these female lines of influence will be shown to exist side-by-side with, for instance, Ní Dhuibhne's references to Joyce, Keegan's tribute to McGahern, or Lavin's appropriation of Turgenev. This Russian master of the short story also brings me to another thorny issue which has to be briefly clarified: the relation between genre and nationality.

THE IRISH SHORT STORY

In his Preface to *New Irish Short Stories*, editor Joseph O'Connor justifies his inclusion of short stories by Richard Ford and Rebecca Miller by noting "I have not been overly focused on passport requirements" since "Literature opens citizenships of affection" (2011, x–xi). Without perhaps going as far as adopting Richard Ford as an Irish short story writer because of "his professorship at Trinity College Dublin", the women writers discussed in this study are 'Irish' in a broad sense. They include Mary Lavin, who was born in Chicago but moved to Ireland as a teenager, as well as Maeve Brennan who permanently moved to the USA at the age of 17. They also include Anglo-Irish Ascendancy writers such as Jane Barlow, Elizabeth Bowen, Edith Somerville and Martin Ross, whom some critics have considered too English to warrant inclusion. In fact, my survey starts with the pioneering short story writer George Egerton, aka Mary Chavelita Dunne, who was born in Australia to an Irish father, spent her youth in Ireland but relocated to England later in life, and it ends with the contemporary writer Claire-Louise Bennett, who went in the opposite direction: born in England, she moved to Galway in the late 1990s.

As with the question of gender, these writers can usefully be grouped together because their life in, or connection to, Ireland grants their work certain shared concerns and perspectives, different from that of other Anglophone writers. Nevertheless, as with the work of women writers, we should beware of essentializing the Irish short story and of seeing it as a tradition entirely separate from that of neighbouring traditions.

In fact, even more than the novel, the short story is as an international genre which easily transcends national and linguistic borders, as its very shortness enables quick magazine publication and encourages rapid translation and dissemination (Turton 2002). Moreover, the modern short story only developed in Britain and Ireland under the influence of French and Russian masters of the form, such as Maupassant, Balzac, Turgenev and Chekhov. This was also something O'Connor recognized when he devoted several chapters of *The Lonely Voice* to the work of American, Russian and English writers. In another way, the short fiction of Irish writers was also affected by its being published by London publishers or in leading American magazines, such as *The New Yorker* or *The Atlantic Monthly*. In short, investigating the Irish short story requires a perspective that is attuned to local topics as well as universal themes, to Irish traditions as well as international trends and influences.

In its focus on more general questions of human connection and community, my study thus differs from existing histories of the Irish short story, which have traditionally assumed a very close link between the Irish short story and questions of nationhood or national identity. This blending of genre and nationality may be due to the perceived special status of the short story in Ireland as a "national genre" or to the fact that the heydays of the Irish short story happened to coincide with the shaping of a distinctive national identity in post-Independence Ireland (Lonergan 2008, 63). Whatever the case, this correlation pervades histories and anthologies of the Irish short story to this day (Ingman 2009, 13). Although I do not want to dispute the validity of such an approach, it is not one I will follow in this study. In my readings, rather, I aim to show how the local and the global go hand in hand in the short stories of Irish women writers, how their investment in the domestic, the parochial, and the regional acquires a far larger human appeal.

BREVITY AND THE SHORT STORY

The last vexed question to tackle in this Introduction is one all studies of the short story have to deal with: What is the short story? Or even, What is it that makes a story short? Ever since Edgar Allen Poe sought to distinguish the effects and characteristics of short tales from those of longer novels, this question has haunted writers and critics of the short story. Poe himself argued that the short story distinguishes itself by "a certain unique or single effect", so that "in the whole composition there should be no word written, of which the tendency, direct or indirect, is not to the one pre-established design" (1994, 61). For much of the twentieth century, the definitions that were given tended to be essentialist: from Brander Matthew's prescription that "a short story deals with a single character, a single event, a single emotion, or the series of emotions called forth by a single situation" (1994, 73) to Charles May's grand claim that "whereas the novel exists to reaffirm the world of 'everyday' reality; the short story exists to 'defamiliarize' the everyday" (1984, 329). Under the influence of genre theory, these prescriptive approaches gradually gave way to more descriptive and pragmatic attempts to outline Wittgensteinian 'family resemblances' among short stories (Friedman 1989; Wright 1989). Moreover, short story theory has recently teamed up with other critical approaches, such as materialist criticism and book studies (Chan 2007; Baldwin 2013), reader-response theories (Gerlach 1985; Lohafer 2003), and stylistics (Toolan 2009). While many of these approaches are highly interesting—and I will draw on some of their insights in what follows—they have not brought us any closer to an exhaustive definition of the genre. As Valerie Shaw notes, "It seems reasonable to say that a firm definition of the genre is impossible. No single theory can encompass the multifarious nature of a genre in which the only constant feature seems to be the achievement of a narrative purpose in a comparatively short space" (1983, 21).

The best we can do, therefore, is to list a number of characteristics which are shared by a significant number of short stories, but are neither totally exclusive, nor absolutely essential to the form. As Austin Wright puts it:

> If a genre is a cluster of characteristics [...] borderline and original works can be handled easily and naturally. We can speak of ways in which a work partakes of the short story and ways in which it does not, and the discrimination will enhance a fine description of what the work actually does. (1989, 48)

In the case of the short story, moreover, many of these generic characteristics can be related, in one way or another, to the distinctive brevity of the form. Indeed, even though this brevity cannot be defined in absolute terms, it can be seen to impact the preferred plot structures, characterization, style, narrative techniques, and publication contexts of this narrative form. In terms of plot, first, the short story typically favours plots of smaller magnitude, focused, for instance, on a single incident, disclosure or moment of change, or on a series of incidents or scenes tied together by a common concern. More than other genres, therefore, the short story depends on a strong degree of focus and unity to carry the reader from the opening lines to the ending. As Gerlach argues, in short fiction, "the anticipation of the ending [is] used to structure the whole" (1985, 3). Still, this end-directedness does not necessarily entail that all stories achieve closure, whether in terms of plot resolution or an O. Henry-like twist. An open ending characterizes many modern stories, as does a beginning *in medias res*. Unsurprisingly, therefore, characterization in short fiction is likely to be less elaborate than in the novel, and to proceed through implication rather than through extensive description, scene-setting or contextualization. This stylistic mode of implication and suggestion has often been considered a hallmark of the modern short story in general. Wright argues,

> The shorter the work, the more prominent the details. Words and images, as well as characters and events, stand out more vividly than they would in a larger context. This attention to the parts, found in all short fiction and poetry, implies recalcitrance in the act of attention, the arresting of notice at every significant point. (1989, 120)

This linguistic economy, which the short story arguably shares with poetry, can perhaps most famously be found in the uses of epiphany, ellipsis and symbolism in modernist short fiction. Yet, in more incident-packed short stories too, small details will often prove significant for the denouement of the plot.

Another corollary of the short story's brevity is its flexibility as a genre. As we will see in the following pages, a short story can take on many different guises. It can be a psychological sketch or fragment, as in some of Egerton's stories, but also a highly plotted comic tale as in Somerville and Ross's R.M. stories. It can take the form of a (one-sided) dialogue, an overheard conversation or a fleeting memory, as in Bowen's stories, but can also condense the story of a life as in O'Brien's well-known story, "A Rose at the Heart of New York". Drawing on earlier tale traditions, the story can also be a parable, a fairy-tale revisited, or an overheard tall tale, while crossovers with other genres can generate short stories in the form of essayistic reflections and dramatic monologues, as in some of Ní Dhuibhne's stories, but also prose poems, letters or diary fragments as in Donoghue's story collections. Historically speaking, this flexibility has often put the short story at the forefront of avant-garde movements and waves of experimentation. Thus, Bowen's modernist stories as well as Enright's postmodernist ones can be seen to try out new narrative or stylistic techniques, often in more radical or extreme ways than in the novel. In terms of publication context, finally, the shortness of the form means that short stories are not usually published separately (Keegan's *Foster* is a noteworthy exception), but rather appear among other texts in magazines, newspapers, anthologies or collections. This "polytextual" publication mode (Monfort 1992, 158) creates meanings and resonances beyond those of the single story. Indeed, readers of a short story are inevitably influenced by the context in which the story appears: reading a short story in a magazine, next to reportage or advertisements, is a very different experience from reading a short story in a single-author collection or in a thematic anthology. This study's focus on important short story writers and their oeuvre means that I read individual stories mostly within the context of the collections in which they first appeared, or as part of collected editions of the author's work. This means that specific attention will be devoted to such polytextual publications contexts as the short story series or the short story cycle, but that the stories' prior publication in magazines as well as their subsequent reprinting in anthologies will not usually be considered. The vicissitudes of Irish women's short fiction in these publication contexts would require a separate study to do it full justice.

A final word on the temporal framework of this study, signalled by the term "modern" in the title. In studying the contributions of Irish women writers to the genre of the modern short story, from the late nineteenth century to the present, I inevitably take up a position in the critical debate surrounding the precise starting point of the short story tradition in Ireland. While O'Connor opens his anthology with George Moore, both Trevor and Mercier include a selection of Gaelic tales in their anthologies and have the short story proper start with Oliver Goldsmith and William Carleton, respectively. Similarly, James Kilroy starts his historical overview with Maria Edgeworth, while Deborah Averill traces the Irish short story's development from Moore to O'Connor. All depends of course on one's conception of the short story as either a specific, modern genre or simply any narrative that is short. Since I take the first view, I agree with those critics who locate the birth of the modern short story around the 1850s in the USA, and around the 1880s and 1890s in Britain and Ireland. For much of the eighteenth and nineteenth centuries, tales—as they were called—were rather long and elaborately plotted. They also seemed strangely unable to record ordinary reality, instead preferring such sub-genres as adventure, exotic or Christmas tales, and ghost stories or didactic stories. Only at the end of the nineteenth century did the consciousness emerge that the short story could be more than a condensed novel, that shortness was a positive quality, which enabled a distinctive focus and opened up different narrative possibilities (Hunter 2007, 6–9). Or as the editors of *A Companion to the British and Irish Short Story* put it, "after 1880 (approximatively) it makes sense to talk about the short story in Britain as a discrete type of text which is taken seriously and, to a degree, thought about by writers and critics" (Malcolm and Malcolm 2008, 9). This study thus follows the consensus among short story critics to date the beginning of the tradition of the short story around 1880 and to consider the tales predating that turning-point as precursors of the modern short story (Hunter 2007, 5; Ingman 2009, 9). Hence, it is with a consideration of George Egerton's *Keynotes* (1893) and Somerville and Ross's *Some Experiences of an Irish R.M.* (1899) that we will embark on our exploration of the fascinating short stories of Irish women writers.

CHAPTER OVERVIEW

Although George Moore is usually hailed as the father of the modern Irish short story, in Chapter 2, I defend the case of alternative mothers for this tradition. I argue that the short fiction of George Egerton, on the one hand, and of Somerville and Ross, on the other, can be considered as starting points of two trends which have dominated the Irish short story throughout the twentieth century. Influenced by Kipling, Somerville and Ross's *Some Experiences of an Irish R.M.* offers the prototype of the popular, plot-bound, magazine story which was hugely successful in the late nineteenth and early twentieth century, and continues to exert its influence to this day. George Egerton's experimental and innovative short stories on the other hand, prepare the stage for the impressionist, mood-dependent, and psychological short story which would flourish in modernist literature. Through a detailed formal and analysis of representative stories, I show how these writers foreground social conceptualizations of the self: Somerville and Ross by depicting individuals as part of a community (albeit one ambivalently defined in terms of class, gender and nationality); Egerton by modifying the Nietzschean conceptualization of the free and strong-willed individual into the ideal of the relational self, shaped by both personal freedom and an ethics of care.

The tension between personal freedom and domestic responsibility recurs in Chapter 3, which explores the poetics of house and home in short stories by two Irish writers who left Ireland to live in Britain and the USA: Elizabeth Bowen and Maeve Brennan. This experience of migration has shaped the critical reception of their short fiction: it has often been read as expressing the alienation, loneliness and longing for the lost home characteristic of diaspora literature. Yet, the overall negative representation of houses and homes in their work at least partly undermines this reading. In a series of close readings, I pick apart the stylistic structures underpinning these representations and I show how they express the female characters' feelings of confinement or emptiness with regard to their houses and homes. Considering the personal, social and national contexts of the work of Bowen and Brennan, I argue that these images mount a profound critique of the domestic ideology that dominated mid-century Britain and Ireland. Interestingly, both authors also offer a few images of ideal homes which attempt to depict an alternative conceptualization of female identity and relations than that offered by the middle-class home and family.

Chapter 4 returns to the historical narrative of the Irish short story, by tracing the development from Bowen's short fiction to the work of Mary Lavin. It does so by comparing the first story Mary Lavin ever wrote ("Miss Holland") with the first story Bowen finished ("Breakfast"). Both stories are remarkably similar in terms of topic, yet their treatment of this topic differs. The comparison provides the starting point for a description of Lavin's short story poetics as well as for an analysis of her obsessive thematic concern with relations, whether those of love, family or community. For Lavin, much more than for Bowen, the individual is defined by a network of relations: to parents, spouses, siblings, children. Through a close reading of a selection of Lavin's stories from different stages in her career, I discuss two different aspects of Lavin's "relational selves" (Gergen 2009): her recurrent staging of character doubles and her representation of the individual's relation to society.

In Chapter 5, I zoom in on a specific aspect of this social context, namely, the idea and reality of community, as it has been expressed in women's short fiction. Although O'Connor and many other critics have argued that community has no place in the short story at all, several Irish writers do stage a concern with community in their stories and represent communal structures in various ways. First, the chapter looks at the different ways in which community is staged in the stories of Egerton and Lavin: as an abstract idea(l), a silent constraint or a polyphonic chorus. Then, I discuss the ways in which Irish women writers have used the literary form of the short story cycle to dramatize community life. Theories of the short story cycle—and its subgenre, the narrative of community—form the conceptual background for a discussion of Jane

Barlow's *Irish Idylls* (1893) and *Strangers at Lisconnel* (1895), Mary Beckett's *A Belfast Woman* (1980) and *A Literary Woman* (1990), and Éilís Ní Dhuibhne's *The Shelter of Neighbours* (2012).

In Chapter 6, I focus on that most iconic and troubled of female relations: the mother-daughter bond. Against the background of psychoanalytic and contextual readings of that relation, I offer a close reading of mother-daughter stories by Edna O'Brien and Claire Keegan. In the case of O'Brien, her recent stories show a departure from the classic Freudian plots enacted in her early stories and instead depict a more intersubjective mother-daughter relationship based on similarity, difference and mutual respect. Like O'Brien, Keegan also usually depicts the mother-daughter relationship from the perspective of the daughter. Yet, while O'Brien's heavily symbolic stories are bent on dramatizing the underlying psychic structures and archetypal myths that govern individual behaviour, Keegan's more realistic stories are less bound by Freudian categories and Catholic or nationalist iconography. Instead, her stories frame the mother-daughter relationship in the light of the gendered hierarchies and power structures that still shape individual identity and family relations in patriarchal societies. Yet, even though these patriarchal structures may appear inflexible and deterministic in Keegan's seemingly timeless rural Ireland, her stories do revise the mother-daughter plot in a way that emphasizes mutual acts of rebellion and the possibility of change. In the case of both authors, moreover, I try to show how their particular use of first-person present-tense narration plays an important part in staging these more positive contemporary variants of the embattled mother-daughter plot.

Chapter 7 continues my exploration of the short story's development by comparing the postmodernist stories of Éilís Ní Dhuibhne, Anne Enright and Emma Donoghue. All three writers combine postmodern techniques with a clear feminist message and this comes across most strongly in their use of metafiction and rewriting. Ní Dhuibhne's stories typically juxtapose contemporary stories with elements from Ireland's rich repository of folk tales and myths to expose both the patriarchal dimension of these folk tales and the danger of setting too much store by the romantic ideals they contain. In her rewriting of stories by Mary Lavin too, Ní Dhuibhne shows how real life is always more complex and ambivalent than literature makes us believe, and it is precisely through postmodern techniques of metafiction and intertextuality that her short fiction tries to get closer to the ordinariness of everyday lives. In her even more experimental early stories, Enright too is engaged in a practice of revisioning, but her focus is on the all-too-familiar plots and patterns of popular culture. Enright's stories often revise the gendered hierarchies that inform these popular plots, so as to open up alternative identities for men and women. The historiographical short stories of Donoghue's *The Woman Who Gave Birth to Rabbits* (2002) and *Astray* (2012) are all hybrid stories, which imagine the lives of women (and, in *Astray*, also men) who figure in the margins of historical documents. Through this mode of rewriting history, I argue, her stories seek to question received views or dominant discourses about women (in *The Woman*) and about emigration (in *Astray*). All three writers also cleverly exploit the form of the short story cycle to stage the singularity and difference of women's lives as well their interconnections and shared social position.

The Conclusion summarizes the thematic concerns and formal characteristics of Irish women's short fiction as they have been traced in the different chapters. It reiterates the importance of making more room in literary historical accounts of the Irish short story for the work of Irish women writers and of opening up established conceptions of the Irish short story to the concerns these writers bring to the form. Finally, the chronological trajectory followed in the book is extended to the present moment by a brief discussion of three promising debut collections, all published by The Stinging Fly Press: Mary Costello's *The China Factory* (2012), Danielle McLaughlin's *Dinosaurs on Other Planets* (2015) and Claire-Louise Bennett's *Pond* (2015).

BIBLIOGRAPHY

Averill, Deborah M. 1982. *The Irish Short Story from George Moore to Frank O'Connor*. Lanham, MD: University Press of America.

Baldwin, Dean. 2013. *Art and Commerce in the British Short Story, 1880–1950*. London: Pickering & Chatto.

Bowen, Elizabeth, and Allan Hepburn. 2008. *The Bazaar and Other Stories*. Edinburgh: Edinburgh University Press.

Brennan, Maeve. 1998. *The Springs of Affection: Stories of Dublin*. New York: Houghton Mifflin.

Brennan, Maeve. 2000. *The Rose Garden: Short Stories*. Washington, DC: Counterpoint.

Chan, Winnie. 2007. *The Economy of the Short Story in British Periodicals of the 1890s*. London: Routledge.

Conlon, Evelyn, and Hans Christian Oeser. 2001. *Cutting the Night in Two: Short Stories by Irish Women Writers*. Dublin: New Island.

Coughlan, Patricia. 2008. Introduction. In *Irish Literature: Feminist Perspectives*, edited by Patricia Coughlan and Tina O'Toole, 1–16. Cork: Carysfort Press.

DeSalvo, Louise, Kathleen Walsh D'Arcy, and Katherine Hogan, eds. 1991. *Territories of the Voice: Contemporary Stories by Irish Women Writers*. Boston: Beacon Press.

D'hoker, Elke, ed. 2013b. *Mary Lavin*. Dublin: Irish Academic Press.

Eagleton, Mary. 1989. Gender and Genre. In *Re-Reading the Short Story*, edited by Clare Hanson, 55–68. Basingstoke: Palgrave.

Egerton, George. 2006. *Keynotes and Discords*. London: Continuum. Original edition, 1893, 1894.

Enright, Anne. 2010. *The Granta Book of the Irish Short Story*. London: Granta.

Friedman, Norman. 1989. Recent Short Story Theories: Problems in Definition. In *Short Story Theory at a Crossroads*, edited by Susan Lohafer and Jo Ellyn Clarey, 13–31. Baton Rouge: Louisiana State University Press.

Gergen, Kenneth J. 2009. *Relational Being: Beyond Self and Community*. Oxford: Oxford University Press.

Gerlach, John C. 1985. *Toward the End: Closure and Structure in the American Short Story*. Tuscaloosa: University of Alabama Press.

Gleeson, Sinéad, ed. 2015. *The Long Gaze Back: An Anthology of Irish Women Writers*. Dublin: New Island.

Hanson, Clare. 1989. *Re-Reading the Short Story*. Basingstoke: Macmillan.

Harrington, Ellen Burton. 2008. *Scribbling Women & the Short Story Form: Approaches by American & British Women Writers*. Oxford: Peter Lang.

Harris, Wendell. 1994. Vision and Form: The English Novel and the Emergence of the Short Story. In *The New Short Story Theories*, edited by Charles E. May, 182–191. Athens: Ohio University Press.

Hunter, Adrian. 2007. *The Cambridge Introduction to the Short Story in English*. Cambridge: Cambridge University Press.

Ingman, Heather. 2009. *A History of the Irish Short Story*. Cambridge: Cambridge University Press.

Kiely, Benedict. 2011. *The Penguin Book of Irish Short Stories*. London: Penguin. Original edition, 1981.

Kilroy, James. 1984. *The Irish Short Story: A Critical History*. Boston: Twayne.

Krueger, Kate. 2014. *British Women Writers and the Short Story, 1850–1930: Reclaiming Social Space*. Basingstoke: Palgrave.

Laing, Kathryn, Sinéad Mooney, and Maureen O'Connor. 2006. *Edna O'Brien: New Critical Perspectives*. Cork: Carysfort Press.

Lassner, Phyllis. 1991. *Elizabeth Bowen: A Study of the Short Fiction*. Boston: Twayne.

Lavin, Mary. 2011. *Happiness and Other Stories*. Dublin: New Island Books. Original edition, 1970.

Lavin, Mary. 2012. *Tales From Bective Bridge*. London: Faber. Original edition, 1943.

Lee, Hermione, ed. 1995. *The Secret Self: A Century of Short Stories by Women*. London: Phoenix.

Lohafer, Susan. 2003. *Reading for Storyness: Preclosure Theory, Genre Poetics, and Culture in the Short Story.* Baltimore: Johns Hopkins University Press.

Lonergan, Patrick. 2008. Irish Short Fiction: 1880–1945. In *A Companion to the British and Irish Short Story*, edited by Cheryl Alexander Malcolm and Malcolm David, 51–64. Chichester: Wiley-Blackwell.

Madden-Simpson, Janet, ed. 1984. *Woman's Part: An Anthology of Short Fiction By and About Irish Women, 1890–1960.* Dublin: Arlen House.

Malcolm, Cheryl Alexander, and David Malcolm. 2008. *A Companion to the British and Irish Short Story.* Oxford: Wiley-Blackwell.

Matthews, Brander. 1994. The Philosophy of the Short-Story. In *The New Short Story Theories*, edited by Charles E. May, 73–80. Athens: Ohio University Press. Original edition, 1901.

May, Charles E. 1984. The Nature of Knowledge in Short Fiction. *Studies in Short Fiction* 21 (4):327–38.

Mercier, Vivian, ed. 1992. *Great Irish Short Stories.* London: Abacus. Original edition, 1964.

Monfort, Bruno. 1992. La Nouvelle et Son Mode de Publication. Le Cas Américain. *Poétique* 90:153–171.

Norris, David. 1979. Imaginative Response vs. Authority Structures. A Theme of the Anglo-Irish Short Story. In *The Irish Short Story*, edited by Patrick Rafroidi and Terence Brown 39–62. Gerrards Cross: Smythe.

O'Connor, Frank. 1957. *Classic Irish Short Stories.* Oxford: Oxford University Press.

O'Connor, Frank. 2004. *The Lonely Voice: A Study of the Short Story.* Hoboken, NJ: Melville House Pub. Original edition, 1963.

O'Connor, Joseph, ed. 2011. *New Irish Short Stories.* London: Faber & Faber.

Poe, E. A. 1994. Review of *Twice-Told Tales.* In *The New Short Story Theories*, edited by Charles E. May, 59–64. Athens: Ohio University Press. Original edition, 1842.

Rafroidi, Patrick, and Terence Brown. 1979. *The Irish Short Story.* Gerrards Cross: Smythe.

Shaw, Valerie. 1983. *The Short Story: A Critical Introduction.* London: Longman.

Somerville, E. Œ. and Martin Ross. 1899. *Some Experiences of an Irish R.M.* London: Longmans, Green.

Toolan, Michael J. 2009. *Narrative Progression in the Short Story: A Corpus Stylistic Approach.* Philadelphia: John Benjamins Pub.

Trevor, William, ed. 1991. *The Oxford Book of Irish Short Stories.* Oxford: Oxford University Press.

Turton, Glynn. 2002. *Turgenev and the Context of English Literature 1850–1900.* Oxford: Taylor & Francis.

Walsh, Caroline, ed. 1993. *Virgins and Hyacinths.* Dublin: Attic Press.

Wright, Austin. 1989. On Defining the Short Story. In *Short Story Theory at a Crossroads*, edited by Susan Lohafer and Jo Ellyn Clarey. Baton Rouge: Louisiana State University Press.

CHAPTER 2

Mothers of the Irish Short Story: George Egerton and Somerville and Ross

In his Preface to the 1914 edition of *The Untilled Field* (1903), George Moore prides himself on having almost single-handedly shaped the modern Irish short story. He notes how he wrote the book "in the hope of furnishing the young Irish of the future with models" and calls it "a landmark in Anglo-Irish literature, a new departure" (Moore 2000, xxix, xxxii). Posterity seems to have agreed with this confident appraisal as Moore is generally considered the father of the modern Irish short story (Averill 1982; Ingman 2009, 84–94). "Moore made the Irish short story a fact", O'Connor wrote in *The Lonely Voice* and he subsequently selected "Home Sickness" as the opening story of his *Classic Irish Short Stories* (O'Connor 2004, 198; 1957). Influenced by Turgenev's *Sketches from a Hunter's Album*, Moore is credited with moving the short story beyond both the Gaelic myths or folktales eagerly collected in the Irish Renaissance and the nineteenth-century tale tradition of Carleton, Griffin and Le Fanu. Moore's use of the short story as a vehicle for psychological and social realism is, in its turn, considered an influence on the work of subsequent Irish short story writers, notably Joyce, O'Flaherty and O'Connor. Without denying the importance of *The Untilled Field* in the history of the Irish short story, I want to make a case in this chapter for two alternative starting points of that tradition: George Egerton's *Keynotes* (1893) and *Discords* (1894) and Somerville and Ross's Irish R.M. stories, first published in *The Badminton Magazine* in 1898. These writers, I will argue, should be revalued as important mothers of the Irish short story, as they stand at the birth of two strands of modern short fiction which continue

© The Editor(s) (if applicable) and The Author (s) 2016   21
E. D'hoker, *Irish Women Writers and the Modern Short Story*,
DOI 10.1007/978-3-319-30288-1_2

to shape the short story today. At the same time, their work foregrounds questions of connection and community which constitute a red thread through the short fiction of Irish women writers. While many of Egerton's stories imaginatively investigate the ethical tensions between self and other involved in being a mother, a wife and a sister, the stories of Somerville and Ross explore the network of relations that constitute a community in the South-West of Ireland.

GEORGE EGERTON'S PIONEERING SHORT STORIES

Although George Egerton, pen name of Mary Chavelita Dunne (1859–1945), published plays, translations and an autobiographical novel, her fame as a writer rests almost entirely on the short stories she published in five collections between 1893 and 1905. Egerton also saw herself primarily as a short story writer. In a 1932 autobiographical essay, she wrote: "I was a short story, at most a long short story writer. For years they came in droves and said themselves, leaving no scope for padding or altered endings; the long book was not my pigeon" (1932, 59). In 1893, Egerton became an instant celebrity with the publication of her first collection *Keynotes*, published by Elkin Mathews and John Lane at the Bodley Head, with a cover design by Aubrey Beardsley. The book caused quite a stir for its innovative style as well as its taboo-breaking subject matter and John Lane subsequently borrowed its title for his notorious Keynote Series. Two years later, Egerton's collection had gone through eight editions and had been translated into seven languages (Stetz and Lasner 1990, 39). In 1894, John Lane and Henry Harland also invited Egerton to contribute to the inaugural volume of *The Yellow Book*, an honour she shared with Henry James, Edmund Gosse and Arthur Symons. Egerton's two subsequent collections, *Symphonies* and *Fantasias*, were also published by The Bodley Head, in 1897 and 1898 respectively. Yet for her last collection, *Flies in Amber* (1905), she struggled to find a publisher. In retrospect, Egerton wondered whether she had perhaps been too reluctant to adapt her work to publishers' demands and to the market which, in the early twentieth century, seemed much less keen on short story collections (1932, 59). At her death in 1945, Egerton had certainly outlived her fame and for much of the twentieth century her work was forgotten, despite the publication in 1958 of *A Leaf from the Yellow Book: The Correspondence of George Egerton* by her nephew, Terence de Vere White (Egerton 1958).

Since the late 1980s, however, Egerton's stories have enjoyed a critical revival. Scholars of New Woman writing have praised her work for its ground-breaking use of literary impressionism and psychological realism, for its novel depiction of women's inner lives and desires, and for its frank treatment of taboo-topics such as female sexuality, adultery, and infanticide (Ardis 1990, 115ff; Pykett 1992, 1995; Heilmann 2000). For Gerd Bjørhovde, Egerton is "a true literary pioneer, from a formal and technical point of view as well as in subject matter and themes" (1987, 131). More recently, Egerton's work has also been recovered in an Irish context. Kate McCullough, Tina O'Toole and Maureen O'Connor have identified Irish elements in her writings, in terms of setting, religious allusions, ideological critique and folkloric beliefs (McCullough 1996; O'Connor 2010, 64–83; O'Toole 2013, 88–109). In her *History of the Irish Short Story*, Ingman also discusses Egerton's short stories, as part of the "*fin de siècle* visions" of such writers as Yeats, Wilde and James Stephens. She writes,

> Though Egerton is not generally admitted to histories of the Irish short story, her stories have many links with other Irish writers. She shares with Yeats the use of the form to convey her artistic and spiritual visions. Her stories anticipate Joyce in their critique of Dublin's narrow-minded materialism and in their use of the Orient as a place of imagined liberation and sexual fantasy. (Ingman 2009, 75)

To this, I would add that Egerton's highly innovative use of narrative techniques, plot structures and stylistic devices has been very instrumental in shaping the modern short story in Britain and Ireland. While her actual fame may not have lasted beyond the early twentieth century, her indirect influence extends much further: from Anglo-Irish contemporaries such as Sarah Grand and Ella D'Arcy, ranging over modernist writers like Moore and Joyce to the work of Elizabeth Bowen, Mary Lavin and Anne Enright. In order to properly gauge Egerton's importance as a pioneering short story writer, however, it is necessary to consider her work in its publication context, the so-called 'golden age' of the English short story, when, as H.G. Wells memorably put it, "short stories broke out everywhere" (1911, v).

It is by now well documented that the development of the modern short story in late-nineteenth-century Britain was in important ways enabled by the exponential growth of the magazine market. As Henry James put it in

1891, "Periodical literature is a huge open mouth which has to be fed—a vessel of immense capacity which has to be filled" (1986, 232). Following the famous example of *The Strand* magazine, moreover, more and more magazines made it their policy to publish only self-contained works of short fiction rather than the serialized novels which had been popular for much of the nineteenth century. As a result, the short story became for the first time a financially viable genre for young and established writers (Baldwin 2013, 9–11). With the growing demand for self-contained short fiction came an increased awareness of the generic specificity of the genre, as distinct from the novel. Before the 1880s, "Victorian editors and readers did not insist upon relatively brief self-contained stories but were content with short fiction that was in essence a condensed novel or that took the form of a joke, fantasy, or thriller" (Baldwin 2013, 10). Yet, influenced by American realist short stories and by the translations of Maupassant, Pushkin and Daudet that appeared in the first issues of *The Strand* (Ashley 2006, 11), a clearer concept of the genre started to emerge, an awareness that the "short story could achieve great richness and complexity as a result of, rather than in spite of its brevity" (Hunter 2007, 2). Writers like Stevenson and Kipling were the first to realize the potential of the new genre: "Combining exoticism, realism, local colour and moralism, first Stevenson and then Kipling—inspired by Bret Harte—found the short story both profitable financially and satisfying artistically" (Baldwin 2013, 11). In the "Kipling boom" of 1889, the latter in particular was praised by his contemporaries for "having reinvented the short story" (Hunter 2007, 20). Inevitably, writers, editors and reviewers eagerly sought to pinpoint the characteristics of this new genre. Poe's insistence on unity—"unity of impression" as well as "unique or single *effect*"—became one of the guiding principles of the short story (Poe 1994, 60, 61). As Brander Matthews summarized it in *The Philosophy of the Short-Story* (1901), "[a] true Short-story differs from the Novel chiefly in its essential unity of impression [...] A Short-story deals with a single character, a single event, a single emotion, or the series of emotions called forth by a single situation" (1994, 73).

If this emphasis on unity was realized by many writers through a tightly controlled plot, character types, and an emphasis on closure, often by means of a final revelation or twist (think of Kipling's mystery stories or Conan Doyle's detective stories), other writers sought to achieve this unity of impression by other means. Chief among this second group was Henry James who experimented with the form and structure of his stories to carefully adjust "every portion of story to the atmosphere, theme, and total effect of the work" (Harris 1979, 86). James himself spelled out the opposition between the two modes as follows:

> [The effect] with which we are most familiar is that of the detached incident, single and sharp, as clear as a pistol-shot; the other, of rarer performance, is that of the impression, comparatively generalized—simplified, foreshortened, reduced to a single perspective—of a complexity or continuity. The former is an adventure comparatively safe, in which you have, for the most part, but to put one foot in front of the other. It is just the risks of the latter, on the contrary, that make the best of the sport. (1898, 652)

In opposition to most incident-bound magazine stories, James advocated plotlessness and an emphasis on a single mood or atmosphere as well as omission and compression to achieve complexity. Critics and writers found in this sense of plotlessness a ready means to distinguish the literary story from its popular counterpart, thus opening up the gap between popular and highbrow writing which would become even more pronounced in the early twentieth century. Particularly *The Yellow Book*, published by John Lane, was instrumental in "redefining the short story against its prevalent mass-cultural identification" (Chan 2007, 55). Styled as a precious art object, with its distinctive yellow cover and drawings by Audrey Beardsley, *The Yellow Book* sought to raise the short story to the status of an elite art form, defining it—in explicit opposition to popular stories—through such terms as compression, suggestion, ambiguity, interiority, and plot-lessness. In one of his provocative "Yellow Dwarf" columns, for instance, Henry Harland contrasts his journal's refined literary stories—"the Cats of Bookland", which "proceed by omission, by implication and suggestion" and "employ the *demi-mot* and the *nuance*"—to the "Dogs of Bookland" with "their boisterousness" and "their low truckling to the tastes of the purchaser" (1896, 15–16). Moreover, Harland, and other *Yellow Book* writers, also associated the popular *Strand* stories with ideological conservativism and, hence, the plotless, experimental short fiction with (Hunter 2007, 39).

Into this coterie of writers, artists and critics, George Egerton was enthusiastically welcomed in 1893. The manuscript of *Keynotes*, which she had sent to John Lane at The Bodley Head, was strongly recommended for publication by Richard Le Galienne and "launched at the head of what became a distinguished list of new writers" (Vicinus 1983, 19). Yet

Egerton had written the stories, for financial reasons, at some remove from the London buzz: in the rural environment of Millstreet, Co. Cork. We can only speculate about the extent to which she had been inspired by the short story boom of the late 1880s and early 1890s: Egerton had lived in London for a short period around that time, before taking up permanent residency there in 1894. Yet critics have mostly traced the extraordinary original and innovative quality of her short stories to the influence of the Scandinavian writers she had read—and met—in the late 1880s when living in Norway. As Harris notes:

> From the Scandinavian dramatists [Ibsen and Strindberg] very likely came the encouragement to treat the questions of love and marriage with frankness and to dare to reveal attitudes strongly at variance with conventional morality. To Hamsun she almost certainly owes her interest in reproducing the indirect, at times wayward progress by which the mind assimilates thoughts and impressions. (1968, 32)

And Ledger concurs, "The intense psychological penetration of Ibsen and Strindberg's drama ... profoundly influenced *Keynotes* and *Discords*, as did the hallucinatory, fragmentary lyricism of Hamsun's early work, and the aestheticism of Hansson's early poetry" (2006, xviii). Although Egerton openly advertised these influences, by translating Hansson and Hamsun or having her characters in her stories allude to Ibsen, Strindberg and Bjørnson, she also made these stimuli very much her own and integrated them in highly original short stories which in many ways anticipate the celebrated modernist characteristics of the form.

In terms of plot, first, Egerton deviates from both the complex and convoluted plots of Victorian tales and the incident-bound plot structure of the popular short stories, by shaping her stories around a seemingly ordinary slice of life. While "An Empty Frame" and "Her Share" evoke a single momentous experience or conversation, a more recurrent strategy is the juxtaposition of a few such scenes, carefully selected to bring out the ambivalent complexity of the protagonist's psychology. "Virgin Soil" juxtaposes two defining moments in a young girl's life: in the first, a frightened girl is carted off by a "proprietory" husband after her wedding (Egerton 2006, 128); in the second, a disillusioned young woman returns alone to confront her mother over the unanticipated horrors of her marriage. The intervening period is only hinted at by means of blank space and four asterisks. In "A Cross Line", similarly, three scenes spread out over a few days show us the protagonist's conflicted desires through a flirtation with a handsome stranger, a comfortable evening scene with her devoted husband and the discovery of pregnancy and maternal feelings in a conversation with her maid. In tri-partite stories such as "Under Northern Sky", "The Regeneration of Two" and "A Psychological Moment at Three Periods", this juxtaposition of discrete scenes is spelled out even more clearly: the effect is again one of evoking the complexity of a woman's life through some carefully selected and often contrasting scenes, which are fully realized in both external and internal details. What happens in between these scenes is entirely omitted or only briefly hinted at, so that plot is de-emphasized in favour of psychology and mood.

On a par with these ellipses and omissions are the abrupt beginnings of Egerton's stories in *Keynotes* and *Discords*. "A Cross Line" opens enigmatically with "The rather flat notes of a man's voice float out into the clear air" and any hard facts about the characters or their context have to be deduced from dialogues or rare descriptions (Egerton 2006, 3). Open endings too are used by Egerton to great effect. "A Cross Line" ends on a seemingly trivial dialogue between the woman and her maid, the significance of which has to be inferred by the reader while "Now Spring Has Come" opens with some lines from a song and ends with the question "Do you really think that crinolines will be worn?" (2006, 23). Other stories end on a moment of insight or symbolic significance similar to Joyce's celebrated modernist epiphanies. In "An Empty Frame", the woman's growing awareness of being imprisoned in an insignificant marriage is symbolized by a dream of her head being "wedged in a huge frame, the top of her head touches its top, the sides its sides, and it keeps growing larger and larger and her head with it, until she seems to be sitting inside her own head, and the inside is one vast hollow" (2006, 43), while "Wedlock" refrains from describing the triple infanticide that closes the story, only hinting at it through the protagonist's dream of "poppies, blood-red poppies [scattered] in handfuls over three open graves" (2006, 126).

In terms of the overall style of her stories too, Egerton often makes use of symbolic patterns to evoke the situation or state of mind of a protagonist. The empty frame, in the story of that title, symbolizes the absence of true passion in the marriage while the "chrysanthemums struggl[ing] to raise their heads from the gravel path into which the sharp shower has beaten them" stand for the young woman who will try to carve out a new life after her disastrous marriage (2006, 128). Throughout the stories, women are often associated with nature and animals: birds, flowers, snakes and horses. Maureen O'Connor reads this symbolism as pointing to a "parallel suffering endured by woman and animal that renders them equally abject" (2010, 65), but there are also many positive images which attribute to her female—and some male—characters a primitive wildness in tune with nature. Another characteristic of Egerton's style that is markedly modernist is her recurrent use of associations to link scenes or memories and to generally evoke a character's thought process. In "Now Spring Has Come" and "A Psychological Moment" a line from a song serves "to jog a link in a chain of association" (2006, 15), while in "A Cross Line" daydreams work in a similar fashion. In many other stories, the associations appear more random and serve to highlight the eccentric meanderings of a private mind.

Of course, these stylistic features of symbolism, association, ellipsis and suggestion are only effective because of the equally innovative mode of narration of Egerton's short stories. If the nineteenth-century tale often worked with gregarious editorial narrators, the popular magazine story favours the more tightly unified perspective of a witness or mediating narrator "whose authority and ordinariness […] served to verify the story's ultimate truth" (Chan 2007, 36). Egerton, to the contrary, is not so much interested in conveying factual truth as in exploring psychological truth. Hence, her stories explore different narrative ways of achieving psychological realism. Some of her stories make use of third-person narration with focalization—and free indirect discourse—to faithfully record the individual protagonist's consciousness. The long and fanciful interior monologue in "A Cross Line" is perhaps the most famous example of this technique, but also much of "Under the Northern Sky" and "A Psychological Moment" is written in this figural mode, which would become the hallmark of the short stories of Joyce, Mansfield and Woolf. Stories such as "Now Spring Has Come" and "A Little Grey Glove", however, achieve unity and authenticity by means of the sustained subjective perspective of a first-person protagonist narrator who relates a significant episode or encounter.

From this first-person perspective, it is but a small step to the unreliable narration that Egerton would use to great effect in her *Yellow Book* story, "A Lost Masterpiece" to evoke the arrogant self-absorption of a male artist figure (who prefigures the artist narrator of Mansfield's "Je ne parle pas français"). Yet another group of Egerton's stories borrows the technique of multiple or embedded narration from the popular magazine stories. In "The Spell of the White Elf", a first-person narrator relates her transformational encounter with another woman, who tells—again in the first-person—of the happiness a child has given her, while in "Her Share", the narration of a woman's love stifled by society and convention is antithetically embedded within the story of the main protagonist "in the first flush of [her] new-found happiness" (2006, 95). Although these multiple, embedded narrations do not serve to cast doubt on the truth of the story (as they would in Conrad's box-like story structures), neither do they serve to emphasize the veracity of the story as in the case of the multiple trustworthy narrators of *The Strand*'s popular detective stories. Rather, the focus of the stories is on the bonds of affinity and sisterhood which are forged between women in an exchange of life experiences. Smaller instances of this can also be found in the maid's telling of her stillborn child in "A Cross Line" or the sad life stories exchanged by the two old school friends in the final part of "A Psychological Moment". Although this emphasis on storytelling may seem to us as a remnant of an older tale tradition in Egerton's otherwise modern stories, it is important to stress the specific—and quite radical—thematic purpose to which this traditional technique is put: that of foregrounding the bonds between women as in many ways more lasting and profound than heterosexual relationships. And it is to this thematic interest in sisterhood and other forms of relationship that I will now turn.

After all, readers of Egerton's stories were—and still are—primarily interested in their quite daring thematic and ideological content. Contemporary reviewers recognized the literary quality and originality of Egerton's short stories—"Nothing more powerful and original has appeared in English fiction for many a day", a review in *The Speaker* claimed (Gill 1893, 611)—but they focused primarily on the issues she addressed. Opinions were sharply divided: some reviewers praised her stories as "true human documents", containing "the authentic bitter cry of suffering" (Anonymous 1894, 684), others saw only "sexual hysterics" in "revolting studies of drink and lust and murder" which "should never have been printed" (Anonymous 1895, 375). Recent critics too have mostly focused on Egerton's critique of the social conventions that restrict women and her exploration of the suffering that comes from suppressed dreams and desires. Feeling trapped by the nineteenth-century gender ideology, Egerton's protagonists often yearn for freedom and escape. In an erotically charged daydream, the protagonist of "A Cross Line" longs "to sail off somewhere too—away from the daily need of dinner-getting, and the recurring Monday with its washing; life with its tame duties and virtuous monotony. She fancies herself in Arabia on the back of a swift steed" (2006, 8). While she is proud of her own "self-sufficiency", "I have been for myself, and helped myself, and borne the burden of my own mistakes", she speaks wistfully of "the freedom, the freshness, the vague danger, the unknown" (Egerton 2006, 10–11). These sentiments are echoed by other women throughout the two collections, where "free woman" or "free spirit" are labels of honour (2006, 39, 77, 169), and they are symbolically underscored by the natural, open spaces in which these women are often depicted.

What chains these free spirits then are, first and foremost, the trappings of social codes and conventions. In a rather Nietzschean speech, the narrator of "Now Spring Has Come" exclaims:

> Isn't it dreadful to think what slaves we are to custom? I wonder shall we ever be able to tell the truth, ever be able to live fearlessly according to our light, to believe that what is right for us might be right? It seems as if all the religions, all the advancement, all the culture of the past, has only been a forging of chains to cripple posterity, a laborious building up of moral and legal prisons based on false conceptions of sin and shame, to cramp men's minds and hearts and souls, not to speak of women's. (2006, 16)

In the stories "Her Share" and "An Empty Frame", women are shown to suffer because they have lacked the courage to follow their own "light": having turned their back on love out of a concern for social propriety, they now lead "hollow" and "empty" lives (2006, 43, 100). In her negative portrayal of characters who curb their personal happiness because of "the world's opinion" (2006, 168), Egerton points forward to Mary Lavin's depiction of lives stunted by a fear of "what the neighbours would say" (D'hoker 2008a, 418).

In several other stories, however, social convention and religious doctrine conspire to chain female characters in an unhappy marriage. "Virgin Soil" and "A Psychological Moment" offer the most explicit indictments of marriage. In the first story, it is rejected as a prison, a "hateful yoke" to which mothers consign their ignorant daughters. In the latter, it is but a commercial transaction, no better than the affair secured through blackmail with which it is juxtaposed. And when marriage is entered voluntarily on the part of the woman, it is usually in a moment of weakness. "We forge our own chains in a moment of softness", the woman in "A Cross

Line" says, and this is echoed by the protagonist of "The Regeneration of Two": "I married without understanding anything about it [...] He just came to me in one of my affectible moods." When her husband dies, her "strongest feeling ... was a fierce inward whisper of exultant joy that I belonged to myself again" (Egerton 2006, 11, 137).

If freedom and self-reliance are a precious good in the stories, Egerton is also careful to distinguish these ideals from individualism and egoism. Even though her protagonists may clamour for freedom and may seek to escape the "bondage" of marriage, this does not mean that they aim for the radical egotism and self-cultivation promoted by Nietzsche (D'hoker 2011, 538). Instead, the ultimate ideal seems to be a self-discovery in the service of others. This slightly paradoxical ideal responds to the central concern with independence and autonomy in the literature of the period. For Regenia Gagnier, *fin-de-siècle* discourse distinguished between independence, which "eliminates all values but self-affirmation and thus gives rise to irreducible differences" and autonomy, which is "relational and compatible with submission to a common need or even common law" (2010, 62). Comparing the depiction of the New Woman in writing by men and women in the late nineteenth century, she argues, "Women-created New Women were not so rigidly independent. They wanted autonomy, individual development, but they wanted it through relationship" (2010, 63). In Egerton's stories too, the emphasis on self-reliance is tempered by the many other relationships which the protagonists willingly engage in. Almost all of the stories contain moments of woman-to-woman bonding: between mistress and maid as in "A Cross Line" and "The Regeneration of Two", between strangers who bond over an exchange of life stories as in "The Spell of the White Elf", "Her Share" and "Gone Under", or between childhood friends as in "A Psychological Moment". Moreover, the darkest stories are precisely those where that sense of bonding is lacking: "Wedlock", where the writer turns her back on her suffering landlady or "A Virgin Soil", where the mother fails to share her knowledge of life and love with her daughter. Although critics have been divided over whether Egerton bases this sense of woman-to-woman relations in a shared female nature, which may or may not cross the boundaries of class and race (McCullough 1996; Jusová 2000; Hager 2006), it is clear that these moments of woman-to-woman bonding are of vital importance for Egerton. A culmination of this sense of sisterhood can be found in the utopian community of women which the protagonist founds in "The Regeneration of Two": "a colony of women managed by a woman, going their own way to hold a place in the world in the face of opinion" (Egerton 2006, 161). Yet, the protagonist's care for these 'fallen women' and their illegitimate children is perhaps not so much sisterly as it is motherly. In this way, it links up with the notion of motherhood, which is also often celebrated in *Keynotes* and *Discords*.

Much has been written about the precise meaning and value of motherhood in Egerton's stories, especially about the extent to which Egerton constructs the "Mutter-Drang" or "maternal instinct" as an essential female characteristic, "the *only divine* fibre in a woman", as it is called in "Gone Under" (Egerton 2006, 108; Fluhr 2001). Yet if maternal feelings are often celebrated in *Keynotes* and *Discords*, providing a moment of bonding between women in such stories as "A Cross Line", "The Spell of the White Elf", and "The Regeneration of Two", mother-child relations themselves hardly figure at all in the collections. And when they do—briefly in "The Spell" and "Regeneration"—the children mothered are not the woman's own. Although stories like "Wedlock" and "Gone Under" sound terrible warnings of what happens when instinctual maternal feelings are crossed, most other stories depict and celebrate an abstract and generalized maternal feeling which encompasses all those in need of care: children, siblings, animals, but also other women and even men. Moreover, also men in Egerton's stories can possess this maternal sensibility: the husband in "A Cross Line" "love[s] young things" and the husband in "The Spell" seems to have an innate knowledge of babies: "she never seen a man as knew so much about babies, not for one as never 'ad none of 'is own" (2006, 5, 30). As Jusová puts it, "If mothering appears to be a matter of congenital instinct with some women, it is described as being at least as 'inherent' in many of Egerton's male characters, whereas with numerous other women, the mothering 'instinct' is clearly a matter of socialization" (2000, 38–9).

However, Egerton goes even further than this social constructivist notion of motherhood. In several stories, motherhood is raised to the level of a moral and social ideal. It is seen as an antidote to egoism and morbid self-absorption, and should therefore be put in the service of society at large. In "Gone Under", the maternal is celebrated as a "moral" value, fostering "the sublimest qualities of unselfishness and devotion" (Egerton 2006, 108) and in "The Regeneration", the protagonist who considers herself "too selfish" for "abstract" "philanthropy" finds her destiny in taking care of other women and children, "all dependent on her in some way" (2006, 136, 154). In this way, Egerton's celebrated "maternal instinct" becomes a generalized human ethical model, anticipating the "ethics of care" developed by contemporary philosophers (Gilligan 1982; Held 2006; Slote 2007).

Given the equally strong insistence on self-reliance and freedom in the stories, one may wonder, though, how Egerton manages to balance the claims of self and others in her ethical model. The longest and most explicit exposition of Egerton's belief system can be found in the last part of "A Psychological Moment", where the protagonist—whose childhood and youth bear clear similarities to Egerton's own life—gives advice to an old friend in need. However, to a contemporary reader, her advice seems not without its contradictions. On the one hand, the woman counsels independence and self-reliance:

> You must find yourself. All the systems of philosophy or treatises of moral science, all the religious codes devised by the imagination of men will not save you—*always you must come back to yourself* [...] You've got to get a purchase on your own soul. Stand on your own feet, heed no man's opinion, no woman's scorn, if you believe you are in the right [...] Work out your own fate. (2006, 93)

On the other hand, this Nietzschean advice is juxtaposed with the decidedly un-Nietzschean exhortation to "Forget yourself, live as much as you can for others" (2006, 92; see D'hoker 2011).

If both self-discovery and self-negation remain largely theoretical ideals in "A Psychological Moment", they receive a concrete, if utopian, application in "The Regeneration of Two" where the protagonist achieves autonomy and self-reliance through a process of self-discovery—"I had found myself all the same, and I said: From this out I belong body and soul to myself; I will live as I choose, seek joy as I choose, carve the way of my life as I will"—but subsequently puts this newly found self-confidence in the service of others, defying ridicule and disapproval to set up a "scheme for helping wretched sisters out of the mire" (2006, 165, 153). Other stories too seem to bear out Gagnier's understanding of relational autonomy, since a strong sense of self seems to go hand in hand with a care for others, at least in so far as these others are women, as in "Gone Under", where the young protagonist, "a free spirit", cares for the wretched Edith, or children, as in "The Spell" where maternal care happily complements the woman's independent working life.

Still, a tension between self and other does emerge when a relationship threatens to overwhelm the self, as it does in the love—and lovesickness—depicted in "Now Spring has Come":

> It is bad enough to be a fool and not to know it, but to be a fool and feel with every fibre of your being that you are one, and that there is no help for it; that all your philosophy won't aid you; that you are one great want, stilled a little by a letter, only to be haunted afresh by the personality of another creature tortured with doubts and hurt by your loss of self-respect. (2006, 21)

If self-containment is not—or not necessarily—threatened by maternal or sisterly bonds, it is often threatened by heterosexual love in Egerton's stories. In "Now Spring Has Come", Egerton also blames conventional morality and gender roles for this: "we repress, and then some day we stumble on the man who just satisfies our sexual and emotional nature, and then there is a shipwreck of some sort. When we shall live larger and freer lives, we shall be better balanced than we are now" (2006, 21). As if to demonstrate this claim, the last story of *Discords*, "The Regeneration of Two" does end on the promise of a perfect balance between self and other in a "free" relationship of equals, where love "will never be more than one note; true, a grand note, in the harmony of union; but not the harmony" (2006, 167). Even if this resolution of all the discords of the previous stories in a grand finale, in which self and other are in perfect harmony, is perhaps too utopian to be really convincing, it is clear testimony of Egerton's ideal of individuation without separation, of a strong self in—rather than at the expense of—relationships.

Hunting with a Twist in Somerville and Ross's *The Irish R.M.*

If the neglect of Egerton's ground-breaking stories in Irish literary criticism may have been due both to the overall disregard of her work as well as to its lack of explicitly Irish settings, subject matters and themes, these reasons cannot be adduced to explain the absence of Somerville and Ross's *The Irish R.M.* in the canon of the Irish short story. Hugely popular when they first appeared, in *The Badminton Magazine* (1898–1899) and in *The*

Strand (1904–1907), the stories have never gone out of print and the authors themselves have obtained a place in the Irish canon on account of their naturalist Big House novel, *The Real Charlotte* (1894). In terms of setting, characters, and language, moreover, the R.M. stories are recognizably Irish—even if the nature of that Irishness was not to everyone's liking. In spite of this, the R.M. stories have, as a rule, not been included in critical accounts of the modern Irish short story. Illustrative in this respect is Frank O'Connor's brief discussion of the stories in *The Lonely Voice* as "an object lesson in the way storytelling develops" (2004, 32–6). While he admits that *The Irish R.M.* is "one of the most lovable books I know", he does not consider it as serious literature: the stories are "yarns, pure and simple", mere "schoolgirl high jinks". Moreover, for O'Connor, they hark back to the nineteenth-century tale tradition and are thus to be dismissed from consideration in the context of the modern short story. Contrasting the book unfavourably to *The Untilled Field*, O'Connor continues, "Though I suspect that for one copy of *The Untilled Field* you can find, you will find a hundred of *The Irish R.M.*, Irish literature has gone Moore's way, not Somerville and Ross's."

Again, critics have unquestioningly taken over O'Connor's verdict, discussing the work, if at all, in the context of nineteenth-century literature. For Heinz Kozok, the stories belong "soziologisch wie literarisch" in the nineteenth century (1982, 131), Julie-Ann Stevens notes that they have little affinity with the modern Irish short story as it would later develop (2007, 162), and in her *History of the Irish Short Story*, Ingman discusses the authors in the context of the nineteenth-century tale tradition, rather than in her chapter on *fin-de-siècle* experiments with short fiction. Surely that is an odd context for a story series that ran from 1898, when the stories were first serialized in *The Badminton Magazine for Sports and Pastimes*, to 1915 when the third collection, *In Mr. Knox's Country*, was published in London. As we have seen, in the 1890s the modern short story came into its own as both a highly popular and a self-consciously literary genre. That Somerville and Ross were familiar with these new developments can be seen from their correspondence with each other and with editors and other writers. They were particularly admiring of Kipling's innovative modern short stories and Kipling himself wrote an enthusiastic letter to Somerville, noting correspondences between their works (Rauchbauer 1995, 172–3, 231). Moreover, James Pinker, their literary agent, also represented such innovators of the modern short story as H.G. Wells, Stephen Crane and Joseph Conrad (Stevens 2007, 161). Further, as O'Connor himself indicates, the novels of Somerville and Ross clearly reveal the authors' knowledge of and adherence to international literary trends. Is it then at all credible that these ambitious authors would, as O'Connor argues, "forg[e]t all they had ever learned from the French Naturalists and wr[i]te [the R.M. stories] just to enjoy themselves" (2004, 33)?

It is of course not hard to see that several characteristics of the R.M. stories offend O'Connor's model for the modern Irish short story. The R.M. stories foreground a community, rooted in a very specific place (West Carbery in County Cork), rather than O'Connor's outlaws and outsiders. As they mostly revolve around Major Yeates's relations to and experiences with the characters that make up this community, loneliness is not an issue. Moreover, while O'Connor's ideal story zooms in on an individual's consciousness, tragically illuminated by a life-changing experience, the stories of Somerville and Ross are comic, rather than tragic. They are peopled by types and too preoccupied with action and dialogue to register the finer shades of mood or consciousness. Nor are they overtly concerned with the themes of politics, religion or ideology which O'Connor considered characteristic of the Irish short story. Finally, they are the product of a close collaboration between two women writers, which in itself was probably enough to offend O'Connor's ideal of the short story as "the lonely voice" addressed by a solitary writer to a solitary reader.

The success of the stories and the collaborative efforts of their authors seem in general to have impeded recognition of *The Irish R.M.* as serious works of art (Jamison 2007) as did the taint of stage-Irishry and upper-class snobbery that clung to the stories for much of the twentieth century (Waters 1984; Deane 2000). More recently, however, the R.M. stories have received closer scrutiny in terms of their social context and politics (Crossman 2000; Stevens 2007), their subversive deployment of gendered conventions (Cahalan 1993; Cowman 1997; O'Connor 2010), and their aesthetics (Garavel 2008). In what follows I would like to add to this process of recovery, by reconsidering the position of *The Irish R.M.* within the Irish short story tradition. In particular, I want to make a claim for the seminal importance of Somerville and Ross's stories as Irish representatives of that other strand of the modern short story: the tightly unified and plot-bound magazine story, which was developed in the British periodical literature of the 1890s by writers such as Kipling, Stevenson and Wells. It continued to flourish in the works of such masters of the short story as Pritchett, Saki and Maugham in Britain, but also infuses Irish short fiction from Elizabeth Bowen's ghost stories and James Stephen's satirical stories over the darkly comic stories of Benedict Kiely and Clare Boylan to the plot-bound stories of Kevin Barry and Colin Barrett.

In short story criticism, the two types of short fiction are often described as plotted vs. plotless stories: "works in which the major emphasis is on plot and those in which plot is subordinate to mood" (Hanson 1985, 5). Although critics have described the development of both types in twentieth-century short fiction, the critical hegemony of the plotless modernist short story has been such that the plot-bound story has often been sidelined as popular or middlebrow, and as harking back to the nineteenth-century tale. However, the popular magazine story which came into being in the late nineteenth century was very much a modern form, quite different from Victorian tales, on account of its brevity and realism, its formal and thematic unity, its self-consciousness about storytelling and narration, and the absence of moralizing didacticism. As we have seen, it was in fact the very popularity of this new, plot-bound, unified short story that provoked a counter-reaction among writers and critics and led to the development of the plotless, open-ended, mood-dependent short stories in avant-garde magazines such as *The Yellow Book* and *The Savoy*. Although these stories—of which Egerton can be considered a pioneer—were at the time "ritually branded as 'mere' sketches, impressions, atmospheric pieces, mood studies" (Baldwin 2013, 131), they were subsequently consolidated in the modernist short story and became, to a large extent, normative for the genre as a whole. Since critics are now increasingly recognizing the importance of the popular, plot-bound strand of short fiction which existed side by side with its more celebrated modernist counterpart for much of the twentieth century, it is important to also acknowledge the place of *The Irish R.M.* within this first strand and within the tradition of the Irish short story as a whole. Far from being mere relics of a dying Victorian tale tradition, I argue, the stories of Somerville and Ross are quintessentially modern. Their first collection, *Some Experiences of an Irish R.M.* (1899), in particular, deserves credit for being one of the first modern Irish short story collections, on a par with—if very different from— Egerton's *Keynotes*.

Compared to the loose, anecdotal plots of most nineteenth-century tales, Somerville and Ross's stories stand out by their concision and remarkable unity. The stories achieve the "single effect" which contemporary critics recommended for the story through a unified setting, time frame and theme. Every detail counts in their stories, and seemingly stray remarks, incidents or side characters in the opening scenes of the stories invariably return with added significance in the closing scenes. In terms of plot structure, the stories typically revolve around a series of mishaps or comical misunderstandings, which reach a, generally disastrous, climax and are brought to some kind of resolution in the end. In this, the R.M. stories follow the "unique poetics for the short story" developed by writers and critics at *The Strand* and similar middlebrow magazines, "of plots unified around a revelation, their complications deriving from negotiations between exposure and suppression of a secret toward an ultimately inevitably 'truth' consisting of objective, irrefutable fact" (Chan 2007, 3). Still, contrary to the detective stories that *The Strand* liked to publish, in which the truth invariably damns the criminal, in Somerville and Ross's stories, a revelation of the true facts of some misdemeanour only rarely results in the true culprits being brought to justice. Instead, Major Yeates and other figures of authority usually draw the shortest end. In "Holy Island", for instance, Major Yeates and Constable Murray are outwitted by farmer Canty, who successfully smuggles illegal whiskey to his brother's pub in Cork under cover of a funeral cortege. As Flurry Knox laughingly notes to Murray, "by the time the train was in Cork, yourself and the Major were the only two men in town that weren't talking about it" (Somerville and Ross 2002, 167). In many other stories, Major Yeates's naïvety—and the manipulations of arch-schemer Flurry Knox—leave him in incriminating situations, where he has to defend his honesty and integrity against witnesses and the reader. Mrs. Knox's pronouncement in one of the early stories, "I acquit you Major [...] though appearances are against you", thus applies to many of the stories (2002, 75). Or as Major Yeates notes wryly in "The Aussolas Martin Cat", "As is usual in my dealings with Flurry, the fault was mine" (2002, 435). The final lines of "When I First Met Dr. Hickey" capture the reversal effected in many stories in another striking image: "'There are those men again!' exclaimed Philippa, coming a little nearer to me. In front of us, deviously ascending the long slope; was the Asylum party; the keepers, exceedingly drunk, being assisted to the station by the lunatics" (2002, 44). As Garavel notes, this reversal typically finds Yeates "manipulated into subverting the standards he has ostensibly been sent to uphold" (2008, 94). In other words, while adhering to the poetics of unity, revelation and closure of the popular magazine story, Somerville and Ross at the same time depart from its attendant affirmation of authority and rationality, instead working towards a comic, sometimes satirical, reversal in which hierarchies are destabilized and authority is undermined.

In spite of these comic and satiric elements, however, there is a great deal of realism in the stories as well. In this too, the stories are distinct from the Victorian tales, with their predilection for the supernatural. Nevertheless, critics have often banned the R.M. stories from the realist tradition of the modern short story, arguing that "they flee reality and take happy refuge in a world compounded of outrageously funny accidents and extravagant Irish folk" (Cronin 1972, 53). Apart from the comic dimension, it is especially their reliance on types that has damned them for many critics, as this seemed to perpetuate the tradition of using stage-Irish characters to please English audiences. While it is certainly true that the mode of characterization in the R.M. stories depends on a shared knowledge of types rather than on moral complexity or psychological insight, it should also be stressed that all characters are treated in this way: Irish, English and Anglo-Irish; protagonists no less than marginal characters. Take, for instance, the description of "the honourable Basil Leigh Kelway" in "Lisheen Races, Second-Hand": "the stout young friend of my youth had changed considerably. His important nose and slightly prominent teeth remained, but his wavy hair had withdrawn intellectually from his temples; his eyes had acquired a statesmanlike absence of expression, and his neck had grown long and birdlike", or our first introduction to Flurry Knox, Major Yeates's scheming but likeable landlord: "He was a fair, spare young man, who looked like a stableboy among gentlemen, and a gentleman among stableboys", "he seldom laughed, having in unusual perfection the gravity of manners that is bred by horse-dealing, probably from the habitual repression of all emotion save disparagement" (2002, 94, 10–11). As these examples make clear, characters are often introduced, and their actions described, through reference to the group or type they belong to: the cook is said to reply "with the exulting pessimism of her kind", a small boy is "stimulating [a] donkey with the success peculiar to his class", an officer is mocked for "the common English delusion that he could imitate an Irish brogue", and Philippa, in one of innumerable generalizations about the "female sex", is said to possess, "in common with many of her sex, an inappeasable passion for picnics" (2002, 96, 124, 90, 158).

What is interesting, though, is that contemporary reviewers did not see this mode of characterization as in conflict with the realist dimension of the stories. To the contrary, they praised the stories for their truthful recording of Anglo-Irish idiom and for their lifelike rendering of characters and scenes. The stories confront us with "life itself", one reviewer observes, "with all the added quickness to its revolutions and intensity to its vision that art can give" (Williams 1920, 563). Moreover, Somerville and Ross themselves were, by their own admission, very averse to stage-Irish buffoonery and considered their characters to be drawn from life (O'Connor 2010, 112). In her Prefaces, Somerville proudly records the response of many enthusiastic readers who thought they "knew" the originals on which the characters were based (Somerville 1991, xix; 2002, n.p.) and she notes that the characters are "composite photographs of the people of Ireland" (cited in Cowart 1994). In the illustrations accompanying her work too, "Somerville stressed the genuine quality of her pictures while noting that they represented particular types" (Stevens 2007, 113). In a letter to Lady Gregory, Martin similarly states that, unlike Romantic revivalists such as Synge or Yeats, her "instinct is for the real" (cited in Lewis 1987, 104).

How then can we square Somerville and Ross's realist aims with their reliance on type in characterization? First, accustomed as we have become to the modernist association of realism with the subjective, the individual, the random and the odd, it is perhaps difficult for us to see that a more Platonic conception of realism holds that a realistic depiction shows what is typical, characteristic or according to the norm (Nuttall 2004, 61). Somerville and Ross certainly subscribe to the latter conception. Second, lest one should simply see this understanding of realism as typicality as a remnant of an older tradition, it is important to consider the central role of character types in the modern short story, particularly in the strand of the plotted story which Somerville and Ross represent. Many short story writers have emphasized the need for stylization of characters in short fiction: Edith Wharton, for instance, has noted that in the short story "Type, general character may be set forth in a few strokes", while the novelistic "unfolding of personality [...] requires space" (cited in March-Russell 2009, 120) and Elizabeth Bowen agrees that, in short story fiction, "character cannot be more than *shown*—it is there for use, the use is dramatic. Foreshortening is not only unavoidable, it is right" (Bowen 1962, 71). A.E. Coppard too can be said to speak for Somerville and Ross's stories when he claims that if the novel starts from characters, the short story's initial focus is on situation and "the writer has to find the character or characters most suited to bring it to a successful issue" (cited in Shaw 1983, 119). This foreshortening or stylization of characters in short stories can be achieved in a variety of ways: through a self-conscious distance between author and characters, as in the works of Maugham, through the creation of "outsize" characters, in the manner of Twain, through staging nameless characters, as in several of Kipling's stories, by making characters the embodiment of certain ideologies, as in Lawrence's stories or, through the reliance on types, as in the stories of Chekhov (Shaw 1983, 134). Viewed in this context, Somerville and Ross's use of stereotypes in the R.M. stories can be seen both as an integral part of their realist project and as an inherent aspect of the mode of characterization of the modern short story.

In the case of the narrator-protagonist of the stories, moreover, this reliance on type in characterization contributes in important ways to the ironic double structure of the stories, which invites the reader to gently mock the narrator and to question his judgements. Like all other characters, indeed, Major Yeates is also composed of types. He recalls the "officious bumpkins of farce" as he is easily duped and frequently finds himself in positions that compromise his authority (Stevens 2007, 131). He is also the "reluctant husband" who complains of his wife's social events, her numerous dresses and former suitors (Somerville 2002, 453). On hunting, fishing or boating scenes, finally, Major Yeates takes on the role of the unenthusiastic sportsman, bemoaning the weather, the ungodly hour and many other small pains and discomforts. Although Yeates resembles the authoritative witness or mediating narrators characteristic of the new magazines stories, "whose authority and ordinariness […] served to verify the story's ultimate truth", as Chan put it (2007, 36), his often farcical experiences and overt stereotyping as a character at the same time serve to undermine that authority and mark him as an unreliable narrator. Indeed, the reader is invited to laugh not just along with the narrator, but also at his expense: at his many complaints, at his frequents bouts of self-pity and his craving for comfort, at his foolish partiality to young women and at his snobbishness. As we have seen, Yeates is also easily dupable: he is a naïve character who often fails to understand what is really going on and hence falls for the traps that Flurry and other characters set for him. Moreover, small hints in the text allow the reader to move ahead of Yeates and to scent the danger or understand the situation before he does. An ironic distance thus opens up between the beliefs, world-view or understanding of the narrator and those of the implied author (or the text itself), which narratologists recognize as the defining characteristic of unreliable narration (D'hoker 2008b, 152). James Phelan has usefully classified unreliable narration on the basis of three axes: (1) unreliable reporting on the axis of facts; (2) unreliable evaluating on the axis of ethics; and (3) unreliable reading on the axis of knowledge or perception (2005, 50). Following this division, we can argue that while Yeates can be trusted in his reporting of events, his frequently naïve readings of characters and events certainly give rise to narrative irony. On Phelan's axis of evaluation, Yeates's unreliability is even more clearly marked. This is indicated by the hyperbolic adjectives or adverbs marking his judgements of people and their actions, as in his disapproval of Sally's "base appeal to my professional feelings"; of Philippa's "preposterous reproach", her "nauseating hypocrisy" or of Bernard Shute's "exasperating health and energy" and the "ridiculous spectacle" he made of himself in courting a McRory girl (Somerville and Ross 2002, 211, 454, 375). In Yeates's many arguments with his wife, certainly, the reader is invited to side with Philippa rather than with her pompous husband and, hence, to disagree with his negative evaluation of Sally's marriage to Flurry ("She can do a good deal better than Flurry") (2002, 223), of Philippa's socializing with the McRorys (he calls the "indissoluble friendship" with the McRorys a "despicable position") (2002, 525), or of Philippa's hunting abilities:

> Any fair minded person will agree that I had cause to be excessively angry with Philippa. That a grown woman, the mother of two children, should mistake the bellow of a bullock for the note of a horn was bad enough; but that when, having caused a serious accident by not knowing her right hand from her left, and having, by further insanities, driven one valuable horse adrift in the country, probably broken the back of another, laid the seeds of heart disease in her husband from shock and over-exertion, and of rheumatic fever in herself; when, I repeat, after all these outrages, she should sit in a soaking heap by the roadside, laughing like a maniac, I feel that the sympathy of the public will not be withheld from me. (2002, 371–2)

Given these markers of unreliability, one would be quite mistaken to charge the authors with the snobbery of their narrator. To the contrary, Yeates's snobbish and pompous attitude towards the Catholic, *nouveau riche* McRory family is clearly mocked and the reader more readily sides with the more welcoming attitude of Philippa or Bobby Bennett. In fact, the reader is later justified for taking this position when Yeates comes to defend the strong and vivacious Larkie McRory against the snobbish disapproval of

Lady Knox, which he initially shared. In "Put Down One and Carry Two", Yeates indeed moves from agreement with Lady Knox's snobbish verdict—"this simple statement indicated so pleasingly our oneness of soul in the matter of the McRorys"—to "compassion" for the "poor little girl" and a resolution to defend her to possible "detractors" (2002, 541, 553).

That Major Yeates is to be considered a comic character, rather than as a trusted guide and reliable narrator, is further highlighted by the numerous illustrations which Edith Somerville drew to accompany the stories in the magazines in which they first appeared, *The Badminton Magazine* and *The Strand*. Since these illustrations often depict Yeates in various unhappy circumstances, the reader is invited to take an outside view on the storyworld and the narrator. In this way, the illustrations support the ironic double structure of unreliability, encouraging the reader to take up a perspective different from the supposedly superior one of the narrator. On the level of plot too, as we have seen, the ironic double structure of narrative unreliability is underscored by the plot of comic reversal that characterizes many of the R.M. stories as authority is undermined and characters come to occupy different positions on the hierarchies of class, ethnicity and gender. Clearly, this ironic double structure, pervading the narrative, plot and textual presentation of the stories, makes them more rather than less modern than the stories of their contemporaries and may well have influenced subsequent uses of unreliable first-person narration, as in Bowen's stories "A Day in the Dark", "The Cheery Soul" and "The Dolt's Tale".

With regard to the use of illustrations in magazine short fiction in general, Sillars has argued that they add "another Bakhtinian voice in the presentation of actions and characters" (1989, 75). For the R.M. stories, this means that the illustrations add yet another voice to the already polyphonic and multi-voiced nature of the stories. Indeed, although Major Yeates is the official narrator of the stories, a substantial part of his narratives consists of embedded stories told by other characters, or by lengthy quotations of dialogue. The story "Occasional Licences", for instance, opens with Mrs. Moloney trying to convince the Major to grant her husband an 'occasional licence' for selling liquor on Saint Peter and Paul's Day: "Sure I know well that if th'angel Gabriel came down from heaven looking for a license for the races, your honour wouldn't give it to him without a character, but as for Michael! Sure the world knows what Michael is!" (2002, 202). The story then records the different conversations the Major has with Philippa, Flurry, Lady Knox, and Slipper about the festivities, before proceeding to describe the sports events of the day. Even there, different onlookers are allowed to voice their perspective on the race:

> "That's a dam nice horse," said one of my hangers-on, looking approvingly at Sultan as he passed us at the beginning of the second round, making a good deal of noise but apparently going at his ease, "you might depend your life on him, and he have the crabbedest jock in the globe or Ireland on him this minute." "Canty's mare's very sour," said another: "look at her now, baulking the bank! She's as cross as a bag of weasels" [...] "I'll tell you what it is," said Miss Sally, very seriously, in my ear, "that chestnut of Sheehy's is settling down." (2002, 212)

Yeates subsequently becomes an "unwilling conspirator" in another horse-related scheme of Flurry—"a part with which my acquaintance with Mr. Knox had rendered me but too familiar" (2002, 214). As the series of mishaps comes to its climax, the story nicely returns to the opening scene, with Mrs. Moloney taking revenge on Yeates for being refused the 'occasional licence' for the day. In the story's concluding paragraph, the narrator refers to alternative accounts of the events:

> The only comments on the day's events that are worthy of record were that Philippa said to me that she had not been able to understand what the curious taste in the tea had been till Sally told her it was turf-smoke, and that Mrs. Cadogan said to Philippa that night that "the Major was that dhrinched that if he had a shirt between his skin and himself he could have wrung it", and that Lady Knox said to a mutual friend that though Major Yeates had been extremely kind and obliging, he was an uncommonly bad whip. (2002, 218)

Such a metafictional closing paragraph is a recurrent feature in the stories. The narrator typically ends his story by quoting other, often more colourful, versions of the facts that are circulating in the neighbourhood. "The Pug-nosed Fox" ends with Yeates excerpting "a paragraph from the *Curranhilty Herald*" and in "A Conspiracy of Silence", he concludes "I understand that Slipper has put forth a version of the story, in which the whole matter is resolved into a trial of wits between himself and Eugene. With this I have not interfered." At the end of "The Bosom of the McRory's", to give another example, Yeates refers to the many different tales that are being told about his scrape: "When, a few days later, the story flowed over and ran about the country, some things that were both new and interesting came to my ears" (2002, 258, 321, 539). By pointing to other versions or interpretations of the events, the narrator effectively cedes narrative authority and invites the reader once again to question his superior insight and understanding. The polyphonic nature of the stories is thus realized at differently levels: stylistically, through the direct rendering of different voices; metafictionally, through a frequent reference to other stories and the act of storytelling, and in a narrative way, through the recurrent use of embedded narrators.

Viewed from yet another perspective, finally, this Bakhtinian polyphony also contributes to the sense of community the stories evoke: a community not just made up of types and classes, but also of voices and stories. As we have seen, this embeddedness in and evocation of a community were reason enough for Frank O'Connor to ban the stories to the nineteenth century. Moreover, the hierarchical and colonial nature of this community led many subsequent critics to reject the stories on ideological grounds (Devlin 1998; Crossman 2000; Deane 2000). It is of course true that the stories' protagonist and centre of gravity is a colonial officer and ex-British army colonel of Anglo-Irish descent and that the stories' most prominent characters belong to the Anglo-Irish gentry. Nevertheless, characters from all classes do feature in the stories, as they gather, across class divisions, on market days, court sessions, fairs or dances, or meet with the narrator on his many travels through the district. As we have seen in "Occasional Licences", for instance, many different characters play a part in the festivities and mischief recorded in the story: from Mrs. Cadogan and Slipper, across the farming and shopkeeping village families (the Sheehys, Moloneys, McConnells, and Cantys), to the different branches of the Knox family and the English Bernard Shute. Moreover, as we have seen, several stories of the third collection, *In Mr. Knox's Country*, revolve around the Catholic, landowning McRory family who are, in spite of Major Yeates's initial snobbish prejudices, quite readily welcomed in the community. The glue that binds these characters together—and allows new ones in—is the hunt, which also has the effect of subsuming class differences to sporting ability and horsemanship. In their more eulogizing descriptions of the excitement of the hunt, Somerville and Ross highlight its communal dimension: in "Philippa's Fox-Hunt", for instance, Philippa is helped in her pursuit on bike by everyone she passes: from the boys who run alongside her to the old women who point the way. In short, even though Yeates gives his name to the stories, it is the community as a whole that is their main protagonist, as the stories typically revolve around communal events, such as markets, fairs, feast days, outings and, of course, the hunt. In this communal focus too, the R.M. stories can usefully be compared to Kipling's *Plain Tales of the Hills* (1888), which sought to depict life in Colonial India to both the British and the Anglo-Indian reader.

Somerville and Ross's proximity to Kipling, the "father" of the modern English short story (Hunter 2007, 20), underlines once again the modernity of their short fiction. Far from belonging to an antiquated nineteenth-century tale tradition, the R.M. stories deserve a prominent place in the tradition of the modern, plot-bound story, as it developed in 1890s Britain. Indeed, although they were probably writing primarily for English and Anglo-Irish audiences, Somerville and Ross deserve credit for being the first Irish writers of this strand of modern short fiction, which would continue to make its presence felt in Irish short fiction, for instance, in the satiric short fiction of James Stephens and Brian Nolan, in the more plot-bound stories of Elizabeth Bowen or the comic stories of Clare Boylan. At the same time, Somerville and Ross's ironic treatment of the narrator and the polyphonic nature of their stories also depart from the typical magazine story's greater investment in the superior stance and reliable rationality of the narrator. In narrative terms, Major Yeates's authority is often questioned and his version juxtaposed to that of other characters. Clearly, this makes the stories more rather than less modern than those of their contemporaries. Moreover, if Yeates's narration often cedes authority to the embedded dialogues, stories and voices of other characters, in plot terms too, Yeates mostly cedes agency to other members of the community: women, servants, and, of course, Flurry Knox, the shadow-protagonist of several of the stories. In this distribution of agency, authority and voice across the different characters, Somerville and Ross effectively use the short story form to depict a community, as a network of different groups and individuals, rather than the lonely hero O'Connor postulated for the short story. In this way too, they anticipate the work of Irish short fiction writers. Indeed, as we will see in Chapter 6, the short stories, and short story cycles, of writers like Mary Lavin, Mary Beckett, Val Mulkerns, and Éilís Ní Dhuibhne also seek to stage community life in a variety of ways. For all of these reasons, in short, the polyphonic, ironic and communal stories of Somerville and Ross deserve a place within, rather than before, the modern Irish short story tradition.

BIBLIOGRAPHY

Anonymous. 1894. Socio-Literary Portents. *The Speaker: The Liberal Review* 10:683–685.

Anonymous. 1895. Short Stories. *The Athenaeum* (3517):375–376.

Ardis, Ann L. 1990. *New Women, New Novels: Feminism and Early Modernism.* New Brunswick: Rutgers University Press.

Ashley, Michael. 2006. *The Age of the Storytellers: British Popular Fiction Magazines 1880–1950.* London: British Library and Oak Knoll Press.

Averill, Deborah M. 1982. *The Irish Short Story from George Moore to Frank O'Connor.* Lanham, MD: University Press of America.

Baldwin, Dean. 2013. *Art and Commerce in the British Short Story, 1880–1950.* London: Pickering & Chatto.

Bjørhovde, Gerd. 1987. *Rebellious Structures: Women Writers and the Crisis of the Novel 1880–1900.* Oslo: Norwegian University Press.

Bowen, Elizabeth. 1962. *Afterthought: Pieces About Writing.* London: Longmans.

Cahalan, James M. 1993. 'Humor with a Gender': Somerville and Ross and the Irish R.M. *Eire-Ireland: A Journal of Irish Studies* 28 (3):87–102.

Chan, Winnie. 2007. *The Economy of the Short Story in British Periodicals of the 1890s.* London: Routledge.

Cowart, Claire Denelle. 1994. Edith Somerville. In *Dictionary of Literary Biography. British Short-Fiction Writers, 1880–1914: The Realist Tradition,* edited by William B. Thesing. Detroit: Gale. Online access: Literature Resource Centre.

Cowman, Roz. 1997. Lost Time: The Smell and Taste of Castle T. In *Nation and Dissent in Irish Writing,* edited by Eibhear Walshe, 87–102. Cork: Cork University Press.

Cronin, John. 1972. *Somerville and Ross.* Lewisburg, Bucknell University Press.

Crossman, Virginia. 2000. The Resident Magistrate as Colonial Officer: Addison, Somerville and Ross. *Irish Studies Review* 8 (1):23–33.

Deane, Paul. 2000. Another Irish Myth: Somerville and Ross's *Some Experiences of an Irish R.M. Notes on Modern Irish Literature* 12:12–17.

Devlin, Joseph. 1998. The End of the Hunt: Somerville and Ross's Irish R.M. *The Canadian Journal of Irish Studies* 24 (1):23–50.

D'hoker, Elke. 2008a. Beyond the Stereotypes. Mary Lavin's Irish Women. *Irish Studies Review* 16(4): 415–430.

D'hoker, Elke. 2008b. Unreliability Between Mimesis and Metaphor: The Works of Kazuo Ishiguro. In *Narrative Unreliability in the Twentieth-Century First-Person Novel,* edited by Elke D'hoker and Gunther Martens, 147–70. Berlin: De Gruyter.

D'hoker, Elke. 2011b. 'Half-Man or Half-Doll': George Egerton's Response to Friedrich Nietzsche. *Women's Writing* 18 (4):524–546.

Egerton, George. 1932. A Keynote to *Keynotes*. In *Ten Contemporaries: Notes Toward their Definitive Bibliography*, edited by John Gawsworth, 58–60. London: Ernest Benn

Egerton, George. 1958. *A Leaf from the Yellow Book: The Correspondence of George Egerton, edited by Terence de Vere White*. London: Richards Press.

Egerton, George. 1905. *Flies in Amber*. London: Hutchinson.

Egerton, George. 2006. *Keynotes and Discords*. London: Continuum. Original edition, 1893, 1894.

Fluhr, Nicole M. 2001. Figuring the New Woman: Writers and Mothers in George Egerton's Early Stories. *Texas Studies in Literature and Language* 43 (3):243–266.

Gagnier, Regenia. 2010. *Individualism, Decadence and Globalization: On the Relationship of Part to Whole, 1859–1920*. Basingstoke: Palgrave.

Garavel, Andrew J. 2008. 'Green World': The Mock-Pastoral of the Irish R. M. *Estudios Irlandeses* 3:92–100.

Gill, T.P. 1893. A Literary Causerie. *The Speaker: The Liberal Review* 8:609–611.

Gilligan, Carol. 1982. *In a Different Voice. Psychological Theory and Women's Development*. Cambridge, MA: Harvard University Press.

Hager, Lisa. 2006. A Community of Women: Women's Agency and Sexuality in George Egerton's *Keynotes* and *Discords*. *Nineteenth-Century Gender Studies* 2 (2). http://ncgsjournal.com/issue22/hager.htm.

Hanson, Clare. 1985. *Short Stories and Short Fictions, 1880–1980*. London: Macmillan.

Harland, Henry 1896. Dogs, Cats, Books, and the Average Man. *The Yellow Book* 10:11–23.

Harris, Wendell V. 1968. Egerton: Forgotten Realist. *Victorian Newsletter* 35:31–35.

Harris, Wendell V. 1979. *British Short Fiction in the Nineteenth Century: A Literary and Bibliographic Guide*. Detroit. Wayne State University Press.

Heilmann, Ann. 2000. *New Woman Fiction: Women Writing First-Wave Feminism*. Basingstoke, Palgrave.

Held, Virginia. 2006. *The Ethics of Care: Personal, Political, and Global*. Oxford: Oxford University Press.

Hunter, Adrian. 2007. *The Cambridge Introduction to the Short Story in English*. Cambridge: Cambridge University Press.

Ingman, Heather. 2009. *A History of the Irish Short Story*. Cambridge: Cambridge University Press.

James, Henry. 1898. The Story-Teller at Large: Mr. Henry Harland. *Fortnightly Review* 63 (374):650–654.

James, Henry. 1986. The Science of Criticism. In *The Art of Criticism: Henry James on the Theory and the Practice of Fiction*, edited by W. Veeder and S.M. Griffin, 232–236. Chicago: University of Chicago Press. Original edition, 1891.

Jamison, Anne. 2007. Plagiarism, Popularity, and the Dilemma of Artistic Worth: E. Œ. Somerville and Martin Ross's Some Experiences of an Irish R. M. (1899). *European Journal of English Studies* 11 (1):65–78.

Jusová, Iveta. 2000. George Egerton and the Project of British Colonialism. *Tulsa Studies in Women's Literature* 19 (1):27–55.

Kipling, Rudyard. 1888. *Plain Tales from the Hills*. Calcutta: Thacker, Spink.

Kosok, Heinz. 1982. Vorformen der modernen Kurzgeschichte in der Anglo-Irischen Literatur des 19. Jahrhunderts. *Arbeiten Aus Anglistik und Amerikanistik*. 7 (2). 131–146.

Ledger, Sally. 2006. Introduction. In *Keynotes and Discords*, ix–xxvi. London: Continuum.

Lewis, Gifford. 1987. *Somerville and Ross: The World of the Irish R.M.* London: Penguin.

March-Russell, Paul. 2009. *The Short Story: An Introduction*. Edinburgh: Edinburgh University Press.

Matthews, Brander. 1994. The Philosophy of the Short-Story. In *The New Short Story Theories*, edited by Charles E. May, 73–80. Athens: Ohio University Press. Original edition, 1901.

McCullough, Kate. 1996. Mapping the 'Terra Incognita' of Woman: George Egerton's *Keynotes* (1983) and New Woman Fiction. In *The New Nineteenth Century: Feminist Readings of Underread Victorian Fiction*, edited by Barbara Leah Harman and Susan Meyer, 205–224. New York: Garland.

Moore, George. 2000. *The Untilled Field*. Gerrards Cross: Colin Smythe. Original edition, 1903.

Nuttall, A.D. 2004. Auerbach's Mimesis. *Essays in Criticism* 54 (1):60–74.

O'Connor, Frank. 1957. *Classic Irish Short Stories*. Oxford: Oxford University Press.

O'Connor, Frank. 2004. *The Lonely Voice: A Study of the Short Story*. Hoboken, NJ: Melville House Pub. Original edition, 1963.

O'Connor, Maureen. 2010. *The Female and the Species: The Animal in Irish Women's Writing*. Oxford: Peter Lang.

O'Toole, Tina. 2013. *The Irish New Woman*. Basingstoke: Palgrave.

Phelan, James. 2005. *Living to Tell About It: A Rhetoric and Ethics of Character Narration*. Ithaca, NY: Cornell University Press.

Poe, E. A. 1994. Review of *Twice-Told Tales*. In *The New Short Story Theories*, edited by Charles E. May, 59–64. Athens: Ohio University Press. Original edition, 1842.

Pykett, Lyn. 1992. *The "Improper" Feminine: The Women's Sensation Novel and the New Woman Writing*. London: Routledge.

Pykett, Lyn. 1995. *Engendering Fictions: The English Novel in the Early Twentieth Century*. London: E. Arnold.

Rauchbauer, Otto. 1995. *The Edith Œnone Somerville Archive, in Drishane: A Catalogue and an Evaluative Essay*. Dublin: Irish Manuscripts Commission.

Shaw, Valerie. 1983. *The Short Story: A Critical Introduction*. London: Longman.

Sillars, Stuart. 1989. The Illustrated Short Story. A Typology. In *Short Story Theory at a Crossroads*, edited by Susan Lohafer and Jo Ellyn Clarey, 70–80. Baton Rouge: Lousiana State University Press.

Slote, Michael. 2007. *The Ethics of Care and Empathy*. London: Taylor & Francis.

Somerville E. Œ. and Martin Ross. 1894. *The Real Charlotte*. London: Ward and Downey.

Somerville, E. Œ. and Martin Ross. 1899. *Some Experiences of an Irish R.M.* London: Longmans, Green.

Somerville, E. OE. 1991. Preface. In *Some Experiences and Further Experiences of an Irish R.M.*, xvii-xx. London: Everyman. Original edition, 1944.

Somerville, E. OE. 2002. Preface. In *The Irish R.M.* London: Time Warner. Original edition, 1928.

Somerville, E. OE., and Martin Ross. 2002. *The Irish R.M.* London: Time Warner. Original edition, 1928.

Stetz, Margaret D., and Mark Samuels Lasner. 1990. *England in the 1890s: Literary Publishing at the Bodley Head*. Washington, DC: Georgetown University Press.

Stevens, Julie Anne. 2007. *The Irish Scene in Somerville and Ross*. Dublin: Irish Academic Press.

Vicinus, Martha. 1983. Rediscovering the 'New Woman' of the 1890s: The Stories of George Egerton. In *Feminist Re-Visions: What Has Been and Might Be*, edited by Vivian Patraka and Louisa A. Tilly, 12–25. Ann Arbor: Michigan University Press.

Waters, Maureen. 1984. *The Comic Irishman*. New York: State University of New York Press.

Wells, H.G. 1911. Introduction. In *The Country of the Blind, and Other Stories*. London: Thomas Nelson & Sons.

Williams, Orlo. 1920. A Little Classic of the Future. *The London Mercury* 1 (4):555–564.

CHAPTER 3

Houses and Homes in the Short Stories of Elizabeth Bowen and Maeve Brennan

In his introduction to Maeve Brennan's *The Springs of Affection: Stories of Dublin*, William Maxwell, Brennan's colleague and literary editor at *The New Yorker* wrote, "The only bone of contention between us I was aware of was that she refused to read the novels of Elizabeth Bowen because Bowen was Anglo-Irish. On the other hand, she venerated Yeats, who was also Anglo-Irish, and she knew a good deal of his poetry by heart" (Brennan 1998, 3). As Maxwell suggests, Brennan may have been only provocative in her dismissal of Bowen. In fact, she did reveal an intimate knowledge of Bowen's work in one of *The Long-Winded Lady* sketches she published in *The New Yorker* between 1953 and 1968. Describing the deserted but expectant air of a film set in front of the Algonquin Hotel, Brennan comments: "Elizabeth Bowen once described a room that was crowded although there were no people in it as looking as if somebody was holding a party for furniture. The scene on Forty-Fourth Street today looked as if somebody were holding a protest meeting for cars" (Brennan 1997, 167). In this remark one can detect the insistent concern with place—with cities and streets, buildings and rooms—which both writers share. "Am I not manifestly a writer for whom places loom large?", Bowen asked in her abandoned autobiography, *Pictures and Conversations* (Bowen 1975a, 34). Brennan's stories too are always clearly located: in Ranelagh, East Hampton or New York City. Moreover, in the short stories of both Brennan and Bowen, the family home stands out as both a common setting and a dominant poetic image. Perhaps then, Brennan's dismissal of Bowen also masks a sense of affinity with her fellow Irish writer.

© The Editor(s) (if applicable) and The Author (s) 2016   51
E. D'hoker, *Irish Women Writers and the Modern Short Story*,
DOI 10.1007/978-3-319-30288-1_3

It is this affinity between both writers that I would like to explore in this chapter.

Apart from the shared concern with place, and with houses in particular, both writers are also alike in their use of the modern short story as a form that combines modernist techniques with an insistence on plot and closure. In this way, they seek to unify the two strands of short fiction which I have traced in Chapter 2: the psychological, mood-dependent, slice-of-life stories initiated by Egerton and the more popular, storytelling tradition of Somerville and Ross, in which a realistic rendering of setting and action goes hand in hand with comic, gothic or satiric effect. As I will show, a combination of those modes can be observed in the short fiction of both Bowen and Brennan. Another aspect linking these writers is the critical reception of their work in terms of displacement and homelessness. Bowen's characters are typically described as "homeless", or "dispossessed" (Lee 1999, 73; Kreilkamp 2009, 15), "out of place, cut off and cut loose from the safety that a final home might offer" (Hand 2009, 65) or as "orphans and wards, homeless lovers, disinherited gadabouts" (Bowen and Lee 1986, viii). Moreover, Bowen's staging of these characters is routinely related to her own experience of dislocation: leaving her ancestral family home in Ireland for England as a child and subsequently losing that home altogether. In a similar way, "homelessness" is a recurring notion in the—as yet much more limited—critical reception of Maeve Brennan's work. In her excellent biography, tellingly entitled *Homesick at The New Yorker: An Irish Writer in Exile*, Angela Bourke finds in Brennan's short fiction a perennial quest for home which reflects the author's own experience of emigration and her subsequent nomadic life in New York (Bourke 2004). For Patricia Coughlan, similarly, "themes of deracination and irreparable loss of home are extremely pervasive in her work, which in this respect is a classical expression of diaspora existence" (2004b, 435). In the case of both Bowen and Brennan, in other words, the critical reception of their work is to a large extent shaped by biographical facts as well as by the traditional representation of Irish migration "as involuntary exile" (Cullingford 2014, 61). As several critics have pointed out, while the Irish have had many different reasons for emigrating to Britain or the USA, the dominant cultural imaginary construes the emigrant as a hapless victim, cruelly uprooted from home and homeland (Akenson 1996, 10–11). In the case of female authors and their characters, these "tropes of victimhood and forced departure" may have been even more insistent (Éinrí and O'Toole 2012, 7–8), as they are compounded by a firmly entrenched domestic ideology that routinely links women to house and home. In this way, being homeless for Irish women writers entails a loss of both domestic and national identity, which is consistently figured as problematical by critics and read as the chief source of unhappiness for authors and their characters alike.

While I do not want to contest that experiences of alienation, unhappiness, and loss of love loom large in the short fiction of Bowen and Brennan, I would like to qualify the persistent framing of these experiences in terms of homelessness or displacement. For, as a close reading of the stories will show, being 'at home' is also a problematic and mostly unhappy experience for Bowen's and Brennan's characters. In many stories, the women characters in particular are shown to be either oppressed or effaced by the homes they help to create, while the nostalgic or idealizing images of home on the part of male characters are satirized or undermined. In what follows I propose to trace these conflicted feeling about home in the work of Bowen and Brennan, by looking at the imaginative depiction of houses in their short stories. For, as Blunt and Dowling argue, home is "a spatial imaginary": "a place/site, a set of feelings/cultural meanings, and the relation between the two" (2006, 2). As the single most important spatial image in the work of both writers, the house certainly carries such multiple and often conflicted meanings: bearing the weight of the characters' feelings, houses are also repositories of cultural and ideological meaning. In the work of Elizabeth Bowen, they even assume a life of their own.

The Horrors of Domesticity in Bowen's Stories

The place of Elizabeth Bowen's short stories in literary history has long been an ambivalent one. For quite some time, her work was not deemed Irish enough to warrant full inclusion in discussions of Irish short fiction. Both Kilroy and Ingman discuss her so-called "Irish stories" (Kilroy 1984, 153ff; Ingman 2009, 142–3, 152–5), but in Rafroidi and Brown's *The Irish Short Story* and Averill's *The Irish Short Story from Moore to O'Connor*, Bowen does not feature at all. In general histories of the short story in English, to the contrary, Bowen has always been a respected figure, not least because of her many astute comments on the short story form. Still, even there, her short fiction was often considered a come down after the modernist short story. For some, Bowen's short story was a "retrogressive form", returning to traditional modes of storytelling (Hanson 1985, 112); for others, she offered at best "a popularized, intellectually desiccated version of modernism", which radically condemned her to the realms of the middlebrow (Hunter 2007, 112). Recent critics have rescued Bowen's fiction from that 'doomed' category of the middlebrow and have praised her work as modernist after all (Ellmann 2003; Kreilkamp 2009). Yet, I would argue that Bowen's short fiction is middlebrow in the sense that it draws on the tradition of the popular magazine stories (of writers like Kipling, Wells, Coppard, and, indeed, Somerville and Ross), even as it also employs modernist narrative modes and stylistic techniques. Hence, Bowen deserves credit for trying to bridge the two strands of short fiction outlined in Chapter 2 and which had become increasingly distant in the early twentieth century: the plot-bound magazine stories working towards a single, often surprising, effect and the plotless, mood-dependent, modernist stories aiming for psychological or existential realism.

In her Preface to *The Faber Book of Modern Short Stories* (1936), Bowen herself connects these two strands to the respective influence of two "foreign masters" on the form: Chekhov and Maupassant. While pointing out the profound influence of Chekhov's exploration of "that involuntary sub-life of the spirit" on the modernist short story (which she calls the "free story"), Bowen suggests that the contemporary short story could now do with a dose of Maupassant's influence, his "vitality", "astringency, iron relevance"—which, incidentally, she finds in the work of Irish writers, particularly O'Connor and O'Flaherty (1950, 39–41). In the same essay, she also takes issue with the binary of "commercial" or middlebrow and "non-commercial" or highbrow and artistic stories, which was cultivated by modernist writers (in the wake of *The Yellow Book*'s example, as we saw in Chapter 2). Bowen writes:

> It is too generally taken that a story by *being* non-commercial may immediately pretend to art [...] The public gets slated by the free short story's promotors for not giving such stories a more grateful reception [...] But why should anyone tolerate lax, unconvincing or arty work—work whose idiom too often shows a touch of high-hat complacency?" (1950, 42)

Turning her back on this pretentiousness, Bowen herself sought to promote the short story as a "modern mass art form" (Hunter 2007, 115). She always published her short stories in many different magazines, from *Mademoiselle* to *The New Yorker*, often selling the same story to several publications "in order to maximize its exposure" (Bowen and Hepburn 2008, 4), and, one might add, its financial reward.

In terms of form too, Bowen aimed for a combination of the popular, incident-bound magazine story, influenced by Maupassant, and the psychological, plotless modernist story influenced by Chekhov. What she took from the former was a striving for focus, sharpness, for the concentrated effect, towards which all the elements in a story should be directed. Yet, she rejected the idea that closure should entail a full explanation or answer, instead favouring Mansfield's and Woolf's idea that stories should be "questions posed" (Bowen 1962, 94). Hence, while she was adamant that "a story, to be a story, *must* have a turning point", she also noted that most of her stories end "with a shrug, others with an impatient or a dismissing sigh" (1962, 87, 94). Similarly, Bowen's greater emphasis on elements of storyness—plot, turning-point, characters and dialogue—goes hand in hand with a modernist preoccupation with what she called "the possibilities of atmosphere" and with an uncanny ability to create a mood that envelops and even guides the characters (1962, 91). As I will describe in more detail in what follows, her realist emphasis on external reality and context as a necessary frame for plot and characters does not prevent that context from attaining symbolic overtones, as in the stories of Mansfield and Lawrence.

Quite unlike these modernist writers, however, is Bowen's reinstatement of the omniscient narrator, which had already been in retreat in the stories of George Egerton. Yet, her stories' peculiar combination of omniscient narration and focalization does not lead to greater objectivity or moral authority, as it did in the popular magazine story. Instead, the narrator's often cryptic descriptions, together with the character's subjective understanding, result in a fragmented, multifocal perspective, which questions rather than affirms reality. Very typical of Bowen's short fiction, finally, is an eclecticism in terms of genre—again, a rather damning characteristic from a modernist perspective. As Hunter notes, "Bowen's fiction is generically diverse, freely plundering the resources of psychological realism, pastiche, the ghost story, the Gothic melodrama, the thriller and the comedy of manners" (2007, 113). More in general, Bowen's idiosyncratic combination of psychological realism and supernatural elements shows the influence of both the fantastic stories of Kipling, Wells and Saki and the modernist emphasis on interiority we find in the stories of Mansfield and Joyce. In her Preface to *The Faber Book of Modern Short Stories*, Bowen makes a firm distinction between the "pure fantasy story" and her own use of "inward, or [...] applied and functional fantasy, which does not depart from life but tempers it" (1950, 44). Influenced by many different strands and traditions, in short, Bowen made the modern short story into an infinitely flexible literary form, well suited to capture the changing realities of the interwar period.

Bowen's characteristic blend of realist, modernist and fantastic elements can also be observed in the house imagery that pervades her short stories and to which I will now turn. Reading through her *Collected Stories*, one cannot fail to be struck by the strong bond that is created between character and house, yet unpicking the stylistic structures that underpin that bond proves more difficult. The first thing to note is that in many of Bowen's stories descriptions of houses function as metonymic expressions of the main characters' status and personality: from the Italian villa with its lush, maze-like garden in the early story "Requiescat" to the stately portraits and massive furniture that darken Miss Banderry's parlour in Bowen's last published story, "A Day in the Dark". This is, in fact, in tune with the popular story's reliance on type in characterization (cf. supra), and readers had become quite adept at deriving the social status and personality of a character from his or her surroundings. A full application of this technique can also be found in "The Disinherited", in which the different characters are introduced by means of their houses. The interior of Mrs. Ashworth's "manor" in the village, is "kindly, crimson and stuffy" (Bowen 1981, 377), while the Harveys' modern house is a "freshly built white rough-cast house with a touch of priggishness in its architecture", its living room "artfully pale and bare", with "steel-framed windows" and "a cold brick hearth" (1981, 377–8). The room of Prothero—the criminal with a stolen identity—is 'bare' in a different way: "the furniture showed by candlelight mean outlines on the whitewash. The man had no belong ings; the place seemed to be to let"; and in the "immense façade" of Lord Thingummy's Palladian mansion, which will host a desultory party of disaffected young aristocrats, the "pilasters soared out of sight above an unlit fanlight like patterns of black ice" (1981, 391, 385). Even in metonymic descriptions such as these, however, we can note the use of some metaphorical devices such as symbol and simile. Details of the context are elaborated into symbols—or "metaphorical metonymies", as David Lodge calls them (1977, 100)—and these similes are mostly drawn from semantic fields associated with the context, as when the narrator notes how the few houses on the Harveys' new estate "stood apart, like Englishmen not yet acquainted" (1981, 376). Through these tropes, however, the houses do acquire a metaphoric meaning, based on correspondence, over and above their metonymic dimension. Thus, the modern whiteness of Marianne's house receives symbolic insistency through repetition and comes to stand for the sterility of her domestic life; the icy coldness that pervades Lord Thingummy's castle, on the other hand, symbolizes the cynicism of the characters who inhabit it.

If this mixture of contextual detail, metonymic meaning and symbolist implication already points to Bowen's combination of realist and modernist techniques, so does her skilful blending of narration and focalization in her construction of place. While the above descriptions were all made by the omniscient narrator, in most stories, these aperspectival descriptions are complemented by the modernist, perspectival approach, whereby space is shown from the perspective of a character. The houses and homes evoked in this way in Bowen's fiction do then not just express their inhabitants' personalities, but also the focalizer's consciousness. Take, for instance, the opening paragraphs of "Daffodils", which has Miss Murcheson walk home after school on a nice Spring day:

> Today the houses seemed taller and farther apart; the street wider and full of a bright, clear light that cast no shadows and was never sunshine. Under archways and between the houses the distances had a curious transparency, as though they had been painted upon glass. Against the luminous and indeterminate sky the Abbey tower rose distinct and delicate. (1981, 20)

Clearly, the metaphorical descriptions of the street are infused with Miss Murcheson's feelings and thus become expressive of them. Most of Bowen's characters share Miss Murcheson's sensitivity to their surroundings, in particular to the houses and rooms they inhabit. In this, they remind us of Woolf's and Mansfield's sensitive focalizers, for whom material reality functions as "a trigger to introspective voyaging and the dilation of subjectivity" (Hunter 2007, 113).

Yet Bowen's perspectival evocations of space depart from this modernist technique in that her focalizers never 'voyage' very far: they stay close to the objects they observe and do not achieve the introspective transcendence or the victory of mind over matter which a modernist writer like Woolf famously demonstrated in "The Mark on the Wall" (Ellmann 2003, 7). In Bowen's stories, rather, the thoughts and feelings evoked by certain objects are projected back onto those objects and translated into characteristics of material reality itself. The trope that typically accompanies this feedback loop between character and object—or house, in our case—is that of prosopopeia or personification. To return to the example of "Daffodils": Miss Murcheson's elated reaction to the air of Spring in the streets around her is projected back onto the houses and buildings which are transformed in curiously animate images of freedom and light. After the delicate transparency of the streets, the house which the protagonist enters appears to her as dark, heavy and cramped. Miss Murcheson's responses to this change of scene are again translated as properties of the house itself: "armchairs and cabinets were lurking in the dusk. The square of daylight by the window was blocked by a bamboo table groaning under an array of photographs" (1981, 21).

This pattern, established from Bowen's earliest stories onwards, is repeated throughout her short fiction: a certain scene or object elicits a character's emotional response which is then, in a kind of feedback loop, projected back onto the scene and translated into an emotion or characteristic of the scene or object itself. Sometimes, the character's subjective investment in the animation is made evident with words like "seemed", "appeared" or "as if", but in many other cases these hedges are simply dropped. In "The Return", Lydia, the paid companion, is displeased by her employers' return home after a six-week holiday during which she had the place to herself and throughout the story her feelings are rendered as reactions of the house. At first, Lydia's projection of her feelings is made explicit: "During her six weeks of solitude the house had grown very human to Lydia. She felt now as if it were drawing itself together in a nervous rigor" (1981, 28). Later these phrases are dispensed with so that the actions and feelings seem to reside solely with the house: "the morning-room beckoned her with its association of the last six weeks" or, after a revelatory confession of her mistress, "The place was vibrant with the humanity of Mrs. Tottenham" (1981, 34).

Although these evocations of space do tell us something about the state of mind of the perceiving consciousness, they do not dilate subjectivity in the way of modernist writers like Woolf or James. In fact, because of the combination with personification, the effect is rather one of enlarging and illuminating the houses and of dwarfing and obscuring the characters. In other words, Bowen's houses bear out what Paul de Man describes as the danger of personification or prosopopoeia, viz. "defacement". "By making the death [sic] speak", de Man argues, "the symmetrical structure of the trope implies that the living are struck dumb, frozen in their own death" (1984, 78). By attributing life to the house, in other words, the characters themselves become lifeless, divested of the very emotions that motivated the personification in the first place. In short, if Bowen's mixture of stylistic techniques installs a strong bond between house and character, it also makes that bond a highly ambivalent one: while the realist and modernist evocations of houses suggest a character's agency in construing domestic space and allow us to read that space as an expression of the character's personality or state of mind, the subsequent personification of houses and domestic objects transfers that agency from character to house, thus dwarfing and defacing the characters. As we will see in what follows, this stylistic mixture of agency and passivity, of illumination and effacement, is revisited in the relation between Bowen's houses and characters on a thematic level as well.

Within an Irish framework, the strong bond between house and character in Bowen's stories has been read as a consequence of her own identification with Bowen's Court, her ancestral home in County Cork. As she notes in her memoir of the place, *Bowen's Court*, "A Bowen, in the first place, made Bowen's Court. Since then, with a rather alarming sureness, Bowen's Court has made all the succeeding Bowens" (Bowen 1999, 32). Tradition and family history strongly tie identity to place and, as several critics have noted, displacement seems to entail alienation and loss of self (Lassner 1991, 5; Lee 1999, 73). Yet, the strong bond between house and character in Bowen's stories far exceeds the link to an ancestral place. While the houses in her stories range from big houses and manors over suburban villas, town houses and apartments to farm houses and small roadside cottages, what they have in common is that they seem to pin down the female inhabitants in particular. I would argue, therefore, that another useful context for reading these houses and homes in Bowen's short fiction is the domestic ideology that reigned supreme in interwar Britain. After all, in the 1920s and 1930s, Bowen herself was living a rather conventional middle-class life as the wife of a civil servant in Oxford and, from 1934, in London. This period was also her most productive in terms of short fiction output: five of her eight short story collections were published between 1923 and the start of the Second World War.

As many historians have argued, Britain turned back upon itself after the war, reviving values of domesticity and tradition. Women were urged to return to "home and duty", to the extent that "the single most arresting feature of the interwar years was the strength of the notion that women's place is the home" (Beddoe 1989, 3). This domestic ideology was supported both by government measures, such as the introduction of the marriage bar in professions or dole office practices that removed women from the workplace, and by the "shining ideal of the stay-at-home housewife" that was celebrated in the many domestically orientated women's magazines (Beddoe 1989, 4). In these magazines, and in popular culture at large, having a house of your own was presented as every woman's dream, while women were also urged to make their homes into an expression of their personality (Humble 2001, 17).

In a way, then, Bowen's symbolic construction of houses that mirror the personality of their characters reflects this domestic ideology. In terms of plot too, having a house is shown to confer a sense of identity on Bowen's female characters, who become "the lady of the house", and in several stories married women are shown to embrace the domestic ideology of homemaking. Marianne Harvey in "The Disinherited", for instance, is described as "house-proud": she has come to live in a carefully designed new house and is happily preoccupied with decorating it following the latest fashion trends: "Since August, Marianne had been cheerfully busy, without a moment for any kind of reflection; the Harveys were nesting over again, after twelve years of marriage, making a new home" (Bowen 1981, 378, 375). Yet through her encounter with the satiric parodies of home enacted by the disenchanted Davina and her friends, Marianne becomes aware of the emptiness of this domestic ideal. One of them keeps "a tea-and-cake parlour called The Cat and Kettle" and mocks the nostalgic ideal home that lures the customers to her place:

> But people would eat a boot if it was home made. They like getting caraways into their teeth and spitting out burnt currants; it feels like the old home. I've had customers drive thirty miles to see the dear old black kettle sit on the hob and kid themselves I made the tea out of it. Neurotic, that's what they are. (1981, 399)

As Eluned Summers-Bremner has pointed out, Marianne is the "real casualty" of the story: more than the actually "homeless" Davina and her friends, she has become the "dispossessed" of the title, deprived of the ideal of home she used to live by (2007, 265).

In two other stories, the vacuity of the domestic ideal is exposed in a more comic manner, through lower-middle-class characters. In "Attractive Modern Homes", Mrs. Watson has made a socially upward move to a new house on a brand new estate. Although women's magazines—to which the title ironically alludes—would present this as a dream come true, Mrs. Watson is shown to be extremely unhappy in her new house, a feeling which she—in a characteristic Bowen move—projects on the furniture: "her things appeared uneasy in the new home. The armchairs and settee covered in jazz tapestry, the sideboard with mirror panel, the alabaster light bowls, even the wireless cabinet looked sulky, as though they would rather have stayed in the van" (Bowen 1981, 520). In the climactic middle passage of the story, Mr. Watson finds the "abject" figure of his wife lying face down in the wood that is "too near their door" and in a halting conversation with her husband, Mrs. Watson tries to verbalize the source of her unhappiness. When Mr. Watson challenges his wife with "you've got a home", she replies bitterly, "Yes, it's sweet, isn't it. Like you see in advertisements." In fact, she continues, it's "awful", "you can't think what it's like when you're in it [the house] the whole time". And when her husband points out, "We're the same as we've been always", she replies, "Yes [...] but it [*sic*] didn't notice before" (1981, 526–8). In short, the move to this liminal position in a new estate has brought Mrs. Watson face to face with the emptiness or "nothingness" at the heart of her domestic life. Yet since this is a story in a comic-satiric mode, the abyss is covered up again at the end of the story when Mrs. Watson meets a friendly neighbour from "Kosy Kot", whose recognition restores her sense of identity again.

A similar combination of satire, comedy and horror can be found in "The Working-Party", which stages the young Mrs. Fisk who is for the first time hosting a working-cum-tea-party for the ladies of her village. While the narrator clearly mocks Mrs. Fisk's domestic aspirations—"She had noted the china, the teaspoons, the doylies and saved herself up to outdo them" (1981, 287)—the horror which subsequently strikes when she encounters a dead man blocking the passage between kitchen and parlour is made powerfully real. Although Mrs. Fisk is at first determined that "Nothing should wreck her" (1981, 293, repeated twice), the nothingness at the heart of her home ultimately does wreck her and she flees from her house into the equally empty fields around it:

> The grey-green fields were uncomforting, the very colour of silence; the sky hung over the valley, from hill to hill, like a slack white sheet. The river slipped between reddening willows, sighing and shining. With the dread of her home behind her she fled up the empty valley [...] Long before he could possibly hear her she was calling out [...] "William! I'm frightened—frightened—I don't dare stay in the house—all alone with him—all alone—*William!*" (1981, 296)

Again, the narrator's ironic final comment—"She had forgotten the Working Party"—cannot dispel the real feelings of loneliness, emptiness, nothingness, even deadness which are in this story symbolically attached to the house, thus again undermining the initially more positive depiction of Combe Farm as an "old and solid" house, "command[ing] the valley" (1981, 286).

If these stories reveal the nothingness and emptiness at the heart of the domestic ideal, in some of Bowen's ghost stories women are shown to lose rather than gain an identity through their identification with the home. Instead of being a means to self-expression, homemaking is shown to result in a loss of self. In "The Shadowy Third", Posy has made great efforts to change and refurbish the house—"It seems so very much our house [...] we have made it so entirely"—yet her husband continues to be haunted by the—now absent—furniture, clock and draperies that his first, dead wife had put in place (1981, 77). And Posy herself is—rightly—afraid of turning into a mirror image of this first wife, for instead of securing her identity through the house, her domestic life threatens to turns her into "Anybody", as the first wife is routinely referred to. In "Foothold", a story which revisits this idea in an upper-class household, Janet is initially staged as the perfect embodiment of the modern housewife. She is repeatedly praised by Thomas, a friend of the family, for the tasteful way in which she has furnished the house:

> Thomas [...] looked round the dining-room. Janet did things imaginatively; a subdued, not too buoyant prettiness had been superimposed on last night's sombre effect; a honey-coloured Italian table-cloth on the mahogany, vase of brown marigolds, breakfast china about the age of the house with a red rim and scattered gold pimpernels. The firelight pleasantly jiggled, catching the glaze of dishes and coffee-pot, the copper feet of the "sluggard's joy". The square high room had, like Janet, a certain grace of proportion. (1981, 297)

A seeming paragon of modern domesticity, Janet has managed to make her house into an expression of personality and Thomas compliments her with, "You've inhabited [the house] to a degree I wouldn't have thought possible" (1981, 302). Yet this homemaking no longer brings Janet any satisfaction. In a typical Bowen move, she translates her own unhappiness into a characteristic of the house, which becomes more empty every day: "I do feel the house has grown since we've been in it. The rooms seem to take so much longer to get across" (1981, 299). In spite of her aspirations to make the house into an image of herself, the house in the end destroys Janet, turning her into a duplicate image of its other, ghostly, inhabitant.

For Lassner, these ghost stories show how "[w]omen become ghosts as a result of being sacrificed to the life and purpose of a house [...] they lose their individuality and keep duplicating each other" (1991, 15; see also Wallace 2004).

In all of the stories discussed so far, the fate of these housewives mirrors on a thematic level the stylistic effect of Bowen's mixture of tropes. Just like the house's metaphoric and metonymic function as an expressive marker of the central character's personality is undermined by its prosopopeic agency which works to divest the character of this personality, so the women's attempts to gain identity and self-expression through home-making are undermined by the emptiness at the heart of the house, which threatens to rob the women of any personality or sense of self. Yet if Bowen's housewives are in danger of being effaced by the nothingness, deadness or emptiness of their houses, Bowen's daughters feel restricted by their home's overpowering presence. In "Aunt Tatty", Eleanor struggles with the impossibility of bringing her London lover into her childhood home: "it seems all wrong here. You see this is my home, Paul, and it's me too." When seated around the fire with "the women of the family", Paul intones sardonically: "This is living, O Daughter of the House, this is how time passes, this is how you approach death!" (1981, 266–7).

In stories such as "Mrs. Moysey" or "The Little Girl's Room", the oppressive, even imprisoning quality of the childhood home is construed as the flip-side of the warmth, order and safety it also offers. In the last story, Geraldine is jealously guarded from all corrupting outside influences in her grandmother's Italianate House and she escapes from its suffocating cosiness in the imaginary battles she enacts in her room. The closing lines of the story read: "Security, feeling for her in the dark, closed the last of its tentacles on her limbs, her senses. When the door shut, when they had gone, she sighed acquiescence into her frilly pillow and once more slept in her prison" (1981, 434). In these stories, the childhood home is realized as the "stifling dominating matriarchal house", which Lassner and Derdiger have also traced in some of Bowen's novels (2008, 209). In several other stories, to the contrary, it is a patriarchal presence that seems to oppress, blight or haunt the house. In "Look at All Those Roses", the cottage by the roadside which looks so appealing to Lou—"I wish we lived *there*"—turns out to be blighted by male violence (Bowen 1981, 513). Although the house appears to be an ideal, all-female domain—inhabited by the tellingly named Mrs. Mather, her invalid daughter and a maid—the home is permanently scarred by Mr. Mather's destruction of his daughter's health.

Hence, while Lou expects the house to be "homely", "extinct paper and phantom cretonnes gave it a gutted air" (1981, 517).

In "Joining Charles", to give another example, Louise first sees her husband's childhood home as the "home" she had never had: "the White House opened its arms to her and she began to be carried away by this fullness, this intimacy and the queer seclusion of family life" (1981, 223–4). Yet she comes to realize that the house is "dominated" by her husband, the absent son and brother of the women in the White House: "The things he said, the things he had made, his imprint, were all over the White House" (1981, 225). That this imprint is as destructive as that of Mr. Mather is suggested by Polephemus, the house cat, for whose loss of an eye Charles is to blame. When leaving the house to join her husband in France, Louise leaves Trollope's novel *Framley Parsonage* behind and with it all her illusions about a happy house and home. Ironically, Charles himself likes to uphold the ideal of the happy home: "The White House seemed to Charles [...] very proper as an institution; it was equally proper that he should have a contempt for it" (1981, 225). In other stories too, a distance opens up between the son's contemplation of home as an ideal, often from a distance, and the daughter's experience of it as an oppressive reality. In "The Last Night in the Old Home", the son mourns the loss of his childhood house—"It had always helped him to think of his old home; after a thick night it made him feel good and squashy", while his sister feels "profound relief" as "its grip relaxed on her spirit" (1981, 372–3). This relief is echoed by Cicely in "The New House", when she counters her brother's nostalgic references to their "happy little home" with: "all my life I seem to have been tied up, fastened on to things and people. Why even the way the furniture was arranged at No. 17 held me so I couldn't get away. The way the chairs went in the sitting-room" (1981, 57).

This juxtaposition of male and female reactions to the home clearly suggests that it is not just the reality of home which turns out to be problematic in Bowen's stories: the very ideal of home as warm, comforting and protective is mocked as a male fantasy. This is quite clearly demonstrated in an early story, "Human Habitation". Two students on a walking tour in the English Midlands have lost their way and are heartened by "lights" in the distance. One of them says, "There'll be people, you know, and they might let us come by the fire. They'd tell us the way, but I expect they'd ask us to stay for a bit" and his companion concurs, "I expect the people are well-to-do, and live there because they like it. It would be rather a jolly place to live" (1981, 151). The narrator comments wryly, "It was extraordinary how happy they felt as they approached the lights, and how benevolent" (1981, 152). The house they imagine and eagerly anticipate is like a Bachelardian oneiric house, including the iconic light in the distance promising warmth and security. As Bachelard wrote in *The Poetics of Space*, "Through its light alone, the house becomes human", "keeps vigil, vigilantly waits", becomes a "refuge", offering "protection against the forces that besiege it"(Bachelard 1994, 35–7). The students also follow Bachelard in constructing their ideal house as feminine when they misread the woman's anxious look out of the windows as a sign of welcome: "Woman, all the women of the world, hailing them home with relief and expectation. Something stirred warmly in both of them; it would be like this to have a wife" (Bowen 1981, 152). The overblown rhetoric of these passages clearly mocks the students' idealizing celebrations of a feminine domesticity and the rest of the story further undercuts these images as the woman, her crying baby, and an elderly aunt turn out to be anxiously waiting for a husband who has never been late before. The house is thus marked by anxiety and absence rather than by the warmth, fullness and safety they anticipated. The most sensitive of the students recognizes the falsity of their ideal and tries to understand the very different perspective of the woman:

> One felt that she had built up for herself an intricate and perhaps rather lonely life, monotone beneath the great shadow of William. Jameson was tapping out his points with his spoon against his cup and clamouring about cohesion, but he would be unable to understand the queer unity that had created and destroyed Annie. (1981, 158)

This early story thus announces what many of Bowen's later stories will confirm: house and husband provide women with an identity, a life, but one which is of necessity lonely, monotonous, and ultimately destructive.

In all, if being homeless is not a desirable state in Bowen's fiction, being at home is certainly not ideal either. While for her male characters, the warm and secure home is a nice ideal to contemplate from afar, for her female characters, having a home is a far more ambivalent affair. Although house and home offer a sense of identity and protection, that identity proves ultimately meaningless or empty for Bowen's housewives, while her daughters experience it as restrictive and oppressive. In both cases, the house becomes an extension of personality—as promised by the domestic ideology and realized through metaphor and metonymy—only at the expense of simultaneously defacing this personality, rendering the characters curiously lifeless compared to the greater agency of the house. Bowen's repeated staging of this process, at both a stylistic and a thematic level, can be read as a critique of the domestic ideology that dominated mid-twentieth-century England. At the same time, several stories also focus specifically on the separateness and individualism that seem inevitable attributes of the domestic "one's home is one's castle" ideal. For what most houses in Bowen's stories also share is a sense of isolation. They are typically on their own in the countryside ("Joining Charles", "The New House", "The Working Party", "Her Table Spread", "Human Habitation" and "Look at All Those Roses") or in a liminal place: on the edge of a new estate ("The Dispossessed", "Attractive Modern Homes", "The Shadowy Third") or at the very end of a crumbling terrace ("No. 16", "In the Square"). In all of those instances, the isolation of the houses symbolizes *and* aggravates the loneliness of the characters.

Already in "Daffodils", Bowen suggests that this loneliness is the flipside of the safety the house also offers: "[Miss Murcheson] stood in the doorway, with that square of light and sound behind her, craving the protection and the comfort with which that dark entrance had so often received her. There was a sudden desolation in the emptiness of the house" (1981, 22). Being closed and isolated, Bowen's houses tend to foreclose rather than enable human interaction. In "Daffodils", Miss Murcheson tries to counter the isolation of the house by opening the window and inviting in three of her pupils, but this does not have the intended effect as they do not understand what she is trying to communicate. In "Attractive Modern Homes", conversely, Mrs. Watson's sense of self is eventually restored by the recognition from a neighbour, rather than by the attractiveness of her new home, and in "The Parrot", Eleanor can only embark on a conversation with her glamorous neighbour on the roof-tops of their houses.

In its ideal form, however, Bowen's house does not shut out this interaction but rather incorporates it within itself. An interesting example of such an ideal house is given in "The Visitor":

> Roger had an imaginary house that, when it was quite complete in his mind, he was some day going to live in: in this there were a hundred corridors raying off from a fountain in the centre; at the end of each there was a room looking out into a private garden. The walls of the gardens were so high and smooth that no one could climb over into somebody else's. When they wanted to meet, they would come and bathe together in this fountain. One

of the rooms was for his mother, another for his friend Paul. There were ninety-seven still unappropriated, and now it seemed there would be ninety-eight. (1981, 126)

Traces of this ideal house can also be found in Bowen's descriptions of Bowen's Court. Both in *Bowen's Court* and in a 1958 magazine piece of the same title, Bowen emphasizes the "isolation" of the house in "lonely country", while at the same time stressing the "social" purposes of the house, "with hospitality as its inbuilt ideal" (Bowen and Hepburn 2010, 140, 149). In a 1940 essay for the Irish magazine *The Bell*, Bowen expresses the hope that this social aspect of the Big House will be able to overcome the barriers that isolate it from Irish reality: "Symbolically (though also matter-of-factly) the doors of the big houses stand open all day; it is only regretfully that they are barred up at night" (Bowen and Lee 1986, 29). In another wartime magazine piece, "The Christmas Toast Is Home", Bowen argues more generally against a conception of home as "a narrow place, from which the family bars out the world's troubles": "One's home is one's castle—yes. But must this mean a castle defensively guarded, with drawbridge always raised? The castle (however tiny this may be) should show above all a confident graciousness. And the first of the graces is hospitality" (Bowen and Hepburn 2010, 130–1). Yet, this idea of an open house which balances shelter and sharing, individuality and communality remains an ideal in Bowen's short fiction, both in terms of the aristocratic big houses that are lost and in terms of the middle-class homes still to be realized.

Open Shelters and Dublin Houses in Brennan's Stories

Maeve Brennan is one of a rare breed: a writer fully committed to the genre of the short story. In Irish literature, she is joined in this only by Mary Lavin and, for the time being at least, Claire Keegan. Compared to Lavin, however, Brennan's output is quite small: she published some 40 stories and about an equal amount of sketches, almost exclusively in *The New Yorker*, for which she worked as a journalist for some 25 years. Yet, in spite of this limited output, Brennan did exploit the full possibilities of the short form and the four books which contain her work display both a great variety and a consummate artistry: from the satirical Herbert Retreat stories and affectionate New York sketches that make up

The Rose Garden (2000) over the tragic Dublin stories gathered in *The Springs of Affection* (1998) to the posthumously published novella, *The Visitor* (2001), which is really not much longer than the longest of her Dublin stories. While these newly constituted collections are to an important extent responsible for the critical rediscovery of Brennan's work in the late 1990s, in their grouping of the stories in terms of type and setting, they are slightly misleading. They give the impression that Brennan wrote these stories in sets and, even, that they represent a certain development in her work. In fact, Brennan seems to have written these story series in tandem rather than in sequence. In the early 1950s, for instance, she wrote the first of the Derdon series, "The Poor Men and Women", as well as two Herbert Retreat stories and a few of the autobiographical childhood stories. In the late 1960s, similarly, she was working on some of her New York animal stories while also publishing further Dublin stories about the Derdons and the Bagots. Her novella, *The Visitor* predates all of that, as it was written in the mid-1940s, but remained unpublished during her life. Throughout her whole writing career, Brennan also published sketches about New York City for her "The Talk of the Town" column in *The New Yorker*. These sketches too are often stories of a kind, little vignettes about ordinary life in New York, which anticipate Lydia Davis's similarly well-observed very short short stories.

In their richness and variety, Brennan's short stories appeal to different traditions and trends. Her Herbert Retreat stories, which derive their name from the fictional upper-class suburb in which they are set, are clearly indebted to the popular magazine story that I have traced back to Somerville and Ross's *Some Experiences of an Irish R.M.* Although a more savage satire usually accompanies the comic events, Brennan's stories are equally tightly unified and neatly close on a final twist which serves to destabilize or reverse the power hierarchies which the story has so far traced. In "The Joker", for instance, Isobel, who has been condescendingly kind to the "waifs" she has invited for her annual Christmas party, becomes the object of kindness and pity herself, while in "The Stone Hot-Water Bottle", Leona's discovery of some half-burned letters reverses the power balance between her and her regular weekend guest, the critic Charles Runyon. As in Somerville and Ross's stories, the relations between the upper-class American masters and their Irish maids are often the occasion for reversals and shifts of power (Palko 2007). Yet, in Brennan's much darker stories, the servants are also shown to be no better than the employers they love to ridicule: they are governed by the same in-group jealousies and rivalries, the same desire for power and the same capacity for spite. Like most magazine stories, moreover, the Herbert Retreat stories—and some related stories like "The Holy Terror" and "The Bohemians"—are consistently narrated by an omniscient narrator, who may verbalize the thoughts of one or more characters, but nevertheless keeps an ironic distance throughout.

Entirely different in terms of tone, style and narration are Brennan's semi-autobiographical sketches about life in New York and New Hampshire. Whether told in the first-person, as in "A Snowy Night on West Forty-ninth Street" and "I See You, Bianca", or focalized through Mary Ann Whitty, a thinly disguised alter ego of the author, as in "In and Out of Never-Never Land" and "A Large Bee", these stories are open-ended and largely plotless. Like *The Long-Winded Lady* sketches, these stories offer ruminations on ordinary experiences: dining in a restaurant on a snowy evening, rescuing a bee from drowning, or losing a cat. Yet Brennan's original or odd way of seeing things often has the effect of heightening or estranging the everyday, as in the stories told from the perspective of animals: "The Door on West Tenth Street", for instance, tries to imagine what life is like for a dog in New York, longing to be taken on an outing. In their emphasis on mood, subjective perspective and reflection, these sketch-like stories draw on elements of the modernist short story, yet they remain much more bound to setting and context, which is rendered with a great attention to detail.

A skilful use of perspectival narration can also be found in the autobiographical Dublin stories which make up the first section of *The Springs of Affection*. The stories all hinge on some incident remembered from childhood and are depicted as seen through the child's eye. Yet, this perspective of the 'experiencing I' is cleverly complemented by the more knowledgeable perspective of the 'narrating I', who can put childhood experiences, such as a visit to the Poor Clares or their house being searched by the Free Staters in a larger context. Brennan's use of perspectival narration achieves its most consummate effect, however, in the mainly tragic Derdon and Bagot stories. In contrast to the Herbert Retreat stories, the narrator has almost completely withdrawn in these stories. Instead, the thoughts, memories and emotions of the main protagonists are foregrounded through sustained focalization and the use of indirect and free indirect discourse. Moreover, in the Derdon stories, Brennan carefully alternates between the perspectives of Hubert and Rose Derdon, so as to offer an even-handed dissection of a marriage between two people who are entirely ill-matched, yet bound to each other for life. In these stories, contextual details—the house where they live or Hubert's work environment—are only evoked as seen through the eyes of the characters and the narrator lacks the ironic or self-reflexive stance that can be found in the Herbert Retreat stories and the first-person narratives and sketches. The result is an enclosed, compelling reading experience that mirrors the claustrophobic closedness of the characters' marriage and world.

The different narrative structures and perspectives offered in Brennan's short stories also result in very different evocations of place: from the satiric description of the pretentious houses in the Herbert Retreat stories, over the loving evocation of the grand but decaying buildings around Times Square to the modernist, perspectival depiction of the modest Dublin house that recurs throughout *The Springs of Affection*. Indeed, while houses loom large in Brennan's fiction, as they do in Bowen's, the variety of homes depicted is much smaller. The three sets of Dublin stories share the same house, an imaginative recreation of Brennan's childhood home: 48, Cherryfield Avenue, Ranelagh. This is a two-storey terraced house, with a small, fenced front garden and a slightly larger, walled-in back garden with a flowering laburnum tree at the back. Critics have often read Brennan's obsessive fictional recreation of this childhood home as expressive of the exile's nostalgic longing for "her one true home", as the biographical synopsis in *The Rose Garden* puts it (Brennan 2000). In this reading, home and homeland become one. Angela Bourke's pioneering biography of Maeve Brennan grounds this reading of Brennan in terms of homelessness and dislocation in Brennan's experience of exile and her nomadic life in New York, where she moved between hotels and rented apartments, "as though she hoped to find again the feeling of home she had left behind in Dublin" (Bourke 2004, 142). Unable to do so, Bourke argues, she then set to recreate that home in fiction. In her Preface to *The Visitor*, Clare Boylan repeats this interpretation:

> The marriage [to St. Clair McKelway] broke up and Maeve became a wanderer. She was an exile in the most painful sense. She had nowhere to call home and no kindred spirit with whom to share her unique vision of the world. It may well have been that her removal from her native country at a vulnerable age established her sense of homelessness. (Brennan 2001, n.p.)

Yet, as in the case of Bowen, the insistent preoccupation with houses and homes in Brennan's fiction must be read in tandem with the narrators' evocation of these houses as well as the characters' lived experience of them. Together with Brennan's more straightforward statements on home in *The Long-Winded Lady*, these perspectival evocations of home will tell us something about the feelings that infuse representations of home in Brennan's fiction. As Blunt and Dowling remind us, "These may be feelings of belonging, desire and intimacy, but can also be feelings of fear, violence and alienation" (2006, 2). In the remainder of this chapter, therefore, I aim to trace Brennan's representation of home as a "spatial imagery", or, as Sara Ahmed has called it, "a lived experience of locality" (1999, 341). As I hope to show, these representations are far more ambivalent than the existing critical binaries, of home–homelessness, belonging–alienation and Ireland–exile, allow for.

Of all the homes described in Brennan's short stories, there are only a few that carry the explicit approval of the narrator. These can be found in the autobiographical New York stories that make up the second half of *The Rose Garden*. It is here, I would argue, that Brennan comes closest to sketching her ideal home. In "I See You, Bianca", she does so through describing the house of a friend, while in "In and Out of Never-Never Land" she fictionalizes a cottage in East Hampton she herself lived in for extended periods of time in the 1960s. The importance of the latter story—and the home it describes—is underscored by the fact that it became the title story of her first collection of short stories, published in 1969. Consistent with the fairy-tale allusions of the title, the cottage of Mary-Ann Whitty, a clear alter ego of the author, is figured in terms of unreality: "It wasn't a summer house, and not a seaside house, and, in fact, not a real house. And it wasn't a real house. It wasn't a bit real. The living room, where Mary Ann stood, had been copied from the set of some opera or operetta—*Hansel and Gretel*, Mary Ann had heard" (Brennan 2000, 293). The fact that it is "not a real house" is precisely what she likes about it:

> The room pleased her. She had grown fond of it. It was improbable and impermanent [...] it did not even represent a dream, but was only the echo of somebody's memory of romantic escape—to a hunting lodge, a mountain hideway in Austria, or a secret place in Switzerland [...] The little house was not real. It was only a façade that stood at the end of somebody's lawn, and Mary Ann thought that it did wonderfully for somebody who wanted to live by the Atlantic Ocean but who only wanted to live there for a while. (2000, 294–5)

Mary Ann also seeks to maintain, even strengthen, the house's "improbable and impermanent" air, by refusing to have a dining-room table:

> She knew that she should have a [...] proper table for eating and that without it her life was makeshift, but she thought that makeshift ways were very well suited to this strange little house, which wore such a temporary air [...] she congratulated herself as sincerely on what the house lacked as she did on what it held. But in spite of all it lacked, and for all its temporary air, the little house had an air of gaiety, about it, even of welcome. (2000, 283–4)

This note of welcome is important to Mary Ann, since the cottage is adjacent and "closely related" to "the great house on the dunes where the seven children lived, all of them Bluebell's friends" (2000, 284). They are Mary Ann's friends too and, as the events of the story make clear, she particularly enjoys the close but separate, playful and not responsible relation she has with them. Important too in making this little cottage a real home for Mary Ann is that "it contained her furniture, her books, her dog and cats" (2000, 283).

Similar elements recur to define the ideal home in "I See You, Bianca", in which the I-narrator describes at great length the perfect home her friend Nicolas has made in an apartment house that is forever about to be demolished: another improbable and impermanent place, in other words. With the greater distance of the observer, the narrator lays bare the elements that make it the perfect home for its owner. There is the cosmopolitan dimension ("his own apartment would look much as it does whether he lived in Rome or Brussels or Manchester"); its air of being at once "cavernous and hospitable"; and its close but distanced relation to where the action is: "what it is like, more than anything, is a private room hidden backstage in a very busy theatre where the season is in full swing" (2000, 250–1). As in "In and Out of Never-Never Land", being close to but separate from the hustle and bustle of life and other people is important for the ideal home as is, of course, the presence of the cat, Bianca, on whom the story turns:

> Bianca and the ailanthus provide Nicolas with the extra dimension all apartment dwellers long for. People who have no terraces and no gardens long to escape from their own four walls, but not to wander far. They only want to step outside for a minute [...] They stand around in groups or they sit together on the front steps [...] They lean out of their windows [...] all of them escaping from the rooms they live in and that they are glad to have but

not to be closed up in. It should not be a problem, to have shelter without being shut away. (2000, 256)

In this generalizing move from Nicolas' apartment to the longings of all apartment dwellers, the narrator again defines her ideal home in terms of the perfect balance between solitude and companionship, safety and openness, separateness and relation.

Turning from these New York homes to Brennan's recreated Dublin childhood home, however, it does turn out to be a problem "to have shelter without being shut away". For while the childhood house offers shelter and protection from a hostile outside world, it also threatens to enclose and imprison its inhabitants. In opposition to the makeshift house in East Hampton, first of all, the Dublin house has an air of permanence and conventionality, of commonplace solidity: "it looked like itself, a small plain house in a row, faced from the other side of the terrace by a row of other houses just like it" (Brennan 2000, 204). It is a stable presence in the life of the family, "the house that would never blow up. Never, never" (Brennan 1998, 239). The solidity of the house is reinforced by its solid and proper furniture and the other domestic objects, whose cleaning and polishing make up a good deal of the daily routines of Mrs. Bagot and Mrs. Derdon.

Two of the Bagot stories in fact revolve around the brief sense of freedom that is created when domestic objects are temporarily removed. In "The Carpet with Big Pink Roses on It", Mrs. Bagot puts the carpet in the garden to give it an airing and thinks wistfully of lying on the carpet and being transported to faraway places:

> But to sit on the carpet and go away somewhere—Mrs. Bagot would have liked that, although she did not admit to Lily that she agreed with her. To get the two children and Bennie, the dog, settled on the carpet and then to vanish and go away somewhere, even if it was only for the afternoon or part of the afternoon. To disappear for a little while would do no harm to anyone, and it would be very restful to get away from the house without having to go out by the front door and endure the ceremony of walking down the street where everybody could see you. (1998, 233)

Yet the thought of the neighbours, who might see her lying on the carpet, restrains her and it is instead Lilly, her daughter, who travels on the carpet "to Paris and to Spain" (1998, 239). In "The Sofa", similarly, the front sitting room is emptied in anticipation of the new sofa which will be delivered. The emphasis is on the sense of freedom this creates ("the room looked very carefree with no furniture in it") and Mrs. Bagot watches elatedly how her children give in to the impulse she also feels, of lying on the now exposed carpet in the middle of the room: "And Mrs. Bagot wanted to lie down on the floor with the children and embrace them both" (1998, 257, 259). She doesn't, of course, but waiting for the sofa does provide her with a rare opportunity of doing nothing: "the clock, which had been so domineering all these years, had no power over her today" (1998, 261).

What Mrs. Bagot's home shares with the ideal houses in New York, is that the house only becomes a home because of the children and, to a lesser extent, the animals that inhabit it. On the birth of her first son, Mrs. Bagot reflects how "the house became a kingdom, significant, private, and safe" (1998, 266) and throughout the stories her happiness seems to reside in being with the children in the safety of the house. Conversely, the absence of the children empties the house of all homely feeling: "without them the house had neither substance nor meaning. The house was lonely, that is what it amounted to, and Mrs. Bagot felt the house was making her lonely" (1998, 240). One can note in these instances that, as in Bowen's stories, the character's feelings infuse her perception of the house and are even projected onto the house. Yet, Brennan's houses do not gain agency through personification, since Brennan keeps reminding the reader of the character's subjective perspective through such hedges as "seemed", "as if", or "Mrs. Bagot felt".

This perspectival evocation of space, characteristic of the modernist short story, can also be found in "An Attack of Hunger", where Rose Derdon's feelings of loss after her son has left for the priesthood infuse her perception of the house: "she saw the walls of her house, and its furniture, the pictures and chairs and the little rugs and ornaments, and the sight of these things hurt her, because she had tried hard to keep the house as it had been when John had left it" (1998, 151). The house is inevitably transformed: where there was presence, there is now absence and empti- ness. In a long passage, Mrs. Derdon surveys the material defects that signal his absence for her: two cups have been broken, one of the cushions is stained, there are worn patches in the stair carpet and the wallpaper had begun to peel. She reflects, "There was no hope for her inside the house", but continues "her entire life was in the house" (1998, 152). Her home has become hostile to her, yet her life and identity are so entirely bound to the house, that she cannot exist outside of it. This is made painfully clear to her when she tries to leave the house and her marriage after a row with her husband, but she has nowhere to go. So, she returns "to home and duty", announcing "I came back because it's my duty to stay here and keep your house" (1998, 169).

In the other Derdon stories too, the opposition outside/inside, public/private looms large: Rose feels insecure and exposed outside the house and this is compounded by her husband's reluctance to be seen in public with her: "she and Hubert never went anywhere or visited anyone [...] he had come to distrust her presence everywhere except in the house", they never go on holiday "because they did not like to leave the house alone" (1998, 150, 96). And although the house had initially promised "safety" and a sense of "belonging", with Rose vowing to "never want to leave this house", this promise has turned sour, the stories suggest, by the deterioration of her relations with Hubert, the loss of her son, and the lack of movement in and interaction with the world outside the house (1998, 188, 189). Rose is enclosed within the house, which is itself closed to the outside world. Her sense of enclosure is also symbolized by her favourite pastime, watching the sky, which she has to indulge in obliquely and covertly, from within the house, for fear of being caught staring, as well as by her nostalgic memories of the walks she and Hubert took in and around Stephen's Green before they had bought the house. Since then, she has "kept close to the house. She might as well have been in a net, for all the freedom she felt" (1998, 183).

Although Mrs. Bagot's experience of the house is more positive, because it is a manifestation of her empowering role as mother, in the Bagot stories too, the boundary between outside and inside, between public and private is clearly drawn. While Delia feels the house shelters her from the inquisitive and hostile stare of neighbours, she is also bound to the house like Rose and feels insecure in the neighbourhood streets and shops. Her favourite place is the liminal, inside-outside place of the garden and her favourite pastime is looking out into the street from behind her ferns, so that she cannot herself be watched by others. The constraints of her existence are clear: "The milkman came early in the morning and the bread man at eleven, but otherwise Mrs. Bagot hardly ever had to open the front door, except for the children when they came home from school at half past three" (1998, 250). In fact, the only people both Rose and Delia can confidently invite into the kitchen are the "poor men and women" whom they can patronize and feel superior to.

If Delia Bagot occasionally feels "hemmed in" by the house, it is her husband who truly feels trapped in his house and all it stands for: "He detested the house when he felt like this, because he felt the house transformed him. When he was away from home he was alright [...] But then the minute he got home he felt harassed and pursued" (1998, 226). Only when he is away, or when his wife and children are asleep, can he think of his home in positive terms: "their sound sleep turned the house into a refuge" (1998, 229). On Christmas Eve, in the story of that title, he also becomes momentarily reconciled with his home when listening to Delia and the children talking in a different room: "He had often thought the house cramped, and imagined it held him down, but tonight he knew that he could stretch his arms up through this hall ceiling and on up through the roof and do no damage and that no one would reproach him. There was plenty of room" (1998, 305). Yet Brennan undermines this image of the happy home again, by juxtaposing Martin's thoughts with those of Delia, who is upstairs, feeling "lonely and afraid [...] in a morbid frame of mind", worrying about the coldness of their marriage (1998, 306).

In short, the house is a powerful but highly ambivalent presence in the Dublin stories: while it may offer safety, solidity and a sense of belonging, it is as often restrictive, oppressive and lonely. As in Bowen's stories, especially the female characters are bound to the house: their sense of identity depends on the house and on the domestic tasks they dutifully perform and they feel insecure when they venture outside. Although the male characters tell themselves that this is how their wives want it, the women's often anxious or constricted feelings of the house reveal otherwise. Through her stories, therefore, Brennan also criticizes the domestic ideology which loomed as large in post-Independence Ireland as it did in interwar Britain (Palko 2010). If being at home in Dublin in the 1920s and 1930s may have been a positive experience for a child, as the more happy memories of home in the autobiographical Dublin sketches suggest, Brennan did come to understand and explore the restrictions the domestic ideal placed on men as well as women, whose lived experience of house and home is shown to be far more conflicted.

There is in fact only one adult character in the Dublin stories for whom 'home' is unambiguously positive and that is the elderly bishop who visits Delia in "Stories from Africa". He is interested in her house as it provides fuel to the imaginary home that he has created on the basis of his memories of the farm of Delia's grandmother. His evocation of the farmhouse recalls Bachelard's description of the iconic house in *The Poetics of Place* (Bachelard 1994, 35–7), complete with the welcoming presence of the woman of the house:

> The lane is so nice, the way it turns around to suit the fields and then goes straight between the hedges [...] and the last big turn you make, that brings you in sight of the house, the lane widens out and gets wider as you get nearer the house, and there are very high trees on each side along that last stretch [...] Your grandmother used to watch for me, the Bishop said, and the minute I came around the last turn she would appear out at the door and stand there waiting for me. I could feel her smiling as I came down the lane. God bless her kind heart, she was never ashamed to show that you were welcome, never ashamed, never afraid. She was very gentle. (Brennan 1998, 293)

As in Bachelard's *Poetics*, the bishop's memories reveal the gendering of home as female. As Doreen Massey has put it,

> The construction of 'home' as a woman's place has, moreover, carried through into those views of place itself as a source of stability, reliability and authenticity. Such views of place, which reverberate with nostalgia for something lost, are coded female. Home is where the heart is (if you happen to have the spatial mobility to have left) and where the women (mother, lover-to-whom-you-will-one-day-return) is also. (1994, 180)

The bishop *knows* that this fantasy of home and homeland has little bearing in reality: "What was he doing inventing and polishing and making phrases that said nothing at all? Anyone listening to him would imagine he thought Ireland to be a pretty little oasis of some kind or another, a kind of family paradise" (Brennan 1998, 296). Yet the fantasy sustains him on his foreign missions. If in the bishop's case, the homesickness is kept in check by his pride and sense of duty as a priest, for the sad protagonist of *The Visitor*, there have been no similar checks on self-indulgence. Her lack of purpose and sense of self have led her to fabricate an imaginary fantasy of home around her grandmother's house in Dublin, which has no bearing in reality, but which shields her from an independent life she cannot face. Early in the novella, the narrator warns of the silliness of indulging in homesickness as it is fuelled by entirely imaginary images of home:

> Home is a place in the mind. When it is empty, it frets. It is fretful with memory, faces and places and times gone by. Beloved images rise up in disobedience and make a mirror for emptiness. Then what resentful wonder,

and what half-aimless seeking. It is a silly state of affairs. It is a silly creature that tries to get a smile from even the most familiar and loving shadow. Comical and hopeless, the long gaze back is always turned inward. (Brennan 2001, 8)

In *The Long-Winded Lady* sketch, "A Daydream", Maeve Brennan also sets down one such nostalgic dream of home in East Hampton only to dismiss it with "The daydream was, after all, only a mild attack of home-sickness. The reason it was a mild attack instead of a fierce one is that there are a number of places I am homesick for. East Hampton is only one of them" (Brennan 1997, 264–5). Brennan's transient and itinerant life in New York was certainly very different from the housebound life of Mrs. Bagot and Mrs. Derdon depicted in her Dublin stories, but equally from the deluded homesickness that characterizes Anastasia King in *The Visitor*. Brennan seems to have chosen and embraced her nomadic existence as a "traveller in residence", as she called herself, perhaps out of an abhorrence of the domesticity that she noted in her mother's life or perhaps out of a sense of restlessness inherited from her father (Brennan 1997, 2). The images of the ideal house which her New York stories portray suggest, moreover, that home for her had to provide only a temporary and make-shift shelter, one that provided seclusion but also interaction and openness to the world. The hotels she often stayed in in New York provided this double need: the need for a room of one's own and the need to social-ize down below—in the lobbies, cafés, restaurants and bars that figure largely in Brennan's New York sketches. Moreover, as Ann Peters notes, hotels also conveniently release working women from domestic tasks (Peters 2005, 77). In the last sketch included in *The Long-Winded Lady*, "A Blessing", published in January 1981, Brennan recalls a very special New Year's Eve in Cherryfield Avenue:

> What happened that New Year's Eve was that in the late afternoon word went around from house to house that a minute or so before midnight we would all step out into our front gardens, or even into the street, leaving the front doors open, so that the light streamed out after us, and there we would wait to hear the bells ringing in the New Year. I nearly went mad with excite-ment and happiness. I know I jumped for joy. That New Year's Eve was one of the great occasions of our lives. (Brennan 1997, 268)

This happy memory again evokes the ideal home as one which provides shelter—with the doors open and the lights on, the houses are ready to welcome their inhabitants again—yet which also allows for interpersonal connection among neighbours, friends and strangers. Precisely this dimension of home is entirely absent in the Bagot and Derdon stories, where houses only keep out a world perceived as hostile and where even next-door neighbours are treated with cold civility. It is also absent from the Herbert Retreat houses, which are similarly individualistic and only designed to impress: "It is of no advantage to repair to a neighbor's house in order to see the water and show it off to visitors; each householder feels he must have a view of his own to offer" (Brennan 2000, 4). If in the Herbert Retreat stories, the essentially solitary and closed nature of the home is satirically undercut, in the Dublin stories, the stresses and strains it places on its inhabitants are tragically exposed. Small wonder then that Brennan herself spent her adult life in makeshift and temporary homes that, contrary to 48, Cherryfield Avenue, offered a woman shelter without shutting her away.

BIBLIOGRAPHY

Ahmed, Sara. 1999. Home and Away. Narratives of Migration and Estrangement. *International Journal of Cultural Studies* 2 (3):329–347.

Akenson, Donald Harman. 1996. *The Irish Diaspora: A Primer*. Toronto: P.D. Meany Co.

Bachelard, Gaston. 1994. *The Poetics of Space*. Boston: Beacon Press.

Beddoe, Deirdre. 1989. *Back to Home and Duty: Women Between the Wars 1918–1939*. London: Pandora.

Blunt, Alison, and Robyn M. Dowling. 2006. *Home*. London: Routledge.

Bourke, Angela. 2004. *Maeve Brennan: Homesick at The New Yorker*. London: Jonathan Cape.

Bowen, Elizabeth. 1950. *Preface to The Faber Book of Modern Short Stories, in Collected Impressions*. 38–46. London: Longmans. Original edition 1936.

Bowen, Elizabeth. 1962. *Afterthought: Pieces About Writing*. London: Longmans.

Bowen, Elizabeth. 1975. *Pictures and Conversations*. London: Allen Lane.

Bowen, Elizabeth. 1981. *The Collected Stories of Elizabeth Bowen*. Hopewell, NJ: Ecco Press.

Bowen, Elizabeth. 1999. *Bowen's Court & Seven Winters: Memories of a Dublin Childhood*. London: Vintage.

Bowen, Elizabeth, and Allan Hepburn. 2008. *The Bazaar and Other Stories*. Edinburgh: Edinburgh University Press.

Bowen, Elizabeth, and Allan Hepburn. 2010. *People, Places, Things: Essays by Elizabeth Bowen*. Edinburgh: Edinburgh University Press.

Bowen, Elizabeth, and Hermione Lee. 1986. *The Mulberry Tree: Writings of Elizabeth Bowen*. London: Virago.

Brennan, Maeve. 1997. *The Long-Winded Lady: Notes from the New Yorker*. Berkeley: Counterpoint.

Brennan, Maeve. 1998. *The Springs of Affection: Stories of Dublin*. New York: Houghton Mifflin.

Brennan, Maeve. 2000. *The Rose Garden: Short Stories*. Washington, DC: Counterpoint.

Brennan, Maeve. 2001. *The Visitor*. London: Atlantic.

Coughlan, Patricia. 2004b. Review of *Maeve Brennan: Homesick at The New Yorker* by Angela Bourke. *Irish University Review* 34 (2):435–442.

Cullingford, Elizabeth. 2014. American Dreams: Emigration or Exile in Contemporary Irish Fiction? *Éire-Ireland* 49 (3):60–94.

de Man, Paul. 1984. *The Rhetoric of Romanticism*. New York: Columbia University Press.

Éinrí, Piaras Mac, and Tina O'Toole. 2012. Editors' Introduction: New Approaches to Irish Migration. *Éire-Ireland* 47 (1):5–18.

Ellmann, Maud. 2003. *Elizabeth Bowen: The Shadow Across the Page*. Edinburgh: Edinburgh University Press.

Hand, Derek. 2009. Ghosts from Our Future: Bowen and the Unfinished Business of Living. In *Elizabeth Bowen*, edited by Eibhear Walshe, 65–76. Dublin: Irish Academic Press.

Hanson, Clare. 1985. *Short Stories and Short Fictions, 1880–1980*. London: Macmillan.

Humble, Nicola. 2001. *The Feminine Middlebrow Novel, 1920s to 1950s: Class, Domesticity, and Bohemianism*. Oxford: Oxford University Press.

Hunter, Adrian. 2007. *The Cambridge Introduction to the Short Story in English*. Cambridge: Cambridge University Press.

Ingman, Heather. 2009. *A History of the Irish Short Story*. Cambridge: Cambridge University Press.

Kilroy, James. 1984. *The Irish Short Story: A Critical History*. Boston: Twayne.

Kreilkamp, Vera. 2009. Bowen: Ascendancy Modernist. In *Elizabeth Bowen*, edited by Eibhear Walshe, 12–26. Dublin: Irish Academic Press.

Lassner, Phyllis. 1991. *Elizabeth Bowen: A Study of the Short Fiction*. Boston: Twayne.

Lassner, Phyllis, and Paula Derdiger. 2008. Domestic Gothic, the Global Primitive, and Gender Relations in Elizabeth Bowen's *The Last September* and *The House in Paris*. In *Irish Modernism and the Global Primitive*, edited by Maria McGarrity and Claire A. Culleton, 195–214. New York: Palgrave.

Lee, Hermione. 1999. *Elizabeth Bowen*. London: Vintage.

Lodge, David. 1977. *The Modes of Modern Writing: Metaphor, Metonymy, and the Typology of Modern Literature*. London: Edward Arnold.

Massey, Doreen. 1994. *Space, Place and Gender*. Cambridge: Polity Press.

Palko, Abigail L. 2007. Out of Home in the Kitchen: Maeve Brennan's Herbert's Retreat Stories. *New Hibernia Review* 11 (4):73–91.

Palko, Abigail L. 2010. From *The Uninvited* to *The Visitor*: The Post-Independence Dilemma Faced by Irish Women Writers. *Frontiers: A Journal of Women Studies* 31 (2):1–34.

Peters, Ann. 2005. A Traveler in Residence: Maeve Brennan and the Last Days of New York. *Women's Studies Quarterly* 33 (3/4):66–89.

Summers-Bremner, Eluned. 2007. Monumental City: Elizabeth Bowen and the Modern Unhomely. In *Modernism and Mourning*, edited by Patricia Rae, 260–270. Lewisburg: Bucknell University Press.

Wallace, Diana. 2004. Uncanny Stories: The Ghost Story as Female Gothic. *Gothic Studies* 6 (1):57–68.

CHAPTER 4

Mary Lavin's Relational Selves

A striking likeness exists between "Miss Holland", the first short story Mary Lavin wrote, and Elizabeth Bowen's first story, "Breakfast". Bowen wrote the story in 1919, when she was 20 and wanted to become an artist: "For me reality meant the books I had read—and I turned round, as *I* was writing, from time to time, to stare at them, unassailable in the shelves behind me. (This was my room, containing most things I owned.) I had engaged myself to add to their number" (Bowen 1962, 84). Twenty years later, in 1939, Lavin similarly moved from reading to writing when she wrote "Miss Holland" on the back of some pages of her Ph.D. thesis on Virginia Woolf (Levenson 1998, 47–9). With remarkable similarity, both of these first stories revolve around a protagonist who dreads the communal meals in a boarding house. To Mr. Rossiter, in "Breakfast", it seemed as if "All his days and nights were loops, curving out from breakfast time, curving back to it again. Inexorably the loops grew smaller, looming more and more over his nights, eating more and more out of his days" (Bowen 1981, 20). He is uncomfortable with the teasing conversation, notes with disgust the eating habits of his fellow boarders—"the rotatory mastication of [someone's] jaws", the way someone else "drained his coffee-cup with a gulp and a gurgle" (1981, 16)—and is very conscious of what he does and says himself. In a similar way, Miss Holland becomes obsessed with mealtimes at her boarding house—"All through supper she would sit in a tight straight rigidity of nervousness, indifferent to the food, waiting for an opportunity to enter the conversation in a striking way" (Lavin 1945, 151). Yet she is confounded by the quick bantering that goes on

© The Editor(s) (if applicable) and The Author (s) 2016
E. D'hoker, *Irish Women Writers and the Modern Short Story*,
DOI 10.1007/978-3-319-30288-1_4

83

between the boarders and is unable to join in. The end of the story also records her disgust at "their ugliness, their commonness, their bad taste": a "dark grey stain of grease on the leg of [someone's] trousers", a "stain of perspiration", "false teeth", a "bit of red bleeding flesh, like an inflamed pimple, between two front teeth", and a "wart on the palm" of a hand (1945, 156). In spite of this similar set-up, however, there are also many differences between "Breakfast" and "Miss Holland": formal differences of style and structure as well as a divergence in thematic perspective and moral implication. Starting from these differences, I will try to outline the main characteristics of Lavin's short fiction in this chapter: the social and psychological realism of her stories and her thematic concern with relations, with the differences between people and with the social context that frames individual lives.

In a partial departure from the comparative set-up of the other chapters, this chapter will be devoted entirely to Lavin's work as she is in many ways an important and unique writer in the context of this study. First, she stands out because of the unrivalled quantity of her short fiction: she published more than a hundred short stories during her lifetime, both in magazines and in 11 short story collections. She is unique among Irish writers too in her dedication to the short form, in spite of the two novels she published in the 1950s, which she would later refer to as failures (Kennedy 1976). A mark of her standing as a short story writer, further, is that she secured a first-reading agreement with *The New Yorker*, an honour which she shared in Ireland only with Frank O'Connor (Hurley 2013). In Ireland too, she was celebrated as an important writer during her life and she received several honours and awards, including being elected as president of the Irish Academy of Letters and as Saoi of Aosdána. Yet, as in the case of many other writers discussed in this study, academic criticism has been slow in recognizing the importance of Lavin's work. For a long time, her name was but an uneasy or belated supplement to 'the three O's' which presided over the mid-twentieth-century heydays of the Irish short story. Indeed, Frank O'Connor himself expressed his uneasiness with her work in *The Lonely Voice*, noting the absence of typically Irish subject matter and the presence of a "certain difference in values which finally resolves itself into an almost Victorian attitude to love and marriage" (2004, 201). Whether or not her perspectives and values are un-Irish, old-fashioned, or "too exclusively feminine", as O'Connor also put it, Lavin's tireless exploration of the triumphs and failures of human relationships certainly belies O'Connor's celebration of the lonely hero and Romantic outsider as archetypes of any short story. This departure from the normative parameters of the Irish short story certainly contributed to Lavin's rather marginal position in late-twentieth-century critical accounts of the Irish short story (see D'hoker 2008a). The centenary celebrations of Mary Lavin in 2012, however, seem to have marked a turning-point in the critical reception of her work. Memorial events were staged in Meath, Dublin and New York, two of her collections were reissued (Lavin 2011, 2012), and Irish Academic Press published a collection of critical essays on her work (D'hoker 2013b). In spite of this renewed critical interest, however, many aspects of her short fiction remain to be explored, which is another reason to devote an entire chapter to her work. Still, that does not mean that the comparative perspective is entirely absent in what follows. Indeed, starting from a comparison between Bowen and Lavin, I will conclude with a reflection on the connections between Lavin's work and that of other Irish women writers she inspired or was influenced by.

THE STRAINS OF THE BOARDING HOUSE IN LAVIN AND BOWEN

In its combination of a modernist character sketch and a satirical story-with-a-twist, "Breakfast" can be considered a typical Bowen story. The twist in this story is not a turning-point for the protagonist, but a trick played on the reader. Throughout the story, the narrator cleverly wrong-foots the reader by describing the breakfast scene in a boarding house as though it were that of an extended family and friends in a large, upper-middle-class household. "The family" is mentioned twice in the first paragraph, there is an "Aunt Willoughby" who reminiscences about the past and the hostess exclaims proudly that "There's nothing so homely [...] as a comfortable sit-down family to breakfast" (Bowen 1981, 15, 19). The twist in the story then reveals satirically that this is "home comforts [...] for which Rossiter paid her twenty-four shillings a week. Being sat round and watched while you were eating. Not being *rushed*" (1981, 19). And the narrator concludes (with characteristic Bowenesque personifications): "The room broke up, the table grew smaller again as they all rose from their chairs [...] The coffee and bacon and the hostility and the Christian forbearance blew out before them into the chilly hall" (1981, 20). Like so many of Bowen's stories, "Breakfast" holds up to ridicule the ideal of the happy home that leads people to artificially recreate it in a boarding-house setting. The narrator's voice in these last lines vindicates Mr. Rossiter's abhorrence of this forced intimacy and supports his desire to escape from both their meddling and their all too close physical proximity.

While "Breakfast" displays the typical Bowen mixture of narratorial descriptions, quoted dialogue, and focalized perceptions of the main character, Mary Lavin shows herself a much more faithful student of the modernist short story by focusing consistently on the thoughts, memories and perceptions of Miss Holland. Except for a few scene-setting descriptions, the narrative is focalized entirely through the eyes of the protagonist. Hence, details about Miss Holland's past life and present situation are conveyed obliquely, through her meandering reflections about the room she is about to rent. We learn that she is a middle-aged single woman, whose rather genteel life with her father has come to an end following the latter's death. For the first time in her life she has to fend for herself and deal with the practical and material aspects of life. Yet, as the memorable first sentence of the story—"The cat decided Miss Holland"—suggests, she approaches these practical demands emotionally and evasively. Contrary to Mr. Rossiter, she ignores questions of money and mattresses, and is swayed by the homely air the neighbour's cat confers on the house. In her approach to the room too, she carefully avoids noticing its ugly features: "the mantelpiece was hideous [...] Oh, it is ugly! she cried, and then she looked away [...] I must not look at it. I must not admit that it is ugly. I must look at the lovely wide window [...] And she ran over to it" (Lavin 1945, 146). Even while remaining faithful to Miss Holland's perspective, the story also shows the highly subjective quality of her perceptions, infused as they are by her hopes, dreams and fears. Thus she idealizes her fellow boarders, who are marked by their "terrible difference" from her:

> They were invested with wonderful qualities in her mind. Primary colours, forceful and alarming but infinitely attractive, and beside these thoughts of them her memories of her old home and her old friends faded into pastel insignificance. She sat on her bed and looked around the room. They don't notice the ugliness of their rooms. They ignore small points of difference between tailor-made and ready-made clothes. They transcend these things. They speak of life with courage and vigour. She remembered fragments of the conversation. She was even more impressed by them in retrospect than she was at supper. (1945, 149)

To Miss Holland, they represent "real life" and she longs to be part of them, trying desperately to find a way into their conversation and into their life:

> She felt aggrieved that her education on the Continent and her travels with her father at home and abroad had left her no training or experience for discussion with real people. I can't talk to them [...] I am forty-four and I don't know the attitude of the Church on divorce. I don't know what constitutes a living wage. What is the right tip to give a porter. I don't know anything... (1945, 150)

Searching for an appropriate and striking topic to bring to the conversation, she prepares a description of the masterful behaviour of the cat, which she likes to watch from her bedroom window. Yet, at supper, her attempt to speak clashes with that of another boarder, who regales his audience with a story of how he took a shot at "that damn tomcat crying in the yard" (1945, 155). This time, the laughter of the boarders strikes Miss Holland not as lively and real, but as "red" and "ugly". Now that the difference between them has become too blatant to ignore, Miss Holland finally confronts and "define[s] their ugliness, their commonness, their bad taste", for "Only by recognising the things which I object to in these people, and giving them a name, can I ever protect myself from coming into contact with them again" (1945, 156).

Unlike in "Breakfast", where the narrator's concluding statements clearly underscore Mr. Rossiter's perspective, the sustained internal focalization of "Miss Holland" makes it far more difficult to decide where the story's sympathies lie. Some critics have read the story as celebrating Miss Holland's final, unflinching look at her fellow boarders and, hence, as privileging her sensitive, imaginative and cultured approach to life over their more materialistic and vulgar concerns (Peterson 1978; Tallone 2013). To me, however, the story remains more even-handed in its depiction of these two radically opposed perspectives and personalities. After all, the list of physical shortcomings which for Miss Holland define the boarders' ugliness seems rather snobbish and superficial. And even though there is a certain coarseness in Mr. Moriarty's account of how he aimed at the cat with a shot-gun, it is especially the contrast with Miss Holland's oft-rehearsed aestheticizing description of the cat—"like a Spanish dancer"—that is made to stand out. In fact, Miss Holland's quite deluded seizing upon the cat, a pathetic stand-in for the male authority she has lost, to help her enter their conversation shows up the absurdly shielded life she has led so far, in the shadow of her father. The end of the story sees Miss Holland flee from the dining room, without any one of the boarders noticing her. If the story condemns the boarders for their insensitivity and lack of care, it also censures Miss Holland for retreating from the more down-to-earth aspects of life and condemning herself to a sterile and lonely existence.

Even in this first story, several of Mary Lavin's central concerns already stand out. First, there is the clash between two opposed perspectives which marks so many of her stories. Here the opposition is between a sensitive, imaginative but escapist approach to life and a more materialistic and down-to-earth one, both of which fall short. Although the precise terms of the conflict as well as its evaluation vary from story to story, the tension created by such a binary opposition structurally underpins most of her work. In "Breakfast", by contrast, Mr. Rossiter does not feel different from the other boarders; he even wonders about the noises he himself makes when eating. All he wants to do is escape from the forced intimacy of the shared meal and be left in peace. If in Bowen, the desire for quietude and solitude is often staged as positive, as an escape from suffocating domesticity, it is rarely so in Lavin, where the desire to escape from human bonds is generally frowned upon. Indeed, Mary Lavin's stories obsessively scrutinize human relationships: between siblings, lovers, and friends; in a marriage, a family and a community. As I hope to show, Lavin's commitment to human relations ties in with her appreciation of the radical differences between personalities and perspectives: only the plurality of human bonds can make up for the inevitable shortcomings of the singular position. Yet, as her stories also show, the different, oppositional nature of personalities often makes relationships degenerative and destructive. A third concern introduced by "Miss Holland" involves the importance of the social context for these personal struggles. The differences in social class certainly add to the gap between Miss Holland and her fellow boarders: she belongs to the genteel, leisured class and has enjoyed the luxuries of art and travel, while labouring under a Victorian morality that shields women from all practical concerns; they belong to the working middle classes, are full of life and zest, opinionated and pragmatic, yet they lack an interest in art and beauty. A question that has preoccupied Lavin's critics, in this respect, is the extent to which Lavin blames the social context for the characters' disappointments. Or in the terms of the story: is Miss Holland staged as a "victim of a restrictive society based on materialism and class differences" (Tallone 2013, 65) or does Lavin allow for the shaping influence of individual agency and personal morality? This question will be explored more in detail in what follows. First, however, I'd like to use "Miss Holland" once more to briefly discuss Lavin's particular use of the short story form.

As the comparison with "Breakfast" has already revealed, Mary Lavin shows herself the better student of the modernist short story because of her greater commitment to the vagaries of the human mind. Like Woolf and Mansfield, whom she greatly admired (Peterson 1978, 151), Lavin narrates most of her stories from the subjective and inherently limited perspective of a single consciousness. Indirect and free indirect discourse are most typically used to convey the character's thoughts and feelings, but these sometimes give way to more experimental narrative techniques, such as the first-person passages of interior monologue in "Miss Holland" or the stream-of-consciousness technique in "Sunday Brings Sunday" and "The Lost Child", which evokes a character's descent in dreams and delusions. As in the modernist story, Lavin's consistent use of focalization goes hand in hand with the withdrawal of the omniscient narrator, who generally refrains from commenting on the action or judging the characters. The necessity of keeping the narrator impartial and at a distance is a central tenet in Lavin's view of the short story. In her American lectures on the genre, she criticized some writers for wanting to impose a moral or emotional truth (Peterson 1978, 85) and in her ceaseless editing of her stories, she often removed passages that appeared too intrusive or moralizing (Kelly 1980, 145–50). Exceptions to this dominant narrative mode immediately stand out. There are the parable-like stories, "A Fable", "A Likely Story", and "The Widow's Son", in which the narrator is a storyteller, self-consciously reflecting on the story and its moral. This emphasis on storytelling also pervades the stories told by a first-person character narrator, usually a witness to the events. "The Small Bequest", "My Molly", "Tom", "A Story with a Pattern", and "The Living and the Dead" are cases in point. A final group is made up of "The Black Grave and the Green Grave", "The Great Wave" and "Bridal Sheets": stories which rely heavily on dialect and dialogue to evoke the beliefs and customs of islanders in a manner reminiscent of Synge's poetic realism (Fogarty 2013, 57). In most stories, however, dialogue is relatively scarce and, juxtaposed with the long passages of inner consciousness, it often shows up the gap between what is thought and what is said in Lavin's fiction.

Lavin's privileging of psychology over plot and internal life over external events frequently lead to charges of plotlessness from readers and critics. In "A Story with a Pattern", a meta-fictional story written early in her career but only published in 1945 (Peterson 1978, 76), Lavin explicitly addresses this criticism. The woman writer in the story is challenged by one of her readers, an older man, for writing "thin" stories, with "hardly any plot at all" and with "very bad" endings: "They're not endings at all. Your stories just break off in the middle!" (Lavin 1999, 205). The writer defends herself with, "Life itself has very little plot [...] Life itself has a habit of breaking off in the middle", yet the reader counters this with a story that aims to prove that "there are thousands of times when incidents in life not only show a pattern, but a pattern as clear and well-marked as the pattern on this carpet" (1999, 205, 207). The echoes of Woolf and James in this story clearly show where Lavin's sympathies lie. While some of her stories do end on a final twist or a quite overt moral, these are typically the stories she either edited for her collected stories or refused to republish altogether. In an interview with Maurice Harmon, Lavin explained her preference for the plotless stories with,

> There are two kinds of stories. One is the plot story which does not really satisfy me, although I have written a number of them with pleasure, such as "The Small Bequest", "Posy", and even "The Great Wave". The other is one in which life itself is put on the page. It can almost stand up without plot and without a resolution, but life is absolutely caught. (Harmon 1997, 288)

Even when not depending on plot, Lavin's stories typically end on a moment of heightened awareness or, to use Joyce's term, epiphany. "For a moment it was not clear, then her ideas became clarified", notes the narrator, and Miss Holland proceeds to verbalize and confront the difference and vulgarity of the boarders which she has long tried to ignore. Still, her understanding is only partial as she fails to grasp the snobbish superficiality of her mental list of warts, stains and false teeth and does not realize the more fundamental self-centredness of the boarders which the narrator does spell out: "The doorknob clattered to the floor. No one noticed her going. No one picked up the knob" (Lavin 1945, 156). Such ironic epiphanies are a hallmark of Lavin's writing: her characters rarely experience a final all-encompassing insight. They are typically granted only a partial or misguided understanding, which does, however, encapsulate the character's personality and situation for the reader. James Heaney calls these moments "anti-epiphanies", as they involve a "sudden understanding of the inevitable failure of the understanding or imagination", but Anne Fogarty rightly points out that for Joyce too the epiphany was "a means of signposting but not fully articulating masked psychological realities" (Heaney 1998, 306; Fogarty 2013, 54). More rare in Lavin's fiction are what Woolf called "moments of being" in which a character briefly experiences a heightened sense of being, a momentary sense of peace with the world, other people and the self (Woolf 1976, 70). "In a Café" ends on such a positive moment as do "Posy" and "The Lost Child", but overall Lavin's moments more often suggest a Joycean experience of paralysis, with characters only partially comprehending how or why they have ended up in this state of disappointment, unhappiness or deadlock. The ending of "At Sallygap" is illustrative in this respect. While Manny Ryan comes to realize the intense hatred that binds his wife to him, he fails to understand the cause of their unhappiness. This lack of comprehension is underscored by his failure to remember what it was his wife had said "when she clattered down the wet cup on the saucer in front of him, a little while before [...] But he remembered, distinctly, thinking at the time that it was true, whatever it was" (Lavin 1945, 99).

Joycean, and modernist more generally, is also Lavin's use of symbols as a means to structure her story and to hint at its deeper meaning. In "Miss Holland", the cat and the doorknob symbolize, respectively, Miss Holland's pretensions and the boarders' lack of care. In "At Sallygap", Manny's smashed fiddle symbolizes his ruined dreams, and in "Lilacs", the repeated juxtaposition of the flowers and the dunghill spells out the central tension of the story. Yet, as Fogarty argues, by an unexpectedly poetic description of the dunghill, Lavin also cleverly complicates her metaphors, adding further layers to their meaning (2013, 56). Still, Lavin's metaphors do not run away with themselves to acquire a vampiric life of their own as we saw in Bowen's stories. Her stories remain bound by a realist impetus, which also keeps Lavin from following the modernists all too far on the path of narrative experiment. Lavin's attempt to truly capture the fluidity and complexity of thought processes is tempered by an adherence to a social realism, which grounds these processes in a material and social reality. Like Bowen, in other words, Lavin departs from the modernist example by foregrounding the social context that frames her characters' lives. Yet, the conservative, Catholic and parochial atmosphere of Lavin's small-town Ireland is mostly conveyed obliquely as it colours the characters' thoughts and influences their actions. The same holds true for the setting of her stories, whether a farm or a small town, Dublin or Italy. These places are seen through the eyes of the focalizing characters, which further underscores the psychological focus that directs all her work. As she stated in an interview, "Short-story writing—for me—is only looking closer than normal into the human heart. The vagaries and contrarieties there to be found have their own integral design" (Lavin 1959, vii). Let us now turn to explore these mental and emotional "vagaries" in the character doubles which are so often encountered in Lavin's short stories.

Lavin's Character Pairs

Lavin's earliest critics already commented on her obsessive staging of character pairs with opposite perspectives, values and feelings. Augustine Martin identifies a recurring opposition between "characters who recoil from the more full-blooded implications of life and settle for a cool, cloistered compromise" and "an equal rank of figures who are characterised by their energetic commitment to the hot realities of living" (1963, 403). Peterson finds this "drama of opposed sensibilities" mainly in Lavin's early stories and sees it in terms of a contrast between "sensitive characters hoping for love and beauty in their lives and insensitive characters seeking their fulfilment within the social and economic conventions of the Irish middle class" (1978, 25, 27), while for Kelly, "the Mary/Martha female types" symbolize "preponderant leanings towards the external or internal worlds" (1980, 30). I would like to revisit this binary structure underpinning Lavin's short fiction, as it forms one of the most remarkable features of her work. Far from being limited only to her female characters or to her early work, it pervades Lavin's fiction from "Miss Holland" to "Eterna". Moreover, as the slightly differing critical readings of this conflict suggest, the dichotomies are not always the same.

Let me first give some examples. Besides the oppositions already traced in "Miss Holland", *Tales from Bective Bridge* contains several other opposed characters. There is gentle, sensitive Manny and passionate, aggressive Annie in "At Sallygap" as well as dry and dutiful Matthew and sensuous and sociable Rita in "Love Is for Lovers". Other famous pairs are "anemic and thin-boned" Kathleen vs. passionate and energetic Sarah in "Sarah" (Lavin 1945, 50), and pragmatic, materialistic Kate vs. sensitive, artistic Stacy in "Lilacs". Versions of the latter pair can be found in Agatha and Rose in "A Gentle Soul", Bedelia and Liddy in "A Frail Vessel", Alice and Liddy in "A Visit to the Cemetery", Flora and Honoria in "The Becker Wives", and Eterna and Annie in "Eterna". The body-mind tension of "Sarah", on the other hand, is revisited in Isabel and Annie Bowles in "A Single Lady" or Maimie and Naida in "The Convert" and "Limbo", who recur as Mina and Leila in "The Mouse". As these final three stories stage triangular relations, they can also be read in terms of an opposition between Maimie and Edgar, or Mina and Arthur. Other conflicting male-female pairs are Robert and Ella in "A Happy Death", Sophie's parents in "A Cup of Tea" and Lew and Bina in "A Woman Friend". Twinned male characters are rarer in Lavin's fiction, but can be found, for instance, in "The Convert", where the gregarious Owen Hickey is the exact opposite of the Protestant, book-loving Edgar; or in the similar contrast between the romantic and sensitive Robert and the "strong" and "coarse" Mat in "A Happy Death" (Lavin 1964, 193). Although the conflict of sensibilities seems to become less important in Lavin's final collections, character doubles continue to appear, even in the semi-autobiographical widow stories where Vera is twinned with career women like the Italian Carlotta in "Villa Violetta" and Della in "Trastevere", or with the younger widow Maudie in "In a Café". A more parable-like treatment of this perennial opposition can be found in "The Bunch of Grape" where two girls, tellingly called "Blue Dress" and "Red Dress", decide to eat the grapes they were supposed to bring home for entirely different reasons: Red Dress simply longs to eat the delicious, juicy grapes, while Blue Dress quietly decides to eat them out of abhorrence for the way their perfect beauty would be defiled by the disgusting elderly ladies of her mother's tea party.

If this survey—though far from complete—does express the pervasiveness of character doubles in Lavin's fiction, it probably fails to show the variety of oppositions that are staged. Indeed, contrary to what some critics have suggested, these pairs cannot be reduced to one single opposition—whether external-internal, sensible-sensitive, or rational-passionate. Although some pairs may recall others, they come in many different guises and share only the fact of their opposition, by which they are defined and in turn define themselves. Thus, Mathew's disgusted recoiling from Rita's feisty and imposing personality is different from Manny's impotent gentleness which makes him an easy target for Annie's frustrations and anger. His sensitivity is different again from Robert's romantic dreams of an all-consuming union with Ella, and even though her nagging may remind us of Annie's, it originates in frustrated dreams of genteel respectability, which are totally alien to Annie. To give another example, if Bedelia from the Grimes stories and Kate from "Lilacs" seem similar in their pragmatism, materialism and social concern, Liddy, who experiences both physical passion and true love, is very different from Stacy, who is kind and caring but whiles away her life in ephemeral dreams of solitude and beauty. In short, the binaries informing Lavin's stories are many—emotions vs. reason, body vs. mind, pragmatism vs. idealism, care vs. calculation, vitality vs. quietude, selfishness vs. selflessness, materialism vs. artistic sensibility, social concern vs. primal desire, refinement vs. strength, dreams vs. action—and they come in many different inflections and combinations. If this variety precludes an easy reduction to a single opposition, it also makes it difficult to singularly fix these binaries into a hierarchical position.

Although some stories may privilege one perspective over another, such a hierarchy cannot be established with regard to Lavin's œuvre as a whole. If in "Sarah", Sarah's physical love and strength carry more sympathy than Kathleen's rationalism and refinement, in "The Convert", Naida's quiet bookishness seems preferable over Maimie's sensuality and physical charm. And if Liddy's romantic sensitivity is vindicated over Bedelia's pragmatism in "A Frail Vessel", in "Lilacs", Kate and Stacy receive a more even-handed treatment. In most stories, in fact, Lavin refrains from attributing blame. She is far more interested in observing these conflicts of personalities than in judging them. Her narrative technique of limited omniscience and focalization underwrites this impartial perspective as the perspective shifts from story to story, or sometimes within one story. I would disagree, therefore, with Peterson who argues that Lavin privileges "her more sensitive and introverted characters", by narrating her stories from their point of view (1978, 25). Lavin rather shows herself admirably impartial, even in the face of such established religious hierarchies as mind over body, spirit over matter, or reason over emotion.

Yet if promoting one worldview or sensibility over another is not what motivates the binary pairs in Lavin's fiction, we may well wonder what other source they have or what other purpose they serve. As Todorov reminds us in his discussion of literary doubles, the double is a highly "polysemic" theme which can variously signify "the victory of mind over matter", "threat and terror", "a dawning isolation, a break with the world", or conversely "the means of a closer contact with others, of a more complete integration" (Todorov 1975, 144). Traditionally, doubles in literature have been interpreted as externalizations of an internal conflict, whether that of a character or, in classic Freudian fashion, of the author. Peterson suggests such an autobiographical interpretation when he links the "drama of opposed sensibilities" in Lavin's work to her childhood experience of the "clash of opposed natures and interests" in her parents' marriage (1978, 17). In an earlier reading of Lavin's author figures, I also suggested that the opposition between mind and body or imagination and materialism in stories like "Eterna" and "The Becker Wives" may reveal an anxiety on Lavin's part about the difficulty of combining writing and motherhood, art and life (D'hoker 2012). However, these autobiographical readings only offer a partial explanation of Lavin's obsessive staging of twinned characters in her fiction. More generally, these doubles seem to denote Lavin's fascination with the differences between people, her awareness of the multiplicity of perspectives and personalities that make up society. Occasionally, these differences are shown to originate in the social context, as in "Miss Holland", or in a religious doctrine, as in "The Convert" and "Limbo". More often, the difference seems inborn, a matter of character rather than context, as the many sibling pairs in the stories suggest. In "A Happy Death", the two daughters are shown to inherit their parents' opposed sensibilities: "Dolly was aware again, as she had been a few days earlier, of a great difference between herself and her sister. Mary was like the dying man. She herself was more like her mother" (Lavin 1964, 239). This seems to echo a passage in "Lilacs" where Stacy wonders about this difference between her and Kate:

> All she wanted was to get the dunghill taken away out of the yard and a few lilacs put there instead. But it seemed as if there were more than that bothering Kate. She wondered what it could be? She had always thought herself and Kate were the same, that they had the same way of looking at things, but lately Kate seemed to be changed. Kate was getting old. Stacy took no account of age, but Kate was getting old. And Kate took account of everything. Stacy might have been getting old too, if she was taking account of things, but she wasn't. (Lavin 1945, 26)

In the edited version of the story published in *The Stories of Mary Lavin, Vol. III*, this has become: "She had always thought Kate and herself were alike, that they had the same way of looking at things, but lately she was not so sure of this" (Lavin 1985, 14). That differences between people are there from the start, but may grow more pronounced and inflexible by age is also shown in other childhood stories, such as "The Sandcastle" and "A Visit to the Cemetery". In the latter story, the contrast between the sensitive Liddy, who worries about her mother's soul, and the more pragmatic Alice, who is concerned about social censure, already suggests opposed personalities, but the differences are easily resolved in "a great feeling of sisterly affection", when both girls share dreams of a happy future as married wives and mothers and impulsively decide to go for a walk together (Lavin 1964, 119). A few years later, these different perspectives have hardened into a conflict between Liddy and her pragmatic and materialistic sister in "A Frail Vessel". In "A Cup of Tea", Sophy feels torn between the opposed sensibilities of her mother and father and although she feels more affinity with her father's intellectual concerns, she still tries to see things from her mother's perspective as well. The story concludes with Sophy's dreamed-up solution to the conflict:

> And then it suddenly seemed to Sophy that she had discovered a secret, a wonderful secret, that wise men had been unable to discover, and yet it was so simple and so clear that anyone could understand it. She would go through the world teaching her message. And when it was understood there would be an end to all the misery and unhappiness, all the misunderstanding and argument with which she had been familiar all her life. Everything would be changed [...] People would all have to become alike. They would have to look alike and speak alike and feel and talk and think alike. What a wonderful place the world would become [...] They would all think like herself and her father. It was so simple. It was so clear! She was surprised that no one had thought of it before. She saw the girls untwine their arms, and lift up the hems of their long dresses and step aside to admit her as she passed into their company. (1964, 155–6)

That this is an ironic epiphany, evoking only Sophy's limited understanding and misguided discovery, is evident by the tone of the passage as well by the final reference to the group of girls she dreams of belonging to. This refers to a photograph of her mother and aunts as young girls, laughing and beautiful in their long dresses. Earlier in the story, Sophy had reflected how the differences between their parents were reflected in their different demeanours in these old photos: her mother's happy face in contrast to her father's "stiff and straight" demeanour (1964, 155). Clearly, if all people became "like herself and her father", inclusion in the frivolous, laughing group of her mother's friends would forever be out of reach.

That Lavin disagrees with Sophy's dream of sameness is confirmed in other stories which celebrate the differences between people as part of the richness of life. Stories of childhood, such as "The Sand-Castle" or "The Bunch of Grape" as well as late stories like "Happiness" and "The Lost Child" bear witness to the rich harmony of voices and perspectives

that can result from the meeting of different perspectives and personalities. More frequent, of course, are stories that show up the tensions,
conflicts and destructive relations that also result from an encounter of
opposites and a progressive hardening of positions. In "A Frail Vessel", for
instance, Lavin admirably captures this solidifying of opposite personalities
as Bedelia's conflicted feelings about her younger sister's marriage hard-
ens into a cold practicality, partly in response to her sister's sentimentality
and lack of social or material concern. Nevertheless, I would argue that
precisely this difference between people makes human relations necessary
in Lavin's stories. Since they always represent only one side of a binary, her
characters are figured as half-men or half-women, who need—and often
desire—an opposite character both to define and to complement themselves. As "Miss Holland" and "A Frail Vessel" show, it is only in a conflict
with another personality that one's identity becomes clarified. Yet, that
sense of self continues to need its opposite to exist. In relations, too, as we
will see in the next part, Lavin's characters are very often attracted to their
opposites, in an attempt to achieve a completeness that usually proves
illusory. In a different way, Lavin's stories themselves also aim for wholeness: while her stories typically probe one particular perspective which is
revealed as necessarily subjective and partial by being opposed to its binary
other, her œuvre as a whole offers an incredible array of perspectives and
characters, who are alike only in that they need an other to exist. Indeed,
if the sets of opposed characters in Lavin's stories were merely an exterior-
ization of inner conflict, a harmonious synthesis of these conflicted traits
would be the ideal to be achieved. As it is, Lavin's most positive stories
do not stage a single, happy, fully balanced character, but rather a happy
meeting of personalities, who complement and enrich rather than destroy
one another. We find this, for instance, in "My Molly" where the narrator's sober and self-effacing perspective matches his wife's impetuous exu-
berance, or in "The Lost Child" where Iris's rational scepticism matches
Renée's instinctive faith. In the widow stories such as "Villa Violetta" and
"Happiness" too, Vera's nervous and scatter-brained energy is stabilized
by the priest's gentle and pragmatic presence. In short, the worldview of
Lavin's stories is one that recognizes the fundamental differences between
human beings, their being only half-creatures with a limited, subjective
perspective that both demands and obstructs engagement with another
perspective. It is therefore time to take a closer look at the relationships
Lavin stages and the costs of trying to evade them.

THE NECESSITY OF RELATIONS

In an early discussion of Lavin's stories, Seamus Deane identified her as a social writer who focuses not on "singular individual relationships with the mediocre world", but on "the closely meshed nexus of feelings in which the protagonists are bound". Love is her subject, Deane argued, and "love demands relation" (1979, 245–6). Indeed, all of Lavin's stories depict characters in relation—whether as husbands or wives, brothers or sisters, fathers or mothers, sons or daughters, actual or would-be lovers. As I have elsewhere already discussed the family relations depicted in the Grimes family saga (D'hoker 2013a), I will here focus on the heterosexual relationships which Lavin probes in several of her stories. Once again, *Tales from Bective Bridge* initiates a recurrent preoccupation in this respect as it chronicles the unhappy marriage of two opposed sensibilities in "At Sallygap", a story which would reappear as the title story of Lavin's 1947 collection. Although the story at first reads like an exploration of Joycean paralysis, as it chronicles Manny Ryan's failed escape from a corrupt and pokey Dublin, a radical shift in focalization to Annie, the girl Manny married instead, fastens the attention squarely on their destructive relationship. Through the thoughts and memories of both husband and wife, Lavin clearly shows how their different sensibilities have deepened in a downward spiral of action and reaction, thesis and antithesis:

> [Annie] had not thought of marriage as anything but a means of breaking the monotony. But she had found it a greater monotony than the one she had fled from, and, unlike the other, it had no anteroom of hope leading to something better. Manny accepted her so complacently from the first day that he bored her in a week with his monotonously kind manner. Soon she began to show an artificial irritation at trifles in the hope of stirring up a little excitement, but Manny was kinder and more gentle on those occasions than he was before. Gradually her irritability and petulance became more daring until they could scarcely be classed as such venial sins. And soon, too, what had been slyly deliberate became involuntary, and the sour expression of her face hardened into the mask of middle age. (Lavin 1945, 92)

Similarly ill-matched pairs are depicted in "A Cup of Tea", where the daughter wonders about her mother's choice, "why did she marry the wrong man?" (Lavin 1964, 152), and "A Happy Death", where Ella's cruelty increases in tandem with her husband's meek suffering. Still, as Robert's final semi-delirious epiphany reveals, a deep and genuine love for

Ella has sustained him throughout their unhappy marriage, while her love for him was too much a love for outward appearances to survive adversarial circumstances.

If these stories chronicle the disintegration of a marriage of opposites, "The Convert" and "The Mouse" reveal how such marriages came about in the first place. Both stories tell of a love triangle, whereby a courtship based on similarity is suddenly overthrown by the man's sudden attraction to a woman who is in every way his opposite. In "The Convert", Elgar falls for Maimie precisely because she is so different from the gentle and serious Naida, and from himself. If they are "two creatures exactly alike", Maimie is "all body" and seduces him with her "boldness", "vulgarity", "vanity" and "all her provocative charm" (Lavin 1964, 97–8). The story is set a few years after their elopement, on the occasion of Naida's death, and Elgar despondently realizes the mistake he has made. "The Mouse" tells the same story from the perspective of the spurned girl and her friend. To the latter, Leila and Arthur seemed made for each other: "they were both Protestants" (like Naida and Elgar), "they were both the moody type—quiet, and happy to say nothing if they weren't pressed. They were great readers too—both of them" (Lavin 1974, 256–7). Yet, to the friend's bewilderment, Arthur suddenly breaks off their relationship and elopes with Mina in spite of their radical differences—"You couldn't imagine two people more unlike than Mina and Arthur"—and the marriage proves "an awful failure" (1974, 257). Again, radical difference and physical attraction motivated the elopement but laid no foundation for a happy marriage. Still, if several of these stories seem cautionary tales against a marriage of opposites, in "The Lucky Pair", a companionable relation based on similarities and shared affinities seems boring compared to stormy love-hate relationship, where the lovers "have some awful effect on each other [...] the minute they're together, they quarrel [...] and yet when they're apart they're miserable too" (Lavin 1985, 82). And although the protagonist agrees with her boyfriend that "it must be anguish for them", "as she said the word, its meaning, which she would have thought immutable, began to change and take on strange inflections that were not all of pain. There seemed even to be implications in it of something like exultation" (1985, 83). Juxtaposed with this impetuous passion, their own relation based on similarity comes to seem rather bland. As in "A Cup of Tea", authorial irony undermines the conclusion that they are "the lucky pair" and a relationship—or world—based on similarity appears not so ideal either.

What is certain, however, is that in Lavin's short fiction relationships, whether bland or stormy, sustaining or debilitating, are preferable to giving up on relationships altogether. As several stories suggest, giving up on love and relationships equals giving up on life and that is a great sin in Lavin's fictional world. Again, *Tales from Bective Bridge* contains the archetype of this story in "Love Is for Lovers". The story's great first line—"At the non-committal age of forty-four, Mathew Simmins began to think about marriage" (Lavin 1945, 100)—already characterizes Mathew as a careful, calculating and earnest man who approaches life through reason rather than emotion. He meets his exact opposite in Rita Cooligan, an energetic young widow who is determined to marry him. Mathew is initially attracted to her effusive nature, her passionate feelings and domestic cosiness. Yet, on a hot Saturday afternoon he feels suffocated by her domesticity and nauseated by her body. Abruptly, he flees and seeks refuge in the coolness of the street:

> The houses were cold and grey. The railings were cold and black. And when he stared at it for a moment, after passing his handkerchief over his eyes, the sky was brilliantly blue again, and clear and calm and cooling. But this time he noticed that his handkerchief was an ugly dirty colour, and he stopped at a draper's, there and then, to buy a new one, a new white one, because he wanted to feel the cold white glaze that was always on new white linen. (1945, 120–1)

As Lavin's imagery makes clear, in fleeing from love and relationships, Mathew also flees from life and the—ironic—epiphany that closes the story is very fittingly one of death:

> And just as he hadn't thought about marriage until very recently, he hadn't thought about death either. But he thought of it then, in his cold, damp room, and the coldness and darkness of death appealed to him [...] Death was the next important step and it was through sweet cemetery grasses, over cold grave-stones. He lay in his chill, white bed, and he watched the moon; young, slender; a beautiful cool green moon. (1945, 121)

Thirty years later, Lavin would revisit Mathew's deliberate retreat from love and life in the story "A Memory". Like Mathew, James fully devotes himself to his work and quite literally escapes from Dublin life to write his books in an isolated cottage in the country. Even though this makes him a

Meath writer like Lavin, he is characterized as a supremely selfish and negative figure because of his callous treatment of Myra, his one remaining friend whom he deigns to visit only when his work doesn't go well. After a sudden emotional outburst from Myra, who has studiously avoided showing her love for years, he also flees from this relationship. Like Mathew, he can only read her emotions and offer of love as "ugly", "distasteful" and "nauseating" (Lavin 1972, 209). His alienation from real life is metaphorically highlighted by his bewilderment in Dublin and, subsequently, by his getting lost in the woods around his house, which will finally lead to his death. His is not the clean and cold death Mathew dreams of, but an almost vengeful confrontation with the materiality he has all his life tried to avoid: "he was almost overpowered by the smell of rank earth and rotting leaves [...] and when he gulped for breath, the rotted leaves were sucked into his mouth" (1972, 222–3). Rejecting love and relationships is clearly not desirable in Lavin's fictional world, not even in the interests of intellectual creativity.

If Mathew and James turn their backs on other human beings out of a fear of physical and emotional intimacy, gentler and more sympathetic characters like Rose in "A Gentle Soul" and Daniel in "Posy" fail love because of a concern with social proprieties, dramatized as a fearful inability to stand up to a stronger sibling. In "A Gentle Soul", Rose Darker looks back bitterly on her wasted life and especially on her betrayal of the man she loved. This man was a labourer on their farm and out of fear for her dominant sister Agatha, their father and social decorum in general, she did not follow her heart and refused him. Worse, when he died after an accident with one of their horses, she gave in to her cleverly scheming sister and betrayed him at the inquest that followed. In "Posy", similarly, Daniel is tricked by his conniving sister Kate into giving up the lower-class servant girl he loved. And although Daniel has been deluding himself for years it was "all for the best", the visit of a stranger, supposedly Posy's son, makes him realize his "cowardice and caution" (Lavin 1964, 93). Yet, in a final epiphany, the knowledge of Posy's success does sustain him:

> He felt curiously elated. He, like Hannah and Kate, had to live out the rest of his life in the dungeon of obscurity and petty provincial existence, but he had not held Posy down, he had let her fly away. And if he never saw the upper sunlit air, nor ever now would see it, by the thrust of her flight he knew that somewhere the sun shone. (1964, 93)

INDIVIDUALS VS. SOCIETY IN LAVIN'S STORIES

In both of these stories, class differences and social concern are seen as obstacles to the love match. As Daniel puts it, "If things had been otherwise I don't suppose I would ever have done better, but considering our position in the town, of course it was out of the question from the start. Even Posy could see that" (Lavin 1964, 89). And Rose Darker notes "Agatha and father would never be able to hold up their heads again if I ran away with Jamey Morrow" (Lavin 1964, 48). This strict and hierarchic social framework, which informs many of Lavin's stories, has led critics to read her work as an indictment of the restrictive social context of post-independence Ireland. For Zack Bowen, for instance:

> Lavin's vision of reality is harsh and closely circumscribed by an acute awareness of social class and society's sanctions and rules [...] In the tightly controlled, sometimes fatalistic sphere in which her characters live, many of them succumb to a life of quiet frustration or desperation, while others try to escape, to rationalize, to hide, or to seek freedom through love, nature, insanity or death. (1975, 23)

David Norris concurs and sees Lavin privilege those characters who, through imagination and love, manage to escape from restrictive "authority structures" (1979, 40), while for James Heaney, Lavin criticizes "the introverted and intolerant culture of post-independence Ireland", precisely by denying her characters the possibility of escape (1998, 304). In an article on Lavin's exiles, finally, Marie Arndt similarly argues that "the constrictive religious and social morality of Ireland in the stories causes suffering and turns those forced to live by these conventions into internal exiles" (2002, 110).

Although there is no denying the pervasiveness of the social context in Lavin's short fiction, I would argue that it functions less as a deterministic force than as a backdrop against which ordinary lives are played out and within which characters can—and have to—take responsibility for their own lives. Far from sympathizing with outsiders, as Heaney, Norris and Arndt suggest, Lavin condemns characters who selfishly and cowardly seek to escape from social ties and responsibilities as stories such as "Love Is for Lovers" and "A Memory" clearly suggest. Or as Weekes has argued about a married couple's escape from family and community in "Loving Memory", Lavin considers it "a mistake to think that one can isolate and separate oneself and a chosen one from the web of life" (1990, 142).

In "Posy" and A Gentle Soul", moreover, Lavin seems to deliberately refrain from staging Rose Darker or Daniel as simply victims of a restrictive, class-obsessed society. Rose's failure to act on her love is shown to be the result of her being "a cowardly creature", no match for her domineering sister and father (Lavin 1964, 46). And her fate is juxtaposed to that of her alter ego, Molly Lanigan—"People often said we were alike, Molly and I" (1964, 49)—who does elope with a labourer. In a similar way, Daniel only has his own cowardice to blame for his failure to marry Posy: he lives in "mortal dread" of his sisters far more than of social censure (1964, 89). Other stories also foreground characters who defy social norms. Think of Molly's unconventional behaviour in "My Molly", or of Isabel's father in "A Single Lady", who proposes to marry his slovenly servant, in spite of the warning tale of social ostracism told by his genteel daughter. Robert and Ella in "A Happy Death" too "had eloped in spite of their parents" (1964, 192) and so has Lally in "The Will". Although Lally's life has not been easy, she remains committed to her choices. In a closing epiphany, Lally ponders:

> As a child [...] it had seemed that the bright world ringed the town around, and that somewhere outside the darkness lay the mystery of life [...] Some day she would go. And one day she went. But there was no mystery now; anywhere. Life was just the same in the town, in the city, and in the twisty countryside. Life was the same in the darkness and the light. You were yourself always, no matter where you went or what you did. You didn't change. (Lavin 1964, 140)

This insight has led to diverging interpretations of "The Will". For Norris, Lally is one of a handful of Lavin's characters who manages to escape from the limits of middle-class Ireland, while for Heaney, Lally is unable to escape, thus demonstrating Lavin's pessimistic vision about the "inability to live positively and imaginatively in post-independence Ireland" (Norris 1979, 40; Heaney 1998, 307). I would rather read Lally's reflections as downplaying the importance of a specific social milieu. Lally realizes that her so-called escape did not matter all that much, because human life, human relationships are essentially the same, whether in a narrow-minded provincial town or in a city. What is important, rather, is the way you live your life and stay true to yourself.

This is also the morale of "The Widow's Son", a story that stands out in Lavin's œuvre because of its metafictional, plot-bound and didactic nature.

It tells the story of a widow with a much beloved son who has won a scholarship at school and cycles home in great haste only to be confronted with a hen upon entering the farmyard. The narrator then provides two endings: one in which the son brakes so hard that he is thrown off the bike and dies; a second in which he kills the hen but is severely scolded by his mother—mainly because the neighbours are watching—so that he leaves the house in the middle of the night, runs off to America and never sees his mother again. The narrator then concludes:

> Perhaps all our actions have this double quality about them; this possibility of alternative, and that it is only by careful watching and absolute sincerity, that we may follow the path that is destined for us, and, no matter how tragic that may be, it is better than the tragedy we bring upon ourselves. (Lavin 1964, 113)

Like Daniel, Rose, and many other Lavin characters, the widow in the second version brings tragedy upon herself through false pride, cowardice, and excessive social concern. Yet they are countered by a host of more positive characters like Posy, Molly, Lally and Vera, who remain committed to their love, values, and convictions, whatever the circumstances they find themselves in. With the exception of young girls who fall prey to the prudish and hypocritical sexual mores of Irish Catholicism, none of Lavin's characters is presented as simply a victim of a restrictive social milieu (Shumaker 1995). Instead her characters' lives are shown to be shaped as much by their own choices and personalities as by their circumstances.

In "Happiness", the moral message formulated at the end of "The Widow's Son" is developed into a full-fledged philosophy that further illuminates the social vision of Lavin's fiction. Part of the so-called widow stories, this story figures Vera Traske's three daughters trying to make out their mother's idea of happiness, which was something she considered crucial and often talked about. Although the story looks back on a number of scenes from Vera's life and ends with a description of her death, the reader gets the impression that the scenes and anecdotes have an explicatory or argumentative role in a philosophical treatise: their primary purpose is to illustrate and prove certain elements of Vera's—and Lavin's—philosophy. The first stage in the treatise demonstrates Vera's indifference to social decorum, for instance in her inability to understand the gossip that surrounds her intimate friendship with Father Hugh. The suggestion is that a certain disregard of what the neighbours think or, conversely, a healthy degree of self-certainty and personal responsibility is a prerequisite for happiness. As we have seen, this is demonstrated by default in several of Lavin's stories where a protagonist throws away personal happiness out of a false pride or misguided concern for social censure and decorum.

A second tenet of Vera/Lavin's philosophy of happiness is that although sorrow is not "a necessary ingredient" of happiness, sorrow and pain can coexist with happiness. Thus the narrator recalls how her mother had the disconcerting habit of asking people who were ill or dying: "But are you happy?" (Lavin 1985, 22). A third problem to be tackled is whether happiness is somehow innate or rather the result of the actions of others or of the vicissitudes of life. Vera clearly believed in some innate quality, and by way of illustration she used to pit her father's fundamental happiness, even in the hour of his death, against her mother's perpetual dissatisfaction. Subsequently, Vera's daughters wonder about the nature of this innate quality as they consider happiness a misnomer: "What was it, we used to ask ourselves, that quality that she, we felt sure, misnamed? Was it courage? Was it strength, health or high spirits? Something you could not give or take? A conundrum, or a game of catch-as-catch-can?" (1985, 24). Is this happiness something hereditary or a freak of fate, the daughters wonder, or something you have to achieve or strive for? From her mother's tales of how she had to struggle after the death of her husband, how she had to make an effort to regain happiness, it can again be derived that happiness requires "an effort", an act of defiance, an act of will and even, it turns out, of control. This becomes evident when Vera's dying moments are described. She is frightened and whispers "I cannot face it", whereupon her daughter Bea tells her "It's alright, Mother, you don't have to face it. It's over" (1985, 32). Happiness, in other words, is the struggle to live your own life and not let it be lived by others. It is a Nietzschean embracing of life, a willing of your own fate, an *Amor Fati* which requires will-power and strength but which makes it possible to be happy in the face of sorrow and pain. How much Lavin's philosophy of life involves courage and control is also evident in the narrative set-up of this story: the author Mary Lavin writes about her own beliefs, life and death—only thinly disguised through the alter ego Vera Traske—but she does so from the perspective of her daughters. In this way, the story becomes an attempt on the part of Lavin to take control over the image of her life and beliefs that will live on with her daughters and with her readers after her death.

To some extent, Lavin's philosophy of happiness recalls Egerton's Nietzschean credo, as voiced by the autobiographical protagonist of "A Psychological Moment":

> You must find yourself. All the systems of philosophy or treatises of moral science, all the religious codes devised by the imagination of men will not save you—*always you must come back to yourself* [...] You've got to get a purchase on your own soul. Stand on your own feet, heed no man's opinion, no woman's scorn, if you believe you are in the right [...] Work out your own fate. (Egerton 2006, 93)

If in Egerton's case, this individualism is tempered by the parallel exhortation to "Forget yourself, live as much as you can for others" (2006, 92), in Lavin's story too, the focus on personal happiness is balanced by the awareness that a whole-hearted embracing of life necessary for happiness inevitably includes an embracing of other people. As the mother in "Happiness" reminds her daughters: "Just remember that I had a happy life and if I had to choose my kind of heaven I'd take it on this earth with you again, no matter how much you might at times annoy me" (Lavin 1985, 22).

As the preceding readings have shown, Lavin's worldview is a fundamentally social one, in which human life is played out within a network of relations—of love, family and the larger community. Moreover, her twinned and doubled characters are by default only half-people, each with his or her own personality, subjective perspective and limited vision and Lavin amply shows how this necessitates as well as complicates relationships. As an author, Lavin herself can and does paint the whole picture, offering us a view of the world as rich, diverse, and complex, while urging us to embrace life and to stay true to ourselves. Lavin's worldview thus seems to anticipate late twentieth-century discussions of "relational being" as the cornerstone of our existence (Gilligan 1982; Nancy 2000; Gergen 2009). Her stories in fact demonstrate what Gergen argues for, namely, "that virtually all intelligible action is born, sustained, and/or extinguished within the ongoing process of relationship" (2009, xv). Moreover, unlike Gilligan, who privileges the relational being of women, Lavin also depicts many men as relational selves in her stories. As Ingman has noted, "She describes men like Robert, Father Hugh, and Clem, comfortable with expressions of intimacy, in ways generally excluded by traditional masculinities" (2013, 44). Hence, her stories also counter Frank O'Connor when, in an his attempt to pin down Lavin's different, feminine values, he wrote: "No man need regard himself as a failure if he has failed with women, but a woman does so almost invariably if she has failed with men" (2004, 201). In fact, stories like "A Memory", "Posy", and "Love Is for Lovers" clearly suggest that men (and women) who fail at relationships, fail at life itself.

These social and relational values are evidently very different from the values O'Connor recognized and promoted in the short stories of his contemporaries. Lavin is far less interested in political, social or religious critique, not does she set the same store by the quest for identity, whether individual or national, as O'Connor and O'Faoláin. Moreover, as we have seen, the rebellious and Romantic outsider who removes himself from society does not figure in her work. For Lavin, loneliness is neither an existential condition nor a proud assertion of independence. It is, rather, the sad outcome of a loss or failure of relationship. This failure can either be the result of an individual lack of courage or effort, or the consequence of a mutually destructive hardening of oppositions. It is no doubt this lack of correspondence with the dominant norms of the short story at the time that made Peterson decide that "Mary Lavin's stories have had little influence on contemporary Irish fiction" (1978, 159). Yet, one need only take a superficial glance at the way the vicissitudes of human relationships are a constant preoccupation in the short fiction of contemporary women writers to disprove this point. Indeed, in exploring relations between lovers, married couples, mothers and young children, daughters and elderly mothers, bickering sisters or best friends, writers like Anne Enright, Claire Keegan, Éilís Ní Dhuibhne, Emma Donoghue, and Evelyn Conlon continue on the paths that Mary Lavin first showed them was possible within the confines of the short story. In her collection *The Pale Gold of Alaska*, Éilís Ní Dhuibhne explicitly acknowledged Lavin's influence, by rewriting Lavin's "At Sallygap" and "The Widow's Son" as "At Sally Gap" and "The Banana Boat", respectively (Ní Dhuibhne 2000; Tallone 2004), and in her Preface to the 2012 edition of *Tales from Bective Bridge*, Evelyn Conlon praised the "broad map of human relationships", given in this collection (Lavin 2012, vi). As we will see in the remaining chapters, many other writers show themselves to be influenced by Lavin's social and psychological realism as well as by her compelling moral vision.

BIBLIOGRAPHY

Arndt, Marie. 2002. Narratives of Internal Exile in Mary Lavin's Short Stories. *International Journal of English Studies* 2 (2):109–122.

Bowen, Elizabeth. 1962. *Afterthought: Pieces About Writing*. London: Longmans.

Bowen, Elizabeth. 1981. *The Collected Stories of Elizabeth Bowen*. Hopewell, NJ: Ecco Press.

Bowen, Zack. 1975. *Mary Lavin*. Lewisburg: Bucknell University Press.

D'hoker, Elke. 2008a. Beyond the Stereotypes. Mary Lavin's Irish Women. *Irish Studies Review* 16(4): 415–430.

D'hoker, Elke. 2012. Writers, Artists, Mothers: Author Figures in the Short Fiction of Mary Lavin. *Short Fiction in Theory & Practice* 2 (1–2):129–140.

D'hoker, Elke. 2013a. Family and Community in Mary Lavin's Grimes Stories. In *Mary Lavin*, edited by Elke D'hoker, 152–168. Dublin: Irish Academic Press.

D'hoker, Elke. 2013b. *Mary Lavin*. Dublin: Irish Academic Press.

Deane, Seamus. 1979. Mary Lavin. In *The Irish Short Story*, edited by Patrick Rafroidi and Terence Brown, 237–248. Dublin: Smythe.

Egerton, George. 2006. *Keynotes and Discords*. London: Continuum. Original edition, 1893, 1894.

Fogarty, Anne. 2013. Discontinuities: *Tales from Bective Bridge* and the Modernist Short Story. In *Mary Lavin*, edited by Elke D'hoker, 31–49. Dublin: Irish Academic Press.

Gergen, Kenneth J. 2009. *Relational Being: Beyond Self and Community*. Oxford: Oxford University Press.

Gilligan, Carol. 1982. *In a Different Voice. Psychological Theory and Women's Development*. Cambridge, MA: Harvard University Press.

Harmon, Maurice. 1997. From Conversations with Mary Lavin. *Irish University Review* 27 (2):287–292.

Heaney, James. 1998. 'No Sanctuary from Hatred': A Re-Appraisal of Mary Lavin's Outsiders. *Irish University Review* 28 (2):294–307.

Hurley, Gráinne. 2013. 'Trying to Get the Words Right': Mary Lavin and *The New Yorker*. In *Mary Lavin*, edited by Elke D'hoker, 81–99. Dublin: Irish Academic Press.

Ingman, Heather. 2013. Masculinities in Lavin's Short Stories. In *Mary Lavin*, edited by Elke D'hoker, 30–48. Dublin: Irish Academic Press.

Kelly, A.A. 1980. *Mary Lavin, Quiet Rebel: A Study of her Short Stories*. Dublin: Wolfhound.

Kennedy, Maev. 1976. The Saturday Interview: Maev Kennedy talked to Mary Lavin. *The Irish Times*, 13 March 1976.

Lavin, Mary. 1945. *Tales from Bective Bridge*. London: Michael Joseph. Original edition, 1942.

Lavin, Mary. 1959. Preface. In *Selected Stories*. New York: Macmillan

Lavin, Mary. 1964. *The Stories of Mary Lavin*, vol. I. London: Constable.

Lavin, Mary. 1972. *A Memory and Other Stories*. London: Constable.

Lavin, Mary. 1974. *The Stories of Mary Lavin*, vol. II. London: Constable.

Lavin, Mary. 1985. *The Stories of Mary Lavin*, vol. III. London: Constable.

Lavin, Mary. 1999. *In a Cafe: Selected Stories*. London: Penguin.

Lavin, Mary. 2011. *Happiness and Other Stories*. Dublin: New Island Books. Original edition, 1970.

Lavin, Mary. 2012. *Tales From Bective Bridge*. London: Faber. Original edition, 1943.

Levenson, Leah. 1998. *The Four Seasons of Mary Lavin*. Dublin: Marino Books.

Martin, Augustine. 1963. A Skeleton Key to the Stories of Mary Lavin. *Studies: An Irish Quarterly Review* 52 (208):393–406.

Nancy, Jean-Luc. 2000. *Being Singular Plural*. Stanford: Stanford University Press.

Ní Dhuibhne, Éilís. 2000. *The Pale Gold of Alaska and Other Stories*. Belfast: Blackstaff Press.

Norris, David. 1979. Imaginative Response vs. Authority Structures. A Theme of the Anglo-Irish Short Story. In *The Irish Short Story*, edited by Patrick Rafroidi and Terence Brown 39–62. Gerrards Cross: Smythe.

O'Connor, Frank. 2004. *The Lonely Voice: A Study of the Short Story*. Hoboken, NJ: Melville House Pub. Original edition, 1963.

Peterson, Richard F. 1978. *Mary Lavin*. Boston: Twayne Publishers.

Shumaker, Jeanette Roberts. 1995. Sacrificial Women in Short Stories by Mary Lavin and Edna O'Brien. *Studies in Short Fiction* 32 (2):185–197.

Tallone, Giovanna. 2004. Elsewhere Is a Negative Mirror: The 'Sally Gap' Stories of Éilís Ní Dhuibhne and Mary Lavin. *Hungarian Journal of English and American Studies* 10 (1–2):203–215.

Tallone, Giovanna. 2013. Theatrical Trends in Mary Lavin's Early Stories. In *Mary Lavin*, edited by Elke D'hoker, 65–80. Dublin: Irish Academic Press.

Todorov, Tzvetan. 1975. *The Fantastic: A Structural Approach to a Literary Genre*. Ithaca, NY: Cornell University Press.

Weekes, Ann Owens. 1990. *Irish Women Writers: An Uncharted Tradition*. Lexington: University Press of Kentucky.

Woolf, Virginia. 1976. A Sketch of the Past. In *Moments of Being. Unpublished Autobiographical Writings*, edited by Jeanne Schulkind, 61–159. London: Hogarth Press. Original edition, 1939.

CHAPTER 5

Staging the Community in Irish Short Fiction: Choruses, Cycles and Crimes

The foregoing chapters have revealed a central concern with relations in the short stories of Irish women writers. Lavin's relational selves were seen to be fundamentally tied to partners, children, parents and siblings, the stories of Brennan and Bowen staged the difficult balance between self and other in a marriage or family through the ambivalent imaginary of the home, and in the R.M. stories, Somerville and Ross were centrally concerned with depicting a rural community in the West of Ireland. This chapter proposes to pick up on the communal thread of Chapter 3, by investigating more in general how larger communal networks are staged in Irish women's short fiction. Given the limited scope of the short story and its attendant focus on few characters and a concise plot, the question is not at all a self-evident one. In fact, for many critics, community has no place in the short story at all. As O'Connor put it, only the novel is interested in "man as an animal who lives in a community [...] but the short story remains by its very nature remote from the community—romantic, individualistic, and intransigent" (2004, 20). Even if not all stories show this single-minded focus on the individual, it is of course not easy for the short story to accommodate a large group of characters. As we have seen, Somerville and Ross's solution to this problem took the form of a short story series. This form of serial publication, pioneered by Arthur Conan Doyle in *The Strand*, consists of free-standing, single-episode short stories that are nevertheless linked by means of a shared protagonist and/or narrator and a larger group of characters who recur in several, but not all stories of the series. Another way of staging community in short fiction

111
E. D'hoker, *Irish Women Writers and the Modern Short Story*,
DOI 10.1007/978-3-319-30288-1_5

is by means of the short story cycle or collection of interlinked stories. In the short story cycle, separate stories can be linked in a variety of ways within the confines of the collection. As we will see, short story cycles unified by place have often been used to dramatize and question community life, since separate stories and individual lives can be brought together within a larger communal network. Irish short story cycles which will be discussed in this light are Jane Barlow's *Irish Idylls* (1893) and *Strangers at Lisconell* (1895), Mary Beckett's *A Literary Woman* (1990), and Éilís Ní Dhuibhne's *The Shelter of Neighbours* (2012). In the first section, however, I will consider the way communities can also be staged in individual short stories. Representative examples will be taken from the stories of George Egerton and Mary Lavin, which also connects this chapter to the discussions in Chapters 2 and 4, respectively.

COMMUNAL CHORUS AND COMMUNAL NORMS

Given Egerton's focus on the inner lives of women and on male-female relationships, the vicissitudes of communal living do not as a rule loom large in her work. Still, some of the stories in *Keynotes* and *Discords* contain brief but interesting representations of communities. They fall into three types. First, there is the "colony of women" which the protagonist of "The Regeneration of Two" has set up and manages in her big house in Norway (Egerton 2006, 161). This "New Woman's community of women", as Ledger calls it, represents a utopian ideal where each finds happiness and self-fulfilment through work as care is taken "to find work fitted for each" (Ledger 2006, xxiv; Egerton 2006, 153). Yet, this community is evoked only briefly in terms of "the whirr of wheels and the laughter of children" or "the music of women's voices singing at their work" and remains very much an abstract idea (Egerton 2006, 152, 169). Moreover, the protagonist herself is not really part of this community: although she feels an affinity with the wayward women in her care, as the owner of the colony, she also stands apart from them. The same distance is implied with regard to the community of gypsies which is so wistfully evoked in Part II of "Under Northern Sky". Again, this community is represented by means of music, song and abstract voice: "the whole tribe are gathered round him, begging and screaming with one voice" (2006, 52). And although the protagonist feels a strong affinity with this Romany community, she remains on the outside and can only envy their wild freedom. Both of these communities, the fallen women and the gypsies, are in the end only contemplated from a—safe, superior—distance and construed unproblematically as a unit: as one song, one voice, one people.

A second, quite different reference to community can be found in stories like "A Psychological Moment" or "Her Share", which criticize the hypocrisy of a bourgeois society. The first story satirically exposes the norms and conventions of "so-called Dublin society", the "snobbery" and "bigotry" of "all Catholic Dublin" (2006, 90). Yet, the hypocritical norms and behaviour of this community are seen as but an instantiation of a larger social structure that restricts and submits women. In "Her Share", these social norms are represented and enforced by the community of women on board of a transatlantic steamer: they unanimously condemn and avoid the fallen woman whom the protagonist takes pity on. In the face of this communal and social disapprobation, Egerton's heroines all advocate a spirit of indifference and self-reliance. "Bother what the people say", the protagonist of "A Psychological Moment" counsels and this is echoed by Fruen's defiant drive through the town with her lover in "The Regeneration of Two": "Why should she trouble what the world says—after all one's world is only as big as one can grasp it" (2006, 89, 168).

In both these cases, community remains largely abstract, whether as an ideal unity to be both wary and envious of, or as a repository of social codes and conventions that threatens to reject those who disobey them. In "Wedlock", to the contrary, community takes a third, more concrete form. "Wedlock" tells the horrifying story of a woman who succumbs to drink and murders her stepchildren in revenge for being separated from her own, beloved but illegitimate child. Yet the story starts in a strangely oblique way, by recounting a long conversation between two bricklayers as they observe the drunken woman trying to make it to her house. The men provide background information on her life and help her into her house, but also exchange opinions about whether her alcoholism is her fault or whether it "woz in 'er blood same az the colourin' of 'er skin" (2006, 117). Their heavily colloquial dialogue, conveyed through direct speech, brings out different perspectives on the tragic story. It thus functions as a Greek chorus, commenting on the events and providing a communal frame to the main plot. Unlike in a Greek chorus, however, the dialogic nature of the bricklayers' discussion highlights their differences in opinions, thus creating a more truly communal voice than the unitary constructions of community in the other stories.

Turning to Lavin's stories, we find surprisingly similar constructions of community in a number of her stories. In many of Lavin's stories, first of all, the local community is staged as a mute but deeply felt guardian of social codes and conventions. As we have seen in Chapter 4, Lavin's characters are as a rule very conscious of their status within the community and of the communal sanction or censure their actions might incur. In most stories, though, this communal judgement is presented more as an abstract fear than as a real threat: characters are shown to worry about "what the neighbours might say" rather than about what they actually have said. In other words, these communal strictures are shown to be to a large extent internalized, primarily by characters most concerned with their position within the community. Like Egerton, Lavin counsels defiance in the face of such actual or imagined social censure. As Phelim says to his wife in "Lilacs": "Rose Magarry, if you're going to marry me, you must face up to the people and never be ashamed of anything I do" (Lavin 1985, 7), and this usually guides the action of the most positive characters in Lavin's stories.

In a few of Lavin's stories, community moves from the silent backdrop of characters' life to take up centre stage. Thus, "A Fable" tells of a community's reaction to the perfect beauty of a newcomer to the village: "She was the most beautiful woman they had ever seen and so they hated her" (Lavin 1945, 132). Only when her perfect face becomes scarred in an accident is she accepted as an equal in the community. As I have pointed out already, "A Fable" can be considered one of Lavin's few plotted stories: it is told by a distant, omniscient narrator who summarizes the events across several decades and describes the villagers' thoughts and actions to expose their mean and narrow ways. This judicial tone is already evident in the opening paragraph:

> The women feared that she would dim their own glory, and the men disliked her because they felt she was inaccessible [...] The women need not have feared, for the orchid does not take from the beauty of the bluebell. The men need not have disliked her because they could not possess her body, for had they been wiser men than they were they would have realised that a woman of such incandescent beauty belonged to every eye that looked on her [...] But the men in the village where this beauty came to live were not wise men, nor were they generous, nor were they kind. (1945, 132)

Throughout the story, the villagers are represented as acting in one body, speaking with one voice. Although they are sometimes singled out by their occupation—the postmistress, the teacher, the farmer's lad—they are never individualized by their voice as the story contains no dialogue or direct speech. Like the gypsies and fallen women in Egerton's stories, the village community remains an abstract, unified entity contemplated from a distance by the narrator, who assumes a superior position in the face of "these stupid people" (1945, 142). Hence, if the plot of the story comments on the villagers' hostility to difference, its discourse re-enacts this hostility in a refusal to allow in other voices which could complicate this objectifying representation of the community as one.

More interesting then are the stories which do allow for polyphonic variation in a communal chorus of different voices. Once again *Tales from Bective Bridge* provides an early model of this polyphonic evocation of community in its depiction of the islanders' reaction to the death of one of their fishermen in "The Green Grave and the Black Grave". The story consists almost entirely of dialogue. Tadg Beag and Tadg Mor, together with two neighbouring women, discuss the dead fisherman, his inland wife and the grave he will get. Through this dialogic structure, the story evokes the attitudes of the island community to love and life, death and the sea, but also allows room for the different beliefs of the inland woman:

> "We got no answer to our knocking," said Tadg Mor and Tadg Beag, bringing their words together like two oars striking the one wave, one on this side of the boat and one on that.
> "When the inland woman puts her face down on the feather pillow," said the Sean-beahn O Suillebheain, "that pillow is but as the sea shells children put against their ears, that pillow has in it the sad crying voices of the sea."
> "Is it that you think she is from home this night?" said Tadg Mor.
> "It must be a thing that she is," said the old woman.
> "Is it back to her people in the inlands she'll be gone?" said Tadg Beag, who had more than the curiosity of the night in him.
> "Step into the kitchen", said the old woman, "while I ask Inghean Og if she saw Bean Eamon Og go from her house this night." (1945, 44)

A communal chorus is thus woven out of a polyphony of different voices, which allows for repetition and variation, harmony and (minor) dissent, thus effectively constructing this community through what Jean-Luc Nancy has called "le partage des voix" or the sharing of voices (1991, 29, 158). Since this communal chorus in "The Green Grave and the Black Grave" unfolds after the fishermen are confronted with the dead body of

Eamon Og Murnan, it bears out Nancy's argument that the sharing that constitutes community is based on an encounter with the death of the other:

> Communication consists before all else in this sharing and in this com-pearance (*com-parution*) of finitude: that is, in the dislocation and in the interpellation that reveal themselves to be constitutive of being-in-common— precisely in as much as being-in-common is not a common being -[...] Finitude compears, that is to say it is exposed: such is the essence of com-munity. (1991, 29)

For Nancy, community is emphatically not a common being, predicated on a shared essence or identity, satirically evoked in "A Fable". Rather, it is based on a shared exposure to finitude and, hence, "the sharing of singu-larities" (Nancy 1991, 33). Such a notion of community—with respect for difference and singularity—is also evoked through the communal chorus of Lavin's story as the islanders respect the inlander's different concep-tion of love, but also weave her voice into the story of the community. As Nancy puts it: "The death of lovers, indeed, exposes them, both between themselves as well as outside of themselves to the death of the commu-nity" (1991, 38).

These comments are part of Nancy's seminal study of community, *La Communauté Désœuvrée* [*The Inoperative Community*], in which he responds to Georges Bataille's staging of the immanent communion of lovers as an ideal community, over and against existing social and political communities. Nancy rejects this view, arguing:

> Lovers are neither a society, nor *the* community effected through fusional communion. If lovers harbour a truth of the social relation, it is neither at a distance from nor above society, but rather in that, as lovers, they are exposed in the community. They are not the communion that is refused to or purloined from society; on the contrary, they expose the fact that com-munication is not communion. (1991, 37)

It is interesting to bear these thoughts in mind when turning to a final Lavin story which gives community a voice and explicitly opposes it to the intimate communion of lovers. "Loving Memory" is the last story of Lavin's Grimes saga, yet chronologically it is the first as it depicts the courtship and marriage of the parents of Liddy, Bedelia, and Alice Grimes up until their mother's death (see D'hoker 2013a). The first part of the story is taken up by a representation of the communal context of love and courtship in the small town. The narrator stages a chorus of voices to evoke the good-natured bantering, flirting and singing of the town's young people in the Grimes parlour and concludes:

> Meaningless, idle, leading nowhere, the banter went on inconsequentially until, almost by a slip of the tongue, a remark more pointed than the usual would be acclaimed a kind of public proposal. Then, but not till then, could a couple claim the prize of the parlour: the right to sit on the sofa behind the door [...] The nearer a couple got to marriage the more they were given cover, till finally marriage itself came down like a snuffer over their flame. (Lavin 1974, 266)

Matthias Grimes refuses to participate in these communal courtship practices. Instead he searches for a bride outside of the town and marries her within six weeks. Disregarding social custom and propriety, he keeps the courtship and the marriage private. The narrator evokes the town's consternation through a communal chorus of voices as they speculate about the bride's name, age, money, and family (1974, 268–9). Consternation turns to outrage, when they learn that the newly married couple will not go on the traditional honeymoon, but want to spend their wedding night in their own house. The story dwells at length on the general "embarrassment" that ensues: "Before the couple were home ten minutes, everyone in the town had stolen a glance at that oblong window [of their bedroom]" and the whole town watches how, "Together they contemplated the night for all the world as if they were on a balcony in some Italian resort" (1974, 271). The narrator explains the town's upset with:

> Now, this was not what the town had been led to expect. They'd been told there would be no honeymoon—not that it was to be spent brazenly before their eyes in their own town. After all, it is not only the couple concerned that a honeymoon safeguards. Friends, relations and acquaintances are entitled to a like protection. (1974, 273)

And the married couple continue to give offence by blatantly displaying their love on their daily walks on the outskirts of town, with their hands invariably linked together in Matthias' coat pocket or in Alicia's muff—a clear sexual symbol which is dwelt on at length in the story. In other words, their love is presented as the kind of ecstatic fusion envisaged by Bataille, which remains "private" and stands in opposition to the "public" nature of the community (Nancy 1991, 36).

Although in many other stories, as we have seen, Lavin justifies defying communal censure for the sake of love, in this story, she seems to side with the community's disapproval of the "love-birds", as they are called in the town. For Matthias stubbornly refuses to share Alicia with the community: she is "kept out of the shop" and "spent most of her day out of sight upstairs" (1974, 273). As a result, she remains an elusive figure in the community, "like a lady in a tower", or even "a ghost", as her daughter realizes early on (1974, 273, 264). And this spectral or liminal status is confirmed at the end of the story when after her death, Alice overhears the mothers of the town call out to their children: "'Stay out, so—'the woman said, 'and see what'll happen! Have you forgotten Alicia Grimes? Oh-ho, you haven't! Alicia Grimes will get you! Alicia Grimes will get you!'" (1974, 281). Matthias even keeps Alicia from her children, who are not given a share in their parents' love: "Their house wasn't littered with love [...] Love didn't thunder like a cataract down their staircase. It was all kept stored in their mother's room, and only their father had the key" (1974, 265). After Alicia's death, Matthias completely neglects his children and is only concerned with how he can create a fitting memorial for his wife. In "Loving Memory", Lavin thus valorizes community as the necessary site of social relations, which are made possible by customs, conventions and taboos. As in "The Green Grave and the Black Grave" or in Egerton's "Wedlock", the community is not unified into a single body, but rather represented as a chorus of voices that can accommodate dissension and difference as part of the ongoing communication that defines community. It is only when communication is refused that the limits of the community are exposed as in the case of Matthias and Alicia who deliberately position themselves outside the community. Clearly, not even love justifies such a withdrawal from familial and communal networks in Lavin's world and in this she would agree with Nancy's statement that "Community does not lie beyond the lovers, it does not form a larger circle within which they are contained: it traverses them [...] without such a trait traversing the kiss, sharing it, the kiss is itself as despairing as community is abolished" (Nancy 1991, 40).

JANE BARLOW'S NARRATIVES OF COMMUNITY

From these examples of communal images in individual stories, let us now turn to the more established tradition of representing community through linked stories within a single short story collection. Although the short story cycle, or collection of interlinked stories, is arguably less well known a literary form in Ireland than in the USA or Canada, Irish women writers too have used the form to represent community life in a variety of ways. In the main part of this chapter, therefore, I will discuss three collections which use linked stories to evoke a communal network, whether positively or negatively. These are Jane Barlow's *Irish Idylls*, Mary Beckett's *A Literary Woman* and Éilís Ní Dhuibhne's *The Shelter of Neighbours*. The short story cycle, or short story sequence as it is sometimes called (Luscher 1989), has been seminally defined by Forest Ingram as "a book of short stories so linked to each other by their author that the reader's successive experience on various levels of the pattern of the whole significantly modifies his experience of each of its component parts" (1971, 11). If Ingram placed equal emphasis on authorial intentions, textual characteristics and readerly processing of the short story cycle, subsequent critics have focused more on the formal properties on the form. Susan Garland Mann, for instance, identifies three possible unifying strategies in short story cycles—setting, theme and character—and lists various generic signals which mark out a collection as a short story cycle: a title which does not recur as the title of a short story, genre markers in the subtitle, a preface or authorial statement, an epigraph or motto, a frame or a specific structural organization (Mann 1989: 14–15). In addition, critics have argued that the unique properties of the short story cycle lie in the "simultaneous self-sufficiency and interdependence" of the individual stories (Mann 1989, 15) which results in a characteristic tension between unity and diversity, wholeness and fragmentation, or "between cohering, centripetal forces and separating, centrifugal forces" (Alderman 1985, 135).

Given the popularity of a shared setting as a unifying device, the short story cycle has often lent itself to the portrayal of a local community. With single stories portraying individual characters and plots, and the collection as a whole construing cross-references, a shared fictional universe or other elements of connection, "the short story cycle can express both the plight of an individual and the fate of a community through its very structure" (Pacht 2009, 1). This certainly holds true for the modernist short story cycles which Ingram considered paradigmatic of the genre: Anderson's *Winesburg, Ohio*, Faulkner's *Go Down, Moses* and Joyce's *Dubliners*. More recently, however, critics have argued that the roots of the short story cycle can be found in the nineteenth-century village sketch tradition, which evokes village life through a series of interlinked sketches and stories. Well-known examples of this tradition are Elizabeth Gaskell's *Cranford*, Nancy Mitford's *Our Village*, M.E. Frances's *In a North Country Village*, Sarah Orne Jewett's *The Country of the Pointed Firs*, and, indeed, Jane Barlow's *Irish Idylls*. In a ground-breaking 1988 article, Sandra Zagarell coined the term "narrative of community" for this specific form of regional writing, since these works "take as their subject the life of a community (life in 'its everyday aspects') and portray the minute and quite ordinary processes through which the community maintains itself as an entity" (Zagarell 1988, 499). While Zagarell focused primarily on the ideological and thematic concerns of these late-nineteenth-century narratives of community, subsequent critics have argued that the majority of these works are made up of interlinked short stories and that the narrative of community should therefore be considered as a subgenre of the short story cycle (Harde 2007). Whether these nineteenth-century village narratives should be considered as antecedents or actual exponents of the short story cycle remains a point of contention (Mann 1989, 8; Nagel 2004, 4). It depends of course on whether their component parts are judged to be modern short stories or rather sketches and tales belonging to an earlier nineteenth-century tradition. This is also a question that arises when reading Jane Barlow's *Irish Idylls*. Although written around the same time as Egerton's *Keynotes* and Somerville and Ross's *Some Experiences of an Irish R.M.*, Barlow's stories are more clearly transitional works, which is also the reason I have not included them in the chapter tracing the origins of the modern short story in Ireland. Still, as a first realization of the narrative of community in Ireland, the collection certainly is interesting and deserves to be looked at in more detail.

Although now almost forgotten, Jane Barlow (1857–1917) was a popular writer in her time. She published 19 books—poetry, short fiction and novels—and received an Honorary Doctorate in Literature from Trinity College in 1904. Her best-selling book was *Irish Idylls*, which went through eight editions in her lifetime. It was praised by contemporary reviewers, who connected it to other books in the village sketch tradition. In one review, Barlow was called the "Gaskell of Erin" and in another "the Sarah Orne Jewett of Ireland" (Anonymous 1893, 1898). Yeats included

Irish Idylls in his 1895 "List of Best Irish Books" (Marcus 1987, 286), but subsequently removed it again when he narrowed down his list to 30 books (Hansson 2008, 66). Still, its success prompted Barlow to write a sequel in 1895, *Strangers in Lisconnel: A Second Series of Irish Idylls.* Both collections are set in the fictional Connemara hamlet of Lisconnel from the 1820s to the 1890s and relate incidents in the life of its twenty-odd inhabitants. Apart from the shared setting and recurring characters, the narrative set-up also provides unity to the collection. The stories are all narrated by an editorial narrator who claims first-hand knowledge of the village and frequently voices her opinion on characters and events. Unlike in *Some Experiences of an Irish R.M.*, the anonymous narrator is clearly construed as a reliable and superior judge, who guides the reader through this rural community and through the landscapes, traditions and customs of the West of Ireland in general. This omniscient narrative voice as well as the often meandering and anecdotal plots seem to confine the stories to the nineteenth-century tale tradition. However, some stories are more tightly unified around a single event, such as a widow's unexpected legacy in "A Windfall" or the dangers of selling poteen in "Got the Better of", and this 'single effect', characteristic of the modern short story, becomes more pronounced in the second collection, where the stories are generally shorter and more unified. A telling detail in this respect is Barlow's reworking of "Coming and Going", the final story of *Irish Idylls*, into two separate stories in her second collection. If the ambivalence in the use of plot and narrative voice thus mark the *Irish Idylls* as a transitional book in terms of the development of the modern short story, the same holds true for the qualified realism that characterizes her stories. In the introductory story, the narrator sets out her realist aims: she rejects the revivalist attempt to steep rural Ireland in "legendary lore" and promises to show Lisconnel in "the light of common day, a hard fact with no fantastic myths to embellish or disprove it" (Barlow 1893, 13). The stories are indeed remarkable for their focus on the daily habits and struggles of Lisconnel inhabitants: cutting turf, going to mass or the market, worrying about dinner, digging the steep potato patches, braving cold and rain. Still, while it is true that life in Barlow's village is far from idyllic, it is certainly idealized. As we will see, Barlow's imaginative representation of Lisconnel expresses an ideal of community, far more than its reality. Although this tension between realism and idealism characterizes to some extent all nineteenth-century narratives of community discussed by Zagarell, Barlow's ambivalent position in the embattled reality of turn-of-the-century Ireland makes her idealization of community life especially conflicted and, ultimately, impossible. In Zagarell's definition:

> Narratives of community ignore linear development or chronological sequence and remain in one geographic place. Rather than being constructed around conflict and progress, as novels usually are, narratives of community are rooted in process. They tend to be episodic, built primarily around the continuous small-scale negotiations and daily procedures through which communities sustain themselves. (1988, 503)

Negotiation and neighbourliness are also key terms in Barlow's stories as they depict the villagers supporting each other in their struggle with harsh surroundings and meagre resources. Small conflicts break out occasionally and are resolved again by careful negotiations, and the events of the day (or memorably incidents from the past) are extensively discussed in communal gatherings on neighbouring doorsteps. Interesting in this respect is that, unlike in the women-centred works of Gaskell, Jewett and Mitford, in *Irish Idylls*, men and women seem to share equally in both the domestic tasks and the communal life. Moreover, even though the narrator disapproves of spineless husbands who are being put upon by shrewish wives, she does depict several strong female characters and stages the elderly widows as occupying the highest social standing in the community. In general, the village is represented as a remarkably non-patriarchal and egalitarian community and this is further underscored by the absence of a protagonist or single plot. While the individual stories often revolve around one character or family, the collection as a whole distributes attention equally among the villagers, in keeping with "the predominant focus on the collective life of the community" that characterizes narratives of community (Zagarell 1988, 501). The protagonist of the books really is Lisconnel as a whole, which is linguistically highlighted by such phrases as "Lisconnel opined" or "Lisconnel is not deficient in tact" (Barlow 1893, 209, 20). Yet, this monolithic construction of the community as a single entity, which we also saw at work in stories by Egerton and Lavin, is alleviated by a polyphonic representation of the community through the numerous dialogic passages, recorded in Lisconnel's vivid local dialect. These colloquial conversations are chiefly responsible for the realist, true-to-life effect of *Irish Idylls* and *Strangers at Lisconnel* as they construe the village as a lively community in which members are granted their own individual voice, while also contributing to the communal chorus that constitutes village life.

Another way in which the village of Lisconnel is foregrounded as the protagonist of the books is through the evocation of time and space. Following the conventions of narratives of community, Barlow elaborately describes the village and its surroundings in the introductory opening story of *Irish Idylls*. The emphasis is very much on the isolation of Lisconnel and the bleakness and inhospitality of its surroundings: "There is nothing to shut out the limitless expanses of earth and sky. Travelling on it, a man may learn that a broad hat-rim is not an altogether despicable screen between his imagination and the insistence of an importunate infinity" (1893, 3). The opening story of *Strangers*, on the other hand, evokes a remarkably similar sense of infinity, but with regard to time:

> To Lisconnel, our very small hamlet in the middle of a wide bogland, the days that break over the dim blue hill-line, faint and far off, seldom bring a stranger's face; but then they seldom take a familiar one away, beyond reach, at any rate of return before nightfall. There are few places amid this mortal change to which we may come back after any reasonable interval with more confidence of finding things just as we left them, due allowance being made for the inevitable fingering of time. (1895, 11)

Spatial solitude and temporal stasis serve to construct an image of the community as fixed and unchanging. This is underscored by the treatment of time in both works. While most stories are set in an indefinite present, with frequent references to past events, some other stories, especially in the second collection, are entirely set in the more distant past yet with references to the present as when they relate memorably incidents from the childhood of a character who has reached old age in the other stories. Interestingly, the month or season in which the events take place is specified in each story, but years or decades are not mentioned. The books thus foreground a cyclical notion of time—both in terms of the cycle of life and the cycle of the seasons:

> Thus the generations, as they succeed one another, wave-like present a well-marked rhythm in their coming and going—play, work, rest—not to be interrupted by anything less peremptory than death or disablement [...] And the Lisconnel folk, therefore, because the changes wrought by human agency come to them in unimposing forms, are strongly impressed by the vast natural vicissitudes of things which rule their destinies. The melting of season into season, and year into year. (1895, 12)

For Zagarell, narratives of community emerged as a "response to social, economic, cultural, and demographic changes caused by industrialism, urbanization, and the spread of capitalism", with writers "presenting—and preserving—the patterns, customs and activities through which, in their eyes, traditional communities maintained and perpetuated themselves" (1988, 499–500). Many narratives of community also incorporate modernity's threat against traditional life in the plots of their stories: in *Cranford*, this is symbolized by the advent of the railway, while in *Country of the Pointed Firs*, larger economic changes threaten the traditional lifestyle in the decaying fishing village of Dunnet Landing. No comparable upheavals are announced in Barlow, however. At the end of *Strangers of Lisconnel*, life in the hamlet seems set to continue indefinitely, albeit in a mode of constant struggle against the elements. Even more surprising is the relative absence of past upheavals and political turmoil in Lisconnel. Although there are a few, stray references to the Famine, to distant wars and political unrest, these events do not impinge on life in Lisconnel. In fact, all of the tragic fates mentioned in the stories—murder, starvation, death by fever and famine—happen to outsiders, while all but one of the Lisconnel inhabitants the readers have come to know die, if at all, of old age.

While the absence of a linear plot progression or a clear historical framework are quite common characteristics of narratives of community, the suspension of Lisconnel from the onward march of time is rendered rather more improbable because of the actual political context in which Barlow was writing and in which the stories are set. The final decades of the nineteenth century saw Ireland ravaged by the Land Wars and, as an Anglo-Irish Protestant herself, Barlow was probably not a neutral bystander of the events. Indeed, the idealization of community life, which was a common characteristic of nineteenth-century narratives of community, takes on an additional tinge of unreality in Barlow's works as they neglect to mention this agrarian unrest. In fact, one could speculate that Barlow's idealization of village life in *Irish Idylls* and *Strangers at Lisconnel* may have been a way of justifying the landlord system in Ireland by attempting to demonstrate her characters' contented attachment to life in Lisconnel, in spite of the hardships it presents. In her Preface to the American edition of *Irish Idylls*, Barlow implicitly refers to this intention when she addresses the book to her readers in America,

> to whose shores the wild boglands of Connaught send so many a forlorn voyager 'over oceans of say'. They will perhaps care to glance at his old

home, and learn the reasons why he leaves it, which seem to lie very obviously on the surface, and the reasons, less immediately apparent, why his neighbours bide behind. (1893, v)

In her Preface, Barlow also announces the mediating function of *Irish Idylls* and *Strangers at Lisconnel*, following the general trend of "narratives of community [to] represent the contrast between community life and the modern world directly through participant/observer narrators, [who] typically seek to diminish this distance in the process of giving voice to it" (Zagarell 1988, 501). In Barlow's stories, the narrator mediates not only between traditional, rural and modern, urban life, but also between the Irish protagonists and the English or American readers. In her article on Barlow's works, Hansson discusses the linguistic strategies that dramatize this distance in terms of the contrast between the villagers' "dialect dialogue" and the narrator's own "well-formulated comments" in Standard English, but argues that "these distancing strategies are at least partly countered by Barlow's expressions of belonging" and by her insertion of "dialect words in the narrative without quotation marks or italics, thereby breaking up the firm boundaries between the language varieties she employs" (Hansson 2008, 65). The narrator's use of the first person plural is indeed interesting for the ambivalence it conveys about her position in the community. While phrases such as "our custom in Lisconnel", "our black bogland" or "our customary formula" include the narrator in the community she depicts (Barlow 1893, 50, 158, 178), in other instances, the narrator uses the singular pronoun to dissociate herself from the villagers or uses "we" to refer to another group entirely. An interesting example of the shifting meaning of these pronouns is the following:

> When we meet a stranger or a slight acquaintance on the roads about Lisconnel, we always say it's a fine day, unless it happens to be actually pouring and then we say it's a fine day *for the country*. I do not know exactly what meaning is attached to the qualifying clause […] But it appears to be a mode of speech adopted as a seemly cloak for our uppermost thoughts, on somewhat the same principle that we avoid choosing our own engrossing domestic troubles as a topic of conversation in mixed society. (1893, 76)

If the first "we" positions the narrator as an insider to the Lisconnel community, the "I" that follows suggests her dissociation from that community, while the final "we" refers to the educated community of narrator, author and readers, who may happen to find themselves in mixed society. Throughout the short stories, both uses of "we" clearly testify to the ambivalent position of the narrator who claims to be both an insider to the community she is describing and an insider to the society she is addressing. To a certain extent, this ambivalence is a familiar characteristic of narratives of community, expressive of their mediating role and their double intention to record and explain traditional village life. As Zagarell puts it, "Narrators draw cultural and historical conclusions unthinkable to community members, for whom their life is simply a natural condition" (1988, 516). Yet, in Barlow's narratives of community, the ambivalent position of the narrator as both insider and outsider to the community again approaches the level of impossibility because of the more pressing and more complex political context in which Barlow writes. This very impossibility of the narrator's position becomes evident when we consider the strangely disembodied presence of the narrator in the stories as well as Lisconnel's largely hostile attitude to strangers.

In most other narratives of community, the narrator is also a character: a regular visitor, as in *Cranford*, or a newcomer to the village, as in *Country of the Pointed Firs*, hence ideally placed to negotiate between two worlds. Barlow's narrator does not, however, figure as a character and her status as a regular visitor is only implied. Yet, in *Strangers at Lisconnel*, in particular, these implications are counteracted by the community's negative attitude to outsiders which is described in several of the stories: "Mrs. Kilfoyle's Cloak" justifies Lisconnel's low opinion of the "Tinkers" with a story in which they are indeed revealed to be liars and thieves; in "A Flitting" and "A Return", newcomers to the village are greeted with a suspicion and civilized hostility that prove warranted by their subsequent base behaviour; in "Good Luck", the age-old rivalry between Lisconnel and neighbouring Laraghmena is dealt with at length; and in "Forecasts" the village's callous attitude to a day-labourer, "an other stranger at Lisconnel", is exposed (1895, 63). Although the narrator only disapproves of the community's hostility in the last story, the collection as a whole clearly shows how the community of Lisconnel is defined as much by acts of neighbourly negotiation, daily habits, and a common fount of stories and sayings, as by the setting up of boundaries between the community and "strangers". This familiar form of communal identity construction through opposition to a common enemy can also be observed in Lisconnel's attitude to the police, "the peelers", and to the land agent and the landed gentry more generally, who are dismissively referred to as "Quality" (1895, 109, 181). While the latter never make an actual appearance in *Irish Idylls* or *Strangers at Lisconnel*, the attitude to the police is both demonstrated and sociologically explained at length:

> The men in invisible green tunics belonged completely to the category of pitaty-blights, rint-warnin's, fevers, and the like devastators of life, that dog a man more or less all through it, but close in on him, a pitiful quarry, when the bad seasons come and the childer and the old crathurs are starvin' wid the hunger and his own heart is broke; therefore to accept assistance from them in their official capacity would have been a proceeding most reprehensibly unnatural. To put a private quarrel or injury in the hands of the peelers were a disloyal making of terms with the public foe. (1895, 36)

Lisconnel's general hostility towards outsiders thus further undermines the credibility of the narrator's position as both insider and outsider to the community and helps explain her curiously disembodied voice. Indeed, any concrete embodiment of this inside/outside position—whether as regular visitor, trusted outsider, or even educated inhabitant—would be quite impossible, given, on the one hand, the closed nature of the Lisconnel community and, on the other, the specific situation in Ireland where Barlow's only acquaintance with the village would be as a member or visitor of the Anglo-Irish gentry in the district, in other words as a member of the "Quality" which Lisconnel unanimously despises. While this impossible position of the narrator and, by implication, Barlow, with regard to the community may not have bothered the American or English reader, it must surely have struck the Irish reader and can thus at least partly explain the subsequent disappearance of Barlow's stories from the Irish literary canon—all the more so since the events in the twentieth century would soon deliver a final blow to this idealized version of the communal life of Irish tenants as happy, timeless and unchanging.

COLLABORATION AND CONFINEMENT IN MARY BECKETT'S COMMUNITIES

In American literature, both the short story cycle and its subgenre, the narrative of community, enjoyed renewed critical and popular success in the final decades of the twentieth century, as many writers used it to dramatize the experience of ethnically defined communities in the USA (Nagel 2004; Harde 2007). In Ireland and Britain, by contrast, the short story cycle occupied a much more marginal position (D'hoker 2013c), up until the turn of the twenty-first century when, as we will see in Chapter 7, postmodern writers like Anne Enright, Emma Donoghue and Éilís Ní Dhuibhne turned to the form. Hence, apart from such famous examples as Joyce's *Dubliners* and Moore's *The Untilled Field*, short story cycles unified by setting are also quite rare in twentieth-century Irish literature. Exceptions are Val Mulkerns's *Antiquities: A Sequence of Short Stories* (1978) and Mary Beckett's *A Literary Woman* (1990), both of which are set in Dublin. Because Mulkerns uses the form to explore the political alliances of one Dublin family across different generations, it does not really qualify as a narrative of community. In what follows, therefore, I will focus only on *A Literary Woman*, which explores the connections, however tenuous, between different inhabitants of a middle-class Dublin suburb. The collection thus enables an investigation of how both the idea and the reality of community have changed a century after Barlow's rural idylls.

Despite the relative success of her Troubles novel, *Give Them Stones* (1987), Mary Beckett's work is not very well known. This may be due to the unusual development of her career. She published some stories to critical acclaim in the 1950s and was included alongside Elizabeth Bowen, Kate O'Brien and Mary Lavin in a special "Women Writers Issue" of *Irish Writing* in 1954 (Matthews 2014, 97), but she stopped writing for over two decades, before publishing children's books, short story collections and a novel again in the late 1980s and 1990s (Macken 2006, 15). *A Belfast Woman*, her first short story collection, was published in 1980. *A Literary Woman* followed ten years later. Although *A Belfast Woman* does not consist of linked stories, the collection is interesting for our purposes because its quite negative portrayal of community life can be considered a prequel to the suburban community depicted in *A Literary Woman*. *A Belfast Woman* brings together Beckett's stories from the 1950s and adds a new one, "A Belfast Woman". The stories depict the quiet desperation and occasional acts of defiance of ordinary women in small Northern Irish villages or in Belfast. With the exception of the title story, none of the stories show traces of the Troubles or of religious dissension. Rather, in its psychological emphasis, social realism, and focus on domestic relations, Beckett's short fiction resembles that of Mary Lavin. More than in Lavin's stories, however, the norms and strictures of the local community are shown to frame the protagonists' lives. "During the last year of the war Theresa was so recklessly gay that some of the neighbours began to whisper gossip about her", reads the opening line of "Theresa", while "A Farm of Land" starts with "The entire countryside was horrified last week when the news leaked out that Susan Lavery had sold her father's farm" (Beckett 1980, 12, 32). In most stories, "the neighbours" are simply referred to as a unitary body, feared for its gossip, jealousy and pity, while the female protagonists are shown to defiantly battle this communal censure for what they feel is right.

In "Ruth", however, the community is given a more polyphonic representation in the form of two neighbours who visit Mrs. McGreevy, whose granddaughter has run away. The story is told almost entirely through dialogue: the gossip of the neighbours as they cycle to and from the farm and their conversation with Mrs. McGreevy who surprises them by baring her soul. She laments how pride and shame prevented her from taking in her illegitimate granddaughter immediately after her mother had died and how fear and cowardice kept her from showing her any real love when she eventually did: "There was no sense in hiding what was known, no sense at all. You talked among yourselves but there wasn't one would speak out to me" (Beckett 1980, 64). Kelly Matthews reads the story as an indictment of the culture of shame that rules mid-century Northern Ireland, as behaviour is dictated by fear of the neighbours' judgement (2014, 102). The tragic plot of the story indeed offers a strong denunciation of the hypocrisy, envy and false pride that govern social behaviour in this closed community. Yet, by juxtaposing the voices of the two neighbours in a communal chorus, the story's discourse also leaves room for difference within the community, with one neighbour being far more sympathetic and understanding than the other one. Hence, Beckett's story ultimately offers a plea for a private moral responsibility, even as it acknowledges the courage needed to brave the community's gossip and quick judgements. "Theresa", the only other story of *A Belfast Woman* to sport a woman's name, can be read as a counterpart to "Ruth". In this story, Theresa brings home her illegitimate—and black—baby from the orphanage to raise it herself. While her husband, the priest, her parents and the entire community are quick to accept the child, Theresa herself remains worried about the girl's future prospects for work or marriage. The story thus testifies once again to the way communal norms and judgements have been interiorized, even when they are no longer actually expressed.

In *A Literary Woman*, Beckett continues her exploration of women's inner lives, family relations and community, but the setting of these concerns has changed. Her characters now live in a middle-class Dublin suburb, much like Beckett herself who moved South after her marriage in 1956.

Although the stories in *A Literary Woman* appear at first as separate and self-contained short stories about Irish women, gradually their interconnectedness becomes apparent: they all inhabit the same neighbourhood in Dublin and all receive an anonymous letter which probes or threatens to divulge their innermost secret: a new mother is told her husband has had an affair, an unmarried man is accused of being gay, a mother whose child died in an accident is told that everybody knows of her crime, a woman who enjoys the quietude of her home is accused of being an alcoholic, and a middle-aged woman is suspected of having an affair with her neighbour. The letters are signed "The Watchers" or "A Wellwisher" (Beckett 1990, 47, 130). They can be read as a crystallization of neighbourly gossip, representing the community's most suspicious and censorious voice. Even when the accusations are blatantly untrue, the characters cannot fail to be affected by them, precisely because they carry the power of a submerged social censure, even in an otherwise rather anonymous Dublin suburb.

Interestingly, it is that very anonymity which motivates the letter-writer, as we learn in the penultimate story, "A Literary Woman". Miss Teeling is a middle-aged woman, who, as the illegitimate child of a housekeeper, has spent a childhood "hiding in other people's houses" (1990, 129). Never having enjoyed a normal family life, she feels unwanted and invisible and envies people their "warm comfortable houses", their "smug houses" (1990, 129). So she sets out to wreck their—real or apparent—domestic happiness and to make her influence felt. She watches the people on the road and listens to gossip so as to learn "the tenderest place to aim the blow" (1990, 127). Although the local gossip gives her ammunition for her anonymous sallies, it is also the neighbours' communal sharing that ultimately defeats her. In "Sudden Infant Death", the protagonist is consoled after receiving the poisonous letter by a solicitous neighbour who has detected her anxiety and tells her: "a few people round here have got nasty letters" (1990, 86). It is precisely by sharing rather than fearfully hiding these letters that the women can identify the letter-writer and hand her over to the police. In *A Literary Woman*, Beckett thus construes an interestingly balanced view of community, as potentially both constructive and destructive, supportive and indifferent, caring and cold. As I will show, her clever use of the form of the short story cycle to represent this community serves to further bring out this point.

Although I have so far mainly discussed the plot that binds the different stories together, that plot only plays a minor part in the stories, with the letter a crystallization of inner conflict or a catalyst for action. Instead, the different stories focus on the domestic and family relations of middle-class women: the conflict between motherhood and career in "Inheritance" and "The Cypress Trees", relationship problems in "A Ghost Story" and "The Long Engagement", and never-ending maternal care in "Heaven" and "Under Control". This emphasis on the private lives of women is under-scored by the symbolic insistence on the house in all of the stories. Whether experienced as a sanctuary or a prison, as empty or haunted by ghostly pres-ences, the house forms the backdrop of all the stories and stands for the characters' individuality and fundamental separateness. Unlike in Barlow's *Irish Idylls*, where most of the drama took place on communal doorsteps, in *A Literary Woman* the dramas are private, even if they may be alleviated or aggravated by communal judgement or action. Similarly, if in *Irish Idylls* most of the stories featured several, if not all, of Lisconnel's inhabitants, in *A Literary Woman* the emphasis is squarely on the private struggles of the protagonist of each story, with characters from one story appearing only as minor figures in the next. The image of community that follows from this different treatment is certainly not the idealized, organic and unified community depicted in Barlow's work. Instead, Beckett's approach high-lights the fundamental separateness of her characters even as they become embroiled in the larger plot of the anonymous letters.

This tension between separateness and interconnectedness, between individualism and collectivity in Beckett's late-twentieth-century Dublin suburb is also embodied in the very form of the short story cycle itself. As the different stories in the collection are arranged to form a single sequence, so the different houses are linked up to form a street, and the individual families come together in a neighbourhood community. Nevertheless, the gaps and differences between the stories are as impor-tant as the connections between them and Beckett admirably exploits the short story cycle's characteristic tension "between cohering, centripetal forces and separating, centrifugal forces" to bring out the conflicting cur-rents of individualism and communal involvement within a contemporary community (Alderman 1985, 135). Far from forming an organic col-lectivity as in *Irish Idylls*, Beckett's houses and their inhabitants remain different, distinct and separate, as is suggested in "The Cypress Trees" when a magnet which Gavin steals from a neighbouring house refuses to join his "door key": "They remained separate. Disappointed, he put them both in his pocket" (1990, 75). Still, the contrary pull of separation and connection also allows for a greater openness of the community than could be found in Lisconnel. The quite different lives and experiences of the women in *A Literary Woman* testify to the diversity that constitutes even this middle-class neighbourhood and a story like "Sudden Infant Death" shows this community's more welcoming attitude to outsiders, even though its hospitality did perhaps not extend to Miss Teeling. Yet, by allowing Miss Teeling to tell us her own story, Beckett herself does make room in her story cycle for this sad outsider figure. Significantly, the final word is not for her anti-communal story, but for that of her landlady Maeve, who quietly contemplates the relative peace that has returned to her house and to the neighbourhood. The intertwining of both seems the key to Beckett's vision, with happy homes being constitutive of the community and the reaching out to the community also a necessary part of the happy home. Mary Beckett's representation of individual, family and community may remind us again of Jean-Luc Nancy's concept of community as a "being-in-common" rather than a "common being", or as "a plurality of singularities" rather than an impossible, organic entity (Nancy 1991, xxxix; 2000, 85). As Beckett's *A Literary Woman* shows, the short story cycle—itself a conglomerate of singularities—is eminently suited to realistically capture this day-to-day experience of community.

CRIME AND COMMUNITY IN ÉILÍS NÍ DHUIBHNE'S *THE SHELTER OF NEIGHBOURS*

Although the short fiction of Éilís Ní Dhuibhne will receive a more detailed examination in the last chapter, I will conclude this chapter's investigation of community in short fiction with a discussion of Ní Dhuibhne's 2012 collection, *The Shelter of Neighbours*. As the blurb explains, the title draws on "the Irish proverb, *Ar Scáth a Chéile a Mhaireann na Daoine*—people live in one another's shelter or shadow" (Ní Dhuibhne 2012b). The thematic focus on community announced by the title is confirmed by the individual stories, which often focus on the interactions between neighbours and friends in contemporary Ireland. Although the collection as a whole does not qualify as a short story cycle or narrative of community, six of the 14 stories are linked together in various ways, thus constituting a mini-cycle within the larger collection. In an interview, Ní Dhuibhne herself commented on the interconnectedness of the stories in *The Shelter of Neighbours* as follows:

> And then there is the fact that "tarraingíonn scéal scéal eile": one story suggests another. Therefore, common themes run through the collection and

will be easily identifiable to readers, but that does not mean that I identified them in advance of writing. One theme is writing itself. Another subgroup of stories focuses on people living in one neighbourhood; I'm interested in examining the networking of social groups. (Ní Dhuibhne 2012a)

The six stories of this mini-cycle zoom in on the individual lives of middle-aged men and women, who turn out to live on the same street in a middle-class South Dublin housing estate, Dunroon Crescent. Apart from this shared setting, cross-references between the stories reinforce their interconnectedness: Martha, who is mentioned in "Trespasses" as the neighbour who "has offered to look after Bran, Clara's dog" (2012b, 95), appears as the protagonist in the subsequent story, "The Shelter of Neighbours", which dwells on the interactions between Martha and her other neighbour, Mitzy, but also casually refers to other residents, Finn O'Keefe, the protagonist of "The Man Who Had No Story", and Ingrid Stafford who figures in "The Shortcut Through IKEA". In "Red-Hot Poker", to give a final example, the newly widowed Linda tells of her interactions with a neighbouring couple, Tressa and Denis, but also refers to protagonists from the other stories: "Martha [from] the book club", "Clara, who is inclined to be cynical", and "Audrey", "a nasty piece of work", who is the protagonist of "The Sugar Loaf" (2012b, 191, 192). In this way, the interlinked stories effectively stage the network of individuals that make up a community. That this community is probably not a tightly-knit one, is evident from the fact that the individual stories zoom in on one or two protagonists, as in Beckett's *A Literary Woman*, rather than on a recurring cast of characters, as in Barlow's narrative of community. Moreover, the very name of the estate, Dunroon Crescent does not bode well, as Dunroon may be the Anglicized version of the Irish "Dún Rún", or "Fort of Secrets" (Ní Chonchúir 2012). As we will see, Ní Dhuibhne's characters are generally very adept at keeping their lives and secrets to themselves.

If the use of Irish language and folklore elements in her stories is one of the trademarks of Ní Dhuibhne's writing in general, in *The Shelter of Neighbours*, the Irish sayings also underscore the opposition between traditional village life and contemporary (sub-)urban communities, which recurs throughout the stories. In the first story, this contrast is realized through the contemporary retelling of an old Irish folktale, "The Man Who Had No Story" (O'Cathain 1988). Finn is a Dublin-based writer who has not written anything for years, instead devoting his energy to domestic concerns and to teaching creative writing. His unenviable position thus recalls that of the man who finds himself without a story in the folktale, but who is given the gift of confidence and imagination by the fairies and becomes an excellent storyteller. Finn ponders "In the old days, the storytelling days, they [the fairies] were always there. To frighten ordinary, decent people. And to give the gift of music, or story, or song, to the other ones. To the artists in the community" (2012b, 9). Instead of fairies, Finn has to contend with rats, that typically urban blight, and instead of having an eminent position in the community, he is criticized by his wife for his "selfish" absorption in his "stupid writing" (2012b, 11). A similar juxtaposition of traditional community life and contemporary suburban living is also often made by other characters: Linda in "Red-Hot Poker" muses how, in "the good old days", people "had to be neighbourly because they didn't have a phone, much less Facebook or whatever" (2012b, 192), and Mitzy in "The Shelter of Neighbours" reminiscences about her childhood on a farm:

> 'I loved it,' she said. 'Mucking about. There was a great sense of purpose to it. And you belonged not just to your family, but to a community. Everyone knew everyone. And looked out for them. *Ar scáth a chéile a mhaireann na daoine.*' She quoted the well-known proverb in Irish, about neighbours depending on one another. [...] 'It's so different now for the kids in the suburbs,' Mitzy said. 'I pity them.' (2012b, 120–1)

Here, as in several other stories, traditional proverbs serve to evoke a kind of bygone communal wisdom, which used to facilitate social interaction: "*Is fear an troid ná an t-uaigneas,* [Finn] heard on the radio another day. The fighting is better than the loneliness. They'd a proverb for every situation, the old folks. Finn wonders who made them in the first place, and if anyone does that any more" (2012b, 12). Besides the storytelling and the sayings, praying too drew traditional Irish communities together, as Polly suggests in "The Moon Shines Clear, the Horseman's Here". Revisiting her childhood village in the West of Ireland after a 30-year absence, Polly ponders:

> The family observed other essential religious formalities, some seemingly private in themselves but linked by invisible threads to the social and cultural web that enmeshed everybody. For instance, they said the rosary every night after tea, praying for the souls of the departed dead and also for living souls

to whom they were closely related or who had power and prestige [...] It seemed to Polly that this praying strengthened their connections to these people; it seemed to her that she had some role when the county won the All-Ireland final in Croke [...] and she had a hand, too, in the running of the country. (2012b, 158)

In opposition to these wistful evocations of traditional village life stands life in the contemporary, post-Celtic-Tiger Dublin estate of Dunroon Crescent. Most of the neighbours hardly know one another and communal activities are virtually non-existent. In "The Shelter of Neighbours", Martha gives a sociological explanation for her lack of contact with other mothers in the estate: as working women became the norm, there was no "time to be with the neighbours at all, at all. She rushed through her days from early morning to late at night" (2012b, 117). Yet, quite apart from referring to larger social changes, such as urbanization, secularization, increased individualism, new Celtic Tiger wealth or crisis austerity, the stories also hint at a darker undercurrent of violence, which lies underneath the apparent calm of suburban Ireland. Indeed, in spite of the ordinariness of characters and surroundings, the Dunroon sequence often relates quite shocking events: in "Trespasses", Clara is verbally, then physically abused by an elderly couple in a neighbouring estate for parking in front of their driveway and she retaliates by killing the woman; in "Red-Hot Poker", Linda has an affair with her neighbour's husband and subsequently prevents that neighbour from stealing her savings by burning and breaking the neighbour's hand with a hot poker; and in "The Shelter of Neighbours", Martha is a crucial witness in a murder case involving her neighbour's daughter. The recurrence of such violent acts in the Dunroon sequence creates the impression of a steady stream of violence and hatred, simmering beneath the peaceful and domestic surface reality of the stories and beneath the perfect poise and control of Ní Dhuibhne's prose.

Since the violence in contemporary Dublin is interlaced, as we have seen, with nostalgic images of a warm, supportive communal life in Ireland's rural past, the stories could be read as offering a searing critique of the individualism and materialism of contemporary Ireland and the corresponding destruction of community structures. This critique participates in a wider lament about the disappearance of communal life in contemporary Western societies, as sociologists like Robert Putnam in the USA and Zygmunt Bauman or Ulrich Beck in Germany have extensively documented (Bauman 2000; Putnam 2000; Beck and Beck-Gernsheim 2001).

Yet, even though the binaries of rural–urban, traditional–contemporary, the West–Dublin, communal life–individualism certainly inform the stories, Ní Dhuibhne also complicates these binaries in several ways, thus qualifying this nostalgic and conservative view.

First, in the two Dunroon Crescent stories most centrally involved with relations between neighbours, the antagonistic or individualistic acts are juxtaposed to proofs of neighbourly support. In "Red-Hot Poker", Linda finds comfort with her neighbours after her husband has died and in the title story, Martha recalls how Mitzy helped her during the terminal illness of her child as she is deciding whether or not to tell the Gardaí about seeing Mitzy's daughter on the night of the murder: "So Mitzy came to the rescue. She often sat in the hospital with Luke all day, when Martha was at work. Frequently, Siobhán, who was just six then, sat with her. They did that for eight months" (2012b, 127). Although the end of the story leaves Martha's decision open, the importance of that act of neighbourly support seems to suggest that Martha will not tell on Siobhán after all.

In fact, her silence is anticipated by two similar occasions which are, more casually, referred to in other stories. In "Yeats", the protagonist recalls how her husband's first wife died:

His wife was murdered, stabbed to death by an insane neighbour on the small, almost private, beach below the house, where she liked to skinny dip in the hot summers they used to have […] although they never found the murderer, everyone knew who did it. The son of the best storyteller. He moved to England two days after the funeral, which everyone in the valley, all the Catholics as well as the C of I's attended. (2012b, 64, 66)

In "The Moon Shines Clear, the Horseman's Here", similarly, the death of Paddy is dissembled by the village as an ordinary case of drowning, whereas in fact he had been pushed overboard by another man after a quarrel: "Paddy was dead, anyway, and the fisherman would never inform on one of their own" (2012b, 187). Protecting the murderer, if he's a member of the community, seems part and parcel of village life as well: everyone knows and no one tells. Although both of these crimes took place within traditional villages with a strong community life, they are clearly linked to the violent acts that pervade suburban Dublin, thus suggesting a fundamental similarity to neighbourly interactions in both places. This is also implied in "Trespasses", where the violent clash between Clara and the elderly couple in a neighbouring street is juxtaposed to another act of violence, which Clara hears about on the radio: in a small Midlands village, a farmer "died after being assaulted by [...] his neighbours" after he 'trespassed' into their field chasing after one of his heifers" (2012b, 103).

In short, these juxtapositions within and cross-references between the stories of *The Shelter of Neighbours* suggest a basic similarity to life in contemporary suburban or traditional rural communities, which complicates any easy binary opposition and undercuts the nostalgic longing for traditional community life which the characters often express. Kindness and support, as well as jealousy, hatred and violence are shown to be universal aspects of human relationships, whatever the circumstances. These two sides of human relations are in fact already suggested by the Irish proverb which gave its title to Ní Dhuibhne's collection. Although it is usually translated as "people live in one another's shelter", the original meaning of *scáth*—shadow—carries, in English at least, darker connotations as well: of living in someone's shadow or of being overshadowed by someone's acts or influence. The last story of the Dunroon sequence ends with the character narrator deciding that "no matter how lucky you seem to be, in the end there is nobody taking care of you. No god, no friend, no husband, no lover. No neighbour. In the end you're on your own" (2012b, 201–2). Yet, this pessimistic vision is not borne out by *The Shelter of Neighbours* as a whole. Rather, the plot of the individual stories and their structural integration in the collection suggest that, whether you are sheltered or shadowed by another's presence, no man is an island: human interactions—with friends or strangers, neighbours or family—determine one's life, to the good and to the bad. Linda's dark conclusion thus finds its counterpart in "It Is a Miracle", where Sara experiences a moment of connection with a stranger, whom she had initially sought to keep at arm's length. As he unburdens his personal troubles to her, she consoles him with traditional platitudes—"Everything will be OK" and "A good cry does you a power of good"—but he is truly grateful, exclaiming "You are the one person in this city of two million people I can talk to! Yes, it is a miracle" (2012b, 85–6). It is a phrase that, in spite of her natural distrust and scepticism, Sara repeats in an e-mail: *"Thanks for everything. The lunch and the conversation. It was a miracle"* (2012b, 94).

BIBLIOGRAPHY

Alderman, Timothy C. 1985. The Enigma of *The Ebony Tower*: A Genre Study. *MFS Modern Fiction Studies* 31 (1):134–147.

Anonymous. 1893. Notes on New Books. *The Irish Monthly* 21 (246):655–659.

Anonymous. 1898. A Batch of Irish Learics. *The Irish Monthly* 26 (296):87–89.

Barlow, Jane. 1893. *Irish Idylls*. New York: Dodd, Mead.

Barlow, Jane. 1895. *Strangers at Lisconnel: A Second Series of Irish Idylls*. New York: Dodd, Mead.

Bauman, Zygmunt. 2000. *Community: Seeking Safety in an Insecure World*. Cambridge: Polity.

Beck, Ulrich, and Elisabeth Beck-Gernsheim. 2001. *Individualization: Institutionalized Individualism and Its Social and Political Consequences*. London: Sage.

Beckett, Mary. 1980. *A Belfast Woman and Other Stories*. Dublin: Poolbeg Press.

Beckett, Mary. 1987. *Give Them Stones*. London: Bloomsbury.

Beckett, Mary. 1990. *A Literary Woman*. London: Bloomsbury.

D'hoker, Elke. 2013a. Family and Community in Mary Lavin's Grimes Stories. In *Mary Lavin*, edited by Elke D'hoker, 152–168. Dublin: Irish Academic Press.

D'hoker, Elke. 2013c. The Short Story Cycle: Broadening the Perspective. *Short Fiction in Theory and Practice* 3(2):151–160.

Egerton, George. 2006. *Keynotes and Discords*. London: Continuum. Original edition, 1893, 1894.

Hansson, Heidi. 2008. Our Village: Linguistic Negotiation in Jane Barlow's Fiction. *Nordic Irish Studies* 7:57–70.

Harde, Roxanne, ed. 2007. *Narratives of Community: Women's Short Story Sequences*. Cambridge: Cambridge Scholars

Ingram, Forrest L. 1971. *Representative Short Story Cycles of the Twentieth Century: Studies in a Literary Genre*. Paris: Mouton.

Lavin, Mary. 1945. *Tales from Bective Bridge*. London: Michael Joseph. Original edition, 1942.

Lavin, Mary. 1974. *The Stories of Mary Lavin*, vol. II. London: Constable.

Lavin, Mary. 1985. *The Stories of Mary Lavin*, vol. III. London: Constable.

Ledger, Sally. 2006. Introduction. In *Keynotes and Discords*, ix–xxvi. London: Continuum.

Luscher, Robert M. 1989. The Short Story Sequence: An Open Book. *Short Story Theory at a Crossroads*, edited by *Susan Lohafer and Jo Ellyn Clarey*, 148–167. Baton Rouge: Louisiana State University Press.

Macken, Valérie. 2006. Mary Beckett. In *Irish Women Writers. An A to Z Guide*, edited by Alexander G. Gonzalez, 14–17. Westport, CT: Greenwood.

Mann, Susan Garland. 1989. *The Short Story Cycle: A Genre Companion and Reference Guide*. Westport, CT: Greenwood Press.

Marcus, Phillip L. 1987. *Yeats and the Beginning of the Irish Renaissance*. Syracuse: Syracuse University Press.

Matthews, Kelly. 2014. A Belfast Woman: Shame, Guilt, and Gender in Mary Beckett's Short Stories of the 1950s. *New Hibernia Review* 18 (2):97–109.

Mulkerns, Val. 1978. *Antiquities. A Sequence of Short Stories*. London: Deutsch

Nagel, James. 2004. *The Contemporary American Short-Story Cycle: The Ethnic Resonance of Genre*. Baton Rouge: Louisiana State University Press.

Nancy, Jean-Luc. 1991. *The Inoperative Community*. Minneapolis, MN: University of Minnesota Press.

Nancy, Jean-Luc. 2000. *Being Singular Plural*. Stanford: Stanford University Press.

Ní Chonchúir, Nuala. 2012. Review of *The Shelter of Neighbours* by Éilís Ní Dhuibhne. *The Short Review*. Accessed 11/02/2015. http://www.theshortreview.com/reviews/EilisNiDhuibhneTheShelterOfNeighbours.htm

Ní Dhuibhne, Éilís. 2012a. Interview with Éilís Ní Dhuibhne. *The Short Review*. http://www.theshortreview.com/authors/EilisNiDhuibne.htm

Ní Dhuibhne, Éilís. 2012b. *The Shelter of Neighbours*. Belfast: Blackstaff Press.

O'Cathain, Seamus. 1988. *The Bedside Book of Irish Folklore*. Cork: Mercier Press.

O'Connor, Frank. 2004. *The Lonely Voice: A Study of the Short Story*. Hoboken, NJ: Melville House Pub. Original edition, 1963.

Pacht, Michelle. 2009. *The Subversive Storyteller: The Short Story Cycle and the Politics of Identity in America*. Newcastle Upon Tyne: Cambridge Scholars Publisher.

Putnam, Robert D. 2000. *Bowling Alone: The Collapse and Revival of American Community*. New York: Simon & Schuster.

Zagarell, Sandra A. 1988. Narrative of Community: The Identification of a Genre. *Signs* 498–527.

CHAPTER 6

The Rebellious Daughters of Edna O'Brien and Claire Keegan

Given the thematic emphasis of this study on relations in the short fiction of Irish women writers, a chapter on that most iconic and troubled of female relationships—the mother-daughter bond—seems indispensable, notwithstanding the considerable amount of critical studies on this topic in recent years. Indeed, if in 1977, Adrienne Rich still famously lamented the absence of representations of motherhood in general and of the mother-daughter relations in particular in Western literature (Rich 1986; see also Hirsch 1989, 11; Pelan 2006a), almost 40 years on, this situation has changed. Literary critics and feminist scholars have unearthed numerous dramatizations of the mother-daughter bond in literature and myth, and contemporary women writers have re-imagined that relation in a variety of ways. Yet, contrary to their hopes perhaps, critics have found the mother-daughter relation in literature to be almost invariably problematic, with "maternal representations bound in a pattern of idealisation and defilement" (Giorgio 2002, 30). In Irish literature too, this pattern has been noted, with critics describing the mother-daughter bond in Irish fiction as "embattled" (Chang 2008, 54), "difficult and acrimonious" (Weekes 2000, 120), "tempestuous, problem-laden, and fraught with multiple tensions", "inveterately divided and strained" (Fogarty 2002, 86, 88), riddled by tensions and "rivalries" (Shumaker 2001, 83), or characterized by "mutual hostility and conflict" (Ingman 2007, 76). Although these problems are often framed in a developmental narrative that pushes contemporary fiction towards reconciliation and "the endeavour to discover the reciprocal bonds between [mother and daughter]" (Fogarty 2002, 86),

© The Editor(s) (if applicable) and The Author (s) 2016   141
E. D'hoker, *Irish Women Writers and the Modern Short Story*,
DOI 10.1007/978-3-319-30288-1_6

the troubled relationship is itself interesting for what it reveals about the social, cultural and psychic patterns that shape Western patriarchal societies. The conflicted mother-daughter plot has indeed been interpreted in a variety of contextual and psychoanalytic frames, which I will briefly present before turning to contemporary variations of this plot in recent short stories by Edna O'Brien and Claire Keegan.

THE MOTHER-DAUGHTER PLOT

Since the 1970s, feminist investigations of the mother-daughter plot have mainly developed along two lines: (1) a psychoanalytic perspective, which has drawn upon, refined and criticized theories of Freud and Lacan about psychic development; and (2) a contextual/ideological perspective, which reads mother-daughter conflicts as products of patriarchal societies. Although these frameworks often intersect in actual interpretations, I will introduce them separately in what follows. In an Irish context, these perspectives are complemented by a recognition of the strong influence of the nationalist and Catholic iconography of Mother Ireland and the Virgin Mary, respectively.

Psychoanalytic theories have approached the mother-daughter relation in the context of the child's psychic development, whereby adult conflicts or pathologies are indicative of childhood traumas or of an incomplete individuation. For Freud, as is well known, the maternal is but what has to be repressed and rejected as the child moves from the pre-Oedipal into the Oedipal phase, and from instinct and desire to language and law through the intervention of the father. For Lacan, similarly, individuation and the child's ability to say 'I' are only possible through a rupture of the "Imaginary" or symbiotic mother-child bond which enables the child to enter the realm of the "Symbolic", the realm of otherness and difference. If, for Freud and Lacan, the maternal receives little—and only negative—attention, other psychoanalysts have emphasized the importance of the pre-Oedipal mother-child symbiosis for psychic development. Melanie Klein, for instance, draws attention to the defence mechanism of splitting through which the child divides the mother into a good and a bad object. Literary critics have traced this pattern of splitting in the twin fantasies of the omnipotent and the castrating mother, the idealized and the denigrated mother, which are prevalent throughout the Western cultural imaginary. Several theorists have also pointed to the additional difficulties this process of individuation poses for girls, who have to reject the person they are required to identify with. Hence, as Coughlan puts it, the mother-daughter bond typically

> involves opposite imperatives: in one direction to escape, to form, and free the separate self and disavow the maternal other, and in the other to remain attached, to resist at all costs the process of detachment from and relinquishing of the mother, and indeed to long for a total (re)union with her. (2006, 178)

As Irigaray has argued, the attempt to suppress or "murder" the mother in Western culture, leaves the daughter in a state of "*dereliction*" or melancholia, since a necessary part of her identity and heritage is lost (Irigaray and Whitford 1991, 47). In response to this symbolical matricide on the part of patriarchal culture, feminist philosophers like Kristeva, Cixous and Irigaray have highlighted the way the pre-symbolic maternal order remains present as a subversive, destabilizing undercurrent to the paternal symbolic order, whether in the form of the abject, the semiotic, or the body. However, even while celebrating the subversive potential of the maternal, these philosophers continue to subscribe to the classic Freudian schema of the close, symbiotic bond between mother and child which has to be broken for the child to gain an independent identity. As a result, the maternal remains that which has to be repressed for a successful psychic development.

This psychoanalytic premise has recently been questioned by Jessica Benjamin. Drawing on Daniel Stern's research on neonatal abilities and children's play, she argues that even the early mother-child dyad is already marked by intersubjectivity: "infants do not begin life as part of an undifferentiated unity"; rather, already in the earliest interactions, the mother can "identify the first signs of mutual recognition: 'I recognize *you* as my baby who recognizes *me*'" (1988, 18, 15). This process of recognition is marked by "a paradoxical mixture of otherness and togetherness", "distance and closeness", a balance of self and other (1988, 15, 34). Emphasizing the mutuality of this recognition, which forms a model for relationships in later life, Benjamin notes:

> Recognition is that response from the other which makes meaningful the feelings, intentions, and actions of the self. It allows the self to realize its agency and authorship in a tangible way. But such recognition can only come from a person whom we, in turn, recognize as a person in his or her own right. (1988, 12)

With this theory of intersubjectivity based on mutual recognition, Benjamin replaces the standard view of the child's development as a process of separation with that of a progressive development of relationality: "the issue is not how we become free of the other, but how we actively engage and make ourselves known in relationship to the other" (1988, 18). At the same time, she also supplants the standard psychoanalytic view of the mother as but an object of the infant's needs, attachment or love with an understanding of the mother "as another subject with a purpose apart from her existence for the child" (1988, 23). Thus, "the idea of intersubjectivity reorients the conception of the psychic world from a subject's relation to its object toward a subject meeting another subject" (1988, 20). While Benjamin recognizes that this meeting of subjectivities will be characterized by tensions, she emphasizes that these can only be solved within the intersubjective relationship itself rather than by its rejection or by the intervention of a third. "Resolution of the emotional knot between mother and daughter resides", therefore, "not in the intervention of a third term, but within the relationship itself, when each overcomes the desire for omnipotent control over the other and acknowledges the other's independent existence" (Giorgio 2002, 26).

Apart from its application in psychotherapy, Benjamin's psychoanalytic approach can help to dislodge the powerful myths that have shaped representations of the mother and the mother-daughter bond: the myth of the symbiotic mother-child bond as well as the fantasy of the omnipotent mother. From an entirely different perspective, these myths have also been attacked by feminist critics as "repositories of society's idealism", as expressions of a patriarchal ideology that seeks to hide women's secondary status under a set of images that glorify motherhood as powerful, superior and pure (Hirsch 1989, 15). In this view, the daughter's rejection of the mother, which is so often dramatized in twentieth-century Western literature, comes from a realization of the mother's powerlessness and subjugation. As Hirsch puts it, the emphasis of stories of female development thus comes to rest on

> the heroine's refusal of conventional heterosexual and marriage plots and, furthermore, on their disidentification from conventional constructions of femininity. Mothers—the ones who are not singular, who did succumb to convention inasmuch as they are mothers—thereby become the targets of this process of disidentification and the primary negative models for the daughter. (1989, 11)

Hence, as Adrienne Rich noted, the matrophobia we find in the literature does not signify the daughter's fear of an omnipotent, suffocating mother, as psychoanalysis suggests, but rather the fear of "*becoming one's mother*", since

> a mother's victimization does not merely humiliate her, it mutilates the daughter who watches her for clues as to what it means to be a woman. Like the traditional foot-bound Chinese woman, she passes on her own affliction. The mother's self-hatred and low expectations are the binding-rags for the psyche of the daughter. (Rich 1986, 235, 243)

In many literary texts, therefore, matrophobia is accompanied by a—literal or figurative—matricide which reflects the daughter's anger at the mother's implication in patriarchal law and at her failure to protect or empower her daughter.

Elaborating on this patriarchal critique within an Irish context, critics have focused both on the actual restrictions imposed on women by the conservative, familist, and Catholic ideology of the new Irish state as well as on the negative influence of Catholic and nationalist iconography on the representation of motherhood in Ireland (Weekes 2000, 100–7). As several scholars have noted, Catholic imagery of the Virgin Mary presents the impossible fantasy of a "pure" motherhood (Pelan 2006a, 59) and reinforces maternal ideals of "purity, asexuality, and a self-denying devotion to others" (Fogarty 2002, 87). Within a nationalist ideology, moreover, the figure of the mother is also linked to that of—an equally idealized and long-suffering—Mother Ireland. As Fogarty puts it:

> The images of Ireland as a hapless abandoned maiden, a homeless crone, an exacting, tutelary spirit who needs to be propitiated, and as a melancholic mother who demands unceasing sacrifice and devotion from her children and is herself defined by an unswerving propensity to self-immolation generated by nationalist literature continue to inflect the ways in which femininity is construed in the country today. (2002, 87)

For Irish mother-daughter fictions in particular, this means that the daughter's rejection of the mother often entails a rejection of the motherland, even if an underlying pull to the mother/land always remains. Hence, as Ingman claims, "Irish women's novels of the 1960s, 1970s, and 1980s frequently feature daughters who flee their mothers and their mother country in order to escape repeating their mothers' thwarted lives" (2007, 79).

In more recent women's fiction, however, critics have noted a shift towards a reconciliation with the mother and an attempt to recover her voice. Hirsch has found in African-American fiction an exploration of a maternal heritage and a recognition of the mother's role in the daughter's creative abilities (1989, 162ff), while Fogarty has argued about Irish novels of the 1990s:

> Fictions highlighting the gulf between mothers and daughters give way to narratives that find equal space for stories of filial protest and escape and the otherness of maternal discourse", whereby "the urge to recover the history of the mother seems [...] a necessary concomitant of the daughter's quest for fulfilment and self-knowledge" (2002, 89, 113)

Frequently this movement towards a recovery of the mother's voice seems to take the form of a "contextualization" in an attempt to understand the mother's choices (Giorgio 2002, 29). In contemporary literature, moreover, this increased exploration of the figure of the mother has also led to a shift from daughter-centred to mother-centred stories. In the context of Irish literature, one can think of Éilís Ní Dhuibhne's *Fox, Swallow, Scarecrow*, Mary Morrissey's *Mother of Pearl*, and several of Anne Enright's novels as well as her non-fictional *Making Babies* as cases in point. In short fiction too, this maternal turn can be noticed in such stories as Mary Beckett's "Under Control" (Beckett 1990), Enright's "Yesterday's Weather", "Caravan" and "Shaft" (Enright 2008) or Emma Donoghue's "Expecting" and "Through the Night" (Donoghue 2006).

However, also stories offering daughter-centred explorations of the mother-daughter plot continue to be written. In this chapter I propose to explore a handful of such stories by Edna O'Brien and Claire Keegan. Focusing on the contemporary work of both writers—published after 2000—I hope to investigate how the mother-daughter plot has developed in contemporary Ireland. Taking my cue from the psychoanalytic and socio-cultural perspectives just outlined, I will examine whether processes of intersubjectivity and contextualization have succeeded in leading the embattled mother-daughter relationship beyond the realm of fantasy, with its binary opposition of idealization and defilement, symbiosis and rejection, matrophilia and matricide.

EDNA O'BRIEN'S DESIRING SUBJECTS

A prolific and original writer, Edna O'Brien is one of the major figures of twentieth-century Irish literature. In the development of the Irish short story, moreover, she can be credited with leading the short story beyond the dominant mid-century paradigm of social and psychological realism. Although O'Brien's stories appear to depict complex characters and events in a recognizable social milieu, this mimetic impression is somewhat deceptive. In most stories, this realism is but a thin veneer covering an underlying symbolic structure, which dramatizes recurrent psychic patterns and processes. In this, O'Brien clearly shows herself indebted to Freudian theories of the unconscious (Rooks-Hughes 1996, 78; Weekes 2000, 115) as well as to the archetypal psychic patterns that are contained in the myths and fairy tales of Western culture (Mooney 2009). At the same time, her insistent use of symbolism also points to the influence of Joyce—an influence which O'Brien herself has repeatedly emphasized (Gillespie 2006; Pelan 2006b, 24ff). More generally, Edna O'Brien deserves credit for re-connecting the Irish short story with the more experimental strand of modernist short fiction. O'Brien's narrative experiments with interior monologue, second-person narration and unreliable narration can in fact be traced back to Egerton's proto-modernist techniques and also her frank exploration of women's sexual desires finds a precursor in several stories from Egerton's *Keynotes* and *Discords*. Looking back on these stories in 1932, Egerton would write that they constituted an attempt to map the processes of the unconscious: "the complexes and inhibitions, repressions and sub-conscious impulses that determine actions and reactions", even though she "did not know the technical jargon current today of Freud and the psycho-analysts" (Egerton 1932, 58). O'Brien's mapping of a similar terrain, on the other hand, has clearly been influenced by psychoanalytic theories. It is not surprising, then, that her work has often been interpreted within this framework. This certainly holds true for the problematic mother-daughter bond which features in so many of her novels and short stories. Before turning to the daughter stories published in *Saints and Sinners* (2011), therefore, I will briefly summarize these readings so as to form a frame against which to assess recent developments in O'Brien's short fiction.

Drawing on O'Brien's *Country Girls Trilogy* as well as such early stories as "A Rug", "A Demon", "Cords", "A Bachelor", and—especially—"A Rose in the Heart of New York", several critics have identified a recurrent daughterly development in O'Brien's fiction, which moves from closeness to rejection, or "from unquestioning to resentful love" (Weekes 2006, 312), and from "the maternal idealisation of the child to the matrophobia of the adult daughter" (Mooney 2009, 432). Yet, this rejection of the mother remains forever incomplete, even after her death, and O'Brien's daughters often long for a reconciliation and a return to the original bond. Some critics attribute the daughter's growing disenchantment with the mother to the latter's implication in Catholic and patriarchal mores and her accompanying failure to shield and empower the daughter. As Weekes puts it, "O'Brien's early 'martyr' mothers [...] reflect the impoverished conditions of rural Ireland: trapped on small farms, cut off from intellectual, emotional or social contacts, bitter about the possibility of romantic love, fearful of their brutal husbands, victims of helpless fatalism" (2006, 310). Hence, they are depicted as "primarily responsible for programming daughters into a narrow-minded world of subjugation and imprisonment" (Pelan 2006a, 63). Other critics interpret O'Brien's mother-daughter stories in psychoanalytic terms, as dramatizations of the daughter's failed individuation process following an incomplete severing of the pre-Oedipal bond. As Mooney notes, stories like "A Rug" and "A Rose" are clearly "attempts to narrativize what Freud and others have termed the almost entirely repressed and inaccessible pre-Oedipal imaginary", the close symbiotic bond with the mother which precedes differentiation, language, and lack (Mooney 2009, 434). In these stories, images of food and the body symbolize this communion as well as its subsequent rejection (Graham 1996). For, in a faithful demonstration of Kristevan theories of abjection, the daughters end up forcefully "abjecting" the maternal, which nevertheless continues to haunt them (Coughlan 2006, 186; Mooney 2009, 436). Even as maternal symbiosis turns to suffocation, it continues to determine the daughter's life in the form of an obsessive quest for a complete fusion in romantic love, which nevertheless fails to "live up to the all-consuming totality of maternal love" (Mooney 2009, 435). "Having never achieved the necessary separation from the mother", Rebecca Pelan argues similarly, O'Brien's daughters are forever "stranded at a level of psychological and emotional dependence from which [they] cannot escape" (2006a, 71). They pursue an ideal of perfect union which leads inevitably to disappointment, since "the process of idealisation and search for identity—whether through the mother, a man, or a child—is an illusion", leading to "ultimate disillusion and self-destruction" (Pelan 2006a, 71).

As these psychoanalytic readings demonstrate, mother-daughter rela-tionships in O'Brien's stories remain caught in the binary pattern of ide-alization and defilement, shelter and suffocation, symbiosis and abjection. Clearly, the devouring 'bad' mother is but the flipside of the idealized, omnipotent 'good' mother and, as Jessica Benjamin has argued, both are fantasies which blind us to the intersubjective potential of even the earli-est mother-daughter bond. That these fantasies are firmly entrenched in our cultural imagery is evident, for instance, in the fairy-tale opposition of the good and bad mother, the idealization and denigration of mothers in Western literature and, as Benjamin has noted, the psychoanalytic reading of the early mother-child bond as one of prelapsarian unity and symbiosis. O'Brien's mother-daughter stories are clearly very much indebted to these archetypal fantasies, even as they point to the deadlock and destruction that inevitably result. Two more recent stories, however, seem to seek a way out of this destructive binary through a reconsideration of the pre-Oedipal bond which tries to see the mother no longer as an object of the child's fears and desires, but as a subject in her own right.

These stories can be found in O'Brien's most recent collection, *Saints and Sinners*, which received the prestigious Frank O'Connor Short Story Award in 2011. Reviewers were quick to note the repetition of "old O'Brien themes" in the collection (Kilroy 2011), of "places and people from earlier books" (Shillinger 2011). Or, as a review in *The Times* put it: "Some writ-ers, like painters, return to the same subject again and again. Edna O'Brien is that kind of artist [...]. [She] returns to the theme of sexual repression and motherhood that marked her early works" (Foster 2011). Mothers and lovers do indeed feature in several of the stories: from the opening story, "Shovel Kings", where an ageing London Irishman keeps pining for the motherland he had to leave behind to the dashed romantic dreams of Miss Gilhooly in "Send My Roots Rain", who has been stood up by the poet she arranged to meet. "Green Georgette" and "My Two Mothers" are the stories which most explicitly revisit the mother-daughter plots of O'Brien's earlier fiction. The first story tells of a visit of a mother and daughter to the wife of the town's banker. Although they have high hopes for the visit, as it would raise their status in the community, these hopes are dashed when it turns out that they have only been invited to cover up the woman's flirtations with the local doctor. "My Two Mothers", finally, depicts the familiar, long-suffering O'Brien mother from the perspective of the daugh-ter who dwells on the story of her mother's life after the latter's death. If the high hopes turned sour of "Green Georgette" recall similar stories of disappointment in "The Rug" or "A Demon", the development from matrophilia over matrophobia to attempts at reconciliation traced in "My Two Mothers" echoes the plot lines of "Cords" and "A Rose in the Heart of New York". In spite of these familiar ingredients, however, the tone and atmosphere of "Green Georgette" and "My Two Mothers" are markedly different from the far more negative and fatalistic mood of the earlier stories. In what follows, therefore, I propose to analyse these stories more in detail so as to account for this change in tone. I will argue that the stories do not so much repeat the mother-daughter plot of earlier stories as rewrite this plot through a remarkable rereading of the figure of the mother.

At first sight, "Green Georgette" seems a familiar story of disappointment of a kind with such famous stories as "The Rug", "Irish Revel" and "A Demon". In these stories, dreams and hopes of mother and/or daughter are briefly raised by a luxurious rug, an invitation to a party or a day's outing, yet these never meet the high expectations and the stories typically end on a note of resignation or depression. In "Green Georgette", the mother's desire for social status and recognition and the daughter's longing for glamour and romance come together in their careful preparations for the visit to Mrs. Coughlan who, as the young narrator puts it, "is the cynosure of all" (O'Brien 2011, 112). Other familiar elements in the story are the mother's reminiscences of a stay in America before she married, her hard work on the farm and her tireless serving of a lazy husband, who is prone to "tantrums" and "drinking sprees", even though these "have tapered off a bit" (2011, 115). However, this *Saints and Sinners* story also differs from the earlier stories in significant ways. What stands out, first of all, is the peculiar use of tense and narrative voice in the story. The first section of the story, entitled "Thursday", is told by a first-person narrator in the present tense: "Mama and I have been invited to the Coughlans. It is to be Sunday evening at seven o'clock. I imagine us setting out in good time..." (2011, 111). Although the narrator also dwells on the Coughlans' presence in the village and on how the "miracle" of the invitation came about, she mostly speculates on what the visit will be like, the dresses they will wear, what her mother will say and do:

> Mama says I am to wear my green knitted dress with the scalloped angora edging and carry my cardigan in case it gets chilly on the way home [...] She herself is going to wear her tweedex suit—a fawn, flecked with pink, one that she knitted for an entire winter. I know in her heart that she hopes the conversation will get around to the fact of her knitting it. Indeed, if it is

admired, she will probably offer to knit one for Mrs. Coughlan. She is like that. Certainly she will make Drew a gift of a wallet, or a rug, as she goes to the new technical school at night to master these skills. Nothing would please her more than that they would become friends, the Coughlans coming to us and a big spread of cakes and buns and sausage rolls and caramel custards in their own individual ramekins. (2011, 115)

The second part of the story, "Sunday", chronicles the facts of the visit in the past tense: "We went" (2011, 116). Although the tense-switch heightens the contrast between the bright hopes of the first part and the disappointments of the second, it cannot entirely dispel these hopes and longings. Indeed, their vivid rendering in the present and future tense makes them outshine the disappointment. This is further confirmed when the future tense returns in the evocation of new hopes and desires at the story's close: even though the mother does not give in to the daughter's "insatiable longing for tinned peaches" upon their return, she does "promis[e] that we would have them some Sunday with an orange soufflé, which she had just mastered the recipe for" (2011, 124). Hence, promises, hopes and desire explicitly frame this story of disillusionment, thus testifying to the possibility of renewal. O'Brien's earlier stories, by contrast, are typically framed by disappointment as the initial hopes and longings are already formulated in a past tense, which conveys their essential futility: "Irish Revel" opens symbolically and ominously with "Mary hoped that the rotted front tire would not burst" (2003, 177) and in "The Rug", the first-person narrator starts her reminiscence of the rug with the comment that the smell of new linoleum makes her "both a little disturbed and sad" (2003, 199). The oft-quoted ending of this story further confirms the disappointment:

> As she watched him go down the avenue she wept, not so much for the loss—though the loss was enormous—as for her own foolishness in thinking that someone had wanted to do her a kindness at last. 'We live and learn', she said, as she undid her apron strings, out of habit, and then retied them, slowly and methodically, making a tighter knot. (2003, 206)

The tighter knot aptly sums up the suffering, self-denying mother of O'Brien's early stories, who seeks to suppress the body and its desires, finally succumbing to fatalism, for as the mother in "A Demon" complains, "whenever she looked forward to anything it was always botched" (1990, 134).

If the whole narrative set-up of "Green Georgette" highlights hope over disappointment, the girl's representation of the mother also emphasizes the latter's dreams and desires. As the passage quoted above makes clear, the mother *hopes* for Drew's friendship, *longs* for her talents to be recognized and *dreams* of future feasts. The mother's ceaseless energy is revealed in her tireless making of things, dresses, gloves, purses, meals, as she likes to try new recipes and master new skills. Although traces of self-denial are left in the mother of "Green Georgette", the narrator mostly foregrounds her mother's warmth and generosity, the pride she finds in her hard work and the pleasure she takes in small luxuries such as soft clothes and delicious food. —"Mama's cakes [...] were dusted with caster sugar or a soft-boiled icing that literally melted on the tongue" (2011, 119). There is nothing sinful about food—or the desire for it—in "Green Georgette" and again, that makes for a difference with an earlier story such as "A Demon" where the daughter "offered to make a sacrifice" if the car they booked would come after all: "she would not eat apple tart, she would also decline lemonade if it was offered her, and that night, when they got home, she would get out of bed at least ten times to say several Our Fathers, Hail Marys, and Glorias" (1990, 135). The title of that story also alludes to the demonization of the female body as something that has to be repressed or covered up.

A final difference from the earlier stories concerns the relationship between mother and daughter in "Green Georgette". As we have seen, mother and daughter are very close; they share similar likes and dislikes, hopes and disappointments, moving from "Our being invited is a miracle" to "We were in a gloom" (2011, 113, 124). However, the daughter's accurate reading of her mother's innermost desires, to the extent of predicting her behaviour at the visit, also signal an awareness of her mother as a separate person. Moreover, in her account of the visit, the narrator expresses slight annoyance at her mother's compliance: "Normally she was reserved but her yearning to form a friendship had made her over-accommodating", or "She was too conciliatory, even though she was rattled within" (2011, 120, 124). The final lines of the story further highlight the difference between mother and daughter: while the mother takes comfort in the mundane promise of an orange soufflé, the daughter has much more radical desires: she hopes "for drastic things to occur—for the bullocks to rise up in mutiny, then gore one another, for my father to die in his sleep, for our school to catch fire, and for Mr. Coughlan to take a pistol and shoot his wife, before shooting himself" (2011, 125).

Unlike the symbiotic but suffocating mother-daughter relations in several of O'Brien's early stories, the relationship between mother and daughter in "Green Georgette" is characterized by similarity and difference, by closeness and distance, by mutual understanding and respect. The narrator knows and understands her mother's desires and disappointments, shares some of them, yet ultimately diverges from them, without, however, entirely tearing herself away from the mother in the process. Instead of the pathological mother-daughter bond evoked in most of O'Brien's fiction, "Green Georgette" rather depicts Benjamin's "intersubjective relation" in which the daughter no longer sees the mother as an object, whether of fantasy, need or blame. Instead, she recognizes her as "an independent subject", "as a separate person who is like [her] yet distinct", "different and yet alike" (Benjamin 1988, 23). Indeed, as we have seen, the daughter represents the mother as a desiring subject, with wishes and desires that partly run parallel to her own desires—when they involve food, glamour, clothes—but ultimately diverge from them, as in the ironic juxtaposition of the mother's rather mundane promise of a delicious cake and the far more glamorous dreams of the daughter.

The challenge of seeing the mother as a subject also informs "My Two Mothers", even though the title hints at the opposite, and more familiar, binary pattern of idealization and defilement of the mother. This binary also informs the story's plot as it chronicles the daughter's familiar trajectory from symbiosis with the mother—"we were inseparable"—through separation and estrangement to attempts at reconciliation. In keeping with the status of this splitting as an unconscious fantasy, the devouring mother haunts the daughter's "dreams" even as the "archetypal" image of the omnipotent mother determines her waking life. Freudian theories are explicitly invoked in the daughter's characterization of their early life together as a "symbiosis". Later, she claims to "banish" the mother, "just as in a fairy tale", while Gothic imagery frames her desire to uncover the mother's secret, "like finding a hidden room in a house I thought I knew" (2011, 173, 179). These references hint at the daughter-narrator's awareness of the fantastic nature of this binary, which does not necessarily have a bearing in reality. As the narrator notes:

> We lived for a time in such a symbiosis that there might never have been a husband or other children, except that there were. *We all* sat at the same fire, ate the same food, and when a gift of a box of chocolates arrived looked with longing at a picture on the back, choosing our favourites in our minds.

That box might not be opened for a year. Life was frugal and unpredictable, the harvests and the ripening hay subject to the hazards of rain and ruin. (2011, 170, my italics)

The narrator thus acknowledges the partly fabricated nature of her memories of symbiosis as they are contradicted by the knowledge that the whole family shared in the joys as well as the hardships of family life. As the stuff of fairy-tales and Freudian theories, the fantasies of the good and the bad mother come to be seen as a restrictive binary which the narrator longs to transcend, yet seems doomed to repeat, much like the recurring dream of the devouring mother which she longs to leave behind: "I wait for the dream that leads us *beyond* the ghastly white spittoon and the metal razor, to fields and meadows, up onto the mountain, that bluish realm, half earth, half sky" (2011, 180). Even though this wish is presented as a daydream at the end of the story, I will argue that the narrative itself already enacts this movement *beyond* destructive maternal splitting.

First, although the narrator of "Two Mothers" refers to her mother as "real mother and archetypal mother", she creates a far more personal and mundane mother figure than the larger-than-life maternal icons that figure in "Cords" and "A Rose in the Heart of New York". As several critics have noted, the nameless "mother" in "A Rose" is staged as an incarnation of Mother Ireland and the Virgin Mary (Graham 1996; Mooney 2009). In the harrowing birthing scene which opens that story, the "poor poor mother" is cast as a veritable sacrificial figure: brutalized by her husband ("prized apart [...] rammed through and told to open up"), worn down by domestic drudgery, and now bloodied and wounded, symbolically linked to the half-cooked goose the drunken men downstairs have torn apart (2003, 375–6). The rather overblown imagery of the first pages connects the mother not just with the Virgin Mary but also with Christ: "The mother roared again and said this indeed was her vinegar and gall. She bit into the crucifix and dented it further. She could feel her mouth and eyelids being stitched, too; she was no longer a lovely body, she was a vehicle for pain and insult" (2003, 379). How different then, the much more personal tone of "My Two Mothers" in which the first-person narrator recalls very specific details about her mother:

Her fingers and nails smelt of food—meal for hen and chickens, gruel for calves and bread for us—whereas her body smelt of myriad things, depending on whether she was happy or unhappy, and the most pleasant was a lingering smell of a perfume from the cotton wad that she sometimes tucked under her brassiere. At Christmas time it was a smell of fruitcake soaked with grog and the sugary smell of white icing, stiff as starch, which she applied with the rapture of an artist. (2011, 169)

The emphasis on food and the maternal body is of course familiar from "A Rose", where it served to symbolize the pre-Oedipal mother-daughter symbiosis: "the food was what united them, eating off the same plate, using the same spoon, watching one another's chews, feeling the food as it went down the other neck" (2003, 380). Yet, in "My Two Mothers", the mother's body is evoked in a far more detailed and particular way. Significant too is the daughter's recognition of the mother's feelings: this already marks her out as a subject, rather than as an object of veneration. As in "Green Georgette", the mother is primarily depicted as a warm and generous person, with a love of food, clothes and luxuries, shared by the daughter. On summer evenings, for instance, they don their best clothes and take a walk:

Those walks bordered on enchantment, what with neighbours in some sudden comradery, greeting us profusely, and always, irrationally, the added possibility that we might walk out of our old sad existence [...] On those walks she invariably spoke of visitors that were bound to come in the summer and the dainty dishes she would prepare for them. There was a host of recipes she had not yet tried. (2011, 171)

Although the shared indulgence in walks, daydreams, food and small luxuries recalls those of "A Rose", they do not come with the strictures that invariably dampen enjoyment in the early stories. In "A Rose", the girl's enjoyment of an orange cake her mother has made elicits the warning that she'll get fat, and a gift of a "most beautiful lipstick in a ridged gold case" is admired for a while, but then shut away in its case where it "dried out and developed a peculiar shape" (2003, 384, 388). The emphasis in these early stories is on self-denial, whereas the emphasis in "Green Georgette" and "My Two Mothers" is on small pleasures and enjoyment in spite of harsh circumstances.

However, also in "My Two Mothers" this childhood happiness is followed by a period of rebellion and escape on the part of the daughter and of disappointment on the part of the mother, who openly disapproves of her daughter's writing, her marriage and subsequent divorce. As in

"A Rose", further, the narrator seeks a reconciliation through another form of maternal splitting which postulates a more rebellious, passionate mother—another 'good' mother—under the apparent, conventional and conservative one, the 'bad' mother she quarrels with. In "A Rose", the daughter thus hopes to unearth "a long-sustained hidden passion" of the mother, which would allow them "to be true at last", with no more need to "hide from one another's gaze" (2003, 398). What the daughter wants, in short, is for the mother to be like herself and, hence, for her marriage, divorce and love life to be accepted at last. Yet, the mother quells all such hopes when she sternly states that "there was no such thing as love between the sexes [...] there was only one kind of love and that was a mother's love for her child" (2003, 399).

In "My Two Mothers" too, the narrator senses a "secret" inside her mother which she hopes to uncover (2011, 175). Significantly, the secret is linked both to a lost child—a pregnancy aborted in ominous circumstances—and to a lost sweetheart. Unlike the daughter in "A Rose", the narrator does not want to pry the secret from her mother in a conversation. Instead, she tries to find this secret self through acts of rereading. She rereads both her own memories of her mother and the hundreds of letters her mother has sent her over the years. "Her letters were deeper, sadder than I remembered", writes the narrator, "but what struck me most was their hunger and their thirst" (2011, 175). The narrator uncovers in these letters her mother's wishes and desires—for a trip to London, for her daughter's return, for a chandelier or newly made jam she can offer to her daughter: "Her letter kept wishing that she could hand me a pot of clear jelly over a hedge and see me taste and swallow it" (2011, 176–7). What these letters reveal, therefore, is neither the mother's hidden self, nor her underlying similarity to her daughter. Rather they paint a picture of the mother that largely confirms the daughter's earliest memories of her: that of a warm, generous, energetic woman who wants to enjoy life in spite of the hardships and who expresses her love for her daughter through food, confidences and small luxuries.

If in "A Rose" the girl had only wanted for the mother to understand and accept her life, the narrator in "My Two Mothers" comes to recognize a similar desire for acceptance in her mother—"a woman desperately trying to explain herself and to be understood" (2011, 176). This mutuality recalls again Benjamin's intersubjective relationship which is founded on "the need for mutual recognition, the necessity of recognizing as well as being recognized by the other", hence "the child has a need to see the mother, too, as an independent subject, not simply as the 'external world' or an adjunct of his ego" (Benjamin 1988, 23). Moreover, by recognizing the mother, the daughter also comes to understand herself: "what I admired in her most was her unceasing labour, allowing for no hour of rest, no day of rest. She had set me an example by her resilience and a strange childish gratitude for things" (O'Brien 2011, 179). What the story also, be it more implicitly, suggests is that the writer-narrator owes some of her creativity and writing skills to her mother, even though her literary career has always been a bone of contention between them: "She who professed disgust at the written word wrote daily, bulletins that ranged from the pleading to the poetic, the philosophic and the common-place" (2011, 175).

Still, "My Two Mothers" ends, like "A Rose", with the death of the mother symbolizing a final failure of communication. In "A Rose", "an envelope addressed to her in her mother's handwriting" only contains "some trinkets, a gold sovereign, and some money" and although the daughter desperately "wanted something, some communiqué", "there was no such thing" (2003, 404). The mother's death radically stops all understanding or reconciliation: "A new wall had arisen, stronger and sturdier than before [...] silence filled the room and there was a vaster silence beyond, as if the house itself had died or had been carefully put down to sleep" (2003, 404). In "My Two Mothers", the mother's death is also symbolized by an "unfinished" last letter (2011, 181). Yet, this ending is not as final. The narrator keeps the conversation ongoing, by continuing to reread her mother in memories and letters, all the while waiting for the understanding that "that leads us beyond the ghastly white spittoon and the metal razor, to fields and meadows, up onto the mountain [...] to begin our journey all over again, to live our lives as they should have been lived, happy, trusting and free of shame" (2011, 181). As in "Green Georgette", moreover, the present tense used in this passage is future-directed and emphasizes hopes and dreams over failures and disappointments.

In short, both "Green Georgette" and "My Two Mothers" realize subtle revisions of the mother-daughter relationships even within the confines of familiar plotlines. As we have seen, the larger-than-life, archetypal mother figures of the early stories are replaced by more down-to-earth and personalized mothers, who disturb the dualistic patterns of fairy-tales and Freudian myths. More in general too, the binary dialectic of illusion and disappointment that is a familiar one in O'Brien's fiction is reconfigured through the narrative set-up which emphasizes dreams over despair. This emphasis also affects the representation of the mother, who emerges above all as a desiring subject, propelled by dreams, hopes, desires and love. In recognizing their mother as a subject—rather than as the object of love or hate—the daughters also come to an acceptance of the differences and similarities that bind them to their mothers. While they share this investment in dreams and are similarly marked by strong desires, the objects of their arduous dreams are shown to be different, determined as they are by the contexts that divide them: the rural, Irish, Catholic, and domestic world of the mother versus the urban, cosmopolitan, secular and literary life of the daughter. By thus "contextualising" her mother's life, as Adalgisa Giorgio put it (Giorgio 2002, 29), the daughter comes to better understand it, even while condemning the "shame" that sadly curtailed it (O'Brien 2011, 181). Moreover, the daughter's recognition of her mother's different life is matched by the mother "forgiv[ing] [the daughter's] transgressions, whatever they might have been" (2011, 179). Hence, by recognizing her mother's desires as similar and different from her own, the daughter is able to establish an intersubjective relationship with the mother that moves her beyond the paralyzing fantasies of the omnipotent and castrating mother.

Moreover, although the stories still show how high hopes often end in disappointment, the act of desiring itself is revalorized as one of defiance and "resilience". A telling story in this respect concerns the mother's two dogs in "My Two Mothers":

> She always had two dogs [...] They were named Laddie and Rover and always met with the same fate. They had a habit of following cars in the avenue and one, either one, got killed while the other grieved and mourned, refused food, even refused meat [...] and in a short time died and was buried with its comrade. She would swear never to get another pair of dogs, yet in a matter of months she was writing off to a breeder several counties away and two little puppies in a cardboard box, couched in a nest of dank straw, would arrive by bus and presently be given the identical names of Laddie and Rover. She gloried in describing how mischievous they were, the things they ate, pranks they were up to. (2011, 177–8)

This little story highlights the mother's stubborn defiance of "fate" in her desire for new dogs, even as she knows that they are likely to be killed again. It is this defiant investment in dreams, hopes and desires in the face of disappointment that Voltaire valorized when he wrote that "Illusion is the queen of the human heart", a quote which the daughter reads to her uncomprehending mother in "My Two Mothers". Not reason, but dreams and illusions are what makes us human for Voltaire and, as the ending of "My Two Mothers" shows, they can even sustain us beyond death.

In *The Shadow of the Other*, Jessica Benjamin calls for a new psychoanalytic theory which would "theorize maternal psychic work as an aspect of subjectivity" and would see the mother as "more than merely a mirror to the child's activity" (1998, 57). Only when the mother's status as a sexed subject is given expression in the symbolic economy, she argues, can we move beyond the unconscious fantasies that imprison the mother in the realm of the imaginary. As we have seen, "Green Georgette" and "My Two Mothers" already make a start on such symbolization by reconfiguring the mother-daughter relation as an intersubjective relationship, based on the daughter's recognition of the mother as a desiring subject, who is at once like and unlike herself. Within an Irish context, the stories' staging of the mother's desires and enjoyments gains an added significance as they rewrite the traditional Catholic iconography of the pure and self-denying mother. As Gerardine Meaney has noted, the idolization of the Virgin Mary entailed a "refusal to countenance any representation of the mother's body as origin of life" (2010, 8). This "derealisation of motherhood in the ideology of the southern Irish state", she argued, created a culture that sought to "exclude the sexual, maternal, nurturing, ever-hungry body" (Meaney 2010, 10). "Green Georgette" and "My Two Mothers" clearly break with that repression, by representing the mother as, indeed, hungry, nurturing, and sensual—if not, or not explicitly, sexual. The mothers in these stories, then, are neither the saints nor the sinners referred to in the title, but rather ordinary human beings, "desperately trying [...] to be understood" (O'Brien 2011, 176).

CLAIRE KEEGAN'S REBELLIOUS SUBJECTS

The author of two collections of short stories, *Antarctica* (1999) and *Walk the Blue Fields* (2007), and one long short story published separately, *Foster* (2010), Claire Keegan is one of Ireland's most promising short story writers. A measure of the critical acclaim she has received is the almost routine comparison that is made between her work and that of John McGahern, one of the grand masters of the genre (Kiberd 2004; Enright 2007; Battersby 2010). What invites this comparison, first of all, is the rural Irish setting of most of her short stories. Although *Antarctica* also contains stories set in Britain and the USA, the most intensely felt stories of this collection are set in rural Ireland and the same holds true for *Foster* and all but one of the stories in *Walk the Blue Fields*. These Irish stories feature outlying family farms, village priests, hard-working mothers and feckless fathers. Only small, sly details reveal that this is not mid-twentieth-century Ireland we are reading about, but the Ireland of the 1990s, in which people have avocado starters at a wedding, airports smell "of perfume and roasted coffee beans, expensive things" and a Chinaman in a caravan rivals the local priest (Keegan 2007, 24, 13, 34). In addition, Keegan seems to share with McGahern an interest in what O'Connor has called the "moment of change", when a development is crystallized, a new awareness dawns, or a new turn is taken. As O'Connor famously put it: "It's a bright light falling on an action in such a way that the landscape of that person's life assumes a new shape. Something happens—the iron bar is bent—and anything that happens to that person afterwards, they never feel the same about again" (cited in Ingman 2009, 147). This concentration of a story on a particular moment or scene which grounds characters, development and plot also comes, as in McGahern's stories, with an understated, almost minimalist style in which meaning is conveyed through suggestion and subtle symbolism. Following Joyce's strategy of "scrupulous meanness", context, motivation and explanations are suppressed and the reader has to fill in the gaps. As Keegan has put it:

> [The short story] is very difficult. It's very challenging. It's intense. The level of intensity is very high. You've got to leave most of what could be said, out. It's a discipline of omission. You are truly saying very little. People say very little anyway. We talk a great deal, of course, but we actually say very little to each other. I think the short story is a very fine place to explore that silence between people, and the loneliness between people and the love that is there. And I think they all come organically out of the short story. (Keegan 2009)

However much Claire Keegan may owe to John McGahern, James Joyce, or even William Trevor (Fitzgerald-Hoyt 2015, 280), her short fiction also betrays the influence of the other writer discussed in this chapter,

Edna O'Brien. As Éilís Ní Dhuibhne notes in her review of *Walk the Blue Fields*,

> [Keegan's] interest in flowers, in colours, in natural beauty, finds plenty of parallels in O'Brien's writing. The account of the wedding [in the title story], with the emphasis on its more amusing aspects, and its precise and witty descriptions of the food consumed, remind me of the hilarious hotel scenes in 'Irish Revel'. (Ní Dhuibhne 2008)

Like O'Brien, Keegan often infuses her stories with powerful symbols which at times escape the dominant, realist mode. In O'Brien, they often border on the grotesque or the mythic; in Keegan, they cross over into the surreal, as in "Night of the Quicken Trees" or "The Forrester's Daughter". Most important for my purposes is, of course, the shared concern of O'Brien and Keegan with mother-daughter relationships, as seen from the perspective of the daughter. Indeed, most of the Irish stories from *Antarctica* as well as "A Parting Gift" and "The Forrester's Daughter" from *Walk the Blue Fields* tell stories of young girls, trying to negotiate their identity within the confines of family and local community in rural Ireland. This plot is revisited in *Foster* as a young girl describes a summer she spent on the farm of her mother's relatives. As in O'Brien's stories, mothers are crucial figures in the girl's development. Yet, while O'Brien's heavily symbolic stories are bent on dramatizing the underlying psychic structures and archetypal myths that govern individual behaviour, Keegan's more realistic stories are less bound by Freudian categories and Catholic or nationalist iconography. Instead, her stories frame the mother-daughter relationship in the light of the gendered hierarchies and power structures that still shape individual identity and family relations in patriarchal societies. Even though these patriarchal strictures may appear inflexible and deterministic in Keegan's seemingly timeless rural Ireland, her revision of the twentieth-century mother-daughter plot does open up the possibility of change.

Before turning to the daughter stories, however, I will briefly consider two stories, "Surrender" and "Dark Horses", which encapsulate Keegan's position within the Irish short story tradition. In these stories, Keegan pays tribute to, and moves beyond, the two major influences on her work: John McGahern and Edna O'Brien. As explained in the subtitle, "Surrender" is inspired by an anecdote in McGahern's *Memoir* which describes how his cold, authoritarian father ate a whole box of oranges as a final act of indulgence before "surrendering" himself to marriage. In the story, Keegan cleverly shifts attention from this selfish, gluttonous act to the scenes that precede it. They show the sergeant cruelly belittling everyone he meets: the guard in the barracks, a young couple he meets on the road, and, finally, a little boy in the shop where he buys the oranges:

> The sergeant felt the boy's hungry gaze. He took the tissue off each one [orange] and lifted it to his nose before he pushed back his cape and reached into his pocket for the money [...] She counted out the money on the kitchen table, and when he offered her something extra for the loaf, she looked at the boy. The boy's face was paler now. His skin was chalky. When he saw his mother wrapping the loaf in the brown paper, he began to cry.
> 'Mammy,' he wailed. 'My bread!'
> 'Hush, *a leanbh*. I'll make you another,' she said. 'I'll do it just as soon as the sergeant leaves.'(Keegan 2007, 113)

The power triangle this scene evokes is a familiar one: the sergeant cruelly asserts his authority by flaunting the oranges before the boy and buying the fresh loaf which the boy's mother had earlier promised her child. As Ní Dhuibhne points out, the mother, though kind to the boy, gives in to the sergeant's authority, "betray[ing] her own child, for money and a bullying man"(Ní Dhuibhne 2008). As we will see, the mother's collusion in patriarchal power, a recurring feature in twentieth-century mother-daughter plots, also figures in Keegan's stories, even though the daughters will not always so easily be defeated as the little boy in "Surrender". This is already suggested by Keegan's rewriting of O'Brien's patriarchs in "Dark Horses". The narrator protagonist of this story, named Brady after Cait's father in *The Country Girls*, has all the characteristics of the drunken, feckless husbands of O'Brien's fiction. Yet unlike the mother in O'Brien's stories, his girlfriend has left him and is unlikely to ever come back. In those two stories, in short, Keegan acknowledges the continuing hold of traditional patriarchal patterns and their literary representation, while also highlighting changes that have taken place in contemporary Ireland. As we will see, this tension between tradition and change, acquiescence and rebellion also informs Keegan's mother-daughter stories.

Given Keegan's formal interest in the moment of change, it is perhaps not surprising that most of her daughter stories revolve around that crucial phase in any child's development: the threshold between childhood and adolescence. This is the focus of "Men and Women", "Storms", and "The Ginger Rogers Sermon" from *Antarctica*, "The Forrester's Daughter" from *Walk the Blue Fields*, and *Foster*. "Quare Name for a Boy" and "The Parting Gift", to the contrary, centre on another threshold: the movement from adolescence into adulthood. In the first story, the narrator is about to become a mother herself and considers anew her relationship to her mother and grandmother. In "The Parting Gift", the 18-year-old daughter is moving to the USA, to escape her tyrannical and abusive father. This movement represents a second attempt to achieve the individuation she failed to realize in her teens, blighted as they were by sexual abuse. Trying to recall one positive thing about her father before she leaves, she remembers:

> It was before you had begun to go into his room. He had gone into the village and stopped at the garage for petrol. The girl at the pumps came up to him and told her she was the brightest girl in the class, the best at every subject, until you came along. He'd come back from the village and repeated this, and he was proud because you were brighter than the Protestant's daughter. (Keegan 2007, 12)

What all of Keegan's daughters share, indeed, is that they are—or were— eager, clever and imaginative young girls with ambitions that initially cut across the gender divide. In "The Forrester's Daughter", the girl of the title comes home from school, telling her mother:

> that she solved a word problem in mathematics, that long ago Christina Columbus discovered the earth was round. She says she'll let the Taoiseach marry her and then changes her mind. She will not marry at all but become the captain of a ship. She sees herself standing on deck with a storm blowing the red lemonade out of her cup. (2007, 66)

In "The Ginger Rogers Sermon", the protagonist proudly describes how she joins in the work of her father and the other lumberjacks in summer even though her mother "says it is no job for a girl" (1999, 187). And the slightly naïve narrator in "Men and Women" wishes that she will become like her brother and father when she grows up, since they are being served while she and her mother do all the chores in the house: "I wish I was big. I wish I could sit beside the fire and be called up to dinner and draw triangles, lick the nibs of special pencils, sit behind the wheel of a car and have someone open gates that I could drive through" (1999, 25).

Yet, as the stories proceed to show, the movement into adolescence requires learning about gendered norms and expectations, about how to behave as a girl in a patriarchal society. In the rural world of the stories society is still strictly divided along gender lines: women work within the house, men conduct their affairs outside; men drive cars, women don't; sons are allowed to study, girls have to help. That this division is a hierarchical and lopsided is what the girls increasingly come to realize, witness the following exchange between mother and daughter in "Men and Women": "'How come they do nothing?' I ask [...] 'They're men,' she says, as if this explains everything. Because it is Christmas, I say nothing" (1999, 24). As the narrator of this story gradually comes to learn, the privileges of manhood do not just entail being served, but also being entitled to sleep around, to boss and belittle women—in fact treating them little better than the farm animals (O'Connor 2010, 152). When her brother and father discuss the women at the New Year's Eve party, the narrator notes "I think about the mart, all the men at the rails bidding for heifers and ewes" (1999, 33) and in *Foster*, the father says of his daughter: "She'll ate but you can work her" (2010, 12). As in "Surrender", moreover, mothers often seem to collude in this patriarchal set-up, by acting as the guardians of gender divisions. They teach their daughters to do the chores around the house, to serve and obey the men. They also instruct them into the codes and norms of proper femininity. When the narrator in "The Ginger Rogers Sermon" gets her first period, her mother warns her: "Don't let yer father see them [the towels]" and the narrator comments resentfully on "Her always hiding women away, like we're forbidden" (1999, 192). Resentment and anger at the mother are, as we have seen, common reactions of daughters when confronted with the submissive and secondary position of women in patriarchal family structures. As Hirsch and other critics have argued, the daughter's rejection of the mother can be read as part of a desperate attempt to avoid repeating her fate.

This also the plot we find in "The Parting Gift", the story that stands out among Keegan's daughter's stories because of its different vantage-point and its striking second-person narration. As the long-suffering wife of an abusive and cruel husband, the mother in this story has literally forced her daughter to take her place, by sending her to her father for his monthly allowance of sex. The girl is now poised for escape and ponders her mother's situation: "In her bedroom your mother is moving things around, opening and closing doors. You wonder what it will be like for her when you leave. Part of you doesn't care. She talks through the door" (2007, 3). The title of the story refers to the money the father does not give to his daughter when she leaves, even though the mother believes he will. Yet, the girl has taken her own "gift"—and exacted revenge—by secretly selling one of her father's heifers to pay for her ticket to New York: "She's a red chestnut with one white stocking. You sold her to buy your ticket but she will not be collected until tomorrow. That was the arrangement" (2007, 10). The story ends ambivalently poised between hope and despair as the girl locks herself in a toilet cubicle at the airport to cry: "You pass bright hand-basins, mirrors. Someone asks are you all right— *such a stupid question*—but you do not cry until you have opened and closed another door, until you have safely locked yourself inside your stall" (2007, 13). Although the girl has taken revenge and managed to escape, she will take her trauma with her. As Vivian Lynch has argued, the second-person narration "suggests a profound emotional detachment in the narrator" (2015, 140). The girl's inability to narrate her own story in the first person points indeed to her failure to realize a confident and independent sense of self.

Yet this familiar mother-daughter plot, which finds predecessors in women's writing throughout the twentieth century, is not repeated in Keegan's other daughter stories. Unlike in "The Parting Gift", the daughter's acts of rebellion are supported and even enabled by the mother in the other daughter stories. Hence, there is no longer any need for the daughter to reject the mother—along with patriarchal norms and strictures—in order to carve out her own identity. Instead, the relationship between mother and daughter is strengthened and the daughter seems ready to enact change, to live rural life with a difference.

In "The Forrester's Daughter", for instance, the mother takes revenge for her husband's betrayal of their daughter's trust by telling the 'story' of her adulterous affair to the neighbours, thus upsetting both the power relations in the family and the iron Irish law of keeping everything within the family unit and not letting "the neighbours" know (2007, 82). In "Men and Women", the daughter is similarly empowered by her mother's rebellion after the New Year's village dance where she has been treated with even more than the usual contempt by her philandering husband. For the first time, the mother refuses to get out and open the gates for her husband as they drive up the lane to the farm and her children follow suit. When the father gets out of the car at last, the mother takes the wheel herself (only the daughter knows that she has secretly been watching driving programmes on television). The closing paragraphs of the story read:

> My father is getting smaller. It feels as though the trees are moving, the chestnut tree whose green hands shelter us in summer is backing away. Then I realize it's the car. It's us. We are rolling, sliding backwards without a hand brake and I am not out there putting the stone behind the wheel. And that is when Mammy takes the steering. She slides over into my father's seat and puts her foot on the brake. We stop going backwards. She revs up the engine and puts the car in gear, the gearbox grinds, she hasn't the clutch in far enough, but then there's a splutter and we're moving. Mammy is taking us forward, past the Santa sign, past my father, who has stopped singing, now through the open gates. She drives us through the fresh snow. I can smell the pines. When I look back, my father is standing there watching our taillights. The snow is falling on him, on his bare head while he stands there, clutching his hat. (1999, 34)

Although it describes but a small act of resistance, the symbolism of this passage highlights its epiphanic potential for the daughter whose perspective on life has fundamentally changed: Santa and the father are left behind, while the fresh snow and open gates suggest new hopes for the future.

In another story from *Antarctica*, "The Ginger Rogers Sermon", the mother shifts the blame for the lumberjack's suicide from her young daughter (who seduced him) to the man himself by pointing the finger to his lack of dancing skills. Hence, she insists on "teaching Eugene [her son] as a precaution, as if knowing these steps will carry him through, prevent him from tying a noose around his neck later on" (1999, 200). The whole family starts dancing in the sitting room, with mother and daughter "mov[ing] him [Eugene] into the places he should go". In the dancing, brother and sister parodically stage the gender roles that are expected of them: "The last picture I remember is the roll-on flying across the room with the snap of elastic and Eugene asking, 'Can I interest you in a snog at the gale wall?' as he swings me in a perfect twist" (1999, 201). Dancing is not just a liberating performance for the mother—witness the discarded roll-on—but also an empowering one for the daughter as its parodic enactment of gender roles may enable the daughter to survive in a gendered world.

"Storms", on the other hand, tells the story of a mother who is not herself able to survive in this world, but nevertheless ensures that her daughter will. While the extremely sensitive mother loses her bearings after her own mother's death and succumbs to madness, she also protects her daughter

by telling her stories, making her see the stars, and teaching her about difference: "She told me about my father, how he'd bruised her for fifteen
years, because she was not the same as other women. She taught me the
difference between loving and liking somebody. She said she didn't like
me any more than him because I had the same cruel eyes" (1999, 66). The
mother shows her daughter that she is both like and unlike her, and she
also directs her to her dual inheritance: from father as well as mother. The
daughter starts to explore the heritage of her "father's people", a box with
old books and papers, but also combines it with her mother's knowledge
of stars, animals and burns (1999, 62). The daughter concludes her story
as follows: "I run the house now. The last man who said I was old enough
got scalded. My mother always said there was nothing as bad as a burn.
And she was right. It's turning out that I'm taking no nonsense from
anybody." And although she proudly claims her father's "cruel" eyes, she
visits her mother every Sunday: "Maybe I need a little of what my mother
has. Just a little. I take a small share of it for my own protection [...] you
have to face the worst possible case to be able for anything" (1999, 68).

This emphasis on matrilineal heritage, on being part of a line of mothers
and daughters, is a central element in most of Keegan's daughter stories.
In "The Ginger Rogers Sermon" this is realized through the metaphor
of the dancing, being passed on from mother to daughter. In "Men and
Women" and in *Foster*, the household duties shared by mother, or foster-
mother, and daughter are evoked both as rituals being passed on from
generation to generation and as moments of mother-daughter bonding, as
when the narrator of "Men and Women" describes their Christmas morning ritual:

> Nobody's up except Mammy and me. We are the early birds. We make tea,
> eat toast and chocolate fingers for breakfast, then she puts on her best apron,
> the one dappled with strawberries, and turns on the radio, chops onions and
> parsley while I grate a plain loaf into crumbs. We stuff the turkey and waltz
> around the kitchen. (1999, 23)

In "Quare Name for a Boy", the older—and pregnant—daughter decides
to return to rural Ireland, taking over the ways and knowledge of her
"female relatives", but with a difference:

> Green wood hisses in the grate, the resin oozing out from under the bark.
> Lines of connecting sparks, what my grandmother called soldiers, march
> across the soot. She said that was a sign of bad weather [...] I will live out of

a water barrel and check the skies. I will learn fifteen types of wind and know the weight of tomorrow's rain by the rustle of the sycamores. Make nettle soup and dandelion bread, ask for nothing. And I won't comfort you. I will not be the woman who shelters her man same as he's a boy. That part of my people ends with me. (1999, 107)

This idea of similarity with a difference which is explored here is in fact a crucial one in all of Keegan's daughter stories. It applies not just to the acts of rebellion which empower the daughter to do differently or to the matrilineal heritage with a twist which the daughter takes on, but it also characterizes the relationship between mother and daughter in general. For if the emphasis on similarity and the shared Christmas rituals in "Men and Women" might seem to suggest a pre-Oedipal symbiotic mother-daughter bond, familiar from Edna O'Brien's stories, this is belied by the mutual respect that also marks this relationship. The daughters in these stories do not see the mothers as omnipotent objects, to be feared or loved, possessed or rejected, but rather as subjects and individuals in their own right. In "Men and Women", for instance, the young girl—unlike her brother—comes to recognize her mother's feelings at the New Year's Party and tries to step in and "rescue" her (Keegan 1999, 29). In "The Ginger Rogers Sermon", daughter and mother enact another gendered ritual every Saturday when they are dressing up for an evening out:

> In the kitchen, Ma sets her hair. We call it the Salon [...] I hand her an old *Woman's Weekly* and imagine it's *Vogue*. The last page is ripped out so Da can't read about women's problems. 'Do you want a coffee?' I shout above the noise. There was never any coffee in that house. She stays under there, deaf and talking out loud like an old person, and I hand her a cup of frothy Ovaltine [...] Pot Belly, I call her. 'Are ya going dancing now, Pot Belly? Where's the beauty contest, Pot Belly?' [...] She calls me the Terror: 'Shut up, ya Terror.' (1999, 185)

This clearly points to what Benjamin's intersubjective relation of "*mutual* recognition" in which the other is recognized as "a separate person who is like us yet distinct" (Benjamin 1988, 23).

The message of hope and change which most of Keegan's daughter stories thus convey is also supported by their narrative set-up. With the exception of "The Forrester's Daughter", they are all told by a confident first-person narrator, the opposite of the split and alienated "you" used in "The Parting Gift". As in the first part of Edna O'Brien's "Green Georgette", large parts of these stories are told in the present tense. In "The Ginger Rogers Sermon" and "Storms", this present tense can be interpreted as the fairly conventional historical present, since it is embedded within past-tense narration. Such tense shifts in narratives are usually recognized as having a "highlighting impact", in terms of an "enhanced vividness, dramatic effect or presentification" (Cohn 1999, 99) and in these stories they foreground the lasting importance of the changes and events that unfold: the lumberjack's suicide in "The Ginger Rogers Sermon" and the mother's madness in "Storms". In *Foster*, "Men and Women" and "Quare Name for a Boy", however, the first-person present tense is used throughout the story. This type of "simultaneous narration", as Cohn first called it, is recognized as "an unnatural form of narration" which "doesn't have a clear, real-world analogue" (DelConte 2007, 429), and which seems to violate the general rule that "narrative is past, always past" (Scholes 1980, 210). Distinct from interior monologue which directly transcribes a character's thoughts in the first person, simultaneous narration has the first-person narrator relate the events as they happen. Although this narrative mode is readily naturalized in the reading process (Fludernik 2002, 256), narratologists have highlighted some of its special functions and effects, which Keegan also cleverly draws upon in her daughter stories.

First, as Fleishman points out, "the range of temporal references that the PR tense can have is greater than that of any other tense category" (Fleishman 1990, 34). It can refer to the present, the past and the future, as in the case of the "irrealis present" which represents "fantasies and imagined dream-scenarios" (Cohn 1999, 107). In addition, the present tense is characterized by an aspectual fluidity, which can make it difficult to decide whether "it signif[ies] the singular moment of the speech-act or its durative-iterative context" (Cohn 1999, 106). In her use of the present tense, Keegan plays especially with these hazy borders between the 'now' and the 'often'. On the one hand, the present tense evokes the sense of ritual, habit and cyclical time present in the rural surroundings but also the domestic duties of the women or the recurring social events of dances and marts. Consider the opening paragraph of "Men and Women":

> My father takes me places. He has artificial hips so he needs me to open the gates [...] I open the gates, my father freewheels the Volkswagen through, I close the gates behind him and hop back into the passenger seat. To save petrol, he starts the car on the run, gathering speed on the slope before the road, and then we're off to wherever my father is going on that particular day. (Keegan 1999, 19)

Almost imperceptibly the iterative present changes into the singular present to describe the transformative experiences on New Year's Eve: "For the first time in my life, I have some power. I can butt in and take over, rescue and be rescued" (1999, 29). The multiple semantic possibilities of the present tense allow not just for an easy slide from the now into the often, but also for a surprisingly fluid transition between the often and the now, between fixed habits and the changes that are made. In this way, Keegan's use of simultaneous narration supports the hopeful dimension of the daughter stories which open up the possibility that action and change, however small, are possible, even within conservative rural communities, seemingly fixed in timeless rituals and rigid habits.

A second important aspect of simultaneous narration is the radical absence of retrospection. The temporal distance between experiencing and narrating, the hallmark of traditional past-tense fictional autobiography, is "literally reduced to zero: the moment of narration *is* the moment of experience, the narrating self *is* the experiencing self" (Cohn 1999, 107). As a result, the possibility of a backward glance is cancelled out. In opposition to the disillusionment that governs McGahern's and O'Brien's early stories, Keegan's simultaneous narrations thus underscore hope and the possibility of change. The future is left open as a realm where dreams, hopes and resolutions may be realized, as is further indicated by the shift to the future tense—"I will"—at the end of *Foster* and "Quare Name for a Boy".

In "Men and Women" and *Foster*, thirdly, the simultaneity of first-person present-tense narration also reinforces the naïvety and confusion of the narrators, as they carefully observe an adult reality they do not fully understand. As narratologists have noted, simultaneous narration radically dispenses with the narrative functions of interpretation and evaluation, instead transferring these roles to the reader (DelConte 2007, 430). Through these naïve narrators, Keegan engages the reader's cooperation in decoding these descriptions and supplying the necessary interpretation and evaluation. Especially in *Foster* this dimension of simultaneous narration is used to great effect. Since this story brings together many of the formal and thematic characteristics of Keegan's daughter stories, I will analyse it in some more detail in the remainder of this chapter.

"Foster" was first published in *The New Yorker* in February 2010. An only slightly revised version was then brought out as a separate book by Faber later in the year. In an interview for *The Scotsman*, Keegan objects to the term "novella" being applied to the book and calls it instead a "long short story", which she felt to be the right form considering the length of time—one summer—the story covers (Black 2010). The rural Irish setting of the story seems again timeless and unchanging, even though a small reference to the death of Northern-Irish hunger strikers points to a more precise historical moment: the summer of 1981. In *Foster*, the narrator— a 10-year old girl—is quite literally dropped by her father with relatives of her mother for the duration of the summer, while her mother has yet another child. Careful observation and registration are the narrator's life-line as she learns to negotiate this different life and, by extension, life in a gendered, patriarchal society. Thus, her first impression of her relatives' farm suggests that this might be a good place—clean, warm, well-cared for: "Under the smell of baking there's some disinfectant, some bleach. She lifts a rhubarb tart out of the oven and puts it on the bench to cool: syrup to the point of bubbling over, thin leaves of pastry baked into the crust" (Keegan 2010, 8). She concludes, "this is a different type of house. Here there is room, and time to think. There may even be money to spare" (2010, 13). Like the naïve narrator in "Men and Women", whom she strongly resembles in age and sensibility, the girl's observations primarily teach her about differences: differences between men and women, but also differences among families and households. Thus, she notes that Mrs. Kinsella—mostly called "the woman"—is like her own mother but with a difference: "She is even taller than my mother with the same black hair, but hers is cut tight like a helmet" (2010, 7). The girl also notes that her hands are "softer than [her] mother's" and that Mrs. Kinsella is better able to stand up to her father: "A stalk falls to the floor and then another. He waits for her to pick it up, to hand it to him. She waits for him to do it. Neither one of them will budge. In the end, it's Kinsella who stoops to lift it" (2010, 7, 14). The difference between the kind and caring Kinsella and her own cold and improvident father is especially marked, as the girl turns to Kinsella for the love and recognition she does not get from her father:

> Kinsella takes my hand in his. As soon as he takes it, I realise my father has never once held my hand, and some part of me wants Kinsella to let me go so I won't have to feel this. It's a hard feeling but as we walk along I begin to settle and let the difference between my life at home and the one I have here be. (2010, 61)

The girl also learns to negotiate the gendered divisions which do exist on this farm, although she is more readily allowed to cross over from one realm into the other. During the first few weeks she helps the woman around the house, while wearing clothes of the Kinsellas' dead son. After learning of the death of the son, she starts wearing her new frocks and dresses—while keeping his jacket—but follows Kinsella around on the farm. As in "Storms", the idea seems to be that both paternal and maternal heritages have to be integrated for a successful development— if not those of your own family, then those of a foster family. At the end of her stay, the narrator has learnt the twin virtues of resistance and respect from both of her foster parents. Resistance she learns from the woman's small defiant actions and from Kinsella who tells her, "You don't ever have to say anything [...] Always remember that as a thing you need never do. Many's the man lost much just because he missed a perfect opportunity to say nothing" (2010, 65). Respect she learns from seeing the deep mutual respect between the Kinsellas, so different from the perennial tension between her own parents, and from Mrs. Kinsella's reticent respect for the girl's feelings, when laughs away the girl's bedwetting as a case of an old, "weeping" mattress (2010, 28). The girl returns this respect by acknowledging the woman's very own weeping at the end and promising she "will never, ever tell" about the accident that happened: "'Nothing happened.' This is my mother I am speaking to but I have learned enough, grown enough, to know that what happened is not something I need ever mention. It's my perfect opportunity to say nothing" (2010, 88, 86). The female development sketched in *Foster* is thus again a hopeful one, as the girl's stay with her foster parents has taught her about differences and choices, about responsibility and respect. Having observed different possibilities enables her to envisage and realize a life different than that of her mother, in the same way as she is "making up something different to happen at the end" of the books which Kinsella has taught her to read (2010, 78).

In all, as the previous analysis hopes to have shown, this similarity with a difference is central to Keegan's daughter stories and in particular to the mother-daughter relationship these stories focus on. In spite of her apparent return to a traditional, timeless and often clichéd rural Ireland, Keegan is actually interested in recording change—even if it is a form of change which acknowledges the importance of ritual and tradition. Most of Keegan's daughters, therefore, are able to move beyond their mothers without repudiating them, as was the case in earlier Irish fiction. In a similar way, one might say, Keegan herself moves her short stories also in formal term beyond her predecessors even while learning from and paying tribute to their particular achievements.

BIBLIOGRAPHY

Battersby, Eileen. 2010. Beauty, Harshness, Menace and the Spine of Steel Worthy of High Art. *The Irish Times*, 28 August. http://www.irishtimes.com/culture/books/beauty-harshness-menace-and-the-spine-of-steel-worthy-of-high-art-1.644017

Beckett, Mary. 1990. *A Literary Woman*. London: Bloomsbury.

Benjamin, Jessica. 1988. *The Bonds of Love: Psychoanalysis, Feminism, and the Problem of Domination*. New York: Random House.

Benjamin, Jessica. 1998. *Shadow of the Other: Intersubjectivity and Gender in Psychoanalysis*. New York: Routledge.

Black, Claire. 2010. Interview: Claire Keegan—'A Child's Senses Are Not Dulled by Experience'. *The Scotsman*, 12 December. http://news.scotsman.com/arts/Interview-Claire-Keegan--39A.6525806.jp

Chang, Ann Wan-lih. 2008. Daughters on Hunger Strike: The Irish Mother-Daughter Resistance Plot in the Stories of Edna O'Brien, Mary Lavin, Eilis Ni Dhuibhne and Mary Leland. *Estudios Irlandeses-Journal of Irish Studies* 3:54–64.

Cohn, Dorit. 1999. *The Distinction of Fiction*. Baltimore: Johns Hopkins University Press.

Coughlan, Patricia. 2006. Killing the Bats: O'Brien, Abjection, and the Question of Agency. In *Edna O'Brien. New Critical Perspectives*, edited by Kathryn Laing, Sinéad Mooney and Maureen O'Connor, 171–195. Dublin: Carysfort.

DelConte, Matt. 2007. A Further Study of Present Tense Narration: The Absentee Narratee and Four-Wall Present Tense in Coetzee's *Waiting for the Barbarians* and *Disgrace*. *Journal of Narrative Theory* 37 (3):427–446.

Donoghue, Emma. 2006. *Touchy Subjects: Stories*. Orlando: Harcourt.

Egerton, George. 1932. A Keynote to *Keynotes*. In *Ten Contemporaries: Notes Toward their Definitive Bibliography*, edited by John Gawsworth, 58–60. London: Ernest Benn

Enright, Anne. 2007. Dancing in the Dark. *The Guardian*, 25 August. http://www.theguardian.com/books/2007/aug/25/featuresreviews.guardianreview19

Enright, Anne. 2008. *Taking Pictures*. London: Jonathan Cape.

Fitzgerald-Hoyt, Mary. 2015. Claire Keegan's New Rural Ireland: Torching the Thatched Cottage. In *The Irish Short Story. Traditions and Trends*, edited by Elke D'hoker and Stephanie Eggermont, 279–296. Oxford: Peter Lang.

Fleischman, Suzanne. 1990. *Tense and Narrativity: From Medieval Performance to Modern Fiction*. Austin: University of Texas Press.

Fludernik, Monika. 2002. *Towards a 'Natural' Narratology*. London: Routledge.
Fogarty, Anne. 2002. Mother-Daughter Relationships in Contemporary Irish Women's Fiction. In *Writing Mothers and Daughters: Renegotiating the Mother in Western European Narratives by Women*, edited by Adalgisa Giorgio, 85–118. Oxford: Berghahn Books.
Foster, Aisling. 2011. *Saints and Sinners* by Edna O'Brien. *The Times*, 5 February. http://www.thetimes.co.uk/tto/arts/books/fiction/article2898007.ece
Gillespie, Michael Patrick. 2006. Edna O'Brien and the Lives of James Joyce. In *Wild Colonial Girl: Essays on Edna O'Brien*, edited by Lisa Colletta and Maureen O'Connor, 78–91. Madison: University of Wisconsin Press.
Giorgio, Adalgisa. 2002. Writing the Mother-Daugher Relationship: Psychoanalysis, Culture, and Literary Criticism. In *Writing Mothers and Daughters: Renegotiating the Mother in Western European Narratives by Women*, edited by Adalgisa Giorgio, 10–46. Oxford: Berghahn Books.
Graham, Amanda. 1996. 'The Lovely Substance of the Mother': Food, Gender and Nation in the Work of Edna O'Brien. *Irish Studies Review* 4 (15):16–20.
Hirsch, Marianne. 1989. *The Mother/Daughter Plot: Narrative, Psychoanalysis, Feminism*. Bloomington: Indiana University Press.
Ingman, Heather. 2007. *Twentieth-Century Fiction by Irish Women: Nation and Gender*. London: Ashgate
Ingman, Heather. 2009. *A History of the Irish Short Story*. Cambridge: Cambridge University Press.
Irigaray, Luce, and Margaret Whitford. 1991. *The Irigaray Reader: Luce Irigaray*. Oxford: Blackwell.
Keegan, Claire. 1999. *Antarctica*. New York: Grove Press.
Keegan, Claire. 2007. *Walk the Blue Fields*. London: Faber.
Keegan, Claire. 2009. An Interview with Claire Keegan, Celtic Studies Writer in Residence, edited by Kate Van Dusen. Website of St. Michael's College, University of Toronto. http://stmikes.utoronto.ca/news/archives/09_stories/09_0330_claire_keegan.asp.
Keegan, Claire. 2010. *Foster*. London: Faber.
Kiberd, Declan. 2005. Fruits of the Second Flowering. *The Irish Times*, 30 April. http://www.irishtimes.com/news/fruits-of-the-second-flowering-1.436732
Kilroy, Thomas. 2011. Our Great Teller of the Short Story. *The Irish Times*. 12 February. http://www.irishtimes.com/culture/books/our-great-teller-of-the-short-story-1.570611.
Lynch, Vivian Valvano. 2015. 'Families Can Be Awful Places': The Toxic Parents of Claire Keegan's Fiction. *New Hibernia Review* 19 (1):131–146.
Meaney, Gerardine. 2010. *Gender, Ireland and Cultural Change: Race, Sex and Nation*. London: Routledge.
Mooney, Sinéad. 2009. Edna O'Brien: 'A Rose in the Heart of New York'. In *A Companion to the British and Irish Short Story*, edited by Cheryl Alexander Malcolm and David Malcolm, 431–439. Oxford: Wiley-Blackwell.

Ní Dhuibhne, Éilís. 2008. Give a Thing and Take it Back. *Dublin Review of Books* 5. http://www.drb.ie/essays/give-a-thing-and-take-it-back

O'Brien, Edna. 1990. *Lantern Slides*. London: Penguin.

O'Brien, Edna. 2003. *A Fanatic Heart: Selected Stories*. London: Phoenix. Original edition, 1985.

O'Brien, Edna. 2011. *Saints and Sinners*. London: Faber & Faber.

O'Connor, Maureen. 2010. *The Female and the Species: The Animal in Irish Women's Writing*. Oxford: Peter Lang.

Pelan, Rebecca. 2006a. Edna O'Brien's 'Love Objects.'. In *Wild Colonial Girl: Essays on Edna O'Brien*, edited by Lisa Colletta and Maureen O'Connor, 58–77. Madison: University of Wisconsin Press.

Pelan, Rebecca. 2006b. Reflections on a Connemara Dietrich. In *Edna O'Brien: New Critical Perspectives*, edited by Kathryn Laing, Sinéad Mooney and Maureen O'Connor, 12–37. Dublin: Carysfort.

Rich, Adrienne. 1986. *Of Woman Born: Motherhood as Experience and Institution*. New York: Norton.

Rooks-Hughes, Lorna. 1996. The Family and the Female Body in the Novels of Edna O'Brien and Julia O'Faolain. *The Canadian Journal of Irish Studies* 22 (2):83–97.

Scholes, Robert. 1980. Language, Narrative, and Anti-Narrative. *Critical Inquiry* 7 (1):204–214.

Shillinger, Liesl. 2011. Edna O'Brien's Elemental Fiction. *The New York Times*, 13 May. http://www.nytimes.com/2011/05/15/books/review/book-review-saints-and-sinners-by-edna-obrien.html?_r=0

Shumaker, Jeanette Roberts. 2001. Mother-Daughter Rivalries in Short Stories by Irish Women. *North Dakota Quarterly* 68:70–85.

Weekes, Ann Owens. 2000. Figuring the Mother in Contemporary Irish Fiction. In *Contemporary Irish Fiction: Themes, Tropes, Theories*, edited by Liam Harte and Michael Parker, 100–124. London: Macmillan.

Weekes, Ann Owens. 2006. The Mother Figure in Edna O'Brien's Fiction. In *Back to the Present, Forward to the Past: Irish Writing and History Since 1798*, edited by Patricia Lynch, Joachim Fischer and Brian Coates, 309–324. New York: Rodopi.

CHAPTER 7

Double Visions: The Metafictional Stories of Éilís Ní Dhuibhne, Anne Enright and Emma Donoghue

Compared to the American short story, postmodernism in the British and Irish short story is typically judged a rather "half-hearted affair" (Jarfe 2008, 389). "Muted postmodernism" is the term Broich applies to the British short story of the 1970s (Broich 1993), and it also holds for the Irish short story of the period. Postmodern techniques inflect such collections as Aidan Higgins's *Felo de Se* (1960), John Banville's *Long Lankin* (1970), and Neil Jordan's *Night in Tunisia and Other Stories* (1976), but none of these writers stuck to the genre of the short story for very long. By now, postmodernism is also considered a thing of the past. In his discussion of the postmodernist short fiction in Britain and Ireland, Jarfe notes: "this [postmodernist] phase lasted roughly twenty years. After 1985, postmodernist attitudes and practices slowly petered out", to give way to a return to realism, "often called neo-realism" (2008, 384). Most of the Irish short fiction writers I have discussed so far have also preferred a realist mode, whether a social realism as in the work of Mary Lavin and Mary Beckett, a psychological realism as in Elizabeth Bowen and Maeve Brennan, or a symbolical realism as in Edna O'Brien's short fiction. Moreover, the minimalist realism of Claire Keegan's stories seems proof of the continued dominance of the realist story in twenty-first-century Ireland. Yet this account of the short story's brief flirtation with postmodernism in the 1970s and its subsequent return to realism sidesteps the achievements of several contemporary women writers, whose work presents a strong alliance of postmodern practices and feminist concerns. In Britain, the work of Ali Smith and A.L. Kennedy is exemplary in this

© The Editor(s) (if applicable) and The Author (s) 2016   177
E. D'hoker, *Irish Women Writers and the Modern Short Story*,
DOI 10.1007/978-3-319-30288-1_7

respect. In Ireland, postmodernist strategies pervade the short fiction of Éilís Ní Dhuibhne, Anne Enright and Emma Donoghue, which will be discussed in this chapter.

If postmodernism in the short story is thus "neither over, nor only beginning" (Sacido 2012, 22), the same can be said of feminism and the short story. As Ingman has shown, under the influence of international feminism and the Women's Movement, Irish women writers start to explicitly raise feminist concerns in their short stories from the late 1970s on (Ingman 2009, 202–5). The short fiction of writers such as Edna O'Brien, Evelyn Conlon, Mary Dorcey, Maeve Kelly, Val Mulkerns and Julia O'Faolain critically explores the lives and roles of women in patriarchal Ireland and addresses with increasing frankness such taboo topics as domestic violence, adultery and abortion, female desire and homosexuality. Yet, however controversial the themes these writers address, the stories themselves are predominantly written in a realist mode, to examine the psychological and social dimensions of women's lives. Even if O'Brien and Dorcey experiment with more unusual techniques of consciousness representation—stream-of-consciousness, you-narration, or obsessive monologue—their stories remain committed to the suspension of disbelief that is the hallmark of realist writing. This is no longer the case in the metafictional stories published by Éilís Ní Dhuibhne, Anne Enright and Emma Donoghue around the turn of the twenty-first century. In their work, intertextual allusions, parody and pastiche, metalepsis and metafictional commentary all serve to disrupt the illusion of reality and to draw attention to the constructedness and artificiality of the story told. In the work of all three writers, moreover, these postmodern techniques clearly serve a feminist project, geared towards the deconstruction of the accepted norms, roles, stories and histories that shape women's lives in contemporary society. Evidently, Ní Dhuibhne, Enright and Donoghue approach these concerns in different ways. In the following sections, therefore, I will outline the specific forms and inflections this postmodern and feminist project assumes in the case of each writer. First, however, I will briefly dwell on the formal characteristics of their short fiction to illustrate why it can be classified as postmodernist.

Although the status of postmodernism as either a rupture with or a continuation of modernism remains a moot point in literary criticism, it is clear that the postmodern short story seeks to break, if not with the modernist short story itself, then certainly with the way modernist techniques have become normative for the genre of the modern short story in general. The use of symbolism and ellipsis to suggest rather than state, the preference of psychology over plot, the exploration of individual consciousness during a moment of crisis or an apparently random slice-of-life, an open end and *in medias res* beginning, ambiguity and ambivalence, and an emphasis on condensation and unity: all of these had become hallmarks of the modern short story by the 1930s. Some years later, the new creative writing programmes would indoctrinate aspiring writers with such modernist mantras as "show rather than tell" or "every word counts". Or as Ní Dhuibhne ironically puts it in her story "Oleander": "Be concise. Keep your eye on the ball. Create epiphanies. Focus on the single moment of revelation. Cut out all superfluous words" (2000, 174). Although writers like Bowen, Brennan and Lavin tried to combine the heritage of both the plotted magazine story and the plotless modernist story, their short stories remained committed to a realist impulse, to the telling of a story that could very well have happened. Precisely this idea of verisimilitude, this illusion of lifelikeness is what the postmodernist short story tries to break in an attempt to highlight the radical constructedness of life, reality and meaning. As Jarfe points out, this defiance of realism in the postmodern short story can take several forms:

> (1) [writers] can refuse to tell a story or the story told can be inconsistent, pointless; (2) they can compose stories that no longer automatically and inescapably refer to 'reality' (which can be seen as a social construction anyway), but that become self-reflexive or auto-referential; (3) the act of narration is given special prominence or the arbitrary whims of the narrator are focused on. If this becomes the centre of attention it is called metafiction. (2008, 385)

Examples of all three of these strategies—disrupting storyness, foregrounding narration and literary self-referentiality—can be found in the stories of Ní Dhuibhne, Enright and Donoghue.

The stories Enright published in *The Portable Virgin* (1991) offer prime examples of the attempt to frustrate the sense of storyness readers would expect in a short story. As Clare Hanson notes, "an increasing sense of the fragmentation of human experience will necessarily put pressure on conventional notions of the temporal and causal ordering of this experience" (1985, 142), which leads to the postmodern preference for fragmentation and juxtaposition over causality and storyness. Enright's stories often consist of such discrete story nuggets, whereby the relations between the separate fragments are suppressed. This is most obviously the case in stories which bring together different protagonists as in "Men and Angels", "Historical Letters" and "What Are Cicadas?". In some of the stories, the causal and temporal patterning of storyness is replaced by metaphorical or ideological ordering principles: "Men and Angels" offers different takes on the conjunction of famous men and forgotten, angelic, wives, and in "The House of the Architect's Love Story" a classic betrayal story is told and undermined again through a series of scenes tied together by the metaphor of marriage as a house. As I will argue, this fragmentation and lack of causal patterning serve to undermine any sense of wholeness or coherence of the self. Some of the stories in Donoghue's *The Woman Who Gave Birth to Rabbits* (2002) also disrupt storyness through fragmentation, juxtaposition and a removal of causal links. Thus, "Account" consists of a numerical inventory of things (or people) related to the historical figure of Margaret Drummond and "Cured" juxtaposes diary fragments of a doctor and patient in a case of female circumcision. More than in Enright's early short stories, however, Donoghue's reader is encouraged to piece together a more conventional story by reading between the lines. Hence, storyness is complicated but not completely undermined.

If the modernist short story sought to break with the tale tradition by suppressing the omniscient narrator, suggestively showing meaning rather than stating it, the postmodern short story once again foregrounds the act of narration and the process of telling. Of course, the aim is no longer to vouch for the integrity of the narrator and the truth of the story told. To the contrary, the emphasis on narration seeks to highlight the constructed nature of the story and the subjectivity—even unreliability—of every storyteller. The three authors I discuss all foreground processes of telling, yet they do so in different ways. A hallmark of Ní Dhuibhne's stories is the use of an overt third-person narrator who is given to intrusive comments about the stories and the characters, while also being privy to their innermost feelings and thoughts. In *The Inland Ice and Other Stories* (1997), these comments typically appear between brackets and interrupt the indirect rendering of a character's flow of thoughts. Consider, for instance, this passage from "The Inland Ice": "Nobody ever helped. Frank didn't help her to make decisions. Never seemed to care about her in that deep way that mattered. (What she means is, he let her truckle along with her job as an executive in a public service office, a job which meant something to some people, but not to her.)" (1997, 210). In several stories from *The Pale Gold of Alaska* (2000), on the other hand, the narrator intrudes upon the story in order to tell the reader about the Irish context that explains the character's behaviour. In "The Truth About Married Love", there is an aside about the attitude to divorce in modern Ireland and in "The Day Elvis Presley Died", the narrator interrupts the story with a lengthy explanation about the protagonist's reluctance to have sex with her American boyfriend in view of the "social mores, convention, even the law [which] exert a considerable influence over her sexual life" (2000, 163, 57–8). Such narratorial intrusions draw the reader's attention to the story as story, as an artificial construct rather than an actual slice of life.

Another way of foregrounding the narrative act is through the use of a highly subjective, even unreliable, first-person narrator who gives his or her clearly coloured view of the events. As Anne Fogarty notes, Ní Dhuibhne's use of such first-person narrators "allows for a mingling of postmodern dissonance with the immediacy of direct address" (2003, xii). Thus "Fulfillment" is told by a crazy dog-killer and "Spool of Thread" by a murderer, whose narration serves to satirically expose the many misogynistic stereotypes he acts on. This narrator ends his story with a self-conscious reference to his act of storytelling: "Stand on the threshold to the dark labyrinth of human nature and use your own imagination. (And don't forget your spool of thread)" (Ní Dhuibhne 1997, 137). Metafictional comments on the act of narration also abound in the stories of Donoghue and Enright. The many first-person narrators of Donoghue's story cycle *The Woman Who Gave Birth to Rabbits*, for instance, frequently comment on the duplicitous power of words and stories to both state and dissemble truth: "Without words, we move through life as mute as animals", remarks one narrator, while another ponders "Words have always been my undoing" (Donoghue 2002, 29, 65). The narrator of "The Last Rabbit" realizes the power of storytelling as she stops repeating the story she has been ordered to tell and instead narrates her own story: "I turned and walked back to the room where Sir Richard was waiting for my story" (Donoghue 2002, 13).

Enright's *The Portable Virgin* similarly stages highly self-conscious narrators who frequently compare their stories to existing ones: "Of all the different love stories, I chose an architect's love story", the narrator of "The House of the Architect's Love Story" announces and her counterpart in "The Portable Virgin" comments similarly, "This is the usual betrayal story" (1998, 55, 81). In many other stories, processes of embedding and metalepsis draw attention to the process of telling stories and the inevitable distortions or half-truths involved (D'hoker 2011, 39). Thus, the story of a love affair in "Indifference" is interrupted by stories the lovers tell each other and by the girl's account of the affair in a letter back home, while in "Seascape", the story of a young couple's holiday at the seaside is disrupted by the ironic comments about the holiday which the woman writes on a postcard to her friend. In Ní Dhuibhne's "The Search for the Lost Husband", to give a final example, the narrator ends the story with "That is my story. And if there is a lie in it, it was not I who made it up. All I got for my story was butter boots and paper hats. And a white dog came and ate the boots and tore the hats. But what matter? What matters but the good of the story?" (1997, 262). As I have argued elsewhere, these lines echo the rhetorical disclaimers found in traditional folk tales, which suggests that in some cases the postmodern foregrounding of narration can be seen as a return to an earlier, oral storytelling tradition (D'hoker 2004). At the same time, these last examples from Enright and Ní Dhuibhne also bring us to another dimension of metafictionality, and to the third of Jarfe's characteristics: the self-referentiality of the postmodern short story as it points not (or not just) to a reality beyond the story, but to another story, another text which it echoes, parodies or comments on.

This metafictional and intertextual self-referentiality is an important feature of the short stories of the three writers I am discussing. In many of her short stories, Ní Dhuibhne returns to the rich store of Irish and European folk and fairy tales, either rewriting folk stories or juxtaposing them to contemporary settings and lives. In *The Portable Virgin* and a few other early stories published in *Yesterday's Weather* (2009), on the other hand, Enright creates a web of intertextual references to literature, film, and popular culture, thus allowing her stories to rewrite, subvert, or echo existing ones. In *Kissing the Witch*, finally, Emma Donoghue follows Angela Carter's pattern of retelling fairy tales, while in *The Woman Who Gave Birth to Rabbits* and *Astray* (2012) her stories offer a rewriting of anecdotes and stories submerged in historical records. In all of these modes of rewriting, moreover, the writers display a clear feminist sensibility. Their short fiction thus participates in the tradition of feminist rewriting or revisioning. Indeed, following Adrienne Rich's 1972 call for "writing as re-vision", women writers have often used postmodern techniques of metafiction, rewriting, and intertextuality to reclaim ownership of Western culture and history, to subvert its familiar plots and stereotypes and to recover its elisions and silences (Rich 1972). Within the tradition of the short story, the single most famous work of rewriting is of course Angela Carter's appropriation of fairy tales in *The Bloody Chamber*, but as the work of contemporary Irish women writers shows, feminist rewriting can take many different forms. In what follows, therefore, I propose to offer a closer investigation of the metafictional short stories of Ní Dhuibhne, Enright and Donoghue, so as to describe more accurately the different forms of rewriting these authors offer and the feminist projects they embrace.

COMPARISONS AND COMPROMISES IN THE STORIES OF ÉILÍS NÍ DHUIBHNE

Writing in both English and Irish as well as in different genres, Éilís Ní Dhuibhne is a highly versatile writer. She has won widespread popularity and critical acclaim with such novels as *The Dancers Dancing* (1999) and *Fox, Swallow, Scarecrow* (2007). Yet her greatest achievement is, arguably, within the genre of the short story. Collections such as *The Inland Ice* (1997), *The Pale Gold of Alaska* (2000) and *The Shelter of Neighbours* (2012) were widely praised and a selection of the stories of her early collections, *Blood and Water* (1988) and *Eating Women Is Not Recommended* (1991) were collected, together with some new stories, in *Midwife to the Fairies* (2003). Apart from her literary work, Ní Dhuibhne has also produced scholarly books, articles and editions, as she obtained a PhD in Irish folkore at University College Dublin. Her literary work also bears traces of this academic interest: especially her short stories often allude to a rich store of folk tales, fairy tales and myths. In this way, Ní Dhuibhne's short fiction clearly belongs to a larger international trend of rewriting fairy tales with a feminist intent. In her seminal study, *Myth and Fairy Tale in Contemporary Women's Fiction*, Susan Sellers recognizes "two kinds of revisioning" of folk tales: "The first involves the transfiguration of a well-known tale in which the author depicts its familiar ingredients in an unfamiliar manner, so that the reader is forced to consider their negative aspects and perhaps reject them" (2001, 13). Angela Carter's idiosyncratic and feminist retelling of fairy tales would be a case in point. A second type of reworking involves "the fusion of 'classic' configurations with contemporary settings and alternative plotlines". This is the mode followed by Margaret Atwood and A.S. Byatt in their revisioning of fairy tales.

In Ní Dhuibhne's œuvre, the first type of revisioning can be found in "The Story of the Lost Husband", which is told in instalments throughout *The Inland Ice*. This story is a feminist retelling of the Irish fairy tale

"The Story of the Little White Goat", which was recorded from the female storyteller Máire Ruiséal in 1936, and which is itself a version of the international "Beauty-and-the Beast" folk tale (D'hoker 2004; Fogarty 2009). Ní Dhuibhne follows the original quite faithfully, but changes the ending. Rejecting passion with her elusive—and abusive—animal lover, the protagonist opts for domestic happiness with a reliable farmer husband, for as she puts it: "it's time for me to try another kind of love. I'm tired of all that fairytale stuff" (Ní Dhuibhne 1997, 262). Unlike in the original folk tale, Ní Dhuibhne thus foregrounds both the protagonist's desire—in her all-consuming passion for her animal lover—and her independent agency, as she finally takes her life into her own hands again. As Sellers indicates, this type of feminist rewriting also alerts us to the patriarchal structures and gendered roles of the original story (Sellers 2001, 13).

Because of its prominent position in *The Inland Ice*, this feminist fairy tale has attracted quite some critical attention (D'hoker 2004; Moloney 2007; Fogarty 2009). Yet, it is the only actual rewriting in Ní Dhuibhne's œuvre. Her other stories follow Sellers' second type of reworking as they juxtapose or interweave folk tales with contemporary stories. In Chapter 5, we have already seen how "The Man Who Had No Story" interlaces a story of a contemporary writer's block with an Irish fairy legend. "How Lovely the Slopes Are", similarly, borrows scenes from Iceland's *Njal's Saga* as counterpoints to the quarrels of a married couple in present-day Sweden. "Midwife to the Fairies" stages a contemporary version of a folk tale which is also quoted in italics in the text. And "Summer Pudding" revisions "the old Deirdre story found in 'The Exile of the Sons of UIslui'" (Moloney 2009, 105). While such embedded folk tales do not of course occur in all of Ní Dhuibhne's stories, their resonance is reinforced through the slighter intertextual references that appear in many more stories. Indeed, almost all of Ní Dhuibhne's stories contain intertextual allusions to other stories, whether taken from Irish or international folklore or from Western literature at large. This intertextual network functions as an echo chamber which expands and enlarges the meaning of the actual stories. Ní Dhuibhne discussed this in an interview:

> I allude to old stories. I counterpoint my own stories, set in the now, with oral stories, set in the past, or more accurately, set in the never, never or the always, always. I feel, and I hope that this enhances my ordinary stories, gives them a mythic quality which, on their own, they would find it hard

to achieve. It puts it in a larger context—not only an Irish context, since the first thing one learns about oral narrative is its international nature. (St. Peter and Ní Dhuibhne 2006, 70)

Yet, the significance of these allusions exceeds that of mere additional resonance. Ní Dhuibhne allows her new stories to interact with the existing ones: undermining, affirming or questioning them. As Sellers has pointed out, "one of the strengths of reworking fairy tale [in this second type of revisioning] is precisely the interplay between the known and the new" (2001, 14). And this interplay between known and new stories has a profound bearing on what Ní Dhuibhne herself recognizes as the central concern of her fiction: "the emotional lives of human beings and [...] their inter-relationships" (St. Peter and Ní Dhuibhne 2006, 71).

Heterosexual relationships—whether in the form of courtship, marriage or adulterous affairs—are indeed at the centre of most of the stories in *The Inland Ice* and *The Pale Gold of Alaska*, the two collections I will focus on in what follows, and their intertextual dimension shapes that topic in interesting ways. Apart from enlarging the breadth of the stories, the intertextual allusions to existing stories also set up a comparative structure. Sometimes, this comparison can be attributed to the author, as in the interlacing of fairy tale and contemporary story in "Midwife to the Fairies". In many other stories, the comparisons fall to the narrators or characters who assess their lives in relation to stories they have heard or read about. "She was—and is—a compulsive comparatist", the narrator notes about the protagonist of "Hot Earth" (Ní Dhuibhne 1997, 108) and this in fact applies to most of Ní Dhuibhne's characters. The reader of the stories too is invited to take up the role of a comparatist, teasing out similarities and differences between Ní Dhuibhne's 'new' story and the 'older' ones alluded to.

As highlighted by the revisioned 'Beauty and the Beast' fairy tale that frames *The Inland Ice*, fairy tales and romance stories very much shape the dreams and hopes of the female characters. In "Swiss Cheese", for instance, Cliona describes waiting for her Prince Charming: "You trimmed your lap, you bided your time. Your prince came" and being swept away by a "tidal wave of passion" (1997, 155, 147). Or as the narrator of "At Sally Gap" puts it, "There are many kinds of love but one that everyone wants. True passion" (2000, 128). Dreaming of all-consuming love and passion, Ní Dhuibhne's characters believe in the happy-ever-after promised by marriage in fairy tales: "She felt if she were married, all the other problems would fade into insignificance [....] Roads, green and juicy with promise, rainbow ended, would open before her" (1997, 186). When marriage fails to deliver this, the characters turn to an affair to realize these dreams. For some characters, this investment in fairy tale dreams of romance blinds them to the reality of their relationship. In "The Day Elvis Died", Pat's romantic ideals make her ignore her boyfriend's lack of commitment "she heard him and understood what he was saying but she went on imagining another story" (2000, 54). Similarly, Cliona in "Swiss Cheese" and Fiona in "Love, Hate, and Friendship" only dimly realize that their "true love" really is an abusive relationship, in which they are forever submissively waiting for their faithless lovers' occasional gifts. "Why should it be so hard to forget all this romantic stuff", Fiona wonders, and Cliona prefers to think of "the crazy swing from hatred to love, from despair to happiness, rather than of other dangerous, cruel aspects of what is going on" (1997, 42, 162).

In other stories, the characters' realization that life is not like a fairy tale leads to disappointment and unhappiness. In "The Inland Ice", Polly's dreams of a "wonderful" life have foundered in their "up-and-down-marriage" and in "How Lovely the Slopes Are", Bronwyn's hopes of a marriage based on eternal love and passion, inspired by Icelandic sagas and old Swedish kings, have turned sour in the face of everyday domestic reality (1997, 211, 209, 249). Yet, this feeling of disappointment is in both stories also tempered by a sense of realism or pragmatism. "Nobody's life is perfect", Polly's husband tells her, and Bronwyn's husband exclaims "I'm sick of living life as if it were a Bergman film. Life should be peaceful and pleasant" (1997, 211, 255). Both stories end, in fact, with the female characters accepting the value of married love, blemished but beautiful, like the icecap Polly admires in Greenland:

> From a slight distance, or from above, the icecap is as white and glimmering as anything in the world. But when you are close to it, standing beside it, you see that the white ice if full of gravel and sand. It looks dirty, like old snow piled up at the side of a city street. Underneath, however, the ice has formed shapes like stalagmites, and when you peer under you see that they are blue and turquoise, silver, jade, and other subtle, shining, winking colours for which you have no name. (1997, 217)

Several other stories too end on this note of resignation, with Bernadette in "Hot Earth" realizing that "the land of compromise was where she thrived" (1997, 120) and Pat in "The Day Elvis Presley Died" that "in the mysterious borderland that separates dream and reality, the gap called 'anyway', she is happy—more or less" (2000, 120).

If these characters come to accept that life can never live up to their fairy tale dreams of all-consuming love and everlasting happiness, other characters go even further and recognize the inherent dangers and restrictions of their fairy tale ideals. In "Lili Marlene", the protagonist marries a rich husband who makes her feel "like Cinderella", but in the end she does not want to accept the passive role of "princess in the garden" he offers her and opts for independence through work instead (1997, 98). The unequal power balance of the heterosexual relations depicted in patriarchal fairy tales and romance stories are also exposed in stories like "Swiss Cheese", "Love, Hate, and Friendship", and "Gweedore Girl", where the women's abject love for their unreliable lovers threatens to rob them of their sense of self (see D'hoker 2004). The even more sinister fate of women in some fairy tales is also hinted at through the references to Little Red Riding Hood in "The Day Elvis Presley Died", where a girl is found raped and murdered in the forest (2000, 65). These allusions to the dangers inherent in fairy tales—whether in terms of loss of self or loss of life—tie in with Ní Dhuibhne's feminist revisioning in "The Quest for the Lost Husband", where the girl rejects the expected fairy tale ending and decides to "renegotiate happiness on her own terms", exhibiting a "healthy self-interest by definitively repudiating what may be seen as an abusive relationship" (Fogarty 2009, 75).

With regard to the stories' scrutiny of heterosexual love, in short, the juxtaposition of contemporary stories and fairy tales highlights, on the one hand, the continuing hold of fairy tales on the dreams and desires of contemporary women. On the other hand, the juxtaposition also reveals the necessary gap between fairy tales and reality—a gap which is evaluated in different ways throughout the stories. Far from asking us to choose one side of the binary over the other, therefore, Ní Dhuibhne invites us to compare their different visions of life. As in all comparisons, there are similarities and differences to be found between these stories and the real life that inspired them. Or as the narrator of "Lili Marlene" puts it, "What I think is that life is like *Doctor Zhivago* up to a point—more like it than some would admit. People can have a great, passionate love. I have. Probably you have. But it doesn't seem to survive. One way or another it gets done in, either because you stay together or you don't" (1997, 102).

As this comment makes clear, Ní Dhuibhne's revisioning of fairy tales is also part of the larger metafictional dimension of her short fiction, as it insistently reflects on what stories are or should be, how they are constructed and whether we can or should believe them. The gap between fairy tales and real life is therefore also part of a larger exploration of the relation between stories and life, or between fiction and reality. This becomes evident when we consider Ní Dbhuibhne's rewriting of two of Mary Lavin's short stories, "At Sallygap" and "The Widow's Son". In "The Banana Boat", the narrator tells of the near-drowning of her son during a summer holiday in the West of Ireland. The highly literate narrator infuses her story with countless intertextual references to other writers or storytellers: Tomás Ó Criomhthain, Peig Sayers, Seán Ó Dálaigh, E.M. Forster, Erskine Childers, Edward Lear, Alice Munro, and Mary Lavin. Waiting for news about her son, the narrator ponders:

> I realise right now that there are two ends to my story, two ends to the story of my day and the story of my life. I think of Mary Lavin's story about the widow's son [...] The message of the story is that the loss you suffer through no fault of your own is much easier to bear than the one you bring about by your own actions. But it's going to be much more ambiguous than that. (2000, 209–10)

The narrator's story is more ambiguous because there is no clear opposition between doing or not doing something, but rather a complex muddle of half-decisions, possible misjudgements, intuitions and inactions that might or might not lead to her son's death. This distinction between the neat dichotomies of a story and the complex ambiguities of real life is also hinted at in Ní Dhuibhe's rewriting of Lavin's "At Sallygap". As Giovanna Tallone (2004) has pointed out, there are several similarities between the two stories, most obviously the circular journey both protagonists make from Dublin to the mountains and back again. As I have argued in Chapter 4, Lavin's story revolves around the conflict of sensibilities between Manny and Annie and is structured around such binary opposites as country–city, home–exile, Dublin–Paris, love–hate. The story ends in a deadlock as Mannie comes to realize the depth of his wife's hatred of him. In Ní Dhuibhne's "At Sally Gap", the situation is again more complex. Orla is involved not in one but two heterosexual relations, with her husband and brother-in-law, both of whom she loves.

The hatred is located in yet another relationship: that between Orla and her sister. Unlike Manny who regrets not escaping to Paris when he had the chance, Orla has left Dublin and has built a life in Wales, but she also often returns to her lover in Dublin, since "that is all it takes to be in exile. One and a half hours by Seacat" (2000, 146). Contrary to Lavin's story, "At Sally Gap" also ends on an ambivalent note. While Orla decides to renounce her lover and to "make the most" of her life with Matthew, the narrator immediately undercuts this decision with "This is what she believes, for the moment" (2000, 146). With these rewritings, Ní Dhuibhne thus draws attention to the way stories inevitably distort reality, imposing neat endings or clear-cut binaries which life itself usually lacks.

This also points us to Ní Dhuibhne's particular aesthetic project: to tell stories that remain faithful to the grey zones, ambiguities, and complexities of real life, yet that never lose sight of their status as stories. The first of these ambitions is hinted at in an assessment of Richard Ford's stories in "Oleander": "[The stories] meander like real life and the details ring true as bottle water. Close towards the end of each a dramatic thing happens, however—a bad dramatic thing [...] This is the E.M. Forster touch, the false sparkle that screams 'FICTION'" (2000, 175). Ní Dhuibhne, by contrast, keeps the meandering bit but does away with the dramatic twist, which she considers too much of a falsification. For as the narrator of "The Banana Boat'" puts it, "Real life [is] the life that is uneventful, the life that does not get described in newspapers or even, now that the days of literary realism are coming to an end, in books. The protected ordinary uneventful life, which is the basis of civilization and happiness and everything that is good" (2000, 214). As the metafictional comments in this quote suggests, metafiction and intertextuality are a necessary part of that realist impetus for Ní Dhuibhne: it is precisely by advertising the stories' fictional status, by laying bare their subjectivity, and exposing their own inner workings that the stories may get closer to the hesitations and ambiguities of real life. This postmodern stance, which does not aim to reject reality but to get at it more closely, is already at work in an early story like "The Flowering", where Lennie, a contemporary Irish woman, fabricates the story of an ancestor of hers, Sally Rua, who went mad when she could no longer express herself creatively. The story of Sally Rua is told and undermined at the same time to suggest both the need for such stories—"if there is no Sally Rua, at all, at all, where does that leave Lennie?"—and their necessary falsifications

(Ní Dhuibhne 2003, 21). Paradoxically, it is by displaying this fictionality that the story and the embedded story aim to get closer to a reality that is always already infused by stories, old and new, which we believe in even while knowing they are but fictions.

Anne Enright's Short Stories: Making People Different

If Ní Dhuibhne thus challenges us to read her stories as fictions that are also real, Anne Enright's short stories—especially those published in *The Portable Virgin*—can be seen to proclaim their fictionality to an even greater degree. They fully bear out the postmodern impulse to thwart the illusion of reality and to foreground the constructedness of representation. About the realist suspension of disbelief, Enright herself noted in an interview: "For myself I feel I can't do that particular sleight of hand, that trick that says 'all this is real'. Or I don't claim that trick" (Bracken and Cahill 2011, 31). As I have argued already, the stories collected in *The Portable Virgin* quite overtly display the whole storehouse of postmodern techniques: metalepsis and *mise-en-abîme*, parody and parataxis, metafictional self-reflexivity and playful intertextuality. What is perhaps less obvious is that Enright's stories also participate in the feminist project of writing as revisioning as they seek to unsettle the all-too-familiar plots and stories of contemporary culture. "Felix", the first story Enright ever published, constitutes the most blatant act of rewriting. In a parodic twist on the opening lines of Nabokov's *Lolita*, the story begins with, "Felix, my secret, my angel boy, my dark felicity. Felix: the sibilant hiss of the final x a teasing breath on the tip of my tongue" (Enright 2009, 295). In a style replete with literary flourishes and intertextual references (to Poe, Proust, Baudelaire, Keats and Thomas Mann), a middle-aged woman tells of her passionate affair with an adolescent boy, thus turning the tables on the classic plotline of Nabokov's novel. As an early story, published in the Faber anthology *First Fictions: Introductions 10* (1989), "Felix" sets the pattern for the more implicit acts of rewriting that Enright stages in *The Portable Virgin*. Here she does not so much turn to folk tales or to the canonical texts of Western literature, but rather to the archetypal plots and patterns that infuse Western culture. Indeed, most of the stories in *The Portable Virgin* put a subversive spin on classic stories of love and loss, passion and betrayal, by reversing the customary gender roles. In "She Owns (Every Thing)", a young woman working behind the handbag counter in a big department store falls head over heels in love not with a male, but with a female customer and loses her previous sense of order and propriety. "Indifference" puts a twist on the classic seduction story by having a girl seduce a boy on a one-night-stand in which he loses his virginity, and in the adulterous affairs chronicled in "Luck Be a Lady" and "The House of the Architect's Love Story", the female protagonists are shown to be vocal and bold in getting the man they desire. In some other stories, male characters assume traditionally feminine gender roles, as when the single father in "Juggling Oranges" juggles work and domestic life to care for his daughter, even teaching her to apply make-up, or when Frank in "Mr. Snip Snip Snip" dreams of having children while his wife is having an affair. Even stories which stick to traditional gender roles tend to self-reflexively announce their telling as re-telling: "This is the usual betrayal story, as you have already guessed—the word 'sofa' gave it away", notes the narrator of "The Portable Virgin", and she goes on to make references to other betrayal stories, whether in TV ("BBC mini-series where Judi Dench plays the furniture and has a little sad fun"), film ("'But I thought it *meant* something!' screams the wife, throwing their crystal honeymoon wineglasses from Seville against the Magnolia Matt wall"), literature ("Mrs. Rochester punched a hole in the ceiling"), or advertising ("Mary's soap is all whiffy, but *Mary* uses X—so mild her husband will never leave") (Enright 1998, 81–5).

In short, although these stories, unlike "Felix", do not rewrite actual literary texts, they do appropriate many, mostly romantic, plots familiar to us from TV, film and (popular) literature. This general intertext is also tangentially evoked through the countless references to popular culture: from Errol Flynn over Shirley Temple to Woody Allen (1998, 11, 24, 133), and from Tom and Jerry, over Dr Doolittle to *Star Trek* (1998, 24, 180, 175). By rewriting these popular plots with a difference, Enright's short stories question the naturalness of these plots and unsettle the gendered stereotypes they employ. As a feminist writer, Enright's revisioning is primarily geared towards a "breaking up" of "stereotypes and images" within which women are often contained (Bracken and Cahill 2011, 22), yet stories like "Mr. Snip Snip Snip" and "Juggling Oranges" offer counter-stories to masculine stereotypes and roles as well. Enright's main concern, I would argue, is to open up traditional plots, to break archetypal patterns and to imagine different lives and alternative stories. In an interview for BBC Radio 4, she noted in this respect:

> I am very much against a monolithic kind of voice. I want variety. Growing up in an Ireland where you are supposed to be one kind or the other and where there is an agreed way to be Irish, I was strongly of the opinion that there are many ways to go about this—and that variety is a kind of anti-nationalist impulse in me: to make people different. (Enright and Frostrup 2015)

This concern with difference—and its twin antonyms of similarity and indistinction—pervades the collection in other formal and thematic ways as well.

As I have noted already, Enright's stories typically consist of a juxtaposition of discrete fragments and scenes, which disrupts any traditional sense of storyness. At the same time, this paratactic method, common to postmodernist writing, invites the reader to construe coherence and to piece the fragments together (Coughlan 2004a, 185). Some stories thus juxtapose scenes from one character's life or from a single event. Other stories read more like variations on a common theme: "Liking" offers a series of dialogues on violent deaths; "Historical Letters" consists of fragments of love letters that link personal to historical events, ranging from *fin-de-siècle* Berlin over the Spanish Civil War to the landing on the moon; "Men and Angels" proposes different historical versions of the theme announced by the title; and "What Are Cicadas?" presents discrete scenes and stories from the childhood and adolescence of a "sensitive young man" (1998, 148). Following Enright's postmodern sensibility, the stories are explicitly marked as stories and their accuracy is often put in doubt. In a way, they are like the "fifteen stories of falling off his bicycle" which Billy tells his daughter in "Juggling Oranges": imaginative variations on a theme or event which may itself be entirely fictitious in the first place.

On a stylistic level too, Enright likes playing with this tension between similarity and difference, as her paragraphs are often made up of short sentences that repeat each other with a difference. Consider, for instance, the following paragraph from "She Owns (Every Thing)":

> There were also the women who could not. A woman, for example, who could NOT wear blue. A woman who could wear a print, but NOT beside her face. A woman who could wear beads but NOT earrings. A woman who

had a secret life of shoes too exotic for her [...] A woman who comes home with royal jelly every time she tries to buy a blouse. A woman who cries in the lingerie department. A woman who laughs while trying on hats. A woman who buys two coats of a different colour. (1998, 5)

Repetitions such as these—which are abundant throughout *The Portable Virgin*—confer emphasis but also highlight Enright's thematic concern with difference and similarity. In this story, interestingly, the protagonist likes to make distinctions between customers, to "divide her women into two categories", and she is adept at pairing the correct handbag with each singular woman: "Quietly, one customer after another was guided to the inevitable and surprising choice of a bag that was not 'them' but one step beyond who they thought they might be" (1998, 4). Yet, when she falls in love with one of her customers, all her neat distinctions vanish: "Cathy began to slip. She made mistakes. She sold the wrong bags to the wrong women [...] She sold indiscriminately. She looked at every woman who came her way and she just didn't know anymore" (1998, 7). Her neatly organized life falls apart. A similar trajectory from compartmentalized difference to chaotic indifference is charted in "Luck Be a Lady", where the protagonist's exceptional way with numbers—she obsessively separates and counts everything—deserts her when she falls in love with another man:

The numbers were letting her down. Her daily walk to the shops became a confusion of damaged registration plates, the digits swung sideways or strokes were lopped off. 6 became 0, 7 turned into 1. She added up what was left, 555, 666, 616, 707, 906, 888, the numbers for parting, for grief, for the beginning of grief, for getting, for accidents and for the hate that comes from money. (1998, 75)

In the end, she gives in to her desire for him: "He smiled and the numbers of his face scattered and disappeared" (1998, 77).

In two other stories, by contrast, the development is not from rigid distinctions to a pleasurably chaotic indistinction, but from enabling difference to a restrictive sameness. "Dare to be dowdy" is the proud statement that opens "The Portable Virgin", as the protagonist defends her difference from "those women who hold their skin like a smile" (1998, 81). Yet, when she learns that her husband is having an affair with one of these women, she goes to the hairdresser to achieve the same depressingly uniform beauty ideal: "I look 'a fright'. All the women around me look 'a fright'. Mary is sitting to my left and to my right. She is blue from the neck down, she is reading a magazine, her hair stinks, her skin is pulled into a smile by the rubber tonsure on her head" (1998, 86). In "Fatgirl Terrestrial" too, a young "successful" woman who at first prides herself on being "odd"—"she was fat and so felt herself to be beyond the pale—free"—comes to conform to a more conventional femininity in order to find herself a husband, a suitably "public man" (1998, 131). She loses weight, accepts a demotion in the office, stops sleeping around, and ends up with a perfectly conventional marriage. As Ingman notes, the story thus explores why "educated and successful women nevertheless feel pressurized to conform to society's expectations of femininity" (2009, 249). Both of these stories, in other words, contain a critique of the culture of sameness that pervades contemporary society and popular culture.

It is precisely against these images of a uniform femininity that Enright presents her alternatives in *The Portable Virgin*. As we have seen, she does this through a practice of rewriting which presents different versions of the same old story or playful variations on the same old plot. Both in formal and in thematic terms, therefore, her stories offer repetitions with endless variation. In this way, they can be likened to the images produced by the kaleidoscope, the central metaphor of "Men and Angels": "If the object be put in motion, the combination of images will likewise be put in motion, and new forms, perfectly different, but equally symmetrical, will successively present themselves, sometimes vanishing in the centre, sometimes emerging from it, and sometimes playing around it in double and opposite oscillations" (1998, 103). This joining of opposites, this play of sameness and difference, is also highlighted in a scene from "What Are Cicadas?", where a father gives a displaced answer to the question in the title:

> They look up the dictionary. '"Cicatrise"' says his father, who always answers the wrong question—'"to heal; to mark with scars"'—I always thought there was only one word which encompassed opposites, namely...? To cleave; to cleave apart as with a sword, or to cleave one to another, as in a loyal friend. If you were old enough we might discuss "cleavage" and whether the glass was half empty or half full. Or maybe we can have our cake and eat it after all.' (1998, 148–9)

EMMA DONOGHUE'S ALTERNATIVE HISTORIES

A well-known form of postmodern fiction is historiografiction (Orlofsky 2003) or historiographic metafiction (Hutcheon 2003). It participates in a larger epistemological critique of history, propelled by such questions as: "In whose interests and from what standpoint is [a history] conceived? Who is excluded and who is privileged as a result of the particular narrative perspective? How incomplete are particular histories and who is it that benefits and who is it that is disadvantaged by this incompleteness?" (Peach 2007, 31). Often these question are addressed by imagining the "histories of those who had been previously ignored or forgotten, 'history from below' or from the margins" (Geyh et al. 1998, xxv). One such marginalized group is of course that of women, whose lives and achievements have often been silenced in official histories. Hence, many late-twentieth-century women writers have used historiografiction to "to propel them [the silent and the silences] into the space of representation that is also the place of remembrance. Seeking to 'know the past' differently, women's rewriting 'writes back' to silence in an effort to generate usable pasts, answering it with stories of its own" (Plate 2011, 97). The practice of historiografiction thus joins that of feminist rewriting in an attempt to re-visit and re-imagine women's pasts so as to better address present concerns. Hence, historical narratives are often juxtaposed to contemporary ones, in order to "open [the past] up to the present, to prevent it from being conclusive and teleological" (Hutcheon 2003, 110). Unlike older forms of historical fiction, finally, postmodern historiographical fiction is intensely self-reflexive and tends "to thematise the fragmentary, disjunctive, and often contradictory nature of historical evidence and hence of history itself, rather than presenting history as a continuous, unified story" (Geyh et al. 1998, xxv).

As Hutcheon's definition of historiographic metafiction suggests—"novels which are both intensely self-reflexive and yet paradoxically also lay claim to historical events and personages" (2003, 5)—the term is usually applied to novels. Indeed, historical fiction more generally is typically assumed to be the province of longer works of fiction, as the breadth and expanse of a novel seem required for historical development. In that sense, the two short story collections of Emma Donoghue which I will consider in what follows, are interesting exceptions to this rule. In their self-reflexive joining of fiction and historical fact, these stories very much participate in the postmodern movements of historiografiction and meta-fiction. For as Donoghue announces in the Foreword to *The Woman Who Gave Birth to Rabbits* (2002), "I have tried to use memory and invention together, like two hands engaged in the same muddy work of digging up the past". Although Donoghue has published other short story collections as well, most notably *Kissing the Witch* (1997), a collection of revisioned fairy tales, and *Touchy Subjects* (2006), a collection of contemporary short stories about taboo topics, I will focus on the historical stories of *The Woman* and *Astray* (2012) as examples of the historiographic strand in contemporary Irish short fiction. This will also give me the opportunity to briefly revisit the work of Enright and Ní Dhuibhne, as they also use historiographic metafiction in a few stories. Comparing the different approaches of these writers within this larger category will prepare the way for a more detailed account of Donoghue's specific mode of historio-graphic metafiction.

In "The Flowering", first published in *Eating Women Is Not Recommended* (1991), Ní Dhuibhne tackles problems of historiography head-on. The suitably ironic omniscient narrator tells us about Lennie who "wants to discover her roots" (Ní Dhuibhne 2003, 9). On the basis of "clues" from "textbooks", "exhibition catalogues", "school history stuff" (2003, 10–11), Lennie imagines an ancestral farmhouse, her family's Famine deprivation and—in a longish embedded story—the sad life of a creative great-aunt, Sally Rua. The narrator comments "Of course, none of that is true. It is a yarn, spun out of thin air. Not quite out of thin air: Lennie read about a woman like Sally Rua [...] in a history of embroidery in Ireland" (2003, 20). Yet even while undermining the truth value of this personal history, the narrator also vindicates Lennie's efforts by suggesting that fiction necessarily takes over when history falls short: "Archaeology, history, folklore. Linguistics, genealogy. They tell you about society, not about individuals. It takes literature to do that" (2003, 12). Lennie herself takes an even more radical postmodern attitude:

> She does not see much difference between history and fiction, between painting and embroidery, between either of them and literature. Or scholar-ship. Or building houses [...] The essential skills of learning to manipulate raw material, to transform it into something orderly and expressive, to make it, if not better or more beautiful, different from what it was originally and more itself, apply equally to all of these exercises. (2003, 21)

Moreover, by placing the story of Sally Rua in the larger framework of a contemporary woman's quest for identity, the story also shows how history is always already informed by the concerns and needs of the present. In short, in typical postmodern fashion, Ní Dhuibhne questions the truth value of any historical account, while at the same time asserting the continual need for new and more varied historical imaginings.

Like "The Flowering", Anne Enright's "Men and Angels" also juxtaposes historical stories to a contemporary one. The first two sections of the short story deal with the wives of famous scientists and inventors, Christiaan Huygens and Sir David Brewster, respectively. The third section stages a female artist and offers a twist on the traditional 'men and angels' trope that informs the first two stories: the story ends with "She really was a selfish bastard (as they say of men and angels)" (Enright 1998, 110). The first two stories invite being read as classic examples of feminist historiographic revisioning, as they recover the lives of those marginalized in traditional histories: the wife of Huygens, the inventor of Huygens' endless chain, is said to have given up her wedding ring for the sake of her husband's invention, but "could not rid herself of the shame she felt for her bare hands" (1998, 100) and the wife of Brewster, the scientist who invented the kaleidoscope, the story tells us, to console his sad young wife on her deathbed. Both women are thus presented as forgotten muses and sacrificial figures, living in the shadows of their great husbands. Following the conventions of historiographic metafiction, moreover, the narrator also self-consciously questions the truth of these imagined lives: "Of his wife, we know very little", the narrator notes or "It is difficult to say what broke her" (1998, 102, 106). So far, the two stories neatly observe the staples of historiographic metafiction and feminist revisioning. Yet, the story plays a further twist on these conventions by also fabricating the historical facts of these stories. Thus, Christiaan Huyghens, the inventor of the watch chain, was Dutch rather than German and was not married at all. Similarly, the actual Mrs. Brewster lived a long life, only dying in 1850, while her husband invented the kaleidoscope in 1815. In characteristic fashion, Enright thus stages a parodic, playful version of historiographic metafiction, freely fabricating the past for the sake of a powerful image (the wedding ring in the clock and the refractions of the kaleidoscope) or overall aesthetic structure (the ironic reversal of the 'men and angels' trope). As in the kaleidoscope, historical facts can be twisted and turned to create "new forms, perfectly different, but equally symmetrical [...] sometimes vanishing in the centre, sometimes emerging from it, and sometimes playing around in double and opposite oscillations" (1998, 103).

Compared to Enright's playful and parodic historiografiction, Donoghue's short stories take history far more seriously. In both *The Woman Who Gave Birth to Rabbits* and *Astray*, all the stories are based on historical facts, which are duly acknowledged in a note at the end of each story. In the Foreword to *The Woman*, Donoghue writes "My sources are the flotsam and jetsam of the last seven hundred years of British and Irish life: surgical case-notes; trial records; a plague ballad; theological pamphlets; a painting of two girls in a garden; an articulated skeleton" (2002, n.p.). And in *Astray's* Afterword too, we learn that "Most of these travelers are real people who left traces in the historical record; a few are characters I've invented to put a face on real incidents" (2012, 263). The fictional story and the historical note also work together to form a larger—hybrid—whole: the story gives life to the names and facts mentioned in the historical note and the note itself goes beyond the boundaries of the story, providing it with a larger historical context and relevance. In this way, the stories achieve the kind of "double vision" which Michele Morano attributes to nonfiction stories, as readers are encouraged to see "an imaginative space infused not just with verisimilitude but with reality, a place where fact and fancy are locked in a complicated embrace" (Morano 2003, 38).

In the case of Donoghue's stories, however, this double vision is also a sceptical vision, informed as it is by a postmodern awareness of the limits of history and truth. In *The Woman*, indeed, Donoghue warns the reader that this is "a book of fictions, but they are also true", while quoting Monique Wittig's dictum "Try to remember, or, failing that, invent" (2002, n.p.). The notes also question the truth of historical documents, by pointing to inconsistencies and contradictory versions, or by alerting the reader to a discrepancy between the official facts and the fictional story. In the stories themselves, moreover, narrators and characters often self-consciously reflect on the hazy border between truth and lies, fiction and facts. In the opening story of *The Woman*, for instance, a character comments "And if who can tell what's true and what's not in these times, Mary, why then mayn't this rabbit story be as true as anything else?", while in "The Necessity of Burning", the protagonist questions the truth of the scholarly books in Cambridge, and especially of their representations of women: "No wonder, Margery reckons, seeing as it's men who write the books" (2002, 2, 187). This remark also reveals the ideological dimension of Donoghue's historiographic metafiction. In *The Woman*, Donoghue's revisionary project is clearly a feminist one, as she re-imagines the lives of female characters who have been forgotten, marginalized or misrepresented in official histories. In *Astray*, her rewriting is centred on histories and stories of migration and attempts to question the standard account of Irish emigration. As I will show in some more detail in what follows, the historiographic and metafictional dimensions of both collections can thus be said to serve a larger project of rewriting, which aims to question, unsettle and complicate existing narratives, fictional or otherwise.

As the title of the collection already suggests, all of the 17 stories of *The Woman Who Gave Birth to Rabbits* revolve around female figures. In some stories, these women are the forgotten wives or daughters of famous husbands (Effie Ruskin in "Come, Gentle Knight" or Dido Lindsay in "Dido"), in other stories they are well-known historical figures in their own right (Mary Wollstonecraft in "Words for Things" or the poet Frances Browne in "Night Vision"). In yet other stories, the characters are wholly unknown, derived from footnotes in historical records, such as the patient undergoing a cliterodectomy in "Cured" or, indeed, the woman who pretended to give birth to rabbits in "The Last Rabbit". The women portrayed vary in many other ways as well: their lives span seven centuries and different locations in Britain and Ireland; they come from different social classes and walks of life, and they differ in age, beliefs and sexuality. What they all share, however, is being confined by patriarchal structures. Even if some women occupy positions of power with regard to their servants, children, or even—as in "Revelations"—an entire community, they are all shown to labour under the gender norms and gendered hierarchies of a patriarchal society. Sometimes these gendered restrictions are quite blatant as when the blind girl Frances in "Night Vision" is told by the Minister that "a stunted little girl" like her is not entitled to an education, or when the niece in "Acts of Union" is married off against her will. In other stories, the women are so cowed by men in power, men who know the correct "words", that they easily submit to exploitation (2002, 196). In "Cured", "A Short Story", "The Fox on the Line" and "The Last Rabbit", men of science especially are shown to abuse their authority by reducing women to objects of study, experimentation or fraudulent financial schemes. In many stories, interestingly, the women's subordinate position in a patriarchal society is symbolized by bodily defects: they are crippled, blind, pregnant, too small, or have terrible back- or headaches.

Still, although most women in the collection are shown to suffer either from the gendered restrictions of patriarchal society in general, or from more specific acts of deceit or violence on the part of some men, Donoghue takes care to also highlight acts of resistance or rebellion, however small, in every story. To give some examples: in "The Last Rabbit", the protagonist finally revolts against the plot that has been forced on her and decides to tell her own story; the victim of circumcision in "Cured" self-consciously plays the role of the submissive patient in order to be released; in "Come, Gentle Night", Effie Ruskin reacts against her husband's idealization of her into a disembodied aesthetic object by filing for a divorce; and in "The Necessity of Burning" Margery burns the clergy's books in retaliation against the priest who was too drunk to give her stillborn son a Christian burial. By thus highlighting the characters' agency in the face of patriarchal oppression, Donoghue avoids staging her female protagonists as those "weeping piteous victims who flock across the pages of history", as the narrator of the closing story mockingly puts it (2002, 204). In this way, she skilfully avoids one of the pitfalls of feminist historiography, that of repeating rather than reversing women's marginalization by showing only their wrongful victimization in the hands of men. Donoghue's emphasis on women's agency within a structure of confinement and oppression thus offers a correction to this tradition of victimization: some of her characters use and abuse power themselves, while even those who suffer at the hands of men find ways of resisting patriarchal structures and oppression.

This is demonstrated most clearly in the closing story, "Looking for Petronilla", which both enacts and criticizes the feminist historiographic project as it metafictionally stages a woman's contemporary quest for the maid she abused many centuries earlier. The story's narrator, Dame Alice, went down in history as a witch and murderer of several husbands, yet she only repents her responsibility for the death of her innocent maid, Petronilla. Hence, she is looking for traces of her maid in her hometown of Kilkenny, trying to find a way of re-imagining her, of bringing her to life. In this way, her quest resembles that of Donoghue herself who scoured historical records to give life—and often a voice—to silenced female figures. And even though Dame Alice knows that "there is nothing left", that she will "never fully understand" Petronilla, she continues on her quest: "My one faith is that I will find some trace of Petronilla. My one hope is that she will teach me how to die" (2002, 208, 212). Yet, in spite of her commitment to this woman-centred recovery project, Dame Alice is also dismissive of the revisionist accounts of her own life which she finds in history book:

> "Alice Kyteler [...] was a victim of a combination of the worst excesses of fourteenth-century Christo-patriarchy [...] As in so many other 'witch trials', powerful men (both church and lay) projected their own unconscious fantasies of sexual/satanic perversion onto the blank canvas of a woman's life." I can't help smiling: *blank canvas*, my eye. There is a grain of truth there of course: before she ever trafficked with darkness, the citizens of Kilkenny resented the Kyteler woman's fine house, bright gowns, every last ruby on her fingers. But that hardly makes her innocent. (2002, 206)

A clear *mise-en-abîme* to the collection as a whole, "Looking for Petronilla" spells out the aims of Donoghue's own project of rewriting, as it re-imagines the often forgotten lives of historical women living within the gendered restrictions of a patriarchal society, without falling into the trap of reducing them—once again—to the role of innocent, piteous victims. By foregrounding acts of complicity or rebellion on the part of her female characters, Donoghue shows her historical figures to be, above all, ordinary and complex human beings, who always exceed the neat binaries of witch and angel, aggressor and victim, with which history has often sought to contain them.

Like the stories in *The Woman*, the stories in *Astray* are also hybrid compounds of fiction and fact, with the historical note at the end of the story joining up with the story itself to form a larger whole that encompasses both the private and the public faces of historical events. Again, the stories range widely from the seventeenth to the early twentieth century and stage characters from different nationalities, classes, races and religions. Unlike in the earlier collection, however, men and women are staged as protagonists in the stories, which share a thematic focus on issues of migration. As Donoghue notes in her Afterword: all the stories deal with "travels to, within, and occasionally from the United States and Canada. Most of these travelers are real people who left traces in the historical record; a few are characters I've invented to put a face on real incidents of border crossing" (2012, 263). Yet, the stories go further than a mere imaginative staging of historical incidents. The historiographic dimension of *Astray* is again part of a project of revisioning: not, this time, of silenced women's lives, but rather of the traditional tropes of Irish emigration.

As has been briefly noted in Chapter 3, the iconography of emigration is very central to the Irish imagination: "Emigration and exile, the journeys to and from home, are the very heartbeat of Irish culture. To imagine Ireland is to imagine a journey" (O'Toole 1997, 77). In Irish short fiction, emigration figures in such iconic stories as George Moore's "Exile" and "Homesickness", Liam O'Flaherty's "Going into Exile", and Frank O'Connor's "Uprooted". As the titles of these works suggest, Irish literature typically stages the emigrant as exile, forever yearning for the motherland he left behind. Tropes of homelessness, alienation, outsiderness and loss figure large in these stories. In this way, the Irish short story has helped shape the traditional understanding of Irish emigration as both involuntary and exceptional, with emigrants staged as victims of colonial oppression, religious persecution or economic hardship. The central image here is of course the trauma of the Great Famine which sent many Irish to America on the so-called coffin ships to escape starvation. As I noted in Chapter 3, recent historical research has questioned the "tropes of victimhood and forced departure" that inform discourses of Irish emigration, by highlighting the many different reasons that led people to cross the Atlantic or the Irish Sea towards a new life (Éinrí and O'Toole 2012, 7–8). Moreover, as Akenson argues, imaginatively construing "the Irish diaspora as tragedy and as having been largely an involuntary movement" is "condescending to the migrant generation (who have for the most part been capable of strong and conscious decision-making and were not mere passive bits of flotsam on some alleged historical tide)" and "also unconsciously demeaning to the various new homelands in which the Irish migrants settled, for it treats the New Worlds as a set of Elbas where no one would settle by choice" (Akenson 1996, 10–11). At the same time, diaspora studies have juxtaposed the Irish diaspora to many other diasporas, thus qualifying exceptionalist representations of Irish emigration (Kenny 2013). Nevertheless, the intensified emigration after the collapse of the Celtic Tiger seems to have given new lease to the powerful metaphorical construct of the poor unwilling exile. In a recent article for *The New York Times*, for instance, the novelist John Banville compares the migration of young Irish people today to "the repeated waves of emigration" which Ireland "suffered", "much of it compulsory, ever since the Flight of the Earls at the beginning of the 17th century, when English forces defeated the army of the Irish aristocracy and drove its leaders into exile" (Banville 2011). He adds that "The violent poetry of leave-taking is ingrained in

Irish consciousness", and this appears to be borne out by such recent Irish short stories as Edna O'Brien's "Shovel Kings", Claire Keegan's "The Parting Gift", or Colm Tóibín's "One Minus One" (McWilliams 2013).

Within this pervasive imaginative framework, I will argue, the stories in *Astray* sound a critical, new note. With the individual stories staging the very diverse experiences of migrants to North America, the collection as a whole demonstrates its revisionary power by unsettling the received images of Irish emigration. While the collection is not singularly focused on Irish migratory movements, its Irish dimension stands out in various ways. In her Afterword, Donoghue explicitly calls herself an "Irish writer who spent eight years in England before moving to Canada" (2012, 261). She talks about her own experience of migration and compares it to the iconic image of the 'Irish writer in exile'. Several stories have Irish or Irish-American protagonists, while several others make minor references to Ireland or Irish characters. Because of this Irish dimension, *Astray* can be read as commenting not just on migration in general, but also—and more specifically—on Irish emigration. At the same time, the multifaceted picture of emigration offered in *Astray* serves to complicate the Irish emigration-as-exile trope in various ways.

First, the temporal and spatial breadth of *Astray* opens up the traditional discourse on Irish emigration by placing the Irish case in a larger context. The stories themselves range from 1639 to 1967, while the epigraph from Virgil and the Afterword's references to contemporary migration extend the temporal scale even further. Indeed, as is common in historical fiction, Donoghue's stories can be seen to comment on contemporary processes, as when the fate of the Irish emigrants in "Counting the Days" is linked to that of contemporary "economic migrants" and "their passionate wish for a better life [...] no matter how terrible the journey. When I read headlines about human traffic gunned down crossing a border, or found suffocated in container trucks, I think of the Johnsons" (2012, 266). This temporal reach is matched by a spatial one as the migrants in the stories come from many different European countries as well as from Africa, the West Indies and the Middle East. By thus juxtaposing stories of Irish migrants next to those of many other migrants, *Astray* unsettles the exceptionalist strain in discourses of Irish migration.

A second strategy Donoghue uses is that of displacing familiar tropes and rhetoric by applying them in unusual contexts. For instance, the emigrant's wistful yearning for the home, familiar from Irish literature, is in

Astray most explicitly voiced with regard to the elephant Jumbo who is transported from London to the USA:

> Of course, you'll miss England, and giving the kiddies rides, that's only to be expected. And doing headstands in the Pool, wandering down the Parrot Walk, the Carnivora Terrace, all the old sights. You'll find those American winters a trial to your spirits I shouldn't wonder. And I expect once in a while you'll spare a thought for your old pa. (2012, 11)

In the second story, "Onward", the character feels "she lives in the crack between two worlds" (2012, 32). This could easily be taken to describe the exile's sense of being suspended between two countries, no longer truly at home in either, which has been evoked so hauntingly in Moore's "Homesickness" or O'Brien's "Shovel Kings". Yet, here it is applied to the protagonist's feeling of being caught between the domestic life she tries to uphold and the prostitution she has to stoop to, so as to secure a living for her child and her brother. It is precisely this state of homelessness she hopes to cure by migration. On the whole there is little pining for the motherland in *Astray*—an Irish character even claims "there was nothing set his teeth on edge more than an emigrant sniveling for home" (2012, 237)—while "Vanitas" shows the debilitating effects of homesickness, the "nostalgia for a lost Eden" (2012, 269). The protagonists of this story are not Irish emigrants, holding on to a mythic ideal of a lost Erin, but a French family in Louisiana for whom France "is all things gracious and fine and civilized" with Paris "that pearly city", the "apex of civilization" (2012, 191, 198). It is an impossible ideal that will blight the family's life in different ways.

When Donoghue does tackle the iconic Irish emigration to America during the Famine years, it is again in a displaced or atypical way. The story "Counting the Days" interlaces the memories and eager anticipation of a couple from Antrim: the man has gone ahead to Quebec and the wife is now making the crossing to join him with her two children. The journey has been hard for both of them and as they are about to meet again, Henry succumbs to the cholera epidemic and dies. Yet the protagonists of this sad story of love and loss are not the iconic Catholic Irish tenants escaping starvation, but rather Protestant middle-class shopkeepers escaping a life blighted by debts and the husband's alcoholism. Henry thinks of emigration as a new start for both of them, even though Jane ponders: "What choice have any of them made, when all they know is what they are running from, when Henry with his exasperating enthu-siasm is leading them into the dark?" (2012, 85). In this, and many oth-ers stories, Donoghue clearly alludes to the debate about the voluntary or compulsory nature of (Irish) emigration. Several of the characters see their leaving for "the land of the free" as "a fresh start", or "a new begin-ning" (2012, 18, 36, 35). They migrate looking for better opportuni-ties—like the women sculptors in "What Remains" or the gold-diggers in "Snowblind", or for a freer, happier, better life. Still, Donoghue also shows that there is always something that propelled their decision: an unhappy marriage, debts or poverty, a feeling of alienation or restriction. Some of the migrations are indeed compulsory, such as the elephant's transatlantic journey in "Man and Boy", the child sent on the so-called orphan trains to the American West in "The Gift" and the young German soldier who is forced to go and fight in the American Civil War in "The Hunt". Yet, as in *The Woman*, Donoghue again complicates any straight-forward victim-narrative. In "The Hunt", the boy who has been "sold" by his Prince to the Redcoats becomes a perpetrator himself when he takes part—even if unwillingly—in the soldiers' gang rape of local girls, while in "The Body Swap" a group of Irish emigrants is involved in large-scale counterfeiting and other criminal activities. In "The Widow's Cruse", to the contrary, a Jewish woman from the West Indies who is in an unhappy marriage in early eighteenth-century New York, cleverly uses the aura of victimhood to become a victor instead. She impersonates a hapless and bereaved widow so as to trick her not-yet-dead husband out of his con-siderable fortune.

These examples also point to the other forms of border-crossing which Donoghue explicitly foregrounds in many stories. As the title sug-gests, her migrants and travellers often 'stray' in a moral sense as well, even going 'astray' in the process. The English Puritan in "The Lost Seed", for instance, is set on making his settler community on Cape Cod into the new Eden, by enforcing strict rules to eradicate all evil. Yet he is shown to lose any sense of human sympathy and ultimately himself in the process. In "Last Supper at Brown's", the protagonists cross the heavily policed boundary of race as a black slave and his white mistress kill their abusive master and set off on a journey to freedom. In other stories, migration empowers characters to cross boundar-ies of gender and sexuality. In "What Remains", migrating to Canada empowers the two protagonists to assert their worth as important art-ists in the face of patriarchal prejudices: "Canada was a young country;

there seemed infinite room [...] The towns needed so many memorials, they had to stoop to hiring women" (2012, 253), while the relative lawlessness of mid-nineteenth-century Arizona allows Mollie Monroe in "The Long Way Home" to cross-dress as a man and engage in various masculine activities, even while upholding a personal sense of morality and responsibility. In "Daddy's Girl", similarly, Mary Hall uses the transatlantic crossing to become Murray Hall: with wife and child, fat cigars, a gruff demeanour and a string of mistresses, he becomes "an important man in New York, a pillar of the Democratic Society"—and only after his death is his—or her—actual sex discovered (2012, 230).

As these examples indicate, these border-crossings never constitute clean breaks. Rather, the characters keep identity markers or consciousness constructions related to two genders, nationalities, or races. With regard to actual migrations as well as more symbolic forms of border crossings, Donoghue thus emphasizes the hybridity and creolization involved in migration, with identities combining, colluding and clashing in various ways. In this way, *Astray* substitutes the Irish emigration-as-exile discourse for a transnational take on migration, one which emphasizes "dual or multiple identifications" (Vertovec 2009, 6). Indeed, Donoghue replaces the 'neither–nor' sentiment inherent in the trope of exile, with a view on migration as an 'and–and' story. Unlike the exilic identity, which sees itself as bereft of both homeland and adopted country, the transnational identity foregrounded in *Astray* is made up of a mixture of both identities. In highlighting this perspective, *Astray* effectively rewrites the dominant story of Irish emigration.

Just as in *The Woman*, however, Donoghue shows herself conscious of the pitfalls of this revisionary undertaking. As critics of the transnational turn have pointed out, migration does not always result in a subversively hybrid and anti-essentialist "third space", nor are all transnational ventures to be equated with a progressive politics that moves beyond the nation-state (Vertovec 2009, 11). In *Astray* too, some stories sound a cautionary note to this celebration of hybridity and transnational identity. First, the stories set in the seventeenth and eighteenth centuries remind us that slavery and colonialization were also decidedly transnational ventures, while "The Lost Seed" shows that the transnational consciousness of the Pilgrim Fathers did not entail a liberating progressivism but rather the enforcing of a rigid, conservative and patriarchal morality. A story like "Vanitas", further, usefully reminds us that migration can also lead to an entrenchment of national identity rather than its creolization as the Locoul family stubbornly refuses to mix with non-French neighbours. In the Afterword, finally, Donoghue suggests seeing migration as a metaphor for humanity itself:

> Migration is mortality by another name, the itch we can't scratch. Perhaps because moving far away to some arbitrary spot simply highlights the arbitrariness of getting born into this particular body in the first place: this contingent selfhood, this sole life. Writing stories is my way of scratching that itch: my escape from the claustrophobia of individuality. It lets me, at least for a while, life more than one life, walk more than one path. Reading, of course, can do the same. (2012, 270–1)

Yet if migration exemplifies the limits of the self, Donoghue's stories also show it to represent various efforts to transcend these limits: to cross borders, encounter alterity, explore a different view. And even if the outcome of these efforts may not always be desirable, the efforts themselves, Donoghue shows, are invariably laudable and worthwhile.

Whether they are rewriting folk tales, popular plots or historical narratives, the three writers I have discussed in this chapter all combine postmodern techniques with feminist concerns. Their feminist aesthetics of writing as rewriting allows them to question, undermine and open up the inherited stories, traditional plots and stereotypical images that all too often steer our worldview into predictable grooves. All three writers are committed to telling the other story, presenting the alternative viewpoint, substituting multiplicity for the "monolithic voice" (Enright and Frostrup 2015). Like all forms of rewriting, their work also depends of course on the tension between "the known and the new" (Sellers 2001, 14), between repetition and variation, or similarity and difference. Interestingly, this very tension between sameness and difference also manifests itself on the structural level of the short story collections. Indeed, Ní Dhuibhne's *The Inland Ice*, Enright's *The Portable Virgin*, and Donoghue's *The Woman* and *Astray* can all be said to belong to the genre of the short story cycle, which I already introduced in Chapter 5. In *The Inland Ice*, stories about women from different classes, periods, countries and ages are united by their focus on the vexations and vicissitudes of marital and extra-marital love, and in *The Portable Virgin*, the different stories offer as many variations on the theme of female—and occasionally male—desire. In *The Woman Who Gave Birth to Rabbits*, Donoghue underscores her characters' shared entrapment in patriarchal structures by a distinctive formal structure as well as by threading recurring symbols (e.g. the rabbit, the crippled body), phrases, and names through the individual stories (see Brouckmans and D'hoker 2014). In a similar way, the repetition of tropes and experiences connected to migration unites the different stories in *Astray*. I would argue, therefore, that these story collections achieve their feminist revisionary aims in an important way through their use of the short story cycle and its characteristic tension between unity and diversity or similarity and difference.

BIBLIOGRAPHY

Akenson, Donald Harman. 1996. *The Irish Diaspora: A Primer.* Toronto: P.D. Meany Co.

Banville, John. 1970. *Long Lankin.* London: Secker and Warburg.

Banville, John. 2011. The Grim Good Cheer of the Irish. *New York Times*, 17 December 2011. http://nyti.ms/1DZDJra

Bracken, Claire, and Susan Cahill. 2011. An Interview with Anne Enright. In *Anne Enright*, edited by Claire Bracken and Susan Cahill, 13–32. Dublin: Irish Academic Press.

Broich, Ulrich. 1993. Muted Postmodernism: The Contemporary British Short Story. *Zeitschrift für Anglistik und Amerikanistik* 41 (1):31–39.

Brouckmans, Debbie, and Elke D'hoker. 2014. Rewriting the Irish Short Story: Emma Donoghue's *The Woman Who Gave Birth to Rabbits. Journal of the Short Story in English* 63:213–228.

Coughlan, Patricia. 2004a. Irish Literature and Feminism in Postmodernity. *Hungarian Journal of English and American Studies* 10 (1/2):175–202.

D'hoker, Elke. 2004. The Postmodern Folktales of Eílis Ní Dhuibhne. *ABEI: The Brazilian Journal of Irish Studies* 6:129–140.

Donoghue, Emma. 1997. *Kissing the Witch.* London. Hamish Hamilton.

Donghue, Emma. 2006. *Touchy Subjects.* London: Virago.

Donoghue, Emma. 2002. *The Woman Who Gave Birth To Rabbits.* London: Virago.

Donoghue, Emma. 2012. *Astray.* Basingstoke: Picador.

Éinrí, Piaras Mac, and Tina O'Toole. 2012. Editors' Introduction: New Approaches to Irish Migration. *Éire-Ireland* 47 (1):5–18.

Enright, Anne. 1998. *The Portable Virgin.* London: Vintage. Original edition, 1991.

Enright, Anne. 2009. *Yesterday's Weather.* London: Vintage.

Enright, Anne, and Mariella Frostrup. 2015. Open Book: Anne Enright on *The Green Road.* In *BBC Radio 4: Books and Authors.*

Fogarty, Anne. 2003. Preface. In *Midwife to the Fairies. New and Selected Stories*, edited by Eilis Ni Dhuibhne, ix–xv. Cork: Attic Press.

Fogarty, Anne. 2009. 'What Matters But the Good of the Story?': Femininity and Desire in Eilis Ni Dhuibhne's *The Inland Ice and Other Stories*. In *Eilis Ni Dhuibhne: Perspectives*, edited by Rebecca Pelan, 69–86. Galway: Arlen House.

Geyh, Paula, Fred G. Leebron, and Andrew Levy. 1998. *Postmodern American Fiction: A Norton Anthology*. New York: Norton.

Hanson, Clare. 1985. *Short Stories and Short Fictions, 1880–1980*. London: Macmillan.

Higgins, Aidan. 1960. *Felo De Se*. London: John Calder.

Hutcheon, Linda. 2003. *A Poetics of Postmodernism: History, Theory, Fiction*. New York: Routledge. Original edition, 1988.

Ingman, Heather. 2009. *A History of the Irish Short Story*. Cambridge: Cambridge University Press.

Jarfe, Günther. 2008. Experimental Short Fiction in Britain Since 1945. In *A Companion to the British and Irish Short Story*, edited by Cheryl Alexander Malcolm and David Malcolm, 384–399. Oxford: Wiley.

Jordan, Neil. 1976. *Nights in Tunisia and Other Stories*. Dublin: Irish Writers' Cooperative.

Kenny, Kevin. 2013. *Diaspora: A Very Short Introduction*. Oxford: Oxford University Press.

McWilliams, Ellen. 2013. *Women and Exile in Contemporary Irish Fiction*. Basingstoke: Palgrave.

Moloney, Caitriona. 2007. Reimagining Women's History in the Fiction of Éilís Ní Dhuibhne, Anne Enright, and Kate O'Riordan. *Postcolonial Text* 3 (3). http://postcolonial.org/index.php/pct/article/viewArticle/709.

Moloney, Caitriona. 2009. Exile in Éilís Ní Dhuibhne's Short Fiction. In *Éilís NiDhuibhne: Perspectives*, edited by Rebecca Pelan, 87–112. Galway: Arlen House.

Morano, Michele. 2003. Facts and Fancy: The 'Nonfiction Short Story'. In *The Postmodern Short Story: Forms and Issues*, edited by Farhat Iftekharrudin, Joseph Boyden, Mary Rohrberger and Jaie Claudet, 35–46. Westport, CT: Praeger.

Ní Chonchúir, Nuala. 2012. Review of *The Shelter of Neighbours* by Eilis Ni Dhuibhne. *The Short Review*. Accessed 11/02/2015. http://www.theshort-review.com/reviews/EilisNiDhuibhneTheShelterOfNeighbours.htm.

Ní Dhuibhne, Éilís. 1988. *Blood and Water*. Dublin: Attic Press.

Ní Dhuibhne, Éilís. 1991. *Eating Women is Not Recommended*. Dublin: Attic Press.

Ní Dhuibhne, Éilís. 1999. *The Dancers Dancing*. Belfast: Blackstaff Press.

Ní Dhuibhne, Éilís. 2007. *Fox, Swallow, Scarecrow*. Belfast: Blackstaff Press.

Ní Dhuibhne, Éilís. 1997. *The Inland Ice and Other Stories*. Belfast: Blackstaff Press.

Ní Dhuibhne, Éilís. 2000. *The Pale Gold of Alaska and Other Stories*. Belfast: Blackstaff Press.

Ní Dhuibhne, Éilís. 2003. *Midwife to the Fairies: New and Selected Stories.* Dublin: Attic Press.

O'Toole, Fintan. 1997. Perpetual Motion. In *Arguing at the Crossroads: Essays on a Changing Ireland*, 77–97. Dublin: New Island Books.

Orlofsky, Michael. 2003. Historiografiction: The Fictionalization of History in the Short Story. In *The Postmodern Short Story: Forms and Issues*, edited by Farhat Iftekharrudin, Joseph Boyden, Mary Rohrberger and Jaie Claudet, 47–62. Westport, CT: Praeger.

Peach, Linden. 2007. *Contemporary Irish and Welsh Women's Fiction: Gender, Desire and Power.* Cardiff: University of Wales Press.

Plate, Liedeke. 2011. *Transforming Memories in Contemporary Women's Rewriting.* Basingstoke: Palgrave Macmillan

Rich, Adrienne. 1972. When We Dead Awaken: Writing as Re-Vision. *College English* 34 (1):18–30.

Sacido, Jorge. 2012. Modernism, Postmodernism and the Short Story. In *Modernism, Postmodernism, and the Short Story in English*, edited by Jorge Sacido, 1–25. Amsterdam: Rodopi.

Sellers, Susan. 2001. *Myth and Fairy Tale in Contemporary Women's Fiction.* Basingstoke: Palgrave Macmillan.

St. Peter, Christine, and Éilís Ní Dhuibhne. 2006. Negotiating the Boundaries: An Interview with Éilís Ní Dhuibhne. *The Canadian Journal of Irish Studies* 32 (1):68–75.

Tallone, Giovanna. 2004. Elsewhere Is a Negative Mirror: The 'Sally Gap' Stories of Éilís Ní Dhuibhne and Mary Lavin. *Hungarian Journal of English and American Studies* 10 (1–2):203–215.

Vertovec, Steven. 2009. *Transnationalism.* London: Routledge.

CHAPTER 8

Conclusion

In her Introduction to *The Long Gaze Back: An Anthology of Irish Women Writers*, Sinéad Gleeson explains her title, a quote from Maeve Brennan's *The Visitor*, as an attempt to capture "the sense of looking back over the long arc of Irish women's writing" (Gleeson 2015, 6). Such a long gaze back has also been the aim of this book, not through a selection of representative stories, but by means of close textual analyses of the formal characteristics and thematic concerns of the short fiction by Irish women writers. In this way, this study has attempted to place this writing firmly on the literary map, to secure it a place in the history of the modern Irish short story. Through the loosely chronological trajectory of my six chapters, I have traced the development of the modern short story in the hands of Irish women writers from the two, somewhat oppositional, strands that emerged in the late nineteenth century: the plot-bound magazine story and the proto-modernist, plotless story. Both of these strands found important early representatives in Irish women writers, with the popular R.M. stories of Somerville and Ross embodying the condensed and unified "story with a twist" and the ground-breaking, psychological sketches of George Egerton early examples of the "slice-of-life" story favoured in modernism. Even though these plotless stories emerged in part as the result of foreign influences, in part as a reaction against the phenomenal success of the magazine story, in the course of the twentieth century, the two strands came to represent the extreme ends of a spectrum, rather than radically distinct modes. Following the example of Bowen, many writers freely mixed techniques and forms from both traditions or wrote stories

© The Editor(s) (if applicable) and The Author (s) 2016   211
E. D'hoker, *Irish Women Writers and the Modern Short Story*,
DOI 10.1007/978-3-319-30288-1_8

on different ends of the plotless-plotted continuum. In Lavin's œuvre, as we have seen, a handful of plot-bound stories stand out against the open-ended psychological realism of the rest of her stories, while also Maeve Brennan's short stories range from satirical, plotted stories over single-episode-based realist stories to plotless, speculative sketches.

A similar hybridity marks the realist dimension of Irish women's short fiction. Although realism remains the dominant mode, this realism comes in many different variations and combinations. A mixture of realism with comedy, irony and even satire can be observed in the stories of Somerville and Ross, but also in Brennan's Herbert Retreat stories and in some of the sharper stories of Bowen and Enright. Realism interlaced with fantasy characterizes the ghost stories of Bowen and, in a different way, the folktale-based stories of Ní Dhuibhne, while an idealized realism marks Barlow's transitional short stories as well as Egerton's utopian stories, even as the realism of some of her other stories verges on naturalism. However, the strong psychological impetus of most of Egerton's short fiction seems to have been most influential in the development of Irish women's short fiction. Bowen, Brennan, Lavin, Beckett, O'Brien, Ní Dhuibhne, Donoghue, Enright and Keegan: all of these writers are interested in exploring the different shades and vagaries of human consciousness as it engages with other people in complex world. What differs is the relative importance of a specific social and historical context in the short stories, as well as the specific techniques used for exploring consciousness, witness the highly symbolic realism of O'Brien, the minimalist realism of Keegan, and the meta-fictional or self-conscious realism of postmodern writers like Enright, Donoghue and Ní Dhuibhne.

Apart from this overall concern with exploring the human mind, the short fiction I have discussed in the foregoing chapters also shares many other common interests. First, an interest in woman's place in society, in the roles and norms that define and often oppress her, can be found in many short stories. In my survey, this concern was pioneered, once again, by George Egerton, but it also infuses those Bowen stories that scrutinize the fraught relation between women and the home and attack the reigning domestic ideology. The stories of Mary Beckett and Edna O'Brien too explore women's roles in a changing society, as do the stories of contemporary writers, influenced as they are by the women's movements of the 1970s and 1980s. As I have tried to show throughout the different chapters, further, the one preoccupation common to all short fiction by Irish women writers, is the concern with human relations, whether those of love, the family or the larger community. Inevitably, many stories stage male-female relations in all their different inflections: love, loss and hatred; courtship, long-standing marriage, and divorce; adultery, death and betrayal. This concern is especially prominent perhaps in Brennan's compulsive analyses of a stale marriage, in O'Brien's staging of the self-destructiveness of obsessive love, and in Ní Dhuibhne's chronicling of the attractions and inequities of extra-marital affairs. Second, as we have seen, the affinities and tensions within a family too are often explored in Irish short fiction. I am thinking of the close family bonds in Lavin's short stories, which compellingly depict the rivalries between siblings, the crippling hold of parents on their children, and the strength of family loyalty and motherly love. The troubled mother-daughter bond is also a recurring topic in Irish women's short fiction, from the childhood stories of Maeve Brennan, through the archetypal mother-daughter symbiosis staged in O'Brien's stories to the more enabling mother-daughter relations in the fiction of Claire Keegan. Finally, communities and communal relations too have found a place in Irish women's fiction. Given the brevity of individual short stories, this concern has often, if by no means exclusively, been explored through short stories series or cycles as in *Irish Idylls, Some Experiences of an Irish R.M., A Literary Woman, The Shelter of Neighbours* and Lavin's Grimes sequence.

This central concern with relations does not of course preclude the exploration of other themes in the short stories of Irish women writers. Emigration and exile feature in stories by Donoghue, Ní Dhuibhne, O'Brien, Bowen and Brennan; the restrictive hold of social norms and religious beliefs is explored in stories by Lavin, Beckett and O'Brien; and Irish history and politics play an occasional role in stories by Lavin, Bowen, Ní Dhuibhne, and Donoghue. Similarly, my investigation of the rich and variegated treatment of our relational being in Irish women's short stories does not aim to set their fiction apart from that of male authors on the basis of some innate, sex-specific interest in human connection. While my focus on this aspect of relationality initially grew from the observation that the O'Connor's lonely outsider is rarely the central hero in the short fiction of Irish women writers, I have become increasingly sceptical of the value of this paradigm in general. Short fiction by male Irish writers too, I would argue, is often preoccupied with human relations—whether loving and enabling or cold and hostile—but the very dominance of O'Connor's mantra of the lonely voice has made critics read the difficulties and breakdowns of relationships invariably in terms of alienation, loneliness and lack.

In other words, with my investigation of the challenges, problems and rewards of human relations as depicted in the short fiction of Irish women writers I have tried to redress a double blind spot in the critical understanding of the Irish short story: the lack of attention to the work of women writers as a central component of the Irish short story tradition and the lack of attention to the pressing problem of human connection that haunts many Irish short stories. By training my light on both of these blind spots in particular, I hope they have gained sufficient attention to secure a permanent place in the history of the Irish short story.

In the process of doing so, of course, my own study is likely to have gained its own lacks and blind spots. Having come to the end of my survey, the one I am most conscious of is the omission of many other Irish women writers whose short fiction also deserves more critical attention. My method of close textual analysis as well as my double, formal and thematic, focus have indeed served to limit my corpus to only a dozen of short story writers. Although all of these writers have distinguished themselves in the history of the short story through a combination of innovation, popularity, aesthetic excellence, and dedication to the form, their numbers could have been added to by several other interesting Irish writers. Alongside the pioneering work of George Egerton, I could have discussed the short fiction of other Irish New Woman writers, such as Sarah Grand and Katherine Cecil Thurston (see O'Toole 2013), even if they are better known as novelists. Similarly, the now largely forgotten novelist Norah Hoult published three short story collections between 1928 and 1950 which betray the influence of Egerton but also provide interesting counterparts to the better-known short fiction of Elizabeth Bowen. A contemporary of Edna O'Brien whom I wish I could have found space for is Julia O'Faolain, whose often brutal and unsettling short stories depict the lives of women in the conservative and Catholic countries of Italy and Ireland. The women's movement of the 1980s also encouraged many women writers to expand and explore female experiences in short fiction. Feminist concerns can be found, to lesser or greater extent, in the short stories that writers like Ita Daly, Clare Boylan, Eithne Strong, Mary Dorcey, Evelyn Conlon, Helen Lucy Burke and Leland Bardwell published in magazines, collections and in the New Women's writing anthologies that appeared in the 1980s and 1990s (cf. Pelan 2005). Investigating their short fiction would require a study on its own, hence my focus, in Chapter 6 on the work of Ní Dhuibhne, Enright and Donoghue, who are similarly influenced by the woman's movement yet continue to publish short story collections to great popular and critical acclaim today. Again, however, that meant excluding other excellent contemporary writers, primarily perhaps Nuala Ní Chonchúir, who has already published five highly original short story collections.

As the bias towards contemporary writing in Gleeson's new anthology suggests (22 of the 30 stories are by living writers), the short story scene in Ireland is an exceptionally vibrant one at the moment and women writers are a strong presence on that scene. Although part of a larger international trend, the renaissance of the short story in Ireland is particularly marked. Several factors play a role here: the short story's amenability to the new digital media as suggested by the twitter stories, interactive storytelling and short shorts that proliferate on the internet, the abundance of small and larger short story competitions as well as the major literary prizes dedicated to the form, the emergence of small publishers willing to take a risk with short story collections of new talents, and the success of new print or online magazines offering a forum for new short fiction. Of crucial importance in Ireland in this respect is *The Stinging Fly* magazine. Founded by editor Declan Meade in 1997, this literary magazine has for almost two decades encouraged new writers and promoted the short story form. The Stinging Fly Press founded in its wake has published short fiction anthologies as well as highly acclaimed story collections by new Irish writers. Three of its most recent publications are brilliant new short story collections by Irish women writers: *The China Factory* by Mary Costello (2012), *Pond* by Clare-Louise Bennett (2015b) and *Dinosaurs on Other Planets* by Danielle McLaughlin (2015). It seems fitting, therefore, to end my survey of Irish women's short fiction with a brief discussion of these three promising and original new voices.

"I think of our blood tie sometimes, mine and Gus's, and of the ties that bind us all", muses the narrator of Mary Costello's title story, as she looks back on her job in the local china factor in the summer before going to college (Costello 2012, 19). "The China Factory" details the mixture of affinity and disdain she felt for her co-workers, and especially for Gus, a distant relative, who is an alcoholic and outcast, but is gentle and thoughtful to the narrator during her summer job. The retrospective dimension of this story, its juxtaposition of different time frames, can be found in many of Costello's short stories. Several of her protagonists are middle-aged men and women, who look back on lives that have been shaped by accidents, choices and the whims of fate. In "Things I See" the female protagonist's brief glimpse of her husband's infidelity continues to blight their relationship; in "This Falling Sickness" the protagonist obsessively returns to the deterioration of her first marriage following the accidental death of their son; in "And Who Will Pay Charon?" the narrator ponders the derailing of a woman's life following a sexual assault; and in "The Sewing Room" Alice's retirement as a primary school teacher has her reflect on her life-changing decision to give up her son for adoption:

> She thinks of her life, her whole existence, as a catastrophe. She drops her arm and the bag slides off and she thinks how everything has sprung from one moment, one deed—the insane beauty and the shock of the flesh, the fire of the soul—with consequences that have flowed out and touched and ruptured every minute and hour and day of her life ever since. That brought her to her own crime, her own awful act, on a Belfast street, the *relinquishment*. Greater than all that had gone before or would ever come after. Making her heart grow small, making extinct everything that was essential for a life. Was it all fated, she wonders? Was the desire fated? And the shame? And the crime—was the crime fated too? (2012, 156)

The question of fate preoccupies many of Costello's characters. With it comes a painful awareness of the fragility of life, which can easily become unravelled because of one accident or wrong turning. Although not all of her characters would think of their lives as a "catastrophe", most of the stories are pervaded by a sense of disappointment, offset only by brief moments of happiness, wholeness or true communion.

Interestingly, the stories offering the most profound sense of human connection and communion are those that depart from the retrospective mode of the other stories and are told throughout in the present tense. "You Fill Up My Senses" is a moving account of a child's all-encompassing love for her mother, reminiscent of O'Brien's symbiotic mother-daughter bond. That this strong bond is doomed to sever is hinted at in the future tense of the story's closing lines, "She is afraid her heart is turning. And that her mother will know this, and then her mother's heart will turn too" (2012, 32). The protagonist of the second present-tense story, "The Patio Man", is a gardener who is moved to a profound empathy with his employer, a lonely, newly-married housewife, whom he takes to the hospital when she miscarries:

> Something has been forming, cell by cell, limb by limb in the dark of her […] Now, it had fallen away, a substraction of her being […] He thinks of things he has not thought of before, about women's lives. It is not the same

for men at all [...] She will be stricken, no longer intact. She might need to touch walls when she gets out. She might not trust the ground anymore. She might slide her foot along the pavement, like a blind person. Trying out the world again. (2012, 53)

If told from the retrospective vantage point of the woman, this could easily become another story of the way fate has cruelly shaped a life, but the perspective of the gardener turns it into a story of compassion and connection, of a meeting that may also affect a life in a more positive sense.

Sensitive and gentle male characters occur quite frequently in Costello's collection and five of its twelve stories feature a male protagonist. In general, men and women can be seen to share the same experiences of love and loss, hope and disappointment. Both "Sleeping with a Stranger" and "The Astral Plane", for instance, contrast the mundane routines of a long marriage with the thrill of a new love and show their respective protagonists, a man and a woman, torn between loyalty and love, between guilt and exultation. Costello's primary concern with 'universally' human experiences and emotions also shows in the lack of emphasis on setting or social context. Although her stories are nominally set in contemporary Ireland, the precise geography, economic situation, or social structure of that Ireland has but little impact on the inner lives of the characters chronicled in the stories. Similarly, there is hardly any trace of the patriarchal power relations and gendered norms that proved all-pervasive in so many short stories by Irish women writers. More important than these gendered divisions, Costello seems to argue, is what we share: our finite human life, the randomness of fate, the beauty and terror of the human condition.

To anyone who would think that the absence of feminist concerns in Costello's short fiction is evidence of a supreme gender equality in contemporary Ireland, Danielle McLaughlin's *Dinosaurs on Other Planets* can easily be offered as a corrective. In the opening story, "The Art of Foot-Binding", this age-old Chinese practice is linked to the protagonist's silent acceptance of her husband's affairs in an attempt to keep him and to the repeated injunctions that her teenage daughter lose weight to become more attractive. The desire for male attention and love is the common denominator of these female acts of endurance and self-denial. Yet, this shared oppression does not inspire solidarity among the female characters in the story. Rather, the women see each other as rivals in the struggle for male attention and, following the classic pattern of the mother-daughter plot, Becky turns against her mother in order not to become like her: "well maybe I'm silly, but at least I'm not fucking pathetic. No wonder Dad hates you" (McLaughlin 2015, 19). The story clearly shows how the anger of these girls and women is misdirected, turned against each other rather than against the men or against the patriarchal patterns that oppress them.

Several other of McLaughlin's stories too bear witness to this rivalry between women, the very opposite of the female bonding chronicled in Egerton's early stories. In "The Smell of Dead Flowers", for instance, the narrator returns in memory to her stay with her aunt in Dublin and to the silent battle for the favours of the male lodger that ensued. In a failed attempt at bonding, the aunt shows her niece photographs of the young girl she used to be and comments wryly, "That's what women do […] they do it all the time; they worry about men. We did it, your mother and I, we were fools for men" (2015, 139). Yet, only in hindsight does the narrator recognize the sad truth of this. The prime importance of female youth and beauty in this contest for men, even at a time when women have high-powered jobs, is also demonstrated in "In the Act of Falling", in which the protagonist is jealous of a preacher woman, resembling "Angelina Jolie", who comes to visit her unemployed husband and son when she goes to work in the city (2015, 157). In "Silhouette", similarly, the elderly mother berates her daughter for losing her looks: "She's gotten very fat […] She didn't used to be that fat […] She'd want to watch out […] or Richard will look elsewhere. I always wondered about her marrying a younger man. I worried about it" (2015, 100).

The double standards, gendered norms and unequal power-relations that continue to shape women's lives in contemporary Ireland are also powerfully expressed through the animal metaphors that recur in almost every story of the collection. In "All about Alice", the sad, constricted life of a 43-year-old spinster is dramatized by means of the bluebottles that her father tries to kill and that "rise up in a last frantic salute to life and summer. And they buzz and ping and beat their gauzy wings against the glass" (2015, 42). In "Along the Heron-Studded River", Cathy's tenuous hold on life, after suffering from a postnatal depression, is symbolized by the fish in their pond, which have little defence against the heron in the cold water of winter. In "Night of the Silver Fox", the tough life of a girl who prostitutes herself in order to save her father's mink farm is linked to that of the young silver foxes her father keeps penned up for their fur. And in "A Different Country", the protagonist identifies with the seals that her boyfriend and his brother kill on an Inishowen beach, because "they've got brazen [...] they've been eating through the nets, destroying the catch" (2015, 123).

Both the sustained symbolism of these stories and their feminist dimension recall Donoghue's *The Woman Who Gave Birth to Rabbits* and Enright's *The Portable Virgin*, even if the lyrical realism of McLaughlin's stories has more affinities with the work of Keegan and Ní Dhuibhne. Like all of these writers, moreover, McLaughlin is careful not to lay the blame for the submissive and difficult position of women in her stories with the male characters. Next to the inveterate adulterers of "The Art of Foot-Binding" and "Those That I Fight I Do Not Hate", McLaughlin also stages sensitive and gentle male figures, such as the husband in "Along the Heron-Studded River" who cares for his mentally ill wife and their little daughter or the young boy in "Night of the Silver Fox", who sympathizes with the girl's plight. Instead, McLaughlin shows the problem to lie with the continued hold of traditional gendered norms and expectations in contemporary society, which leaves women struggling to meet the demands of motherhood, work and romance, all at the same time. Unlike Costello's stories, the stories in *Dinosaurs on Other Planets* are firmly embedded in the social context of a contemporary Ireland, characterized by ghost estates, economic hardship, and unemployed men. Most of her stories also have a very specific geographic setting: small towns in the West of Ireland, but also Ranelagh, Drumcondra or the Inishowen peninsula. The natural surroundings of these mostly rural settings are lyrically evoked and often serve to puncture the characters' busy lives with a moment of transcendence, providing both solace and terror. The closing lines of "A Different Country", for instance, leave Sarah standing amidst the dying seals in a scene at once gruesome and sublime:

> She looked down at the seal and saw its half-closed eyelid flicker. All around her, the shore glittered like a sequinned cloth, tiny shells and pebbles luminous in the moonlight, even as the blood darkened the sand. She stood there, the timber held high above her head, the seal bleeding out at her feet. And all the time the waves rushed in, remorseless, and beautiful across the water, steadfast and unblinking, shone the lights of Magilligan. (2015, 124)

A similar epiphanic moment can be found at the end of the title story, when Kate contemplates the night sky:

> There were stars, millions of them, the familiar constellations she had known since childhood. From this distance, they appeared cold and still and beautiful, but she had read somewhere that they were always moving, held together only by their own gravity. They were white-hot clouds of dust and gas, and the light, if you got close, would blind you. (2015, 195)

The stars' mix of familiarity and profound strangeness also symbolizes Kate's relation to her family members in the story: her estranged husband, her daughter who is about to move to Australia and the grandson she hardly sees and finds it difficult to connect to. Like many other female protagonists in McLaughlin's stories, Kates yearns to establish closeness, to really connect with the people around her, but she is often baffled by their strangeness and rebuffed by the distance they keep. The difficulty of really knowing another person and the challenges of true connection are central themes in McLaughlin's collection, themes that place her work squarely in the tradition of Irish women's short fiction I have been describing.

A collection that seems, at first glance, very much at odds with that tradition is *Pond*, by Claire-Louise Bennett. *Pond* consists of 20 sketches or stories of varying length: some only a few lines, others a paragraph or page, the longest stretching to 20 pages. They offer the reflections, memories, anecdotes and observations of an unnamed female narrator, who has gone to live in a cottage in the West of Ireland to seek solitude and to contemplate the world. Formally, the combination of stories, prose poems, and sketch-like stories recalls the short fiction of Lydia Davis, but the set-up of the collection, and its title, are reminiscent of Thoreau's *Walden Pond*, with its archetypal figure of the Romantic artist seeking to escape from society. As Bennett notes in an interview, "In literary history the lone figure of the man has many archetypes […] but the lone woman is something that is still uncomfortable to many." She is routinely seen as lonely, defined "in terms of what she lacks, e.g. she's single, or she's childless" (Stitch 2015). In *Pond*, conversely, Bennett creates a narrator who is mostly alone, but not lonely, who seeks new, more profound ways to connect to the world. Her narrator is then not simply a female version of the male Romantic outsider. If Thoreau left society to find himself, to gain a deeper form of self-knowledge, Bennett's narrator uses her solitary existence to open up to the world. Instead of a Romantic inward turn then, *Pond* is about turning away from the self to the surrounding world. As Bennett puts it in an *Irish Times* essay on the writing of *Pond*: "In solitude you don't need to make an impression on the world, so the world has some opportunity to make an impression on you" (Bennett 2015a).

Hence, although *Pond* seems a very personal book, we actually learn very little about the narrator. Instead, we learn about the narrator's everyday surroundings: her kitchen, the fruit bowls on the window sills, the rusty knobs on her cooker, the banana she eats in the morning, the stir-fry dinner she cooks, and the pieces of furniture she buys or throws away. Each of these commonplace material objects are held up for scrutiny until they become strange. We learn about nature too, not in the sense of the Romantic sublime, but in terms of the ordinary natural world surrounding her: the ants she finds in procession on the kitchen wall, the cows in the neighbouring fields, and the pond that is more like a puddle, in spite of the sign beside it. There are people in the stories too. In "A Little Before Seven", the narrator reflects on a past relationship, pondering the "observation that was generally comical yet profoundly concerning: I rarely acquire any enthusiasm for the opposite sex outside of being drunk", in "Finishing Touch" she hosts a "little party. A perfectly arranged but low-key soirée" and in "The Gloves Are Off", she describes the visit of a friend (Bennett 2015b, 55, 73). Yet, these characters are not usually given speaking parts. Hence, they seem to be on the same level as the objects or animals around her, a non-privileged part of the larger world the narrator tries to observe and negotiate.

With all the cleaning, cooking, decorating and hosting that is taking place in the stories, what the collection seems to describe first and foremost is the narrator's attempt at home-making, both literally in the sense of creating a warm place to live and metaphorically in the sense of securing a place as part of the wider world. "Morning, Noon & Night", the first longer story of *Pond*, evokes the two dimensions of this homemaking as follows:

> There were so many flowers already in bloom when I moved in: wisteria, fuchsia, roses, golden chain, and many other kinds of flowering trees and shrubs I do not know the names of—many of them wild—and all in great abundance. The sun shone most days so naturally I spent most days out the front there, padding in an out all day long, and the air was absolutely buzzing with so many different species of bee and wasp, butterfly, dragonfly, and birds, so many birds, and all of them so busy. Everything: every plant and

flower, every bird, every insect, just getting on with it. In the mornings I flitted about my cottage, taking crockery out of the plate rack and organising it in jaunty stacks along the window ledge, slicing peaches and chopping hazelnuts, folding back the quilt and smoothing down the sheet, watering plants, cleaning mirrors, sweeping floors, polishing glasses, folding clothes, wiping casements, slicing tomatoes, chopping spring onions. And then, after lunch, I'd take a blanket up to the top garden and I'd lie down under the trees in the top garden and listen to things. (2015b, 31)

While the title of this story is borrowed from Jean Rhys, the home and homemaking it describes in such detail recall Maeve Brennan's sketch-like *New Yorker* stories, evoking her beach cottage in New Hampshire or a flat or hotel room in New York. Two of the three epigraphs to the collection also confirm the centrality of concepts of home in Bennett's stories: one is from Bachelard's *A Poetics of Space* and the other from the Italian writer Natalia Ginzburg: "Could it be that any apartment, any one at all, might eventually become a burrow? Would any place eventually welcome me into its dim, warm, reassuring, kindly light?" (2015b, n.p.)

The third epigraph, interestingly, is from Nietzsche and laments the loss of unity in the world, both natural and human: "It is as though [...] a sentimental trait of nature were bemoaning the fact of her fragmentation, her decomposition into separate individuals" (2015b, n.p.). Reading the narrator's homemaking in the context of this Nietzschean lament, we can also see it as an attempt to regain a sense of unity with the material, natural and human world around her. In the passage quoted before, her homemaking clearly expresses the desire to become part of the busy natural world, while in "Words Escape Me", she is both terrified and exulted by the sense that things become alive around her: "from time to time, such as today, it [the terror] reappears, just to remind you, perhaps, what you are living with, even if you almost always forget" (2015b, 154). In "A Little Before Seven", the narrator dreams of such a feeling of oneness with a lover: "We'd be better off silently overlapping each other; next to a river or beneath the clouds or among the long grass—somewhere, anywhere, where something is moving. Isn't that right?" (2015b, 61). This image of human communion in, and with, nature recalls similar images in Egerton's Nietzschean story, "The Regeneration of Two", when the female protagonist feels at one in the woods with the sleeping poet and his dog, and dreams of their three souls "floating away" in true "soul communion" (Egerton 2006, 141). In short, the experience of solitude that motivates *Pond* is neither a self-obsessed inward turn, nor a disappointed turning away from other people, as in the classic outsider story. It is rather an attempt to be radically receptive to the outside world—material, natural and human—and to feel at home, if only momentarily, in this strange and beautiful universe.

In spite of the diversity in form and theme of these three recent debuts, this close attention to the ordinary is something they all share: an object, scene, character, emotion or experience is magnified and polished until it begins to glow. This "closer than normal" observation of the everyday (Lavin 1959, vii), with realist, satiric, estranging or playful effect, can be observed throughout the short stories I have discussed in this study. It clearly places these three new exciting voices in the long tradition of Irish women's short fiction I have attempted to trace. The formal and thematic diversity of their work thus testifies to the flexibility of the form as it continues to flourish in twenty-first-century Ireland.

BIBLIOGRAPHY

Bennett, Claire-Louise. 2015a. Claire-Louise Bennett on Writing *Pond*. *The Irish Times*, 26 May. http://www.irishtimes.com/culture/books/claire-louise-bennett-on-writing-pond-1.2226535

Bennett, Claire-Louise. 2015b. *Pond*. Dublin: The Stinging Fly.

Costello, Mary. 2012. *The China Factory*. Dublin: The Stinging Fly.

Egerton, George. 2006. *Keynotes and Discords*. London: Continuum. Original edition, 1893, 1894.

Gleeson, Sinéad, ed. 2015. *The Long Gaze Back: An Anthology of Irish Women Writers*. Dublin: New Island.

Lavin, Mary. 1959. Preface. In *Selected Stories*. New York: Macmillan

McLaughlin, Danielle. 2015. *Dinosaurs on Other Planets*. Dublin: The Stinging Fly.

O'Toole, Tina. 2013. *The Irish New Woman*. Basingstoke: Palgrave.

Pelan, Rebecca. 2005. *Two Irelands: Literary Feminisms North and South*. Syracuse: Syracuse University Press.

Stitch, Susanne. 2015. Claire-Louise Bennett: Modes of Solitude, Embodiment and Mystery. *The Honest Ulsterman*, June. http://humag.co/features/claire-louise-bennett.

INDEX

© The Editor(s) (if applicable) and The Author(s) 2016   225
E. D'hoker, *Irish Women Writers and the Modern Short Story*,
DOI 10.1007/978-3-319-30288-1

Printed by Printforce, the Netherlands